INK

AND

ASHES

VALYNNE E. MAETANI

INK
AND
ASHES

VALYNNE E. MAETANI

Tu Books
an imprint of Lee & Low Books, Inc.

New York

TU BOOKS, an imprint of LEE & LOW BOOKS Inc., 95 Madison Avenue, New York, NY 10016
leeandlow.com

Manufactured in the United States of America by Worzalla Publishing Company, August 2015

MIX
Paper from responsible sources
FSC® C002589

Book design by Sammy Yuen
Cover calligraphy (INK) and chapter numerals by Brian Ray
Japanese translation by Masaji Watabe
Book production by The Kids at Our House
The text is set in Cochin

10 9 8 7 6 5 4 3 2
First Edition

Library of Congress Cataloging-in-Publication Data

Maetani, Valynne E.
  Ink & ashes / Valynne E. Maetani. — First edition.
     pages cm
  Summary: "When Japanese American Claire Takata finds out that her deceased father was once a member of the yakuza, a Japanese crime syndicate, danger enters her life that could end up killing someone."—Provided by publisher.
  ISBN 978-1-62014-211-0 (hardback) — ISBN 978-1-62014-212-7 (e-book)
  1. Japanese Americans—Juvenile fiction. [1. Japanese Americans—Fiction. 2. Fathers—Fiction. 3. Organized crime—Fiction. 4. Love—Fiction. 5. Mystery and detective stories.] I. Title. II. Title: Ink and ashes.
  PZ7.1.M3In 2015
  [Fic]—dc23
                    2015006632

To Ashley, for her birthday

PROLOGUE

People go to hell for what I'm about to do.

The old man glares at me, his face so close I can see the wrinkles on his forehead stretch wide when he speaks.

"Do you know who I am?" he yells.

I choke on his stale, smoke-filled breath. A thick Japanese accent stains his words. "Do you know who you are?"

Claire Takata. Daughter of loving parents. Devoted sister. Loyal friend.

He strikes me with the back of his hand, the force almost tipping the chair I'm tied to. The sting sends a burning shiver down the side of my face.

"Answer me!" he demands.

I am the heiress to a legacy I wish I'd never discovered.

The cold night prickles my skin. I twist my hands, trying to escape, but the rope cuts into my wrists. I swallow hard and try again.

All the terror he's put me through makes anger storm inside. I want to hurt this man as much as he has hurt me. If I were free, I could kill this man right now.

Without guilt.

I STARED AT my pink walls, wishing away the smell of death. Jasmine incense, used at every funeral I had ever attended, hovered in the air. I imagined the wispy smoke snaking its way through the narrow spaces around my closed door, the tendrils prying at tucked-away memories.

A breeze drifted through my open window, bristling the hair on my neck. My chest wrenched tighter.

It was time.

The morning sun hadn't found its way into the hallway yet, so I flipped on some lights and wandered into my older brother's room. Parker faced a wall crowded with overlapping soccer posters. He stuck the final pin into another picture, covering the last glimpse of light blue paint. "Hey, Claire," he said without looking at me.

"Ready?" I said.

"I was just thinking," Parker said, "I'm not going to be here next year."

"Yeah, yeah." I waited for him to crack a joke, but he didn't.

Parker turned his stocky body. "No. I mean, I won't be home to do the ceremony with you guys."

Every day since school had started, he'd made sure we all knew he couldn't wait to go to college. And I couldn't wait to get rid of him. But somehow the sadness in his voice made the hollow space grow larger.

Parker paused for an expectant moment, then said, "Do you remember the time he took us fishing at Pokai Bay, and I caught five fish?" He removed his black-rimmed glasses and cleaned the lenses with the hem of his shirt.

I'd forgotten about that, but now I could picture the rainbow of color dancing off the water and the way my body rocked in rhythmic waves long after we had gotten off the boat. Sometimes I wasn't sure if a memory was really mine or if it was something I thought I remembered because someone else had talked about it.

"That was a good day." I tried to summon happy experiences to push away the bad memories flooding my head, but I couldn't break the good ones free. I clenched my fists and kicked at an ink stain on the gray carpet. "Mom's probably waiting for us."

"Let's get Avery," Parker said.

He lumbered past me, and I followed him down the hallway. Pictures of all three of us kids at different ages and events lined the walls. The oak floorboards creaked beneath our feet, and we found our younger brother stretched on his bed, his shaggy black hair strewn across the pillow. His walls were papered with posters of skateboarders and snowboarders, but unlike Parker's random clusters, Avery's wall hangings were hung with precision.

Before Parker even opened his mouth, Avery announced, "I'm not doing it this year. It's a dumb tradition and doesn't mean anything anyway."

"He was our father," Parker said. His plump cheeks flushed pink.

My jaw started to tighten. "Show some respect."

Avery shivered a surrendering sigh and rose, as if getting out of bed took all the energy he could muster.

When we got to the butsudan in the corner of the living room, Mom was already at the lacquered shrine, her hands in prayer position, palms together, held at chest level. Parker gave her hip a gentle bump and put an arm around her, eclipsing her slight frame.

After squeezing Mom's shoulder, Parker took a few steps forward and began the ceremony to commemorate the anniversary of our father's death. The familiar smoky smell overpowered me, forcing my mind to awaken with unwanted memories: the suddenness of my father's passing just before my seventh birthday. The invasion of people I'd never met. The weeks it took before Mom could get out of bed.

Willing myself to follow Parker's example, I moved toward the altar, placed my hands together, and bowed. I pinched some ground incense, dropped it in the burner, and bowed again. Once back in place, I bowed a final time, the twinge of my father's absence weighing on me.

Avery repeated the ritual so quickly that he almost dropped his prayer beads. After his final bow, he mumbled, "Until next year, Henry," and slouched away.

I shook my head. Did he really just call our father by his first name?

Mom closed her eyes.

"You'd think he'd at least act like he cared a little more," Parker said.

I caught Avery's hurt expression as he started up the stairs.

"Sometimes," Mom said, "it's the memories we should have had that are most painful." She chased after Avery, but I heard his door slam before she could reach him. I didn't remember much about my father, but Avery, even though he was only a year younger than I was, probably remembered even less.

Parker meditated a few more moments before he left. I lingered behind, brushing my toes in an arc along the patterns of the Oriental rug. Mom came back downstairs and announced she was going grocery shopping. The garage door rumbled open, and then closed.

I sat at the grand piano in the far corner. Because I had quit lessons a couple of years ago, the selection of pieces I could play from memory had become more limited, but I still had some favorites. I settled on a nocturne by Chopin and let my mind wander along the soft and lilting phrases. By the time I finished, my head felt less crowded.

In the distance, the sound of thunder strummed. Dad was up—his light was on in his study across from the living room—but he never joined this ceremony. I guess he wanted to give us some space. I walked across the cold wood floor of the hallway and made my way to my room. At the top of the stairs, I glanced at a picture of five-year-old me, in the time before we moved here, dressed in a lavender Hawaiian floral-print muumuu with an orchid lei around my neck. I barely remembered that life—the life with our father.

Whether it was a picture of us with my father or stepdad,

Mom never displayed pictures of our whole family. Not on this wall, not in this house, not even in old baby albums. She had mentioned she didn't want to be living with a ghost in her marriage to my stepdad, but since she didn't have pictures of him either, I figured it was fair for both of my fathers.

While I loved the comfort of my room, the pink color of everything was overwhelming. Pink was my mom's version of a girl's room, not mine. When we first moved here, I refused to decorate the walls until they were a different color, but had never convinced her to budge. As I got old enough to paint it myself, I still hated pink but no longer cared enough to do anything about it.

I dug behind some shoes in my closet to get to a box where I kept some of my father's things. The cardboard was marked with smudges, and the lid was starting to come apart at one corner.

Inside the box was a worn old notebook bound in burgundy leather. My father had journaled in it, recording inspirational quotes and making notes.

Technically, it shouldn't have been in my possession. When we moved to Utah, Mom had had movers box up some of my father's old things because she couldn't bring herself to do it. She figured she could sort through everything when she was ready. But before she had the chance, I went through the boxes myself. She never noticed the journal—and a few other things—was missing, and I never mentioned I had it.

I sucked in a deep breath, the smell of old paper and leather filling my lungs. The entries about us kids were the ones I loved the most. I flipped to one in which he had written about the time he took me to see hula performances at the Merrie Monarch Festival. I didn't remember that festival, but I'm pretty sure I was his favorite child.

When I turned to a page toward the end to read another entry, I sliced my finger on a cardstock edge that had come unglued from the back cover. I dropped the journal.

A bead of blood formed on the tip of my pointer finger. I couldn't believe how much those tiny things could sting. I grabbed a tissue from my desk and pressed it against the cut.

Blood hadn't gotten on the notebook, and I hadn't smeared anything, but there was a piece of paper sticking out from a pocket between the unglued cardstock and the back cover. I slid my finger into the tight opening and pulled it out. It was an envelope, addressed to George Takata, my stepdad, but it wasn't sealed and had never been postmarked, so it must not have been sent. Inside was a letter.

George,
返事どうも。こんな風に連絡取るのは一昔前のようだね。でも俺の経験では郵便で来る手紙はめったに疑われないもんだよ。
これがお前の欲しい情報さ。
15-8192-45
15-8192-46
15-8192-47

81-80-50722259
やつの電話番号もあげるよ。もし連絡したかったら。。。

お前の助け改めて感謝するよ。このことは俺にとって何よりも大切なんだ。死ぬ前にどうしても片付けなければと思っていたんだ。
Henry

I set the letter down. The taste of blood splashed across my tongue, and I realized I had bitten my bottom lip.

My fathers knew each other?

I READ THE names on the paper again, slower this time, to make sure. But it was definitely my father's handwriting, which I recognized from his journal. And, thanks to snooping in Mom's drawer and stumbling onto old love notes she had kept hidden, I knew he signed the *H* of his first name as if it were written in one stroke.

Thoughts whirled in my head, unearthing questions that would only grow louder unless they were answered. Why wouldn't my parents have said something earlier? Mom must have known they were acquainted.

Unable to read Japanese, I'd have to go to the source and do some probing.

I slid the letter into my back pocket, put the empty envelope and notebook back into the box, and put it away. A faint nervousness hummed under my skin as I walked down the stairs and into Dad's study.

I slumped into a leather chair in front of the man who had

been my new dad almost since mine had passed away. Without glancing up, Dad folded the papers he held and shoved them into a file folder, which he placed in a drawer of the cherrywood credenza behind him. He closed it and took a key from his pocket to lock the drawer.

"What was that?" I said.

Dad shifted in his chair. The scent of his cologne, a mixture of wood and cool winter air, crossed the room. "Don't worry. It's not for your birthday."

"Good," I said. "Because you know how I hate celebrating my birthday."

Right after my father died, Mom forgot about my birthday. Parker's too. Since then, birthdays for me and Parker had become a muted affair that neither of us wanted to celebrate. Avery, however, had no problem making sure Mom pulled out all the stops for his birthday a month later.

I eyed the locked drawer. If he was hiding something, it wouldn't be for long. The whirlwind of thoughts was already in full force. Whether it was a surprise for my birthday or something else, I had to know what was in there, or the spinning would never stop—even though it was most likely insignificant. Even though I shouldn't.

Dad nodded and gave me his full attention. "So how are you doing, princess?"

I shrugged and compelled my mind to focus. If he really knew my father but hadn't said anything, I would have to be very careful in my approach to determine whether not telling us was an oversight or on purpose. Depending on how he answered, I'd have to decide if I wanted to show him the letter I'd found.

"I'm fine," I said, "considering what day it is."

He combed his fingers through his dark hair. "It's still hard, isn't it?" His voice fell at the end as if it was more of a statement than a question.

My heart fluttered faster. I stared at the grain in the dark wood of his desk. "It's been ten years. A long time since it happened. I'm fine."

He nodded.

"I mean, I don't even think about him anymore," I said. "Not much. But I think you really would have liked him." I glanced up to get a good read of his expression.

"I know I would have." Dad's voice was soft, his face unchanged.

"He was such a good person." I kept my eyes trained on his.

He cleared his throat. "I've heard he was one of the best."

"And seriously I'm fine, but you know, every now and then I miss him," I said. "A lot."

Dad nodded and removed his glasses, rubbing both eyes as if tired, then placed them back on the bridge of his nose.

I hadn't sensed anything unusual yet from his body language, so I decided to push further. "Did you happen to know my father?" I asked. "I mean, since you were both in Hawaii?"

Dad shrugged, but I couldn't detect any discomfort or surprise cross his face. Not even the tiny wrinkles at the corners of his eyes or the small sunspot above his left brow shifted.

"I did know of him," he said, "but a lot of people knew who your father was because he was a judge." He folded his arms, and his leather chair creaked as he leaned back. "I'm sure if he were here, he would love watching you play soccer. You have a big game this week, don't you?"

I smiled. "Yeah. We're playing Haven High. They beat us last year."

He brought his chair forward and rested his elbows on the desk. "I know you've been practicing hard, and the team is looking pretty strong. If I were Haven, I'd be nervous."

My team had been practicing hard, and I had to admit we looked good on the field. "Yeah," I said. "Haven should definitely be scared."

"I know it's been a tough morning, but I have to run some errands." He jumped to his feet. "Do you need me to pick up some more energy bars while I'm out, or do you have enough?"

"I'm good."

Before he dashed out the door, he kissed my forehead.

Uneasiness thrummed through me. I tapped my fingers on the arm of the chair and tried to replay our discussion. I wasn't sure if I had any more answers than when I first sat down, and I realized I'd never seen my dad in such a hurry on a weekend.

At some point, Dad had read an article on how one of the best ways to prevents sports injuries was by cross-training. We had all played soccer from a young age and didn't have a lot of time to fit in another sport, so Dad came up with the idea of spending some time on Saturdays learning martial arts and self-defense from him, since he'd grown up practicing karate and jujitsu.

Even if he had other things to do, he always made sure we practiced for an hour or two. But today, he seemed to have completely forgotten. Why would he have offered to pick up energy bars when Mom was at the grocery store anyway?

Outside, the wind howled, the high-pitched whistle sending a flutter down my spine, but I stayed seated, waiting to hear the finality of the garage door rumbling closed. If my phone hadn't vibrated, I would've already been rummaging through Dad's desk. I had a text from my best friend, Forrest Langford.

> **Forrest**: Hey, I remembered what day it was. Are you ok?
> **Me**: I'm fine.
> **Forrest**: Really?
> **Me**: Would I lie to you?
> **Forrest**: Yes. I'll be there soon.

I smiled and returned the phone to my pocket. Then I eyed the corner of a crumpled piece of paper, sticking out of the side of the drawer he had just locked. Without hesitation, I grabbed two paper clips and went to work behind his desk.

Over the past few years I had taught myself how to pick any lock that wasn't electronic. In the sixth grade, Parker locked me out of my own bathroom so I would be late for school. Out of frustration, I shoved a metal skewer in the little round hole, and the door popped open. The euphoria of besting him motivated me to learn how to pick all kinds of locks with all kinds of tools. I had even made my own tension wrench by grinding down an Allen wrench in shop class. Learning the art wasn't easy, and it took a lot of practice to get a feel for tension range and the different pressure that needed to be applied, but the more I practiced, the more I found interesting information no one wanted me to know, so I kept at it.

I shaped the paper clips, placed them in the lock, and started to turn. I'd practiced on this lock many times when I was first starting to learn—all I had to do was apply enough tension and listen for the pins. The lock turned, and I was in. The folder Dad had been holding only minutes earlier stood up a bit from the rest. In my previous searches, I'd never come across it before. I yanked it out, placed it on the desk, and plopped in his high-backed chair.

Even though I'd done this many times, I worked to slow my pulse. Dad had caught me going through some papers on his desk a few years ago, looking for a consent form for a biology field trip to Red Butte Gardens. He told me I should have asked and anything in his office was none of my business. The consent form was a legitimate excuse. Dad would kill me if he knew I was snooping again, this time in a locked drawer.

But if he never found out, it wouldn't hurt him. I opened the file, expecting to find the receipt for a birthday gift he had ordered online or the guest list for a surprise party.

All I found was an envelope with FUNERAL written across the front, containing several photographs. I pulled them out and stared at the picture on top. I didn't know how to make any sense of seeing the two men together, but it was my father, Henry, and my stepdad, George, both of them much younger.

I looked closer at the picture. I replayed the conversation I'd just had with my dad and studied the picture again, but it was both of them, side by side, arms around each other. Dad's face was fuller, his muscles more toned.

My fathers seemed to have known each other a long time, which meant keeping this information from us couldn't have been an oversight. I tried to quiet the sting pinching at my heart, but I still felt like I had been slapped. As the title on the envelope suggested, the next picture was from my father's funeral. Parker and Avery stood at the Buddhist temple doors in their little black suits. I spread the small stack of photos on the floor and took a quick picture of each with my phone. Then I shoved the photos back into the envelope and placed it in the folder, making sure everything appeared as Dad had left it, before relocking the drawer behind me.

After I tidied up, I broke into a sprint up the stairs, passing Avery's room first. "Get into Parker's room," I said. "I need to show you guys something."

DESPITE A FEW grunts, Avery hiked up his soccer shorts, hanging below his boxers, and followed me down the hall. He tightened a bandana around his head before he sprawled on Parker's bed, his wiry body spread-eagle.

Parker stopped tightening screws on his latest contraption, which involved a bicycle seat and a skate deck. He scrunched his nose. "Dude, you stink. Off my bed. Now."

"Just chill." Avery scowled but stood up and leaned against the wall.

Parker slumped into the rolling chair at his desk. "So whassup, shorty?" he asked, focusing on me with eyes that appeared gigantic through his magnifying visor.

I closed the door behind me so Mom couldn't hear if she came back. "Our fathers knew each other," I said. "Isn't that crazy?"

Parker shook his head. "Whatever." Sometimes my obsessive investigations had led to theories, which had sometimes been considered "ludicrous" (Parker) or "stupid" (Avery). Given the evidence, and in some cases lack of evidence, the theories had always seemed plausible to me, but getting access to information for better proof was another reason I had learned how to pick locks. "I found a picture of the two of them together. And there was also this note." I walked to the desk and handed him the piece of paper.

He replaced the magnifying visor with his usual glasses and studied the letter. The smile on Parker's round face fell into a thoughtful expression. "Where'd you get this?"

The thought of sharing our father's notebook made me pause. "Dad's desk," I lied.

Avery dragged himself off the bed to take a peek. "Why does Dad have that?"

"How would I know?" I said. "And it's weird because I just talked to Dad, and he sat there as I went on and on about our father. But he didn't say anything." Up until now, I never thought my parents would lie to me. To us. They must have had a good reason, and I intended to find out what that reason was. Even though I didn't have much evidence yet, I knew the reason couldn't be a good one.

"What're you all staring at?" The boy's voice from behind startled me, but at least it wasn't my mom. I hadn't even heard the door open.

Forrest laughed and gave me a one-armed side hug. In his other hand was a plate of Spritzkuchen. My brothers each grabbed a German donut before I could.

"Whoa," Forrest said and lifted the plate out of their reach. He was about a foot taller than me, and his naturally tan skin had a glow that my mom says comes from clean, healthy living.

His dimpled smile and deep blue eyes sent the hearts of stupid girls everywhere into a flutter. But not mine. Around Forrest, I felt an immediate easiness.

He presented the plate, and I took one, explaining what I'd found between bites.

Forrest shoved a huge chunk of Spritzkuchen in his mouth and shrugged. "Is this theory related to past theories you've had about your dad's travels?" He wiped away some stickiness at the corner of his mouth.

"No," I said. "Maybe." I shook my head. "I don't know."

Parker returned to his tinkering. "I'm sure it's not a big deal."

"I never said it was a big deal." My voice sounded a little whinier than I expected. If they had kept this from us intentionally, was there more they were hiding? "But aren't you the least bit interested in finding out why they never said anything to us?"

The rattle of the garage door announced Mom's arrival home. I needed to hide the evidence, but before I could get the letter, Avery stole it from Parker. "Why don't we ask Mom? I'm sure she'll have a simple explanation, and you'll realize how not-interesting it is, and then I can go back to working hard at being lazy."

"But then she'll I know I was going through Dad's—" I swiped at Avery's arm, but it was too late. He'd already jumped up and headed into the hall.

I raced to catch up to Avery, arguing with him all the way down the stairs.

"Do you know how hard my life is?" he asked. "I have to fit hours of watching TV, playing video games, and napping in one weekend day, all because weekdays are too laborious to let me space these things out. Let's get this over with, so I can get back to my life."

I grabbed at the note again, but he held it out of reach. "You're going to get me in trouble." Stupid little brothers growing taller.

"Yes, but think how peaceful my life will be once your questions are answered." Avery slinked over to the refrigerator and rested against its stainless-steel doors, a smirk playing on his lips.

Parker dropped himself onto a barstool at the island in the middle of the kitchen. After a few more failed attempts to get the paper away, I gave up and sat next to Parker, with Forrest at my back.

Mom came in then, oblivious to our argument, and flitted around emptying grocery bags, shelving spices into the worn oak cabinets, and stacking cans in the overfilled pantry. "Just in time to help me." She shoved a carton of orange juice into Avery's arms.

Instead of putting it in the fridge, Avery set it on the counter. "So, did our dads know each other?" he asked.

Mom's back stiffened. She lifted her shoulders and raised her head, a cantaloupe in her left hand and her right hand reaching into another bag. She put down the fruit, but her wrist caught on the handle of the plastic bag. She ended up yanking it off, wadding it into a ball, and throwing it on the counter before she turned to face us.

"Actually—" She paused. "Yes. Why do you ask?"

Avery glanced at me sideways. "Because Claire said they did."

I darted a murderous glare at him.

Mom's small eyes hardened and narrowed on me, waiting for an explanation.

"It's just that I . . . um, happened to see Dad looking at a picture of the two of them this morning." There was enough of the truth there that I prayed she could tell I wasn't lying.

"Well," Mom said, "he often does his own private ceremony on this day, which I think is very good of him." She fumbled for something in one of the drawers. "He doesn't want to intrude."

"So they were good friends?" Parker asked.

"More like . . ." Her eyes flickered to Forrest, but she knew that by now there wasn't anything I wouldn't tell him anyway. "Acquaintances. I mean, I wouldn't have met George—your dad—otherwise." She unzipped the jacket of her gray tracksuit, slipped it off her thin frame, and draped it over a chair at the kitchen table.

"So you met Dad through"—I took a hesitant breath—"our father?"

"I did. He contacted me after the funeral." She grabbed a carton of eggs off the counter and put it in the fridge, as if what she had told us was the most normal thing in the world.

We waited for her to offer more, but she stacked apples in a bamboo basket until they almost spilled over, her lips remaining tight.

Avery brushed away some long hair strands and finally broke the silence. "So, did you have an affair?"

I sucked in a quick breath. That had never even crossed my mind.

"What?" Mom pressed her palms on the counter.

Avery didn't seem to notice the sharpness of her reply, but Forrest gripped my shoulder. Parker's leg jiggled up and down. I was amazed Avery's mouth hadn't gotten him into more trouble by now.

"That's ridiculous," she said. "Dad and I only got together *after* your father died." Her eyebrows pinched in. "I can't believe you would even ask me something like that."

Avery relaxed his body against the side of the fridge. All of us gave him a look. I shook my head. He lifted his hands and widened his eyes, mouthing, "What's the big deal?"

"Why didn't you guys tell us this before?" Parker asked.

"I didn't think it mattered," Mom said. "And it's not like I never said anything. I told you I met your dad through someone I knew, and that someone happened to be your father." She placed a hand at the back of her head and massaged her neck. "Seriously, kids. They barely even knew each other."

"How do you explain this?" Avery yanked the note from his pocket and stretched the paper in both hands like an open scroll.

My breath caught in my throat. What was he thinking?

Forrest buried his forehead in the back of my hair and muttered, "Idiot."

I took a step in his direction, but Forrest grabbed my arm, and I stopped. Heat flushed my cheeks. I didn't know how long I was going to get grounded, but I was, without a doubt, going to ruin Avery's life.

Mom's face lost color. She snatched the letter from Avery and glanced over it. Her body went still. And then her forehead crinkled, and her eyes narrowed.

Avery waved his hand in front of her face. "Mom?"

"Where did you get this?" she said in a soft voice.

No one said anything. She folded her arms and swept her glare over each of us.

I shot my brothers a look to say we were all in this together, but neither of my brothers lasted longer than a few moments. Parker and Avery shifted their eyes on me. I couldn't believe they were throwing me under the bus without even a second thought. Okay—Avery, yes, because he didn't care if it meant I was getting into trouble, but Parker usually had more staying power. I raised my eyebrows and scowled at them both. Mom rotated and locked onto me with a blazing expression.

I wasn't ready to part with the notebook, but I'd have to give her a good reason to be in Dad's office. I cleared my throat. "I found it in one of those boxes in the garage with Otochan's old stuff, and I know you guys said not to touch them, but that's the only thing I found."

Mom skimmed the note, and as she read, her hands shook. Not a lot, but enough that I could tell she was struggling to keep the paper steady. She didn't say anything, and the moment drew out as I waited for her judgment.

"So?" Avery demanded, still oblivious. He snapped his fingers twice.

Parker stood from his stool and delivered a backhand to Avery's chest.

Avery looked around the room. "You all saw that, right? Domestic violence?" He turned his attention back on Mom. "So?"

She whipped up her head and frowned. "I don't know. I've never seen this before." Her hand gripped tighter, her fingers digging into the paper. "This could be about a lot of things," she said. "I know about as much Japanese as you guys do, so it's not like I can read it. I mean, obviously I can read the numbers, but how would I know what they're for?"

Avery held out his hand so she could return the note.

"I'll hang on to this," Mom said, wetness pooling in the corners of her eyes. She creased the paper in half and jammed it in the pocket of her jacket, still hanging on the chair. "All of you need to mind your own business, and I think this conversation is finished unless you want me to tell your dad what you were up to."

"But Claire was the one who . . ."

Avery's voice faded when Mom's stony expression turned on him. We all hurried to help put the rest of the groceries away, and though I tried to make light conversation, Mom responded with one-word answers. I edged closer to the kitchen table, and when her back was turned, I slipped my hand into the pocket of her jacket. Mom wasn't going to share anything else, but the letter might.

After we finished, we herded upstairs and gathered in my bedroom.

"That was awkward," Forrest said. He perched on the edge of my desk and crossed his long legs at the ankles.

Parker collapsed on the bed among several Hello Kitty pillows, his wide feet hanging off the edge. "It doesn't make sense," he said. "If they were friends in their early twenties, he would have known Dad years before he married Mom."

Avery stretched out facedown on the floor, drawing in the rose-colored carpet with his finger. "Mom's probably thinking of a punishment as we speak. You have totally ruined the rest of my day, Claire. And to think it started out so nicely."

I stood over him, my hands on my hips. "I ruined your day? This only happened because you decided to show Mom—"

"Stop," Avery said. He sat up and waggled his finger at me. "All these accusations are hurting my feelings. I'm very sensitive, you know?"

I forced myself away, fighting the urge to kick him and help him truly find his "sensitive" side. Forrest patted the spot next to him, so I sat on the desk, conflicted between thinking of all the ways I would make Avery's life miserable and the thought that my parents could be hiding something from us.

The unknown made me most uneasy. If I had never found the letter, would they ever have said anything?

"Mom's obviously not going to tell us anything," I said, "but I have this." I reached into my pocket and retrieved the letter. "And these." I tapped my phone and held it up.

"What are those?" Parker asked.

"Pictures from the funeral," I said, "and the letter, but it's in Japanese. If we can get it translated, it might give us more information."

"How'd you get that?" Parker asked.

"Stole it while she wasn't looking."

"Parker!" Mom yelled from downstairs. "Get down here right now!" She must have realized the note was missing from her jacket.

Parker climbed to his feet. "Why am I getting blamed?" he mumbled. "You're the one who took them."

"It's not my fault you're the eldest son," I said.

Avery huffed and stayed on the floor. "Hide it!"

I scanned the room for a good hiding place. "Stall her as long as possible," I said to Parker.

"Now!" Mom screamed. Only on rare occasions did her voice ever reach such decibels.

"Dude, you gotta stop her from coming up here," Avery said in a quiet, rough voice.

Parker tore out of the room just as I heard her footsteps coming up the stairs. "Yes?" he sang as if innocent.

I heard Mom questioning Parker, and then their footsteps began to climb the stairs. My thoughts whirled all over the place, contemplating the places where Mom wouldn't think to look.

Forrest opened a copy of Taming of the Shrew. "How about in here?"

And then it occurred to me: All we needed was a copy of the letter. As far as she knew, we didn't have anything else. "Duh." I laid the letter on the desk next to Forrest and snapped a picture with my phone. I yanked the note off my desk, folded it, and threw the paper like a live grenade at the floor in front of Avery. He whipped his hands behind his back.

Mom crossed through the doorframe. The paper fluttered to the floor like an autumn leaf.

AVERY GLANCED UP at Mom, lunged for the paper, stuffed it in his mouth, and started to chew.

My heart skipped around my chest. What was Avery thinking? Next to me, Forrest's jaw fell. Parker leaned against the doorframe for support, his face strained from trying to hold in laughter.

Mom stalked over until she towered in front of Avery. "Spit." It was only one word, but her voice crackled and sizzled in the air.

Avery pushed himself up on his elbows. "Spit what?" Drool spilled from the corner of his mouth. He wiped at it with his sleeve.

She placed her hands on her hips. "The letter."

He swallowed with a loud gulp. "What letter?"

Mom drew in a deep breath and held it for what seemed an eternity before exhaling. She turned around to burn a scowl into me, then Avery, and finally Parker. "We'll talk about the consequences when your dad gets home." Her voice trembled with irritation.

We all nodded, trying to look properly chastised.

On her way out, she bumped into Parker in the doorframe. I couldn't tell if the nudge was on purpose, but she was mad enough that Avery didn't take the opportunity to make a joke about it.

I let out the breath I'd been holding.

"Oh man, that was too close," Forrest said, relaxing his broad shoulders.

Avery rolled over and sat up straight. "You. Are. Such. A. Loser," he said to me in a low gravelly voice. "That was nasty."

"No one said you had to *eat* it," I said.

"That's how you get rid of evidence. Don't you learn anything from watching all those detective movies?" He whipped his long hair behind him. "Most people would have just said thank you."

I ignored Avery and made Forrest get off the desk so I could work at my laptop comfortably. Once the computer came to life, I downloaded the letter and the pictures. "Let's take a look at the pictures first."

Parker and Forrest positioned themselves, one on each side. Once they were in place, Avery finally lifted himself from the floor and joined them at my back.

I pulled up the images in extra-large thumbnails on my desktop so everyone could see. I pointed to the first picture. "I think this was the first day of the funeral. The incense made me really sick, and I almost threw up."

"Oooh." Avery shuddered. He pointed to a picture on the bottom row. "This one's creepy. Someone actually took a picture of him in the coffin. Probably the first day of the service, before they cremated him."

My mind went to other memories of him before he died. I

remembered the University of Hawaii sweatshirt he liked to wear and how his mouthwash smelled like black licorice.

A new anguish settled inside me. I tried to shake it off and gestured to the picture in the bottom corner. "I can't believe how young we look."

Three pictures in the second row had us surrounded by other Japanese people. "I have no idea who these people are," I said.

Forrest's face twisted into a sour expression. "Hey, there's one of your dad. Not your dead one. Your dad now."

"Maybe it just looks like him," Parker said, squinting at the image.

"It can't be." I opened the picture in a viewer so we could see it in more detail. "Mom just said we didn't meet Dad until after the funeral, so there's no way he could have been—" I stopped. It *was* my dad, standing next to the younger versions of us.

"Why don't I remember him being there?" I whispered.

Had my mom lied, or had she just forgotten Dad was at the funeral? There *were* a lot of people there.

"I don't remember anyone either," Parker said. "But maybe it's because our father was a judge. A lot of people knew him, and I remember there were so many people at his funeral that not everyone fit in the temple."

"This one on the far right doesn't make sense," I said. "Avery and I are passing something to each other with our chopsticks."

"Mom always gets mad at us when we do that," Avery said. He studied it closer. "Says it's bad manners. Kinda looks like we're passing a . . . a bone."

I pointed to the next picture. "And in this one, Dad's putting a bone into the urn with chopsticks. Look who's behind him."

Grandpa, Dad's father. And Mom off to the side.

Mom hadn't forgotten. She had just lied to us downstairs.

My parents might be unwilling to give me answers, but I knew someone who could. I took out my phone and dialed.

"Who are you calling?" Parker asked.

"Grandpa," I said. "Since he's a Buddhist priest, he should be able to tell us what's going on in those pictures."

"Hey, it's Claire," I said when my grandfather answered. Technically he was my step-grandfather, but I loved him as much as I loved my stepdad. "How are you?"

His voice sounded groggy. I had forgotten it was four hours earlier in Hawaii, so I apologized when I realized it. He told me he was happy to talk to me at any hour, and I assured him I was fine.

"Parker and Avery are here with me, so I'm going to put you on speaker." I placed the phone on the desk and motioned for them to gather closer.

"Uh, I'm here too," Forrest muttered.

I gave him a look. "Forrest's here too."

"Hi, Grandpa," Forrest said with enthusiasm.

"Hi, Forrest," Grandpa said.

"I was going through some family photos," I said, "and I saw you next to Dad in one of the group pictures at my father's funeral. But . . . how did you even know my father?"

"Ahh, Henry." Grandpa sighed. "I loved him like a son. But the answer to that question is a little complicated. You'll have to ask your dad to explain everything to you."

Maybe Grandpa wouldn't be giving me answers like I had thought.

"If you loved him like a son," I said, "why didn't we know you before Dad married our mom?"

Grandpa chuckled. "You did," he said. "You just don't remember. Parker, ho, he was so *kolohe*, always getting into trouble. But you don't remember because I left to spend a few years at a monastery in Tibet right after Avery was born. All of you were just babies."

"I see," I said.

"Grandpa, why are there pictures of us passing bones to each other with chopsticks?" Parker asked. "Mom always tells us it's bad manners to do that."

"Mmmm. That I *can* tell you. It's bad manners because the tradition is associated with death. You see, in Japan, bodies are usually cremated. And then the family picks the bones out of the ashes and passes them to one another with chopsticks to put them in the urn. We start with the feet bones and then work up to the head bones so that the dead can be upright."

"Only family do that?" Parker asked.

"Or people considered family," he said.

Grandpa talked a little more about the funeral, and I made some mental notes, quiet rage simmering beneath the surface. I thanked him and promised I would call again soon. But before I ended the conversation, he cleared his throat. "Kids," he said, "can I offer you some advice?"

"Sure," I said.

"Before your father died, everything he did was for you. He loved all of you very much. And your dad now, he loves you as his own. Everything my son and your mother have done has been in your best interest." He cleared his throat again. "Claire, you have always been my little elephant. You are courageous and strong, but sometimes you charge into things too quickly. All of you need to make sure you are prepared to hear the answers before you ask the questions." Then he hung up.

I didn't know what my grandfather meant by that, but the lies my parents were telling were only getting bigger.

"So what now?" Forrest asked.

"Grandpa just called her an elephant," Avery said.

I swatted at him, but he dodged just in time.

"I guess we know Mom was lying," Parker said.

I swiveled my chair around to face all of them. "I think we've got to try to translate this letter and see if it tells us anything,"

"We could find someone who teaches Japanese, or there has to be someone around here who served a mission there," Parker suggested.

Avery punched Parker in the arm. "You're so stupid," he said. "If Mom and Dad weren't willing to tell us that Dad knew our father, there might be other secrets in that letter. Did you not see how mad Mom was a few minutes ago when she realized we—I mean *Claire*—had taken it? Do we really want someone else to see our family's dirty laundry?"

"Why don't we try to use one of those online translation sites?" I suggested. I turned around and opened my Internet browser. After typing in the address for the translating website I sometimes used for my German class, I realized how flawed my thinking was.

"What are you waiting for?" Avery asked.

"I have no idea how to type Japanese characters with this keyboard," I said.

We sat in silence for a moment.

"Do you need a special keyboard?" Forrest asked.

I shrugged. I did a search for "Japanese keyboard" and there were multiple sites that sold them. But we needed a credit card to pay for it.

"Use the prepaid card Grandpa sent you last Christmas," Parker said.

Parker and Avery had both spent theirs the next day on after-Christmas sales. I had saved my card for emergencies. This seemed to qualify, but I had to try other options first. I didn't want to wait for a keyboard to be shipped.

"I wonder if there's software or something we can download," I said and did another online search.

"*Free* software," Avery said.

I amended my search.

The computer screen filled with enough results that we were able to sort through and pick the one that seemed the easiest to use. Once we had downloaded the program, it automatically opened, and a table with Japanese characters appeared.

I clicked on the table and moved it to the right side of the screen, then placed the image of the letter on the left so we could see both at the same time. "All we have to do now is look at the picture of the letter, find the character that matches in the table, and when we click on it, the program will type out the character. We can cut and paste that into the translation site, and then when we have all the words together, we can have it translate the sentence."

Avery grunted. "Yeah, I just realized I don't care about this that much."

I turned around and found Forrest shaking his head. Avery had already irritated me enough today that I wanted to smack him. He started to leave, but Parker grabbed his arm.

"Are you saying you don't care our parents might be keeping other secrets from us," Parker asked, "or are you saying you're lazy?"

"Aw, you know I hate multiple choice," Avery said. "Okay, eeny meeny, miney . . . let's go with option B."

Parker and Forrest both struggled to maintain a straight face. I think they normally wouldn't have held back if I weren't already annoyed.

"Get out of my room," I said to Avery.

Avery skipped out of the room, arms swinging like a five-year-old. A few moments later, the sound of the Xbox booting up in the family room floated up through the vents.

Parker let a laugh slip. He glanced at my rigid expression, cleared his throat, then said, "I'll be right back."

He returned with a couple of folding chairs from the linen closet, which he set up on either side of me. They both sat down, then Forrest said, "Claire, why don't you take the first character, Parker you take the second, and I'll take the third. That way we can work as fast as possible."

I found mine and clicked on it, and then Forrest and Parker pointed to their characters on the table. We continued this way until we had formed a word and then a couple of sentences, but the process was slow and about as fun as cleaning toilets.

In the middle of the third sentence, Parker stood up. "How about we continue this tomorrow?"

"That's fine," I said. We had been working for two hours, but it felt like days had passed. The sun was high in the sky, and my stomach was starting to growl.

I watched Parker leave and then turned to the screen again. The two sentences we'd completed told me nothing: *Thank you for your answer. It seems old to communicate this way.*

Forrest rested his head on my desk with a blank expression.

"You don't have to do this anymore," I said. "But I want to try to finish this sentence."

Forrest pushed his chair away from the desk and stood. "I'm going to get us something to eat."

I nodded and kept working even though a break would've been nice. But if I stopped and went downstairs, Avery would give me a hard time about being lazy. It wouldn't matter that he had spent the last few hours playing video games.

I matched and clicked and matched and clicked, and when I had the last of the words in the sentence, I raised my fists in triumph, then pasted the sentence into the translator. It hadn't been translating everything perfectly, but there seemed to be enough correct here that I wanted to find out what the rest of the letter said.

Forrest returned with a plate in each hand. He set one down next to me filled with a peanut butter sandwich and carrot sticks.

"Look at this!" I pointed at the screen.

He sat down and read.

In my situation, they do not often suspect letters sent by post.

"WHO'S *THEY*?" Forrest asked.

"And why would anything sent from my father be 'suspect'?" I said.

Forrest tore off a corner of his sandwich and threw it in his mouth. He barely chewed before he swallowed. "Let's finish the rest of the letter and see if it gives us more information."

"How about we each translate every other character?" I said. "You take the first one, and I'll be looking for the one that comes next until we've matched all the characters in the word."

"Let's do it."

We took turns pecking at the keyboard, the timing evolving into a steady rhythm. The sound of machine guns and horrifying deaths sailed up through the vents from time to time, reminding me there were better ways to spend a weekend. By early evening, Forrest and I were able to merge our sentences to complete the letter.

Dear George,

Thank you for your answer. It seems old to communicate this way. In my situation, they do not often suspect letters sent by post.

Here is the information.

15-8192-45
15-8192-46
15-8192-47

81-80-50722259
This is his telephone number if you need to contact him.

Thank you for helping me. It is much importance to me. I always feared I would not be able to take care of this if at all times.

   -Henry

"Maybe the translator got it wrong," Forrest said. "Was anything else with the letter?"

I shook my head. From what I could tell, the letter suggested my father trusted my dad. The translation could be wrong, but I couldn't shake my mom's reaction in the kitchen. There had to be a reason for her to hide this relationship from us. Did she have an affair with my dad? And if so, is that something I would I want to know?

"What do you want to do?" Forrest asked.

"Maybe my parents are hiding something, and maybe they aren't," I said, "Either way, I know the questions will fester until I know for sure."

"You didn't answer my question," Forrest said. "I already knew you weren't going to let this go. What do you want to do?"

I pressed my back against the chair. Theories tangled in my head, yet I couldn't ask the very people who could give me answers. "I'm calling the phone number."

"But you don't even know who that is," Forrest said.

"I can find out." I turned back to my laptop, went to a reverse phone number lookup website, and entered the phone number. All it gave me was a location: Tokyo, Japan. I attempted several other sites, and all of them gave me the same information.

"Maybe I don't know who this person is, but it sounds like he was important to my father, so I figure they must have been good friends. And if they were good friends, he must know something about my father, right?"

"Makes sense, but how do you know if he speaks English?"

"He's in Tokyo. Everyone in Tokyo speaks English."

"Are you sure?"

Butterflies danced in my stomach. "I guess there's only one way to find out."

I picked up my phone and had just entered the number when Forrest said, "Wait." I ended the call.

He reached for his wallet in his back pocket and dug around until he found a white plastic card. "Use this. It's an international calling card that I use to call Oma in Germany. Otherwise it's going to be really expensive, and I think your parents are going to notice the charge on the bill."

"And your mom won't notice a charge to Japan?"

"The card has a certain amount of money, so depending on where you call and how long you talk, it deducts different amounts. When the card runs out, Mom gets me a new one."

"Good thinking." I took the plastic card from him and followed the directions on the back, dialing 011 first and then the rest of the number. "And thank you."

Each passing second propelled my pulse faster.

After six rings, I had decided to hang up, when a man's gruff voice answered. *"Moshi, moshi."*

THE MAN ANSWERED in Japanese. My lips went numb, words frozen in my throat. Even though I had been the one who had called, I hadn't actually prepared myself to speak to anyone. Forrest rustled my sleeve.

"Uh, hello," I said. "You don't know me, um, but my name's Claire Takata."

Silence.

"And uh, I don't know if you speak any English, but if you do, I was just wondering if you might happen to know my father, Henry Sato."

Silence.

"Can you tell me who I'm speaking to?"

Silence.

"Okay, I'm guessing you don't understand what I'm saying. I'll just hang up now, so, um . . . good-bye." Another thought occurred to me. Something my grandfather had told me. "Wait! His Japanese name was Hideki. Maybe you knew him by that name. Hideki Kawakami."

Silence.

"Or maybe not. Okay. Bye."

"Yes," he said.

Not expecting a response, I panicked. "Yes you knew him, or yes you want me to hang up?"

The line went dead.

Forrest searched my face for answers. I set down my phone.

"Nothing," I said, but wondered if the silence of *nothing* might mean *something*. I brushed away the thought. "Apparently not everyone in Tokyo speaks English. Probably a wrong number anyway."

I plunged onto the bed, sorting through what my next step would be as I stared at the ceiling.

The silence had almost made me forget anyone else was in the room when Forrest said, "Claire, let all of us help you."

I sighed and sat up. "No, I can do this. I just—"

Forrest rose from his chair and left my room. When he returned, Parker was with him. Parker crossed the room and came over to my laptop. He read the full translation before he sat on the floor with his back against my closet door. "We need to call a meeting."

"This is a family matter," I said. "Why get everyone involved?"

"Because we're all family." Forrest placed himself next to me on the bed. He scooted himself toward the headboard so he could stretch his long legs. "You're the one who always says we need an APM. Call Nicholas and make sure he brings Fed. Fed knows a lot of Japanese from those comics he reads."

APM: Axis Powers Meeting, a meeting used for strategizing and discussing important things. When Parker and Nicholas were in the sixth grade, they learned about three countries that had joined forces during World War II. They then dubbed our three families the Axis Powers, and it had stuck ever since. Nicholas and Fedele Russo were the Italians; Forrest Langford represented the Germans; and the Takatas—Parker, me, and Avery—were the Japanese.

The next year, when Forrest and I were in sixth grade, we learned the Axis powers had not only been defeated, but they had done really terrible things—atrocities so despicable, I was convinced Parker and Nicholas hadn't paid any attention in class at all. But by then, the name had stuck, and we decided we'd write our own history.

"We know how you are, Claire," Parker said, "and you aren't going to be any fun until you feel like you've done everything you can to get answers."

Though I didn't want the help, Parker and Forrest wouldn't be satisfied until a meeting was called. Most likely Parker just wanted to get everyone together to play their new video game, *Song of the Assassin*. So I fumbled for my phone. "Fine. Get Avery, and I'll call." I pressed speed dial for Nicholas, and when he answered, I said, "APM. Now. Bring Fed."

Nicholas Russo was a year older than me, a senior like Parker, and Fedele, who went by Fed, was a year younger than me, a sophomore like Avery.

Within a few minutes, they arrived. Avery trailed behind them and headed directly to a rug in the middle of my floor. He lay facedown and rested his head on his folded arms, ready to sleep.

Nicholas pushed past Parker at the door and planted his thick body at the side of my bed. His deep mahogany hair was hidden beneath a Seattle Seahawks hat, and his dark eyes peered down at me with a serious expression.

"Who hurt you, Kiki?" Nicholas asked. His low voice filled the room. At six foot four and with the body of a linebacker, most found him intimidating.

Not me.

I grabbed a pillow and swung it at him. "That's not why I told you guys to come over," I said. "And even if someone had hurt me, I wouldn't need you to fix it."

He shoved my shoulder. "I know, I know. I've taught you well, Kiki."

I ignored him and turned to face my computer.

Forrest pointed at the letter on the monitor. "*Claire* called you over to look at this." I don't remember when Nicholas nicknamed me Kiki, but Forrest had never cared for it.

Fed bounced over and plopped into the chair at my desk. A million freckles splashed his pale cheeks, and his hair had a lot more red than Nicholas's, but his eyes were the same dark brown. He was almost as tall as his brother, but he hadn't inherited the same muscular frame, so his gangly ape arms swung from one side to the other when he situated himself to get a better look at the screen. "So what is it?"

I tried to explain everything the best I could.

"This is so cool," Fed said when I'd finished. "Totally reminds me of Yama Katana volume one: *Incipient Soul*. The ghost of Kaito's dad comes back and says, 'You have to protect your mother and sister,' and Kaito's all like, 'I'm only fourteen. How am I supposed to do that?' And then ghost-dad says—"

Avery lifted his head from the floor. "Fed, can you help or what?"

Sometimes I wondered how they had ever become friends. Fed glared at Avery, then returned his focus to the note.

His eyes moved from side to side as he looked at the image of the original letter on one side and our translation on the other. "So we have numbers . . ."

Fed mumbled to himself for some time. Then he gasped and pointed to one of the last sentences. "Okay, I could be wrong, which I'm not, but I'm pretty sure this part right here is translated incorrectly. Your translation says 'I always feared I would not be able to take care of this if at all times.' But it's not *if at all times*. This phrase means, 'if I die early' or 'if I die an early death,' which I know 'cause Kaito's mom says this in volume seven."

Early death? I swallowed hard. Fed had to be wrong. Maybe it should have been "before I die" but even then, something concerned my father enough to want it handled if he couldn't.

"Are you sure?" Avery said.

Fed nodded. "Almost sounds like he knew he was going to die or something—I mean, before he, you know, actually died."

Nicholas and Parker walked over to the computer and surrounded Fed.

If he died an early death.

My heart drummed faster. "There's no way he could've *known* he was going to die of a heart attack."

"Maybe he didn't die that way," Fed said. "You know, like how Kaito's dad was murdered by the Gushi Clan?"

Nicholas jabbed Fed's bony side.

Fed glanced up and cringed. "What was that for?"

Nicholas wrangled Fed into a chokehold. "I think what

Fed meant is that if your father knew someone was after him, it might explain how he also knew his death was coming." His voice was steady, even though Fed wriggled against him.

"There's no way that's true," I said. "You're saying my father knew but didn't leave a note behind for his kids? That he actually could have said good-bye in case something happened, but didn't?"

Avery's face grew tight, his eyes narrowing. "This is messed up." He dropped his head back to the carpet.

Fed broke Nicholas's hold. "In Yama Katana volume forty-three," he said, lit with excitement, "the ghost of Kaito's dad comes back and says, 'You gotta get shards of yellow crystal from the heart of Mount Hakai.' But Kaito says—"

Avery sat up. "So are you suggesting we get shards of crystal from a mountain?" His face puckered into a deathly look. "This isn't a manga. This is reality."

Fed turned in my direction. "All I'm saying is that Kaito goes on this journey." He brushed his dark hair out of his eyes over and over again as it fell with each head bob. "And in the end, it turns out Kaito woulda been better off if he'd never gone looking for answers in the first place. I vote we forget about all of this."

"Because of your manga?" I said. "Who knows what else my parents have been hiding?"

Fed bit his lip, then said, "I'm just saying . . ."

The air felt too thick to breathe. "Okay," I said, "meeting adjourned."

"We're not finished," Parker said. "We need to discuss a plan."

I shut my eyes. "What's left to discuss?"

"How about making sure we know how our father really died?" Parker asked.

"So we'll find out how he really died," I said. "Meeting adjourned."

Parker sighed and shook his head. "Don't you think we—"

"Nope." I rotated my chair around and stared at the letter on the screen of my laptop.

My room felt crowded. I didn't know what to do with all this information. I needed to get out of here. If I left now, I could drive to somewhere in California and be relaxing on the beach tomorrow.

Like that would ever happen.

Parker folded his arms. "We should at least consider—"

"Not now."

Parker dropped his arms to his sides and motioned for everyone to follow him out of the room.

Only Forrest stayed behind. He straightened his back, hung his arm around my shoulder and pulled me closer, the scent of fresh linen mixed with musk washing over me. "You okay?"

The words froze in my throat when I tried to speak, so I shrugged. His chest moved with steady, even breaths. I focused until my rapid breaths slowed to match the pace of his.

"I know this could end up being nothing," I said. "But I can't get rid of the twisted knot in my stomach telling me something isn't right. At the very least, my parents have lied to us about my dads knowing each other, and it's hard to trust—" Anger forged a path through my head and chest. My neck and shoulders stiffened. My breaths quickened again. I struggled to regain focus.

Forrest squeezed my shoulder and put his chin on the top of my head. "Do you remember when we were in the fifth grade, and someone stole the model airplane Oma sent me from Germany?"

"Yeah." I grabbed a Hello Kitty pillow and hugged it against my chest.

"You told me you were going to help me figure out who stole it, no matter what it took. And then you asked Mrs. Banks if you could make an announcement, and you stood in front of the class and said your dad was in charge of the whole US military, and if the plane wasn't returned to my desk by the end of the day, you would have your dad hunt them down and take them to jail."

"And you got your plane back," I said, smiling a little.

"It was sitting on my desk by lunch." He pulled away so he could face me. "I'm going to help you figure this out no matter what it takes."

I looked down. The pillow was in my lap. My breaths had slowed. The tension in my muscles had melted. I glanced at him and stared into eyes that were soft and lips that knew the right thing to say even when I didn't. Always.

My hand reached up to touch his cheek, but I caught myself and pulled back. "Thank you." I vaulted off the bed and threw myself into the chair in front of my laptop.

He sat next to me in the same folding chair he'd been using for hours.

If there was any chance my father knew he was going to die, I needed to know. I typed my father's name, Henry Sato, into Google, like I'd done many times before during moments when I wanted to remember him. Previously, I'd avoided some sites, run by people who had been in his courtroom, who didn't like him.

What would give him a reason to fear an early death? Would any of those people have had a grudge?

I scrolled through page after page, until I got to the link of one of my favorite articles, written when my father died. The writer listed all the wonderful things Henry Sato had accomplished, including the fact that he was the youngest judge ever appointed in the first circuit. A quote from his clerk said how my father had made a difference in Hawaii. She said he was always the first one there, usually arriving at 6:00 A.M. with a coffee in one hand and Zippy's Loco Moco in the other. His bailiff mentioned how respected my father was by fellow judges and coworkers despite his playing elaborate pranks on them every April Fool's Day. One of the people on the maintenance staff said my father never forgot a name or a birthday, and on his own birthday, he would bring Dobash cake for everyone in the courthouse because it was his favorite.

Forrest's hands fell on my shoulders. I lifted my chin to see his blue eyes gazing down at the screen.

My heart grew heavy. "They all knew him better than I did."

Dear Otochan,

Mom made me help her clean out the garage today. I don't understand why we couldn't do it next Saturday instead when Avery and Parker would be home to help. You'd think we could've done some fun mother-daughter bonding thing. But no.

And then when we were organizing the shelves, there were three boxes that had your old clothes in them. Mom wanted to donate them to Goodwill, but I wanted to keep them. I told her if I kept the boxes in my closet, she'd still have space on the shelves to store other stuff. She said to give her one good reason why I needed them, and I couldn't. What if I want them because they were yours? She told me I could choose ONE (!!!) of your old shirts. I chose your University of Hawaii sweatshirt that says "Go Rainbow Warriors" on the front. Mom shook her head and said, "You're just like your father sometimes." So I said, "Good-looking?" That's funny, right? And then I got grounded for being "sassy."

So I'm sitting here in my room, wondering what Mom really meant when she said I'm like you. I think she meant I'm stubborn, but I don't remember you enough to know how I'm like you. I'd like to think I have some of your good qualities. You must have been brave because you moved to America even though you didn't speak English. And you must have been smart because you were a judge. I wish Mom talked about you. She gets all weird whenever I ask too many questions, so I don't bother anymore. I may not remember much about you, but I'm pretty sure you wouldn't have grounded me today over something that stupid. She's going to miss me when I move to London.

Love,
Claire, age 13

THE GARAGE DOOR clattered open, making my bedroom floor vibrate. I wasn't sure where Dad had been all day, but I was happy he hadn't been there when Mom discovered I'd stolen the letter back. I knew Mom had started cooking dinner when the smell of steamed rice and marinated beef swept up the stairs and into my room.

"I think we should go downstairs," Forrest said and patted his stomach.

A million thoughts raged in my head on our way down the stairs. I slid the bead on my necklace back and forth along the chain.

Dad walked through the door from the garage and smiled when he saw me at the bottom of the stairs. At just under six feet, he was taller than most Japanese men. Parker and Avery often wished they had gotten his genes for height rather than the ones they inherited from our biological father.

I crossed the short hallway and met him in the kitchen. "How's my princess?" Dad asked. He put his hands on my shoulders and kissed my forehead. "Better?"

My heart softened. How many fatherless kids like me only longed to have a stepdad like mine? I let go some of the anger from the secrets that had been kept and wrapped my arms around his waist.

"Great." If I was going to confront my parents, I would need to find more information on my father.

Forrest joined Mom at the stove and helped her stir meat and vegetables in a wok.

"Are you serious?" Nicholas shouted at a video game on the TV in the family room. I looked over and saw a race car with a crumpled hood, crashed into a concrete barrier.

Parker thundered down the stairs and was about to pass us, but Dad held out his hand to stop him.

"Did you get everything done?" Dad asked.

Parker pushed up his glasses and looked at the ground. "Uh, not really."

Dad folded his arms. "Parker, you can't actually go to college if you don't put in the work to get accepted. I want a spreadsheet of all the colleges you plan to apply to, along with application due dates, the number of teacher recommendations requested, which test scores they accept, and the reason you think it's a good fit. By tomorrow morning."

Parker grunted.

Dad gave him a look.

"I'll have it on your desk by tomorrow morning," Parker groaned. He wandered into the family room, startling Nicholas when he threw himself on the couch.

Nicholas glanced up and, realizing Dad was home, hopped to his feet. Dad opened the fridge and took out a bottle of Coke. I could never taste the difference, but he insisted his drink had to be from a glass bottle, not a can. He uncapped his bottle and took a sip.

Dad called over to Forrest. "You boys staying for dinner?" He loosened his top shirt button.

Nicholas edged next to Dad and gave him a one-armed hug. "If you insist."

My brothers and I liked to joke that Nicholas was my dad's favorite son. In Nicholas's eyes, my dad could do no wrong. Nicholas was always the first to volunteer if my dad needed anything. He took my dad's side no matter what.

Most of the time it was endearing, except when it involved me. Dad always told Parker he needed to watch out for his little sister, and Nicholas acted as if a direct order had been given to him instead.

Forrest held his nose only inches from the pan of frying meat on the stove, breathing in the savory, curling steam. "We're definitely staying," he said. "I'll help Claire set the table." He reached into the cupboard and grabbed some plates.

I went to the cabinet to get drinking glasses and met Forrest at the table.

"I assume your application is ready to go," Dad said to Nicholas.

"Yep," Nicholas said. "I put everything on your desk earlier this afternoon, so it's ready for you to review." Ever since Nicholas and Fed's father had walked out on them, Dad helped their mom out with stuff like this because she was always working.

"Good." Dad clapped Nicholas on the shoulder.

Mom nudged them to the side so she could get what she needed from the fridge. She rinsed some lettuce at the sink and tore off leaves to make a salad. Forrest and I circled the table, arranging dishes, cups, and utensils at each seat.

"You could at least try to make yourself useful, Parker," Mom said with a sharp edge in her voice. Parker moaned and got off the couch.

She finished the salad with some cherry tomatoes and placed it on the table harder than necessary, the plates and glasses rattling.

Everyone stopped moving.

"And if you're not going to help, at least tell your brother to come down for dinner," she said. "I assume Fed's here too, so get both of them."

Parker stepped backward a couple of yards, his feet light as if walking on eggshells.

When he returned with Avery and Fed, we all took our seats around the table.

"Itadakimasu." Dad clasped his hands together and did a slight bow.

"Itadakimasu," the rest of us said and bowed.

The guys piled their plates high, their food almost spilling over the edge. Avery passed some meat with his chopsticks to Parker's chopsticks, and Mom slapped Parker's hand. The meat dropped to the table.

"Bad manners," she said.

And now, we all knew why. I caught a smirk flash across Avery's lips. Avoiding Mom's gaze, Dad asked all of us how the week had gone at school. The rest of the guys answered without much prodding, but my brothers and I shared some glances, not sure what to make of everything we'd discovered today.

Mom remained silent, barely touching her dinner. Every now and then I caught Dad asking questions with his eyes, but she would only lower her head and pretend to eat again. After several helpings, the guys thanked Mom for the meal and excused themselves to go home and do homework. I suspected they were really excusing themselves from the forced conversations and awkward glances across the table.

"Call me if you need anything," Forrest said, before he said good-bye.

My brothers and I helped clear the table. As much as possible, we tried not to cross paths with Mom. We finished without either parent saying anything to us, and I prodded them back into my room.

Parker sat on top of my desk and couldn't stop smiling.

"What's with you?" Avery asked. He dropped to the carpet in his usual spot and stretched out.

"Mom forgot to give us a punishment," Parker said, swinging his legs in the air.

Though it seemed as if we had gotten off scot-free, I wasn't ready to celebrate yet. I'd expected the letter to give us answers, but it only raised more questions.

At 1:36 A.M., I crawled into bed and stared at Forrest's bedroom window, located directly across the yard from mine. His curtains were still open, but the lights were out. For him, sleep trumped pretty much anything, so he had gone to bed hours ago.

Outside, the night was still. The cool air had probably chased all the chirruping crickets away. Only a small part of my parents' room was below mine, but I could hear them arguing as parts of their muffled words drifted through a shared vent.

How could you not tell me about the letter? Mom sounded hurt.

I didn't know about it. I have no idea where it came from. Dad's voice was soft.

What are we going to tell the kids? Now they know you knew Henry. Worry had trickled into Mom's voice.

You should consider telling them the truth. I think they're old enough.

I'm not ready. Her voice trembled.

I slid out of bed and pressed my ear to the vent.

Are we safe here? Maybe we should have moved somewhere farther like Alaska or Maine.

I'll make sure nothing ever happens to our family.

My stomach lurched. Why wouldn't we be safe? I leaped back in bed, curling my knees to my chest. Their voices quieted almost immediately, but I couldn't relax long enough to fall asleep.

If I could figure out what they were hiding, maybe I could find a way to keep us safe.

To calm my mind, I reached into my pillowcase, took out my father's old sweatshirt, and set it next to me on the bed. It was one of only two connections to him that were solely mine—the sweatshirt and his journal.

Mom was alone in the living room the next morning when I found her. She patted fresh rice into a metal cup with her small hands and set it in front of the butsudan, barely stirring when I moved next to her. The urns I saw on TV always looked like a vase, but my father's urn was a specially crafted wooden box that sat on top of the shrine.

I wanted to ask her what Dad thought we were old enough to know, but I didn't want to confirm I had overheard them and prevent future discussions they might have.

She tilted her head toward me. Her face was exhausted and puffy.

"Does it get any easier?" I asked. "Missing him?"

Her eyes sagged into an even more tired expression. "A little. I still miss him so much it hurts, but fortunately I have your dad. He's saved me and our family in so many ways. I don't know what I'd do without him."

I nodded. "Is there . . . is there any way our father knew he was going to die?"

She hugged her chest as if cold. "How could he have possibly known that?"

I picked at a hangnail. "Then how did he really die?"

"Huh?" Mom's eyes glanced to my dad's study. She hesitated. "You already know he died of a heart attack."

"Really?" I asked, my voice wavering.

"Really," she said and left before I could ask any more questions.

"But he was only forty-five," I said to an empty room.

Dear Otochan,

I was sent to the principal's office today. It's the first time I've ever gotten into trouble at school, but I don't regret it.

Last week, Nicholas found out Chase Phillips had started a bet to see how far he could get with me. Chase got some guys to pool money together, and at the end of the month, he would get a certain percentage of the pot depending on what base he got to. A couple of days later, Nicholas took Parker and Forrest to go deal with him. They won't tell me what they did or what they said to Chase, but Nicholas told me they made sure Chase won't bother me again.

On the one hand, I'm grateful they were watching out for me. But I was mad because they made it look like I need them to fight my battles, which I don't. Ever since then, Chase has been glaring at me every time we pass each other in the hallway. People started spreading rumors about me and Chase, and even if he wasn't the one who started them (which he probably was) it's still his fault. It makes me want to move to Canada. Everyone I've met from there is nice.

Anyway, at the end of fifth period today, I confronted him, and he started calling me all these names. Honestly, I don't even know what some of the words meant. But they sounded bad. So I punched him right in the eye. For a second I thought he was going to cry. And then I thought I was going to cry because I thought I'd broken my hand. But there was no way I was going to give him that satisfaction.

Mom says I have to apologize, but I'm not going to. Dad says he agrees with Mom, but I could tell by looking at Dad's face that he's actually proud of me. And, he didn't ground me. What's the purpose of Dad teaching me how to defend myself if I'm not going to use it? Practicing on a punching bag doesn't hurt half as much as the real thing, so technically I've already been punished enough.

Love,

Claire, age 16

UNABLE TO SLEEP, I woke up Wednesday morning at 4:47 A.M. The past few nights had been plagued by the same restlessness.

The sky was black with splashes of purple and a thumbnail moon. The question surrounding my father's death lingered in my mind, pushing out thoughts of much else.

If I could get a copy of the death certificate, I would know for certain how he died. My parents kept personal documents in a file cabinet in Dad's office. Maybe there was something in there.

Since I'd already gotten in trouble for snooping around, I'd need a legitimate excuse to be in there. And I had the perfect one.

Mom was still asleep when I went into their room. Dad's side was empty. He must have left for a business trip before I had woken up. I never knew when he'd be home or away on a trip—he traveled for work so often, and sometimes he didn't know his schedule right away himself.

I tiptoed to Mom's side and gave her a nudge.

Mom's eyes stayed closed. "Mmmm?"

"Coach says I need to bring a copy of my birth certificate."

"What time is it?" she mumbled.

"Almost five. I'm going to get it and make a copy in Dad's office, okay?"

"Mmm," she said. "That's fine." She rolled away from me.

I tried to make as little noise as possible when I left their bedroom.

The file cabinet in the corner of the office appeared locked, but this one never was because the lock was broken. All I had to do was jiggle the drawer until it slid open. I found the file labeled FAVORITE SCRIPTURE PASSAGES. Mom always said if someone wanted to steal our identification, they'd find a way to do it, but this might deter anyone who broke into our house.

The documents were organized from youngest to oldest. Our Social Security cards, immunization records, name change documents when Dad adopted us, birth certificates. At the back were Mom's copies of her marriage certificates to Dad and my father. The last document was my father's death certificate in a weathered envelope.

I'd seen the certificate in the folder before, but I'd never had a reason to look at it. I slid it from the envelope and unfolded two pages, both blank on the backside. I fed both pages through Dad's copier, returned everything to the file cabinet, and went upstairs to study what I'd found.

The sun hadn't risen yet, so I turned on a lamp when I sat at my desk and read the first page: "Enclosed you will find the final, amended certificate of death." I reviewed the next page.

Seeing my father's life reduced to a file number on a sheet of paper made a hollowness inside me swell. I don't know what I expected, but under CAUSE OF DEATH, it said my father had died of an acute myocardial infarction.

I glanced out my window and stared at a black SUV parked across the street. The car started its engine and drove away, leaving a whirlwind of shadowy leaves in the light of the street lamp. I waited for the leaves to settle before I read the pages again. "Final, amended certificate" sounded like something on the document had been changed.

I opened my laptop and did a search.

In cases where the circumstances of death are questionable, an autopsy is ordered, and the cause of death is listed as "pending." The final, amended certificate is issued once the full examination has been completed.

He couldn't have known he might die early if he had died from a heart attack, so how could the circumstances of his death be questionable?

We had just gotten back from a movie when my father collapsed and died soon after. Nothing about that should cause suspicion, but if an autopsy was ordered, there had to be something I was missing. If I had the report, it might give me answers.

I searched again. The progress circle swirled until the results loaded. According to the instructions on the Hawaii government's site, all I had to do was complete information on their website: date of death, his name, my relationship, address, and a few other things.

The fee was small but still caused a slight twinge in my chest as I removed my prepaid Visa card from my wallet. After the purchase, I would still have money on my card, but not enough to buy the soccer cleats I wanted. I'd have to hope Grandpa would be sending me another prepaid credit card for my birthday—I didn't have time to work for spending money, between soccer practice and school.

I typed in the numbers and reviewed them to make sure I hadn't made any mistakes. At the bottom of the page was space for a digital signature. I entered my mom's name, Lynne Takata. The only thing missing before I clicked the submit button was her driver's license number.

Mom had woken up. Even though Christmas was months away, she was in the kitchen whistling "The First Noel." To get the information, I would need help.

My brothers would be up in about thirty minutes. I jumped in the shower and got ready for school.

Avery would never help me, so after I had dressed in a plain T-shirt and jeans, I called out to my older brother.

"Parker!"

He didn't answer, so I yelled again. After several attempts, he finally stretched his head into my room, sleep still in his eyes.

"Distract Mom for me," I said.

He grumbled, but I showed him the death certificate to explain what I was doing, and he made his way downstairs.

"I need advice on girls," he said once he had cornered Mom in the kitchen.

Her face was hidden from me, but I could hear excitement radiating in her voice. Parker had bought me more than enough time. I stole into my parents' bedroom, fished in her wallet, typed the number into my phone, then crept back upstairs.

At the bottom of the online form, I chose the option for an expedited delivery even though it was a little more, and submitted the request.

A car horn honked outside my window—Forrest's Jeep. Forrest had become our designated driver because the Russos only had one car, and their mom needed it for work. Parker had totaled three different cars and had his driving privileges taken away by my parents. I was the only one left with a license, but I hated driving and avoided it whenever possible. Forrest was kind enough to absolve me of carpool duty.

In a dash to the car, I grabbed a bagel off the counter without stopping to toast it. The Russo boys were already there by the time Avery and I arrived, Nicholas in the passenger seat and Fed in the back, but waiting for Parker was part of the morning ritual. I slid into the seat behind Forrest, who was eating the usual banana Creamie for breakfast. He claimed it was healthy because it was like a frozen fruit smoothie on a stick. I argued that fruit smoothies weren't necessarily healthy, but it never stopped him.

At the end of the street a black SUV, like the one I had seen hours earlier, appeared. A car like that was common in Utah, but no one on our street owned one. The driver wheeled past us slowly, but all I could see was a hooded man with reflective-lens sunglasses. The driver turned my way, almost like he'd sensed my stare by instinct, but a moment later he whipped his focus back to the road as if he hadn't even seen me.

Avery laughed. "Maybe that's why you don't have a boyfriend. You scare them off."

I caught my reflection in the side mirror. "Maybe I don't have a boyfriend because my whole life has been spent with you guys."

The car had come with specially installed rear-facing seats in the trunk area, and since Avery and Fed were the youngest, they always got banished to the back where the space was small. Avery climbed over the seat and joined Fed.

Still sour, I grew impatient with Parker's daily tardiness. "Come on, Parker!" I shouted through the open front door. I didn't know how he managed to be late when I had woken him up earlier than usual. Distracting Mom hadn't taken *that* long.

Parker toddled out of the house with his shoes and socks balanced in one hand and backpack in the other. He hopped in and pushed me to the next seat.

The school was only a few minutes' drive from home. We had all climbed out of the car when Chase Phillips pulled into the spot next to us in his Mustang convertible. I had heard quite a few girls at school mention how cute he was, but his nasty personality and self-absorption stood out more to me.

Before Chase stalked off toward the entrance, we shared our normal glares at each other, but his was marked by bags under his eyes. His bleached-blond hair was disheveled. If he'd had a bad night, it was certainly well deserved.

Nicholas dropped his brawny arm around me and began to walk me to class. The sleeve of his flannel shirt smelled musty. I tried to push him away, but his arm had a little more muscle than mine. A lot more. He hung on.

"Not that I care," I said, "and not that I want Chase asking me out again. Ugh. But do you realize no one's ever going to ask me out with you draped on me like this?" I hoped the irritation in my voice would cause him to feel at least a little bit guilty.

"Yep, that's the plan," he said.

"You're worse than my dad," I said.

"No one's worse than your dad."

"Okay, fine." I'd only been to a few dances, but Dad had done a professional job of intimidating my dates.

Nicholas stopped and adjusted his Seahawks hat, letting me go for a moment. "Claire." He caught me enough off guard when he called me by my actual name that I stopped too. I made a slow turn to face him, an eyebrow quirked.

"Parker and Avery may take you for granted," he said, "but for the rest of us . . . well, you're the closest thing we have to a sister. We're guys, Kiki. We know how guys think. And we don't want you dating anyone who thinks like we do. Trust me."

Nicholas never really got serious with me. I hadn't expected him to say something thoughtful.

He placed his arm around my shoulder again and resumed walking toward the school's main entrance, pulling me along with him. "Worried you're not going to get asked to the Halloween dance?"

"No." I tried to brush him off again. "Only idiots ever ask me to these stupid dances."

"That's the plan."

I stopped, squatted down, and leaned forward to shrug off his hulk of an arm. "What's that supposed to mean?" When Dad taught me that move, he probably didn't think I would need to use it on Nicholas. I turned around to face him.

"Uh, nothing," he said. "I just meant that I'm surprised no one's asked you yet, but I'm sure it'll happen. I'd hate to think you were at home by yourself while we were having a good time. We would never want to be at a dance without you."

I tried to process what he'd said. Something wasn't clicking. "Why is it that I only get asked to dances? Why not regular dates?"

He looked above him, eyes searching the sky. "You had a date with that Adams guy once."

"And none since then, unless it's a dance, and that's because you and Parker don't want me to feel left out, right? You probably think it's safe because you'll be nearby and you've handpicked the guy that asks me to the dance and warned him not to touch me. Are you paying these people? What do they get out of it?"

"They get a date with a very fun, but very crazy right now, girl." He smiled.

I blinked. "Crazy?" I said, shoving his shoulder. A few girls I didn't know passed us and looked at me like I really was as crazy as Nicholas suggested.

Nicholas laughed and put an arm around me. "Aw, you know I'm just playing with you. You're not crazy."

A frustrated sigh escaped as we started walking again. "Is something wrong with me?" I asked in a quiet voice.

He shook his head. "Of course not. Why would you think that?"

"It's not that I have anyone in particular in mind, and if all I cared about was going on a date, I could ask someone myself, but I hate that I don't know if I'm not getting asked out on dates that aren't dances because you and Parker are intimidating guys or if it's because something is wrong with me. Aren't people supposed to go on dates in high school?"

When we first moved to Utah, there were too many times I wished I had blonde hair so I could look like everyone else. Sometimes it seemed like every girl here was drop-dead gorgeous. Even now, I wondered every so often if I wasn't getting asked out because I didn't look like the group of girls Nicholas surrounded himself with. I hated myself for thinking that. Maybe I was just too awkward.

Nicholas shook his head. "Claire, nothing is wrong with you. You have some misconceptions, but nothing's wrong with you."

"Misconceptions?"

"About dating in high school." He pointed to a group of beautiful girls gathered by the entrance. "Do you see those girls over there?"

"Yeah."

"I promise you they don't get asked out as often as you seem to think. No one really goes on dates. We hang out at parties instead."

Yeah, everyone hung out; however, several girls on my team had boyfriends. I wasn't sure I believed him. But I probed for the more important piece of information. "So are you saying you and Parker have never meddled with my dating life, dances or otherwise?"

He opened the door, and I went through and waited for an answer. The halls were loud and crowded.

Nicholas dropped his arm around my shoulder again. He took a deep breath and exhaled. "I'm saying there's nothing wrong with you."

I smacked his hard chest with the back of my hand. "I knew it! You guys have been doing this all along."

Nicholas didn't flinch. "And because there's nothing wrong with you," he said, "I'm sure you'll get asked to the dance." He gave my shoulder a quick squeeze and jogged away.

"Hey, wait up," he said to a group of senior girls ahead of us. They stopped, all giggles once he caught up to them.

I loved Nicholas like a brother, but he also annoyed me like a brother.

I HAD ALWAYS been a diligent student but found myself distracted all morning with thoughts of what Parker and Nicholas were up to, my father's past, and the lies my parents had told me. I was staring at the pictures plastered on my locker door between sixth and seventh period when Forrest waved a hand in front of me and snapped me to attention.

"Are you coming to history?" he asked.

I looked at a picture of me and all the guys, and then at the one on top with me and Nicholas at a watermelon-eating contest. How easy it would be to go back to a time when I didn't know what I didn't know? I closed the door and spun my combination an extra time to make sure it was locked, then adjusted my backpack on my shoulder and followed Forrest to class.

Except for a row of windows opposite the door, the brick walls of our classroom were covered in posters of former US presidents and buildings that had historical significance. Forrest and I always sat at the back by the poster of Abraham Lincoln. We made our way down the aisle, and I expected Chase to glare at me, but his desk was empty.

Alex Adams usually sat next to Chase. He'd asked me on a date once but hadn't spoken to me since. His brown hair was cropped short, and his big brown eyes gave him a baby face.

"Hey, Alex," I said.

"Hey." Alex immediately turned to get something out of his notebook.

We didn't have assigned seats, but everyone usually sat in the same places. A few girls from my soccer team surrounded us. Katie Pelo took the desk in front and to my left. Her blonde hair was pulled into a tight ponytail. She waved to us as she sat and put her backpack on the floor. The Miyashima sisters, Mika and Kimi, sat directly ahead, with Ashley Cheung on their right. Though there weren't very many of us, it was nice to see fellow Asians at school.

The bell for sixth period rang, but Mrs. Davenport wasn't here. Lanie Ward sneaked in and sprinted to the seat on the far right of the row. Her strawberry-blonde hair was stuffed into a messy bun. She wiped her forehead, her freckles spreading wide when she smiled at us.

Katie turned around and crossed her long legs. "Hey, I'm having a party this weekend. Do you want to come?"

I looked at Forrest, unsure which one of us she was inviting.

She pointed at me. "You, Claire."

Words caught in my throat. I glanced at Forrest. "I don't know if—"

"She'll be there," Forrest said.

"Can he come too?" I asked.

"I already invited him," she said and winked at Forrest.

"Okay, yeah," I said. "I guess I can be there. Thanks." I grabbed my history book from my bag and held it front of my face, pretending to read. If I sneaked a look at Forrest, I knew I would find him shaking his head at me.

I began to hope we would get a free period when a large man walked through the door. He was about six foot six tall with broad linebacker shoulders. His hair was black with waves that clung to his scalp, and his skin looked like the sun had toasted it to perfection.

Lanie twisted around and mouthed, "He's hot." She acted like she might faint from all the swooning, then turned back around.

The large man set a messenger bag down on the desk at the front of the classroom. "My name is Mr. Tama. Marcus Tama." He took a marker and wrote his name on the dry-erase board.

"I'm Maori, and I was born in New Zealand but moved shortly after that." Mr. Tama stood directly in front of the class, posture straight, arms behind his back as if he had been in the military. "Mrs. Davenport has taken a sudden leave of absence, so I am your new teacher."

I thought I detected a slight accent but wasn't sure. He didn't sound like others I had met from New Zealand.

He clapped his hands and lifted our textbook from his bag. "I've also been asked to take over the debate team since Mrs. Davenport was the debate coach as well, so if you're interested, I'm sure we could use some more students."

I wasn't too surprised Mrs. Davenport had left. She'd always seemed like she hated kids, and I never understood why she'd become a teacher in the first place. Nicholas had almost quit the debate team several times because of her, so he'd probably be happy with the change.

Mr. Tama moved behind the desk and locked his messenger bag in the bottom drawer. Instead of sitting in the chair, he sat on top of the desk and straddled the corner.

"In this class," he said, "I expect you to be prepared. And if you're not prepared, I expect you to be honest about it. For the first few weeks, please state your name before you answer a question if I call on you. My understanding is that you were discussing the Boston Massacre?"

A tall guy at the front confirmed. "People call me Mumps, and that's where Mrs. Davenport left off."

Mr. Tama turned to a different part in our history book. "Can anyone tell me another name for this event?"

Alex raised his hand. Mr. Tama nodded in his direction. "I'm Alex, and I think Paul Revere called it the Bloody Massacre."

Mr. Tama's voice was deep and lyrical as he explained the events leading up to the massacre. I hung on every word until he said, "Eight soldiers as well as an officer and four civilians were charged with murder."

Murder. The word prickled something deep inside me, a sharp and bristly reminder that I didn't know what I could be sure about.

"Paul Revere engraved this famous depiction," Mr. Tama continued. He took a print from his desk and held it up for us to see. "But there are a lot of inaccuracies."

He set it down, went behind his desk, and lifted a model from underneath.

"This is a more accurate replica of what it might have looked like." Figures of British soldiers lined one side, complete with uniforms and rifles. The civilians had little hats, and every person had different clothing.

He placed the replica on his desk and held up the print again. "Unlike Paul Revere's picture, it was actually winter, and there was snow on the ground. If you look at his British soldiers, you'll notice they are the only ones firing shots, but in reality, the fighting broke out on both sides. And this person lying on the ground—" He pointed to a spot on the print of a man lying at the feet of the British soldiers. "His name was Crispus Attucks. In Revere's depiction, you can see the man is white, but in actuality, Attucks was black and one of the most famous black men to fight in the Revolution."

Mr. Tama set the print back down on his desk.

"Did you make that yourself?" Mumps asked.

"I did," Mr. Tama said. "Took me two years."

The bell rang, and I gathered my textbook and put it into my backpack.

"No homework tonight," Mr. Tama shouted over the noise of students getting ready to leave. "And don't forget to think about joining the debate team."

On my way out, I paused to take a closer look at the teacher's handiwork.

"Pretty impressive," I said to Forrest in the hall.

"I hope I still play with toys when I'm his age," he said.

I stopped shy of my locker. The door was hanging ajar—and I was positive that wasn't the way I had left it. I flung open the door.

"What's wrong?" Forrest asked.

"Someone took all my pictures."

ONLY A FEW pieces of tape holding ripped photo corners were left on my locker door. Blood rushed to my head.

"Is anything else missing?" Forrest asked.

I rummaged around to see what had been taken, but everything else seemed to be there. I never left my wallet or anything else valuable in my locker. There was no good reason anyone would need to break in. What would they want with my pictures? Couldn't they have just asked? I wouldn't have necessarily given them pictures, but still . . . it would have been easier.

Anyone trying to get my combination would have had a hard time, but it wasn't impossible for someone who was motivated. The second day of my freshman year, I had forgotten my combination and learned the administrative assistant, Mrs. Davis, kept a spreadsheet on her computer. I'd also heard rumors later she had opened lockers on occasion for students when they wanted to leave birthday balloons or an invitation to a dance.

I pounded my fist on the locker next to me. "This has to be

Chase, and when I find out for sure . . ." I had no idea what I was going to do to him. But it would be bad.

"Are you sure it's him?" Forrest closed my locker door.

The visualization of ripped picture corners was inescapable. "I know I'm not perfect, but I can't think of anyone else who hates me enough to do something like this." Had I offended someone that badly in the past year? If anything, Chase had offended *me*, not the other way around, but he seemed to blame me for his disgrace.

"Maybe the person who took the pictures didn't do it because they hate you," Forrest said. He leaned his back against the lockers. The muscles in his arms and neck were tense, and his eyebrows were pinched in.

I tried to digest what he had said, but that made even less sense. My backpack slid down my arm. "That's kind of creepy." It had to be Chase. Chase and his personal vendetta.

"You should go report this."

I opened my locker, threw my history textbook inside and slammed the door. "I guess."

"Do you want me to go to the office with you?" Forrest asked.

"No, I'll go now," I huffed.

"Sorry this happened," he said. "I'm going to get to class, but I'll see you after school." He gave me a quick hug and jogged down the hall.

IN THE OFFICE, Mrs. Davis lifted her head of short, curly white hair when the door closed behind me. She pushed up her bifocals and typed a few more things on her keyboard before meeting me at the counter.

"Someone broke into my locker and stole all my pictures," I said.

Mrs. Davis tsked, then pulled out a piece of paper. "I'm so sorry, honey. Pictures are irreplaceable." She filled out the incident report form, getting details from me as to what was taken and when. "Who would do such a thing?"

"I don't know," I said. "I can print new pictures, but I don't know why they'd do it."

"You kids and your fancy machines," she said. "What's your locker number?"

"Six eighteen," I said. "Did Chase Phillips stop by here earlier for any reason?"

She put the pen to her thin wrinkled lips. "Only when his

mom checked him out after first period. He looked mighty sick."

"Are you sure?"

She bent her head closer. "Are you sweet on him?"

I thought I might throw up. "No. No, I am *not* 'sweet on him.' He wasn't in class just now and . . . and we are supposed to work on a project together."

"I'm sorry, dear. Didn't mean to make you blush." She opened the attendance book on the counter and lifted her bifocals higher so she could read the notes under the date. "He's not here today."

She glanced at her watch. "There's only five minutes left before school gets out," she said. "Why don't you go home a little bit early, and I'll give you an excused absence in the system for this period."

I checked the time on my phone. There was actually forty minutes of class left. I glanced up. She winked.

"Thank you," I said and left.

I walked down the hall and tried to think of who could have stolen my pictures. If Chase had left after first period, it couldn't have been him. Once I got to my locker, I opened it and gathered everything I would need for homework and soccer practice. Why couldn't they have taken my textbooks instead?

Forty minutes was a long time, and I had nowhere better to be. Fed was probably already wondering where I was since I was supposed to be in study hall with him, so I headed to the library.

The bell rang, and Fed and I parted ways to get to our lockers. He'd tried to help brainstorm possible culprits, but like me, all he could come up with was Chase. Students poured from the classrooms. Someone tapped my shoulder from behind.

I spun around. "Oh hey, Mumps."

The wrists of his long-sleeved black shirt were frayed, and his dark jeans had holes in the knees. I hadn't seen him this close before. He had long, dark ruffled hair and a vacant look in his dark eyes.

"Hey, Claire." He clutched a lacrosse stick in one hand. I had forgotten he was on the lacrosse team.

Forrest sneaked in next to me and rested his hand on the small of my back.

"I was wondering if you wanted to go to the Halloween dance with me," Mumps said, cradling the stick up and down, keeping a ball securely in the net. Forrest's hand twitched against my back.

Other than that Mumps was a senior and was in my history class, I didn't know much about him, including his real name. Neither Mrs. Davenport nor the new teacher had made him introduce himself by his real name. What I did know was this was the last thing I needed. Nicholas gave me a wave from the end of the hall, where Mumps couldn't see him.

"You wouldn't by chance be Nicholas's friend?" I asked.

"Actually, yeah," he said.

"Then no."

"Cool. So I'll pick you up at—wait." He rested the end of the stick on the ground and caught the white ball as it rolled out. "Did you just say no?"

"I'm not going with you because—"

"She's going with me," Forrest said, moving his arm completely around my waist.

"Cool," Mumps said. "Sorry, I thought you guys were just friends."

"We are," I said at the same time Forrest said, "It's a new development."

"It's complicated," I said at the same time Forrest said, "She means an easy transition from being just friends."

Forrest pulled me even closer and kissed the side of my head.

The way Forrest held me tight against him was nice, but it was the kiss that sent an unexpected flutter through me. I put my arm around Forrest in the same way and rested my cheek against his chest. The flutter accelerated, the muscles in my face tensed, and my breaths grew so fast that my lungs struggled to keep up as I stretched my face to smile at Mumps.

What was happening? Whatever it was, it was an act—Forrest really was just my best friend. I thought about my conversation with Nicholas earlier. Maybe Forrest had been colluding with them too. I dropped my arm from Forrest's waist, and urged my body to relax.

I waited for Mumps to stroll away before I whirled and said, "What the hell, Forrest?"

He laughed, but the sound coming from his throat sounded strained, forced. "Oooh, you so owe me. I totally saved you."

I yanked my soccer bag from my locker and slammed the door. "I don't need saving." Without waiting for his response, I stormed to the women's locker room.

On the soccer field, my mind raced nonstop while I stopped to tighten the laces of my cleats. If Chase hadn't broken into my locker, then I needed to find out who had. I sat on the grass with the school at my back, and brought the soles of my feet together. Franklin High kept our fields in pristine shape with lush green grass cut at the perfect length. I leaned forward to stretch and breathed in the earthy smells of dirt and grass.

Mika plunked herself next to me and started to stretch too. Her long black hair was in a thick french braid. I wished I knew how to do that with mine. Putting my hair in a ponytail was the extent of my hairdo abilities.

"Want to be my partner for practice drills today?" she asked.

"Sure." I counted to thirty on this butterfly stretch. Then I stood and spread my feet into a wide stance so I could lunge to one side for thirty seconds and then lunge the other way. Across the field, I noticed the leaves of the large cottonwood trees had changed color almost completely.

The rest of the girls on the team were spread all over. Katie jogged to the middle of the field. "Bring it in, girls. Let's get started." As team captain, she was in charge of warm-up drills.

We divided into two lines, each line dribbling through fifteen cones. Right foot only to the end of the cones and back, then left foot only, alternating each touch with the inside of the right foot and then the outside.

After fifteen different drills, Coach Cesar showed up. "Divide into pairs and practice trapping the ball," he called. Coach was a small guy for a soccer player, but he'd played in college and semi-pro in Europe somewhere. "Ten reps each of inside wedge, outside wedge, top of the foot, and then elevator."

His coaching style was militant but effective. He never called the game soccer—only fútbol—and we gave him a hard time for referring to cleats as "boots."

I paired with Mika, and the rest of the pairs lined themselves down the field. She threw the ball to me from about ten feet away, and I stopped the ball with the inside of my foot and passed it back to her.

"So is Parker dating anyone?" She picked up the ball and lobbed it again.

I passed the ball to her. "Not that I know of."

She trapped the ball with her foot and threw to me again. "Do you think he'd say yes if I asked him to the Halloween dance?"

I trapped the ball and passed it again. "I'm sure he'd be ecstatic."

She looked up and fanned her face with her hand, still holding the ball with her foot after my last throw. "I get so flustered when I think about him."

"Parker?"

"Yeah," she said. "He's so cute and funny."

"Are you sure you're not confusing my brother with someone else?" I looked around, then leaned in. "Parker's pretty short for a guy, and he thinks he's really funny but he's not, and he collects junk—"

"Takata! Miyashima!" Coach yelled. "Run five laps."

"Sorry," I said to Mika.

She shrugged. "I'd rather run than do those stupid drills. Let's take our time."

We started to run along the perimeter of the field.

"Who are you going with?" she asked.

"No one," I said.

"Have you been asked?"

"Yeah." Talking and running at the same time wasn't a good mix. I huffed between words.

We jogged the length of the field, turned the corner and ran past the goal at the north end.

"You don't want to go?" she asked.

"Nope."

She waited. I think she wanted me to explain why, but I didn't want to tell her the whole pathetic story. For the past two years, I'd spent homecoming, Halloween, winter formal, Valentine's, and spring formal dances with dates who barely danced with me and then shook my hand when the evening was over. I even got asked to the Sadie Hawkins dance!

I used to think it was rude to say no because asking someone out takes a lot of guts, which I knew because I never had the courage to do it. This was the year I was determined to change that. But it probably wouldn't be the Halloween dance. I'd have to work up to it.

We ran the rest of the laps in silence. At the end of practice, I gathered my stuff together and dribbled my soccer ball toward the parking lot, where I'd meet the rest of the guys. Our sports practices were all at the same time right after school, soccer and football, so we carpooled home too.

I stopped dribbling when the grass turned to sidewalk, where I looked up and my breath hitched. At the far end of the field was a black SUV.

No one ever parked there unless there was a game.

Dear Otochan,

I really wish you were here right now. Everyone is being so dumb. A few days ago Alex Adams from my English class asked if I wanted to go to a movie with him. Mom said it was fine. So Alex came to pick me up today, and Dad went psycho because he said no one had told him about it. He was arguing with Mom in the kitchen, but we could still hear them in the living room.

And even worse, Forrest was here and sided with Dad because "Alex didn't have a great reputation." Whatever that means. I know him from school and he's nice. I'm so annoyed. Anyway, since Alex was already here, Dad took him to his office and closed the door. They talked for about fifteen minutes. Next thing I know, Parker, Nicholas, and Forrest have been invited to come with us.

I'm so sick of being the only girl. I can't tell you how many times I've wished I had at least one sister.

It's not that I even like Alex that way. I was actually very nervous and didn't know if I even wanted to go. But I'm mad because I feel like everyone thinks I can't take care of myself. I'm tired of not fitting in because I'm a girl. And I'm tired of not fitting in with girls because I'm always with boys.

I really hate when my brothers tell me to stop acting like a girl. But what I hate even more is that sometimes I find myself trying not to do the thing that's making them say I'm acting like a girl. Screw them. Why is acting like a girl a bad thing?

I'm moving back to Hawaii to live with Grandpa. He doesn't care that I'm a girl.

Love,

Claire, age 15

I DIDN'T SEE the SUV again the rest of the week, and the number of theories I had about its presence before soccer practice last Wednesday had dwindled. By the time Monday arrived, the car barely registered on my conspiracy meter. The walk to history class that afternoon was long. All weekend I had obsessed over what had happened with Mumps and shoved the thoughts that included Forrest aside. As much as I wanted to blame Nicholas or Parker, I was the one who had been rude. If someone had rejected me that way, I probably would have wilted.

I could tell Mumps I had changed my mind, but I would lose any ground I'd gained in my quest to find a date with a guy who hadn't been preselected. Was it more important to be decent to someone, or declare my independence?

Forrest caught up with me right before I opened the door. "You okay?"

"Peachy." I went inside. Mumps was already seated. When I passed him, I shifted my eyes away.

"Hey, Claire," he said, acting like nothing had happened.

"Oh." I stopped. "Hi." I forced a smile. I should apologize. What would I say?

"You're holding up traffic," Forrest said.

My mind churned, but I couldn't think of anything. Mumps gave me an expectant look. I darted to my desk and sat down.

Mr. Tama entered the classroom and closed the door behind him. He clapped his hands together. "Take your seats," he said to a few stragglers. "Let's get started."

We had moved on to the Boston Tea Party. "Who can tell me about the Sons of Liberty?"

Chase raised his hand and answered. Then Mr. Tama took off from Chase's answer with a story about the conspirators of the Boston Tea Party, with tension and action and mystery. I almost forgot to take notes because I was so wrapped up in what he was saying.

When the bell rang, I couldn't believe how fast the time had gone by.

"Miss Takata?" Mr. Tama called, glancing at a tablet. His eyes drifted among the exiting students.

"What's up?" Forrest whispered.

I shrugged and raised my hand. "I'm Claire."

Mr. Tama motioned for me to come to his desk. Forrest hung back a few rows, and I weaved between some classmates to get there.

My teacher bent his head and spoke in a hushed voice. "Claire, you've been accused of cheating on the last test Mrs. Davenport gave you before she left, a couple of weeks ago."

"What?" I waited for him to tell me he was joking, but

his expression remained the same, eyes narrowed, eyebrows pinched in.

"I don't cheat. Someone said I cheated? Was it another student?" I asked, each word increasing in volume.

"It was," he said.

"Chase Phillips?"

"The policy is to protect the student's identity, but you'll be able to argue your case in a discussion involving the principal, your parents, and the two of us this Friday." He went behind his desk, unlocked the drawer, and retrieved his bag. "Out of fifty questions, you just happened to miss the same two answers as your accuser. In addition, both of you selected the same incorrect answers for the ones you got wrong. And the answers to your essay questions are almost identical."

"Don't you think it's possible someone else cheated off *my* test instead?" I asked. "I've always had perfect grades in history. Look at their grades. Whose are better? Ask Mrs. Davenport!"

"It's possible." He reached into his bag and removed the multiple-choice test we had taken last week. The copy he held had my name written at the top, but it wasn't mine.

"That's not even my handwriting." My voice started to shake. "Someone's switched the tests."

Forrest took quick steps forward. "That's not her handwriting."

Mr. Tama turned his focus to Forrest. "I appreciate your opinion . . . what's your name again?"

"Forrest."

"Forrest. That's right. Look kids," Mr. Tama said to the both of us. "I am brand-new to this school. Claire, you seem like a nice young lady, and I wish I had been here long enough to recognize your handwriting, but I'm afraid there's nothing I can do."

I yanked my backpack from my shoulder, unzipped it, and snatched my notebook. I dropped the bag to the floor, opened my notebook to a random page, and shoved my notes in front of him. "*This* is my handwriting." Heat flushed up my neck.

Mr. Tama drew in a deep breath. "Claire, I understand what you're saying, and I have faith you will be able to use this to prove that you didn't cheat, but I am not in a position to do anything else. This test was given before I got here."

He clasped his hands together and hesitated. "I also need to inform you that you will not be able to participate in any extracurricular activities until you are cleared. Your coach has been notified."

Forrest sucked in a quick breath. He placed a hand on my shoulder. I swallowed hard. "I can't go to soccer practice?"

Mr. Tama shook his head. "I'm sorry. Not until you're cleared."

"Games?" I asked.

"No," he said. "You can't even step on the practice field."

"Do you realize I could lose my spot as a starter?" I struggled to keep my voice from trembling. I understood why he felt like he couldn't do anything, but I couldn't believe how unfair this was.

"I do," he said. "I played football in high school. I have a lot of sympathy for your situation, and I'm sorry I can't do much to help you right now."

I pressed my lips together and nodded. My knuckles had gone white from my tight grip on my notebook. I lifted my backpack from the floor and put my notebook back inside.

Rather than arguing more, I slung my bag on my shoulder

and marched to the door. "I am going to strangle him and feed him to the sharks."

"Claire?" Mr. Tama called out. "I also received extensive training on the antibullying policy at this school, so given that you are under duress right now, I'm going to pretend you didn't say that. And even if you had, hopefully you meant that metaphorically."

Forrest stopped and turned his head. "Of course she did. Utah isn't really known for sharks."

"I can't believe you said that," I mumbled.

A few students milled outside the classroom. Seventh period had already started, which meant there would be fewer casualties as I stormed down the hall in search of Chase.

Since I was only missing study hall, I didn't feel guilty over the fact that I wasn't there. The school was large, and finding Chase was going to be hard, especially without a hall pass. There were three main halls. I'd have to go systematically through each, starting with east wing because that was closest. Mrs. Spencer approached, so I ducked into the bathroom. I waited a minute before I exited. At the beginning of the east wing, I went from classroom to classroom, peeking in quickly, attempting to avoid being seen by the teacher.

I checked all the classrooms but still hadn't found Chase. On my way to the south wing, I glanced out the windows and saw him on the football field for P.E. I sprinted down the hall and out the doors. As I neared the field, I could hear Coach Cesar yelling at them.

"Five laps! All of you!" he shouted. "Next time listen."

An oval running track encircled the perimeter of the field.

About twenty students started to grumble and jog. When Chase passed, I grabbed him by the hem of his T-shirt and tugged him my way. His eyes went wide, but he didn't resist like I thought he might. He was a lot bigger than me. The students who saw me snickered, and Chase's face grew redder.

I pulled him behind the bleachers to get out of Coach's view. He put his hands on his hips and puffed out his chest, leering. "If you wanted to meet me behind the bleachers, all you had to do was ask."

I wanted to slap the arrogant smirk off his face. But instead I folded my arms. "Are you the one who accused me of cheating?"

He tilted his head and his nose and forehead scrunched up. "Huh?"

"Our last history test. Did you accuse me of cheating?" I said, louder this time.

"No. Why would I do that?" His expression remained the same, and I had to admit it seemed genuine. "Do you really think I'm that petty?"

I stared into his brown eyes, searching for the lie. "I don't know. Are you?"

He bent his face closer to mine. "You're not worth my time."

My jaw clenched, and I remembered why I had punched him before. Chase pulled back and said, "Look, this has been fun and all, but I'd rather run laps than stay here and chat with you. I didn't rat on you for cheating."

I threw my hands in the air. "I don't cheat!"

His lips formed a crooked smile. "Fine, but do you really think I'm the only person at this school who doesn't like you?"

I flinched. Even though I knew Chase was trying to get a rise out of me, that remark stabbed me in the gut. Who else thought of me as an enemy? How would I even know?

He turned and ran back to the track. I began a slow trek back inside.

I could tell my parents had already received a phone call from school by the time we got home. My brothers and I walked through the back door and found Dad reading a newspaper at the kitchen island. Most of the time he read in his office, but reading in the kitchen meant he wanted to make sure he caught us as soon as we came home.

"Claire, could you join me and your mom in the living room?" Dad said.

"Oooh, you in truh-bull," Parker sang. He kicked off his shoes. "What'd you do?"

"Robbed a bank." I slipped off my shoes and set them against the wall. "Took hostages and stole a car to get away."

"You're so stupid." Avery shook his head. "Everyone knows hostages only slow you down."

My brothers went upstairs, and I followed Dad into the living room.

Mom waited for us on the couch. Dad motioned for me to sit in a chair on the other side of the coffee table, and he sat next to Mom.

Mom tilted her head. "The school called today and—"

"I didn't cheat," I said.

"I know you haven't been sleeping well," Mom said, wringing her hands together, "and I know taking all of those hard classes can be stressful, and if there's anything you need to tell us, we want you to feel like you can talk to us, and we'll try not to make any rash judgments."

Mom thought I'd cheated. This couldn't be happening.

Dad shook his head the whole time Mom spoke. "We know you didn't cheat," he said.

"But we would still love you if you did," Mom said, bobbing her head. "Is there anything you would like to tell us?"

"I'd like to tell you I didn't cheat." I tried not to sound too angry. "Someone switched the test. It wasn't even my handwriting."

Dad turned to Mom and put his hand on her arm. "She didn't cheat." He turned back to me. "Is there any reason why someone would make this kind of accusation?"

"Because it's probably Chase," I said, even though I had started to second-guess myself. "And he's an assho—" I saw mom's eyes go wide. "He's a dummy."

"Yes, he is." Dad rose to his feet and clasped his hands. "I'm sure everything will be resolved this Friday when we meet with the principal."

"Can't you talk to the school tomorrow morning?" I stood and spoke to Dad. "If you know I didn't cheat, why can't you talk to my teacher and straighten everything out?"

"I'll call tomorrow, but I don't know if it will do any good." He lifted his shoulders and then let them relax. "There's a reason schools have procedures for these things, and mostly likely I'll come across as the belligerent parent who thinks his kid can do no wrong. Friday is only a couple of days away."

I folded my arms and dropped my head. "But I'm going to miss our game against Haven."

"I'll call the school tomorrow," Dad said again. "All we can do is try."

"Thanks. Can I go now?" I asked.

Dad nodded.

I jumped up and went to my room to get my math homework done. On my way to my bedroom, I checked my phone and saw I already had a few text messages from girls on the soccer team.

Katie: Coach told us the news. I know you would never cheat.

Lanie: So did you do it? I mean, I don't think you did, but I wouldn't tell anyone if you did.

Mika: Sorry. That really sucks.

I sent the same text to all of them—I didn't cheat—and threw my backpack on my desk. When I glanced through my window, I saw Forrest at his. I slid mine open.

From Forrest's irritated expression, he'd been trying to get my attention for quite a while. He'd texted me, but his texts had been pushed down by the girls'. He stood at his open bedroom window, arms folded against his bare chest. He shook his wet hair like a dog and adjusted the towel around his waist.

"So . . . I was thinking we should go to the dance," he said with a voice calmer than his twisted eyebrows suggested. "Like, for real."

"First of all, no. Second, you and me"—I pointed to him and then to myself—"are not speaking until you put some freaking clothes on." I turned away from the window.

Although I had to admit he was nice to look at, I tried not to think of his toned abs while I waited.

Forrest grunted. I heard him scrounging around his room. A few minutes later, he returned to the window. "Dressed. Happy now?"

I swiveled my chair to face him and found him in a wrinkled black Arcade Fire concert shirt and his favorite nasty gray sweatpants.

"So what do you think?" he asked.

"I think those sweatpants have outlived their usefulness."

"About going to the *dance* together. I mean, neither one of us has a date, so you know, we could go together and not have to worry about getting dates." He bit on the collar of his T-shirt.

"I'd rather go with Mumps than be your pity date."

He rolled his eyes. "It's not a pity date."

"Then what is it?"

"I dunno. I think it'll be good to get your mind off everything," he said. "C'mon, it will save me from having to ask someone."

Even with the secrets my parents had been keeping, the cheating accusations, Chase, and everything, being his last resort was insulting. "You want me to go with you because you're too lazy to—"

Nicholas burst through my bedroom door, lifted me from my chair, and tackled me to the bed. His Seahawks hat fell to the floor, and his hat hair alone was enough to scare me.

"Ow!" I screamed. "Get away from me." I beat on his back with my fist.

His dark brown eyes shined with excitement as he began his usual routine. "Body slam! Bam!" He stood up and lunged at me, crushing me facedown against the mattress. From behind me, he hooked his right hand under my armpit and locked the palm of his hand on the back of my neck. "Pow! Half Nelson." With his free hand, he tried to grab my left arm and yank it behind my back, but I wiggled that arm free.

I flipped over onto my back and planted my feet on the bed so I could sit up and break his hold. "Seriously, Nicholas. Finished?"

Forrest watched from his window, entertained.

"I'm just getting started, fool!" Standing on the bed, Nicholas's low voice thundered and stretched to fill the room. He bounded over me and jumped off the foot of the bed, then turned to face me. Though he'd never hurt me, he usually succeeded in irritating me.

I hurled a pillow at him.

He ran and jumped back on the bed, leaning right into my face. "Say uncle! Say uncle!"

I shoved his chest, and he fell onto his back on the bed, flailing his arms and releasing cries of anguish.

"Aw, everyone knows you could kick my butt if you wanted to. So what are we talking about besides your bad hairdo?" He took the pillow I'd thrown at him and made himself comfortable.

Parts of my ponytail had come out, but like he could talk. "You should probably see yourself in a mirror before you make fun of my hair." His hair was a combination of matted hat head and static flyaways. I pulled out my elastic, combed my hair with my fingers, and put it back up.

He sat up. "So you were talking about boys then?"

I glared at him.

"Okay, that's fine. Don't answer." Nicholas got to his feet

and found his hat on the floor. "But you know I'll figure out who *he* is. Max? Patrick? Roarke? Phil? Mohinder Sharma?" He waited for me to react to one of the names as he adjusted his hat on his head.

"I don't even know who any of those guys are," I said.

He pointed at me. "Definitely Phil." I released a frustrated breath, and he sat on the bed, dragging me closer to him by my arm.

"Phil? Get out of my room," I said, shooing him away.

Nicholas jumped off the bed. "I'm going to find out who *he* is!" he shouted, leaping across the hall into Parker's room.

"Phil?" Forrest asked.

I got off the bed and went to the open window. "Who is he?"

"He's a senior on the football team." Forrest put his hands on the windowsill. "Think of the stereotypical jock, and that's Phil. Big, dumb, and thinks he's a lot cooler than he really is."

"It's like Nicholas doesn't even know me. Why would I ever like someone—"

"Claire!" Parker shouted behind me.

I turned around. Both Parker and Nicholas were in my room, Parker waving a white envelope. "It's here."

My fingers were already typing when I said, "I'll text Fed."

APM. The report came.

Dear Otochan,

Forrest is dating Olivia, and it shouldn't bother me, but it does. It's not like he hasn't had other girlfriends before, but this one is different. The girls before seemed temporary, but I think he really likes this one.

Forrest is probably the most important person in my life. He gets me more than anyone I know, and I don't think it's just because we've grown up together. When I'm stressed out or worried and going crazy in my head, he has this way of making me feel like everything's going to be all right. He has my back when Parker and Avery are being stupid, which is all the time. He remembers special dates like the day you died, and he's one of the most thoughtful people I know.

When I get a present from him, I know it's going to be something special. Last year, we were talking about favorite books, and I said mine is To Kill a Mockingbird. Months later, when my birthday came around, he gave me a vintage copy. He said he had to look all over the Internet to find it. Being unselfish and kind comes naturally for him. I wish I were more like that.

And I know he's not perfect. I can't stand being in his room because he's so messy. He reads the last page of a book first, and then gets excited about the story and wants to talk to me about it. I don't know how many times he's spoiled the ending. He has holes in his T-shirts because he bites at the collar when he gets nervous or worried. That's gross. And he can be really stubborn, especially when there's something he wants. Does Olivia know all of these things?

I don't want to be jealous, but there's this tiny sting in my heart. Forrest and I have been friends for a long time, and we have all of these good memories. I don't want him spending time making good memories with some other girl who's not always going to be in his life like I will. I guess that sounds selfish.

Sometimes I wonder if I'm in love with Forrest. I know I feel differently about him than anyone else, but I also think that's how it's supposed to be with your best friend. Even if I knew for sure that I was in love with him, I can't see myself doing anything about it. I'd never want to do anything that would put our friendship at risk. It's just not worth it.

And honestly, I have no idea what being in love feels like. Someone told me you feel like you can't breathe when you're around him. The first time I jumped off the high-dive at the pool, I hit the bottom. But I started to panic on my way up because I couldn't breathe, and I thought I would run out of air. That was pure torture. I've never felt like being around Forrest is pure torture.

When you died, I didn't know if Mom would ever be okay. I've always wondered if she would marry you again if she knew you were going to die. Would she marry you if she knew it would end up causing her so much pain? She never talks about you, and when I ask her questions, I can tell she doesn't want to say anything. Maybe it hurts too much. I don't ever want to feel that way. I don't want to feel like talking about Forrest hurts. I don't ever want to feel like I can't breathe or that I can't think straight when I'm around him. I don't want anything to change between us.

I hate Olivia.

Love,

Claire, age 15

THE AIR WAS heavy with anticipation as everyone gathered in my room. If this APM was as ominous as the last one had been, I didn't know if I was ready. I clenched the envelope and waited for everyone to get situated. Forrest sat next to me on the bed. Parker and Nicholas stood with their backs against the wall by the door. Avery lay in the middle of my carpet, and Fed sat in the chair at my desk.

I inhaled a quick breath and opened the report. Disappointment struck me even harder when I read the first page. "It says he died of a myocardial infarction."

Avery jumped up from the floor and grabbed the file from my hands before I could read on. His eyes scanned the paper. He finished and moved on to the second page. "I guess you didn't see the top of page two?"

Nervousness fluttered to the ends of my fingertips. I retrieved the papers from him and read.

The manner of death is: UNDETERMINED

Parker walked over to the foot of my bed. "What's the difference between cause of death and manner of death?" he asked. "How is it undetermined if they know he died of a heart attack?"

Nicholas reached for his phone in his back pocket and typed something. " 'The manner of death explains how the cause of death arose. It is classified as accident, homicide, suicide, or undetermined.' "

Parker took a step closer to Nicholas and looked at the phone. "Maybe he took some pills that accidentally caused a heart attack."

"Or maybe he took some pills knowing it would cause a heart attack," Avery said and sat back down on the floor. "It'd be hard to tell the difference."

Neither of those was something I wanted to think about.

"There's got to be a way to find out," Parker said.

Nicholas's voice was soft. "Is there a reason you guys need to know?" he asked. "If you think about the reasons for it to be classified as undetermined, none of them are going to make you feel better for knowing."

Parker clapped him on the back. "You're probably right."

I fumbled through some more pages and realized I hadn't seen the worst of it. Under identifying marks, the heading TATTOOS caught my attention. Following that was page after page of pictures of my father's body. Some focused on close-ups of his arms, his legs, his back. Some showed his full body from different angles.

I blinked and blinked again:

- There is a dragon covering all abdominal quadrants
- A koi covering the chest
- Tiger extending from the right shoulder down the right arm just past the elbow.

- 5 black rings circling biceps of left arm
- Cherry blossoms on the right mid pelvis
- Japanese kanji on the left anterior mid pelvis
- Seascape on the right thigh to the right calf
- Samurai warrior on the left thigh
- Mountain landscape covering both the upper and lower back regions

OPINION: The cause of death is due to the effects of heart failure resulting from myocardial infarction. Manner of death is pending toxicology report.

UPDATE: Due to the appended toxicology report, the manner of death has been amended to UNDETERMINED.

I flipped to the toxicology report but didn't understand what any of it meant. Parker walked to the bed and slid the report from my quavering hands.

He read the page aloud. I gripped the chain of my necklace and slid the bead back and forth. Parker's face paled, and for once in his life, words escaped him. My shoulders felt like they were weighted by boulders.

Reaching over, I yanked the report from Parker and threw it across the room as I collapsed against my headboard.

"What's wrong?" Nicholas asked.

"The tattoos." Avery's voice barely wavered, but his dark eyes narrowed. "We didn't—it's just that this is the first time we've ever known about them."

In that moment, I envied Avery's ability to act like nothing affected him.

Forrest slid off the bed and gathered the papers and pictures strewn across the floor. "How could you not know your dad was covered in tattoos?" He came back to the bed and sat down.

"When I think of him," I said, "the only things I can picture him wearing are long-sleeved shirts and pants or board-shorts that went past his knee."

Parker scrunched his eyes. "He never took us swimming."

Fed rolled the chair closer and leaned over Forrest's shoulder to look at the report. "He was a member of the yakuza," Fed whispered, voicing the thing I couldn't bring myself to say.

My brothers and I had seen enough Japanese action movies with Grandpa to know the true significance of irezumi. Most Japanese people didn't get tattoos like that because of their association with corruption. Sure, some people might nowadays, but if they flaunted them in public, people would probably treat them like thugs. Multiple vivid scenes flashed through my head.

"Our father might have been a member of the Japanese mafia," Avery said in a way that sounded like he was trying out the words so he could get used to them. "The five rings on his arm probably mean he killed five people."

As if Fed couldn't help himself, he added, "Fujibara has three rings, which is surprising since he's a flying monk."

My heart dropped to my stomach. *Tokyo Tango.*

My brothers nodded.

"It's a movie we always watch when we go to Hawaii," I said. "There's a prison scene where they talk about the ring tattoos. They don't necessarily have to represent murders though. They can represent major crimes committed."

"Claire," Avery said, gesturing a hand at me. "How many

yakuza movies have we seen? A million? And how many times have the rings represented something other than a murder? Maybe one in never?"

I didn't want to think about it. Was there any other explanation? I couldn't think of one.

Parker took the report from Forrest and adjusted his glasses. "It says there was an amputation above the knuckle of his left pinky. And under CLOTHING AND BELONGINGS one of the items listed is a prosthetic finger." He turned to Nicholas and clarified, "Finger-cutting is a form of punishment for wrongdoing."

"It's called yubitsume," Fed said. "When a trespass has been committed, the offender cuts off the tip of his own finger and presents it to his boss to show penance."

No one said anything, so Fed continued. "The roots of finger-cutting stem back to the old samurai days when the way of the sword ruled Japanese life. I read all about it in—never mind." He disappeared into Avery's room and came back with two sheathed swords. He handed one to Parker. "Take a swing at me."

Avery scooted closer to my closet so he was out of their way.

Parker wound the sword like a baseball bat and swung. Fed blocked the blow with his own sword, but the force almost knocked his scrawny body to the ground.

Fed had Parker lift his pinky from the hilt and try again. This time Fed barely moved when Parker's sword connected to his. "Now try it without your pinky *and* your ring finger," he said.

Parker swung again, but the two swords hardly even clinked together.

"Weakling!" Avery shouted. "Parker's just not used to playing with swords that long."

I scowled. "Avery, what's wrong with you? You like act like this whole thing is a big joke."

Parker threw the sword to Avery. "You try it." Avery rose to his feet.

Fed positioned himself in a fighting stance. "Hit me as hard as you can, but lift all your fingers except your pointer finger and your thumb."

Without a good grip, Avery almost dropped the sword.

Fed mumbled, "Who's the weakling now?"

Nicholas walked over and thumped both of them on the back of the head.

Avery threw the sword to the ground. "Whatever." He paraded out of the room.

Fed rested his weapon against the wall and sat in the chair. "The warriors would lose a finger, starting with the pinky finger, for each thing they did wrong," he said. "And when this happened, it weakened his grip on the sword, which meant he couldn't protect himself very well. With each finger he lost, he got weaker and was forced to rely on the rest of the clan for survival."

Had my father gotten entangled in this warped way of life? Was this what my parents were hiding with their lies?

"We need to confront Mom," Parker said.

"She's going to avoid all of our questions and blow us off again," I said. "We need more proof, so she can't make up more stories. When we know for sure, we can talk to her."

Fed's body went rigid. "Do you think your mom knew about the tattoos? What if she didn't even know he was in the yakuza?"

"Whether he was in the mob or not," I said, "I'm pretty sure she would have seen the tattoos. She did have *three* kids with him."

Fed laughed. "Oh. Yeah."

Parker shuddered. "Gross."

Fed sprung out of the chair. "Claire, what if it's a fake report?"

Parker waved a picture. "This is his face. It's not someone else."

"What if he made a body look like him?" Fed asked.

Nicholas took the file from Forrest and pointed the stack of papers at Fed. "Why would he fake his own death?"

Fed lowered his head. "Because he was in the mafia and in episode—"

"Fed." Nicholas narrowed his eyes. "If you start talking about *Yama Katana* and Kaito and flying monkeys and prophecies and crap analogies, I swear I'm going to pummel you."

"Flying monks, not monkeys," Fed mumbled. "I'm just trying to be helpful."

Nicholas set the report on my desk. "We're crashing here tonight." He left the room, and Parker and Fed followed. I couldn't count the number of nights we had all camped underneath the stars on hot summer nights. Or the times we had slept in the family room together on the couches and floor for all kinds of reasons. A lost soccer game, the time Parker broke up with his girlfriend, Forrest's speeding ticket.

And now, learning our father might have been in the Japanese mafia.

14

AFTER SCHOOL THE next day, I sat at my bedroom desk, attempting to write an English paper, but I still couldn't focus. I had spent the day avoiding anyone who might ask about the cheating accusation. Dad wasn't able to schedule anything sooner, so all I could do was wait. And when that wasn't occupying my head, I was thinking about what we'd found in the report.

I pushed away from the desk and sat on my bed, my mind swimming in a whirlwind of thoughts and questions. My parents had lied to us. Had my father been in the yakuza? How were they able to hide that from us for all these years? How did he really die?

"Hey," Forrest said as he walked into the room. He threw his backpack on the floor and climbed onto the bed.

"Hey." I smiled. Having him there made everything more endurable.

Forrest stayed beside me but didn't say anything at first. He tugged at me until my head rested on his shoulder.

"After everything I've done to find out how he died, I still don't understand," I said. "Why would the manner of death be undetermined?"

"I don't know," Forrest said, "but Nicholas is right. No matter what the answer is, it's not going to make you feel better."

I swallowed the lump in my throat. "Maybe not."

He leaned his head against mine. "Do you think your dad faked his death?"

"No," I said. "I was there. When he died, we wet his lips with water as he lay there in the hospital. Mom said it would help revive him in the afterlife with his ancestors. His lips were still warm. But then I saw him in the coffin, and I remember when I touched him, he was cold. Really cold."

The funeral had lasted several days, and yet I couldn't recall what actually happened except there was one day Mom got mad at Parker because he hit Avery with his juzo and the prayer beads broke. Right after that, I tripped and fell. The string of my juzo snapped and beads flew everywhere, so I sat down and cried because I thought Mom was going to be mad at me. But then this boy about my age came out of nowhere and gave me his juzo. I didn't know who he was, and I'd never seen him since, but I still use those same beads.

The more I thought about what was happening, the more I wanted to throw something, anything, against the wall. Being accused of cheating seemed insignificant in comparison. Almost. I sighed. Thinking of the accusation actually made me feel worse. In some ways, discovering this information was like losing my father all over again.

"I feel like I don't even know the man we buried," I said.

There had to be a way to know for sure that he was yakuza.

"Is there anything you have of his?" Forrest asked. "A journal or notebook?"

I closed my eyes and tried to focus my scattered thoughts. Even though I had the notebook, I had memorized that thing before any of this had ever happened. There was nothing in there that ever made me suspect this.

"I have an idea," I said, harnessing the surge of energy storming inside of me. I rose to my feet.

"Does this idea include doing anything illegal? Will my life be at risk? And-slash-or is there a possibility you might get hurt?"

"No, no, and maybe," I said, pacing the room. "All we're going to do is go up in the attic. I was thinking about the funeral, and there was this boy. I'd never seen him before, and he spoke to me in Japanese. But when he realized I didn't understand what he was saying, he switched to English. He said he would bring me a nicer set of prayer beads from Japan the next time he visited."

I sat back down at the foot of the bed. "If he was visiting from Japan, his family must have been connected to my father's life in Tokyo somehow, and my father must have other friends still there. Anyway, Mom has a trunk full of old pictures and all kinds of things that my father kept. I remember she wrote on some of the pictures and made notes because she wanted to put all of it in a scrapbook someday." I exhaled. "It's a long shot, but maybe we could go through his stuff, collect any names we find, and search online to see if we come up with anything."

He lugged himself off the bed and sighed. "I guess you want me to help pull down the ladder?"

"Thanks."

Forrest got a cane out of the linen closet in the hallway and used it to push up the small square door in the ceiling. He hooked the drop-down ladder with the cane and pulled it down.

I followed him up the ladder and turned on the light. The trunk was in the far corner, but the path was blocked by boxes and unused furniture. Forrest moved an old chair, and I pushed boxes aside until we had enough room to move the trunk.

Forrest brushed off a thick layer of dust coating the box's brocade covering. The particles caught in my throat and made me cough.

"We're looking for names, right?" Forrest asked as we each grabbed a brass handle and carried it to the middle of the floor. We'd have more room to sit there.

"Names and anything that gives us clues about my father's life before he came to America." I flipped open the brass latch on the front and sat down.

Forrest sat next to me on the dusty bare wood floor and removed piles of photos. Some of the pictures had come from "Get to Know You" posters made in elementary school, but most of them were being "saved" until Mom got around to putting them in a scrapbook because she didn't buy into the idea of digital ones. She thought they were too easy to lose or forget.

Forrest thumbed through a few and then flung a picture at my lap like a Frisbee. "The year all of our families started the traditional Easter egg hunts at my house," he said. "Your front teeth are missing."

I laughed. Not much had changed since then. I still wore T-shirts and soccer shorts. Nicholas and Parker each had an arm around the other and had their Easter baskets raised high with their other hands.

"Hard to believe Nicholas was ever a scrawny kid," I said, showing him another picture. "Flag football. *Your* front teeth are missing."

He took it from me. "Forgot my mouth guard that day."

"Halloween." I held up another picture. "I don't even know what our costumes are, but I think we're wearing trash bags."

"Parker and Avery at a karate tournament," he said. "They were always better than I was."

My brothers posed with trophies and bowl haircuts. At the bottom of the trunk, I found a large envelope with old pictures of my father.

"This is a picture of their wedding day," I said, holding it by the corner.

Forrest leaned in. "Your mom's hair is so . . . poofy."

"She says it was the style, but we still make fun of her."

Mom's hair was long back then, and she had curled the ends. Her wedding dress had puffy sleeves and a long train. The veil, attached to a tiara, went halfway down her back. I didn't care for the dress, but she could make anything look beautiful.

I glanced at another picture of the two of them.

"Look at the way your mom is staring at him." Forrest leaned in closer, letting his arm linger against mine. "Her eyes seem to say that even if he were a star scattered among the trillions, she would only see him." He sighed softly. "I want someone to look at me that way."

Forrest had always been a romantic at heart, but his eyes narrowed and fixed on me with a fire I'd never seen before. His lips fell apart slightly, and he tilted his head to the side. The warmth of his skin against mine made my heart pound the way it did when I was watching a scary movie—that point when I was about to find out what monster hid behind the door, and part of me wanted to know what was there. And the other part of me was too scared to know the answer.

Forrest's lips moved as if they might say something, but he pressed them together.

"Forrest?" I hesitated. "Did you break up with Olivia because she didn't look at you that way?"

"I don't know. We started spending so much time together, and the more time I spent with her, the more I missed spending time with you and the guys." He leaned back and rested his weight on his hands. "I know the idea of someone looking at me like I'm the only person in the room may never happen. But at the very least, I want to be with someone who makes me *want* to look at her that way."

"Were you ever in love with her?" I raised a knee and hugged it to my chest.

"No," he said.

How did anyone ever know if they were really in love? I let go of my knee and grabbed a stack of pictures and began to flip through them, barely paying attention. "I haven't found anything yet."

Forrest leaned forward and sorted through some papers and pictures. "All of these newspaper articles are in Japanese. We can try to translate them like the letter, but I think I'd rather eat a spider." He shivered. "Ugh. Spiders."

"That can be our last resort."

My pile had pamphlets that looked like they might be play-bills, as well as tickets. I opened one of the playbills and found a piece of paper that had been torn from a larger piece. Someone had written two words in Japanese on one line and two words on a different line. I placed it in a new pile of things to hang on to.

Forrest handed me a picture. "This one has both of your dads and your mom and grandpa." Mom and my father were sandwiched between my dad and grandpa.

I smiled at the four of them. The next pictures were wedding pictures, and then a handful of pictures from my father's life in Japan. One was a picture of a woman in her twenties.

On the back of the picture, my mom had written EMIKO KAWAKAMI. I recognized the name, but not the face. She died long before I was born. I showed Forrest. "This has to be my grandmother."

Forrest leaned in. "You look like her." He took the photo from me and studied it.

"This is the first picture I've ever seen of her." I lifted the necklace I wore every day. "My father left this for me. It's the only belonging we even have of hers."

Forrest reached over and took the necklace from my palm, the back of his hand resting on my chest as he inspected the bead. "She was very pretty." He let the chain drop to my chest and looked at her photo again.

I snatched the next picture in my pile. My father and a friend standing on a dock by a lake. They smiled with arms in the air as if they were about to jump in the water. On the back of the photo, in my mother's handwriting, was the name Takeshi Sekiguchi.

Another featured a close-up of my father dressed in a suit, posing with a middle-aged man I didn't recognize.

"Is he with your grandfather?" Forrest asked.

"It can't be. His father abandoned him when he was little."

The next was a picture with the same man sitting across from him in a tea ceremony. "This ritual means he was formalizing some kind of new relationship with this man," I said.

Forrest took the last two pictures from me and pointed to the background of the first photo. "See that picture on the wall? I know it's not exactly the same, but it kind of looks like the family crest you guys have hanging above the couch in your living room." He pointed to the other picture. "And that same crest is on both of their lapel pins."

"It looks like a flower," I said. "Let's take these and see what we can find out."

We gathered the rest of the pictures and put them back in the trunk. Though we hadn't found much, it was enough to give us something to go on.

"LET'S SEE IF something comes up in an image search," Forrest said when we got to my room.

I uploaded the image of the crest, but the only matches were to company logos or clubs and none of them were even Japanese.

"There has to be an online library of Japanese crests," I said.

Finding crests was easy, but matching the picture we had was like trying to pair identical snowflakes. Many were similar with only minor differences in the way the flowers were positioned or the size of the geometrical shapes.

When we translated the letter, it had been tedious, but there was a definite path. This was throwing a dart at thousands and thousands of crests in the dark.

"I have an idea," Forrest said. He left, and I heard some mumbling in Parker's bedroom.

When Forrest returned, he had Parker's laptop tucked under his arm. "I'll search for the crests, and you can work on the other stuff." He set the computer on the desk next to mine and sat down.

Between the friend's name and the paper with the four Japanese words, the paper was a lot more intriguing. I used the same software to translate the first two words.

Hibiki Okada

I translated the next two words.

Hanae Sasaki

"I have two names," I said. "How's your search going?"

Forrest grumbled. "Not well. They all look so similar. I might have missed it already."

I ran a search on the first name. Most of the results were in Japanese, so I picked the first link in English, which led me to an article in a science journal. I skimmed the article, but there was nothing helpful.

The next link took me to the *Japan Times*. The article from almost thirty years ago was about a gunman, Hibiki Okada, who hijacked a ferry and killed the captain before fatally shooting himself. Police said the captain had accumulated over $200,000 in debt.

I summarized the article for Forrest. "Let's say the money owed was to a yakuza loan shark, and Hibiki Okada was collecting the debt. What reason would Hibiki have to kill himself? I don't know why my father wrote down Hibiki's name."

"I think it smells fishy, but there's not really definitive proof of anything," he said.

"Yeah, I know." I searched for the second name.

Some of the links were for Facebook posts that didn't seem relevant. I bypassed anything in Japanese and clicked on an article from *Today's Japan* published about the same time as the article about Okada. Hanae Sasaki was a twenty-three-year-old woman who jumped to her death from the twentieth floor of a high-rise building. Evidence from the crime scene suggested someone else had been there.

I showed Forrest the article. "Police found her crying baby on the floor wrapped in a towel. They think she had just finished giving him a bath." The thought made me shudder. "She was taking care of that baby. I can't imagine she would suddenly jump off the balcony. Someone from the yakuza must have pushed her."

"I think it's like the other article," he said. "There's stuff that sounds questionable, but nothing tying any of this to your father or the yakuza."

A search for the two names together didn't result in anything relevant. "I know what my father's handwriting looks like in English, but I don't know if I could recognize something he had written in Japanese with any confidence. Maybe he wasn't the one who wrote this. I think it's a dead end." I slumped against the back of the chair. "Okay, one more name to go."

I searched for my father's friend. Many people named Takeshi Sekiguchi lived in Tokyo, so I began to research them one by one.

"Try doing a search with the name and the word yakuza," Forrest said.

Several links paired Takeshi's name with the name Osamu Sekiguchi. The first link led me to an article almost two decades old in the *Japan Times* about racketeering. The Japanese government had been investigating an investment-banking corporation owned by Takeshi Sekiguchi, son of Osamu.

The article showed a picture of each of them when I scrolled down farther. Forrest gasped. The younger versions of these men were in our pictures. Takeshi was the friend on the dock, and Osamu was the man in the tea ceremony picture.

I refined my search to look for information on Osamu Sekiguchi.

"This article says Osamu Sekiguchi has been charged for racketeering before," I said, "but he has always managed to evade the law."

"That's definitely suspicious," Forrest said.

I clicked the next link and swallowed hard. "Osamu Sekiguchi is the oyabun of the Kobayashi-kai clan in Tokyo. He's the godfather, and this is their crest. It matches the one in our pictures."

Forrest spoke in a quiet voice. "If your father was formalizing a relationship with the godfather, and they're both wearing the crest on their lapel pins . . ."

"And you add these pictures to the missing finger and the tattoos . . ." I rubbed my temples. "I think we have definite proof now." I pushed away from my desk. Every inch of me felt too heavy for my muscles to carry, but I managed to stand and move to the edge of my bed where I threw myself backward and let my head hit the mattress. Forrest planted himself next to me and did the same. We lay in silence, both of us staring at the ceiling, our legs dangling off the bed.

"At least you know now," Forrest said.

"I know this is going to sound stupid, but . . ." I reached above me, grabbed a pillow and squeezed it against my chest. "When I said I wanted to find out the truth . . . I think I was looking for a different truth."

"You were really hoping to find proof he *wasn't* in the yakuza."

"Yeah."

The room felt small, the walls seeming to close in around me. I needed fresh air. I sat up and clutched the bead of my necklace. My eyes wandered around the room.

Forrest sat up too. "Don't run."

"What?"

"When something makes you uncomfortable, you run," he said. "Sometimes you actually get in your car and leave, and other times you change the subject or you shut everyone out."

"No, I don't," I said. "I need space. That's different."

"Sometimes your mind spins when you don't have answers, and it drives you like no one else I've ever seen. But when you're unsure, or scared, or you don't know what to do, you run."

I looked down. My hands were clenched into fists. His words anchored steadfast in my chest. Forrest was right. I just didn't want him to be.

"You don't have to run. It's okay if you don't know what to do all the time. No one does." He put his hand on top of mine on the bed. "Come with me and join everyone else downstairs."

I hated feeling like I had been stripped down with nothing to hide behind. "I think I might stay in my room tonight."

His hand flew off mine when I threw my hands in the air. "I'm not shutting you out. I just need space."

Forrest narrowed his eyes, grabbed a pillow off my bed, and threw it on the floor. "Fine. I'll stay with you, then."

"That's not space."

"It's at least ten feet of space." He pointed to the distance between the bed and the closet.

"Forrest, my parents are home. You know how much they love you, but I don't know what they're going to think if all the other guys are sleeping downstairs, and they find you in my room. Maybe they won't mind, but—"

"I'll be on the floor," he said.

"I know, but—"

"Come join us then." He brushed my cheek with the back of his hand, leaving a trail of heat and longing. He'd never done that before. I nearly leaned in to it, but caught myself. What was he thinking right now?

My head skipped around with so many questions I thought it might burst if I didn't let some of them go. "Forrest?"

"Yeah?" He turned and looked at me—really looked at me, as if he could see something I couldn't.

I tried to hold his stare, hold his blue eyes that reminded me of the ocean, but I had to glance down. I swallowed my questions and let them settle somewhere deep inside me. If I had learned anything, it was that I was happier when I didn't know the truth—before I knew my parents had been lying to me and before I knew my father had been a mobster. Once I knew the answers, I couldn't go back.

I jumped off the bed. "I need to put the ladder away." Because I wasn't as tall as Forrest, I took a folding chair and the cane from the linen closet so I could push the ladder all the way up and slide the attic door back into place.

Forrest walked over and put his hands on the back of the chair. "I could have done that."

"I know," I said, returning the chair and cane to the linen closet.

Forrest went downstairs to join the rest of the guys. To prove I wasn't running, I gathered a pillow and blanket from my room and brought them to the family room.

They had already started a movie. No one paid much attention to the TV. Avery and Fed were sprawled on the floor. Parker and Forrest were on one couch, and Nicholas was on the other.

"So we know for sure?" Parker asked.

I nodded. Forrest had probably shared what we'd found.

Parker leaned back against the cushions. "What now? Do we try to figure out if there's anything else they're hiding?"

"Mom has to know our father was a murderer," Avery said.

"We know he was in the yakuza," I said, "but we don't necessarily know he killed people."

"Five rings," Fed mumbled.

I sat next to Nicholas on one of the couches and picked at fuzz balls on the arm. "Mom has to know he was in the yakuza. We have proof now, so we should talk to her. Ask her about everything." But the thought still tore my insides to pieces. How much more had they kept from us?

"We tried that, and it didn't go so well, remember?" Avery sat up and folded the bill of his hat with both hands.

"But now we have proof," I said.

"Mom didn't even know about the letter," Avery said. "What makes you think it's not our dads who were hiding something?"

Parker leaned on the side of the couch, supporting his head with his hand. "We know that Dad—*George*," he clarified, "knew our father well, which means he would have known our father was a bad man at some point."

The conversation I'd overheard through the vents came to mind, and I tried to tell everyone the parts I could remember. "If Mom was worried we might not be safe, there's something else going on."

"I agree," Nicholas said, resting his arm along the back of

the couch. "No one wants to find out their father was in the mob, but if he's dead, why would it matter if you know? My father's a total loser. You deal with it and get over it, so it seems like there has to be something else."

I understood what Nicholas was trying to say, but I didn't know if he'd ever gotten over the way their father had left them. Their mom kept everything together so well, sometimes I forgot that ever-present wound they carried.

Fed positioned himself between me and Nicholas on the floor, using the couch as a backrest. "I've been thinking, and if he really was a member of the yakuza, then at what point did he become a judge, you now? Either he left before he became a judge, or he was crooked. Doesn't the mob always have judges in their pockets? 'Cause that would be a good reason for your parents to keep all this from you." He looked around. "Or is stuff like that only in the movies?"

My muscles tensed, growing more and more restless. One glance at Forrest made my resolve to stay put stronger.

Forrest leaned forward, placing his elbows on his legs. "What if your parents are the ones who have something to hide? Maybe Avery was onto something when he asked your mom if she'd had an affair. She seemed a little defensive, don't you think?"

Parker jumped to the edge of the couch. "What if George had our father killed, so he could marry our mom?" His eyes were wide, his face had lost color, and the front of his pudgy nose twitched.

The idea was so preposterous that I couldn't even react. Sure, the thought might have flashed through my mind, but there was no way it could be true. Avery took off his hat and threw it at Parker. "Are you saying Dad's a killer too?" His voice had a sharp, condescending tone.

Parker sat straighter. His eyes grew large and his brows slanted up. "What if he is?" He massaged both of his thighs.

Nicholas rose to his feet and folded his arms. "You're being ridiculous, Parker. Your dad would never do that. He's a good man."

I tugged on Nicholas's shorts and urged him to sit down. "And we don't know for sure our father is a killer."

Parker raised his hands, plaintive. "What if he's in the yakuza too? Haven't you ever wondered where he goes all the time on his business trips?"

He was right that Dad didn't talk about work much. And I had to admit a small worry existed. But I was positive our stepdad had all ten fingers. Technically that didn't rule him out as a killer, but I couldn't believe it. Plus, I remembered something important. "Dad takes us swimming every summer, you idiot." We'd been boating at Lake Powell often enough.

"So?" Parker asked. "That doesn't prove anything."

"So he doesn't have any tattoos." Avery glared at Parker as if wondering how it was humanly possible Parker was the older brother. "How can you hide those kinds of tattoos when the only thing you're wearing is swim trunks?"

"Did you see anything *underneath* the trunks?" Parker asked. He stood up, pulled down the back of his board shorts, and mooned us, wiggling his white cheeks until Avery stood and kicked the moving target. Parker tumbled face-first into the couch.

"Ugh," I said and turned my head in disgust. "If he and Dad were like family, Dad wouldn't have killed him."

"For the record," Avery said, "I have wanted to kill both of you on many occasions, even though you're family."

Parker pulled his shorts back up then turned around. "Right back at you."

"Ditto," I said. "But I don't think any of us would actually *do* it."

Avery moaned. "I vote we go to sleep."

"I think all of us could use some rest," I said.

"Let's sleep on it, and make a decision tomorrow," Parker said. He left and went to sleep on the floor in the hallway because the temperature was supposedly cooler there. Eventually, he'd end up in his own room.

The rest of us stayed in the same place: Nicholas on the couch facing the TV, and Forrest on the other couch at a right angle to the TV.

Nicholas slid over to make room on the couch for me, but as we had gotten older and bigger, we didn't fit as well as we used to. Normally these days, we'd both fall asleep, half-sitting and leaning against the arms of the couch as a pillow. At some point I would usually go upstairs.

Except I couldn't sleep. I lay there, thinking about all we learned today. The moon was high in the sky and silver streaks came through the kitchen windows.

After about an hour, everyone else had fallen asleep. While I was staring at the stars, a shadow crossed the window to the back of our house.

16

IF THERE HAD been a shadow, it was gone by the time I got to the kitchen window. I ran to Parker's room to get a bird's-eye view of the backyard, but nothing was there. Walking back downstairs, I stopped halfway. Through the living-room windows, I saw a black SUV parked across the street. My pulse beat a notch faster.

I tiptoed to the window closest to the front door and crouched so only my eyes were above the sill. A silhouette of a man in a sweatshirt with the hood pulled over his head appeared from the backside of the car to the trunk and skulked to my right, heading toward Forrest's house.

He disappeared from my view, so I ran to the living-room window that looked out to the side of our house. From there, I could see the man standing almost on the porch of Forrest's house. He wore sunglasses and held something in his hands. It looked like he was taking pictures, but I didn't notice a flash, so it must have been an expensive camera.

He finished and walked farther away from both of our houses

and started toward the Russos'. Their house was all the way at the end of the street. If that was where he was headed, it would take some time for him to get there and back.

Without thinking anything through, I grabbed a black marker from the kitchen and shoved on some shoes by the front door. I opened the door enough to slip through before I crept down the porch stairs and tore across the street with soft feet.

My pulse thundered in my ears. I crouched to the ground and clutched the marker to my chest, watching down the street to be sure the man didn't see me. He'd gone so far, though, that the streetlights didn't illuminate him. I uncapped the marker and wrote the letters and numbers of the Nevada license plate on the top of my trembling hand. From what I could tell, the man had stopped in front of the Russos' house.

I had just capped the marker when someone grabbed me from behind, covering my mouth so I couldn't scream. Did the man have a partner I hadn't seen? Someone in the car I didn't notice? I was about to bite the hand when the voice whispered, "What are you doing out here?"

Forrest. My chest was sore from the way my heart pounded. It took a moment to catch my breath.

I glanced down the street. The man was still in front of the Russos' house.

"Come on," I said and motioned for him to follow me. I inhaled another deep breath and sprinted back across the street with Forrest at my heels.

I tried to close the front door behind him without making a noise. To catch my breath, I hunched over in the entryway, resting my hands on my thighs.

When I felt like my lungs wouldn't explode, I shoved Forrest in the chest. "Why did you scare me like that?"

"I wanted to know what you were doing."

He took my arm and led me to the living-room couch. I collapsed and put my feet on the coffee table since Mom wasn't around.

Though the last few times I'd seen it, I had managed to convince myself the car was probably nothing, I couldn't find any arguments to chase the fear away. I told Forrest about the SUV and what I had just seen.

"Are you sure? It doesn't make any sense," Forrest said. "Who is this guy, and why would he be interested in us?"

I couldn't think of anything special about the guys, and I was even more boring. "Aren't there laws against this?" I asked. "Stalking or something?"

"Probably not if he was taking pictures in front of the house, although if he went into your backyard that might be different," Forrest said. "But you're not sure where he was, so I don't know."

Was he casing our houses so he could rob us? My heart skipped faster. What could he want?

"What if he's a pedophile? Or a serial killer? Did you think about that?" Forrest asked. "Why would you go by yourself?"

"Because everyone was asleep," I said, but paused to put some more thought into his question. I could have woken someone up. "I don't know why."

"I wasn't asleep yet," Forrest said.

"I know that now." I leaned my head against the back of the couch. "What if all of this is my fault? I started seeing that car right after I found those pictures and the letter. It doesn't feel like a coincidence. Did I raise flags somewhere when I ordered a copy of the autopsy report? My father was in the yakuza. What if I hand-delivered our address when I told them where to mail the report?"

"Maybe," he said. "But that guy was checking out our houses too, not just yours. I think you need to tell your dad."

In the soft light, I could only see half of his face, but his eyebrows were pulled in, and his eyes told me he was more worried or frustrated than he was trying to show.

"I will." I needed to find a way to help fix this.

"I'll let the guys know," Forrest said. "We can make sure they're watching out for it."

He stood and extended his hand to help me off the couch. As I slid my feet off the coffee table and he pulled me up, he said, "I wish you weren't so reckless sometimes." Still holding my hand, he released a frustrated breath. "And sometimes I wish you weren't so cautious." He dropped my hand and shook his head. "I think you should get some rest."

I expected Forrest to stay. I wanted him to say something more—wanted him to make me feel less crazy, less alone. I wanted him to say something that didn't make me ask more questions.

But he walked back to the family room.

Instead of following him, I returned to my bedroom and wrote down the SUV's plates so I could look them up later. Life was never as simple as Forrest seemed to think.

Dear Otochan,

I've been thinking a lot about death lately because Forrest's dog, Flirt, died. Forrest and I loved that animal more than anything. She was this special bond we shared. As heartbroken as Forrest has been, he has this idea that he'll see Flirt again when he dies. He makes everything in life seem so simple, but sometimes things like this are really hard for me to accept the way he does. I think it would be nice to believe there's something after this life because maybe it wouldn't hurt so much. But right now it feels like my heart is being mangled in a meat grinder.

If there is a heaven, are you watching over me? What's it like to be dead? I wonder about things like what food you miss eating the most or if you still need to sleep. I wonder if I will get to see you when I die. If I saw you, would you look really old? Do you still smoke? Would it be awkward if we all end up together in heaven but Mom's married to you and she's married to another guy (aka Dad) too?

It's not that I don't want to see you again, but the whole idea of dying is scary. And right now, death just feels mean. I don't know how God or whatever higher being could take people or animals away when there are people who still love them and need them.

Love,
Claire, age 13

BY MORNING, EVERYONE had scattered to their homes or rooms to get ready for school. Mom was in the kitchen dressed in a light blue blouse and navy dress pants. As an accountant, her busiest times of the year were the months around April when taxes were due and October when people were filing extensions, so her days lately were long.

I grabbed a bowl of cereal and sat on a barstool. Mom stood on the other side eating a banana.

"Where's Dad?" I asked.

"Last-minute business trip to Phoenix," she said. She took the last bite and threw the peel in the garbage can underneath the sink.

"Do you think it ever occurs to Dad we might want to come along?" It would be nice to see other places. Places without mountains, places greener than here. I didn't remember much about Hawaii, and it would be nice to see it again, or at least visit Grandpa.

"We'd just get in the way," she said. "He should be back in

time for your meeting with the principal after school. I'm sorry I won't be there, but your dad is much better than I am at handling these things anyway. Okay, I'm off to work." She grabbed her purse off the counter and made a dash to the garage.

"Bye, I guess." I wasn't necessarily looking forward to the meeting. The last time I was in Principal Alvarez's office was when I punched Chase. But I couldn't wait to get it over with so I could get back on the field. Besides Chase, I still couldn't think of who would have accused me of cheating.

Forrest rolled the Jeep into the driveway, ready to chauffeur us. The fall air had started to turn cold and bit at my ears. Avery trailed behind me on his skateboard, but as usual, Parker failed to grace us with his presence.

Avery picked up his skateboard and maneuvered his way to the back. Before I sat down, I wiped a clear plastic Creamie wrapper from the passenger seat and dropped it to the floor where it joined a pile of matching wrappers.

Forrest drove down the street so we could pick up Nicholas and Fed. He honked the horn, and they piled in. Fed climbed into his usual spot next to Avery and pulled out a comic book, and Forrest turned the car around to make another stop at our house. Parker jogged out of the house, his shoes and socks in hand.

I shook my head as he climbed into the car. Fed set down his book and glanced out of the corner of his eyes. "Nice of you to join us, Parker."

Avery tightened the back of his bandana. "You took that much time to look like that?"

Forrest pulled out of the driveway, Parker still combing his hand through his wet hair. "Hey, perfection takes time. But it's okay. No need to apologize for the bad attitude. You're just jealous. Not my fault I got all the good genes."

"If you had any." Avery's lips pulled back, and he acted like he was going to be sick.

Parker whacked the back of Avery's head and in no time the rest of us were dodging their wrestling moves, and I was getting whiplash from their kicks to the back of my seat. By the time they settled down, we were almost at school.

A bitter feeling rushed across my skin when Forrest turned into the school's parking lot. A black SUV was parked across the street without a driver. I could count at least twenty cars that looked similar, but they were all in the school's lot, and this one had Nevada plates. I couldn't see from here, but I could probably bet the ones in the lot were all Utah plates. To see if he had noticed it, I put a hand on Forrest's shoulder. He nodded to confirm he had.

Before everyone got out of the car, I said, "Hey, do you see that black SUV over there?" I pointed across the street. "I've seen it a lot lately. Last night it was parked across the street, and I think the driver was taking pictures of all of our houses."

"Why would someone do that?" Parker asked.

We all got out of the car. "I don't know."

Avery hiked up his shorts so they hung just below the waist of his boxers. "What's the theory this time, Claire? Drug cartel? Aliens?" He threw his skateboard to the ground and rolled away.

"We'll keep an eye out, Kiki," Nicholas said. He walked ahead of us and was immediately surrounded by a group of giggly girls.

Parker nodded. "I'll do the same."

"Me too." Fed stared at his older brother with a wistful expression, then snapped out of it. "See you in Bio." He ran inside.

I hated the days when my schedule started with Bio because it required me to think too much in the morning, so I took my time getting to my locker, where I grabbed my lab book and safety goggles. I couldn't help worrying about what the guy in the black SUV was up to, and if it truly had a connection to us. I had gotten the license number, so I had a place to start. I just didn't know where to go from there. A few minutes later I was headed to the lab at the end of the hall with a mission in mind. Fed was the perfect guy to help me figure this out.

The smell of formaldehyde overwhelmed me when I walked through the door of the biology lab. The room was decorated with animal skeletons and skulls hanging on the walls; the counter on the far wall had a row of jars with eyeballs, brains, and other animal organs.

Fed was already there. Chase stopped me as soon as I stepped inside. "It's about time you got here," he said. "The kid's been waiting for his babysitter."

I glared at him. "Fed may only be a sophomore, but he's way smarter than you'll ever be." Even though Fed was a year younger, we had similar schedules because he was a lot smarter than most kids his age. "In fact he's so smart that I've never had to punch him for saying something stupid."

"Temper, temper," Chase muttered.

I wasn't positive he was the one who had accused me of cheating, but even if he hadn't, it wouldn't make me like him any better. I pushed past him and continued on to meet Fed at our usual table. He was seated on a barstool, and his long legs were swinging back and forth. His shirt bore an infinity symbol with the caption, MY BRAIN HAS NO LIMIT.

I slammed my books on the table. Fed jumped like a feather swept up by a gust of wind and almost knocked over the test tubes in front of him.

"Hey, Nerdus Maximus," I said, diving right in, "you know all that computer information in your head? And how it's like, just a waste of space right now? Well, I need your help—"

He rolled his eyes. "So, is this like the time we thought your dad was royalty, but he had to keep it secret 'cause he had run away from home to avoid an arranged marriage?"

I dropped into the stool next to him. "Okay, so we were wrong about that. But I *was* in the third grade."

He laughed and rocked back on his stool. "Hey, no need to explain anything. I mean, how often do we even see your dad? Add a few ogres and katanas, and I'm pretty sure I would've come up with the idea myself."

Before I turned on the gas, I made sure the hose to the Bunsen burner was attached securely. "Well, he does travel a lot, so it made sense. And how was I supposed to know what his company does? I mean, the obvious conclusion was that he was secretly visiting a brother or sister who had been banned from seeing him." The smell of natural gas floated in the air, and I lit the burner.

"Obviously." He filled the test tubes with hydrogen peroxide, then looked up at me. "Goggles."

I pulled my lab notes from my backpack and put on my safety glasses.

Mrs. Kenton stood at the front of the lab in a plaid flannel shirt and tan corduroy pants, her lab coat almost as long as she was. "We're doing the same thing as last time, people," she said.

"Make sure you mark this as trial number two in your notes." She went to her desk and sat at her computer.

"So are you going to help me or what?" I asked. Fed was the only one who never thought my ideas were crazy. And if anything, he found ways to take the madness even further.

"Depends," he said. His safety glasses started to slip, so he adjusted them, tightening the sides until they about popped off his pale skin. "We're supposed to be testing different plant and animal tissues to see if they contain the enzyme catalase, not plotting a harebrained scheme." He handed me a test tube.

"Fed, I'm serious. I need your help." I wasn't really begging, but it was pathetically close. "Let's face it. You're totally a super genius when it comes to computers. I mean, you're the only person I know who, if you wanted, could list 'evil super villain' as a possible career choice. Without a doubt it would be *my* top choice if I had your brains, and I guess your goal of becoming an aeronautical engineer is also admirable, but—"

"Claire. Stop." He raised his thin almost-invisible eyebrows. "Who said 'evil super villain' was crossed off the top of my list? Just tell me what you want."

"I have the license plate of that SUV, and I want to figure out who it is." I bent my head forward. "It's a Nevada plate, so I think we'd have to get into the DMV's system there."

Fed's brown eyes widened and his eyebrows went from raised to furrowed. "You mean like hack in?"

"Um, yeah. That." With steady hands, I dropped tissue samples into the tubes and boiled them over the Bunsen burner.

"No way," he said. "Have you heard nothing I've said? I told you to leave this thing alone. In *Son of Tokugawa*—"

"I was listening."

Fed sat straight. "Do you know what would happen to us if we got caught?"

I bent over and recorded some data in my notebook. "But we're at a school with hundreds of students. No one will be able to trace it back to you."

Fed sucked in his hollow, freckled cheeks and blew out a slow breath of air. "It's not gonna work."

He blubbered about firewalls, security, which all sounded like *blah, blah, blah* to me because my head was too clouded to think straight. I remained still.

We worked in silence on the lab project for several minutes, talking only about the numbers we needed to record and what we'd need to report. When it came time to clean up, though, Fed said, "Claire, I don't think this car is anything, 'cause that would be crazy. And we've had crazy ideas before, but super exciting stuff doesn't happen to people like us. But if something ever did, you know all of us would do anything to help you, right?"

He managed to force a smile out of me. "Thanks," I said.

"How are you doing?" he asked. "Like, really."

I shrugged. "I still need to talk to my parents. I think I have a better shot of getting information from my dad, but I've been trying to figure out what I'm going to say. Is there a good way to accuse someone of lying to you your whole life?"

He balled up a paper towel and threw it in the garbage can like a basketball. "You're always quick on your feet. I'm sure you'll think of something."

"I'd trade you for Avery any day."

"And I'd trade you for Nicholas." He laughed, and then he

stopped and his face shifted into a thoughtful expression. "I have an idea, if it will make you feel better."

He reached into his backpack and pulled out a small white disk the size of a quarter. "This is a GPS tracking device. If this car keeps following us around, we can find a way to stick it on the car. It's magnetic, so it should be easy as long as no one sees us do it. We can keep track of it with an app on our phones, and if we watch where it's parked at night, maybe we can get an address and figure out who it is. The app has historical data and everything, so once it's there, we can look at any timeframe we want."

"That's brilliant. But . . . why do you have a GPS tracking device?"

"I know it's brilliant. And Mom's paranoid," he said. We gathered our test tubes and took them to the sink.

"Can't she keep track of you with the GPS on your phone?"

"Yeah, but she got this before I had a phone, and now she wants me to carry both even though it's technically for a girl. They call it GPS jewelry, and you can wear it as a pendant. She never checks it though, so we should be fine." He used the long wire brush to clean out the tube, then handed it to me to rinse. "There's a possibility this could backfire, though, 'cause it works the reverse way too. So if I lost my phone but had the disc, I could press the button on it and it would set off an alarm on my phone until I found the phone. Which means if the owner of the SUV found the disc, he could find you."

"When you say alarm, what kind of alarm are we talking about?" I ran the tubes under the water.

"The app lets you choose between options of a message that

flashes as a banner across your phone's display screen, an actual alarm that sounds like the kind you hear when a spaceship is about to self-destruct, or both. Mom chose both. But don't worry. You have to push it pretty hard before it does anything, so accidentally setting it off shouldn't happen."

"Got it," I said. I set the tubes on the drying rack. "Is your mom going to be mad that I have it?"

"Only if she finds out. For right now, if she happens to check it, it shouldn't matter because we're pretty much together all the time anyway," he said. "And I'm not saying you should use it. Remember, this can backfire in a bad way. This is the absolute last resort. But if you know you have an option, your mind can stop spinning."

We wiped down our table. He gave me the disk and programmed the app in both of our phones before the bell rang.

The disk had a small clip. I attached it to my necklace so it hung next to my bead. "Thanks. I owe you."

"For the rest of your life." He slid an overfilled messenger bag onto his bony shoulder. "I'll need a hot date for the Halloween dance and also every weekend for the next two months. Brunettes are good. And I can't resist gingers because they complement my hair color."

I followed Fed into the hall. "You'll be lucky if I can get a monkey to go out with you," I said.

Truth is, Fed didn't quite have Nicholas's social status, but I didn't know how any girl wouldn't fall in love with him. Finding him a date would be easy.

MR. TAMA WAS speaking to Chase outside the door of the history classroom. Tension set in my shoulders. Was Chase trying to get me into more trouble somehow? I edged a little closer to them on my way into the classroom to see if I could overhear anything, but they were only talking about something for debate. Nicholas had mentioned they were preparing for a tournament.

Mr. Tama grabbed my arm as I passed. "Can I speak to you briefly after class?"

Had Chase said something after all? Maybe he hadn't liked how I'd confronted him about the cheating. I pressed my lips together and reeled back the urge to glare at him. "No problem," I said to Mr. Tama. The best I could manage was a flight-attendant smile.

Mumps was already seated when I walked into the classroom, so I gave him a half wave as I passed his desk to get to mine. I sat at my usual seat and had just unzipped my backpack when Mumps sat down next to me in Forrest's seat.

"Hey," he said.

I stopped what I was doing and looked up. "Hey?"

"I wanted to apologize," he said. "That was really awkward the other day, and I swear if I had known you and Forrest were together, I wouldn't have asked you."

He had gotten a haircut and his dark eyes didn't look as vacant as I had imagined them to be the other day. "We're not," I said. There were enough lies in my life. I didn't want to spread more. "And I'm the one who should apologize. I know it was rude to say no, but I'm sure you can understand why I don't really like Nicholas and my brother setting me up on dates."

The vacant expression returned to his face. Or maybe it was confusion. He shook his head. "I don't know what you're talking about."

Forrest walked through the door, and as soon as he saw Mumps in his seat, I could tell he was irritated. The seats around me started to fill with the girls from my team. I tried to act like I was really into my conversation with Mumps so they didn't ask me any questions about my absence from the field. I felt like I'd let them down, even though I hadn't cheated.

"Nicholas and Parker didn't tell you to ask me?"

"No," he said. "Hey look, Forrest is heading this way, and he probably wants his seat. Are you going to Katie's party?"

Katie flopped into her seat and pointed a finger at me. "You'd better be there." She smiled, then turned to Mumps. "I'm Katie. I know we have this class together, but I don't think we've been introduced."

Katie was the kind of person who knew everyone, so I hadn't realized they didn't know each other. But then again, I guess I hadn't noticed Mumps hanging out with anyone.

Mumps shoved his hands in his front pockets. "I'm Mumps."

"Cool." Katie crossed her legs and swiveled to face the front.

Mumps tapped the top of my desk with his hand. "I'll catch up with you there. And you should consider joining the debate team. I hear they have a really cool guy named Mumps on the team who is a lot of fun to be around." He winked and went to take his seat at the front of the room.

The wink felt more like an inside joke rather than a flirtatious gesture, but I didn't know him well enough to tell. Lanie and Kimi waved at me, but thankfully no one said anything about my alleged cheating.

"What did he want?" Forrest took his seat next to me. His voice sounded tense.

"To apologize," I said.

"He should. Nicholas never said he could—" Forrest opened his notebook and suddenly found something more interesting than our conversation inside.

"Nicholas never said Mumps could what?"

"Nothing." Forrest stuck the front of his T-shirt in his mouth and looked straight ahead at the front of the room.

Nicholas never said he could *what*? Did Forrest really think I would just drop it?

"Forrest," I whisper-shouted. "Forrest." I continued to stare in his direction, but he refused to look my way.

I had a pretty good idea what he was about to say anyway. Nicholas never told Mumps he could ask me to the dance. It made sense considering Mumps's confusion a minute ago.

Mr. Tama walked in. "Let's get started."

Forrest might think he was off the hook, but I would corner

him later. Was Nicholas vetting the guys who were allowed to approach me? Was *that* why I never got asked to dances by anyone remotely interesting?

When I reached into my backpack to get my notebook, I found a small white box on top of it. It was wrapped with a black bow, and my name was written on a white tag in red. When did that get put there? I'd had my bag with me all morning.

I untied the bow and lifted the lid.

When I saw what was inside, I released what sounded more like a yell than a scream. I dropped the box, and it fell into my backpack.

"Is everything all right, Ms. Takata?" Mr. Tama asked.

The last thing I wanted was for Mr. Tama to think I was a troublemaker in addition to being an alleged cheater. "I'm fine. I thought I saw a spider," I said, even though I'm not afraid of spiders. "Sorry."

"No need to apologize," he said.

Chase laughed. When Mr. Tama's back was turned, Chase faced me and spun his pointer finger around the side of his head, mouthing, "Psycho!"

Why was punching him *not* a good decision? I waited for my pulse to slow down before I got out my notebook and pen.

Forrest shuddered. "Was it really a spider? Please tell me you killed it."

"Eyeballs," I whispered.

He raised his eyebrows.

I tried to copy what Mr. Tama had written on the board, but I couldn't stop my hands from trembling. "Someone put four eyeballs in a box. In my bag. Real eyeballs."

Who would have done this? If it was Chase, he was much sicker than I ever could have imagined. But how would he have gotten the box in my bag?

As much as I wanted to run out of the classroom, I steeled my nerves and stayed seated. If there was any chance Chase had done this, I was not going to let him see me squirm.

I couldn't concentrate enough to take notes, so I closed my eyes and drowned out everything by air-playing "Reverie" by Robert Schumann, tapping my fingers against my legs. It wasn't a difficult song, and Mr. Tama wasn't making anyone answer any questions. I'd played it years ago. I let whatever was built up inside lilt away along the melody in my head.

The bell rang, and I gathered myself together. Rather than put my notebook in my bag, I handed it to Forrest. I held my backpack away from my body so I didn't have to touch any more of it than I had to. If I didn't get out of there, I was going to explode. I pushed my way—not gently—through everyone ambling out and sprinted through the door.

"Claire!" Mr. Tama called out. "I still need to speak to you."

When I glanced back, Mr. Tama had followed me into the hall and started after me. For a brief second I thought about turning around. I'd completely forgotten we were supposed to meet after class, but I couldn't go back. Behind me, Forrest shouted my name. My feet kept moving, propelling me through the masses.

Forrest caught up with me at the end of the hall. Either Mr. Tama had given up, or the halls had become too crowded for me to see him.

Forrest grabbed my backpack and unzipped it. He peered

inside and paled, swaying as if he might throw up. It's not like I hadn't warned him what was inside. I was far too angry and confused to get squeamish. And right now, I couldn't control the adrenaline coursing through me.

"I'm going to make a pit stop at the bathroom," he said.

I tugged my backpack from him before he jogged down the hall. We still had seven minutes before the next class started. I marched the opposite way to the biology lab.

Mrs. Kenton was at her desk. I grabbed a couple of paper towels from the dispenser on the wall and brought my backpack over to her.

"Mrs. Kenton," I said, pulling out an eyeball with a paper towel. "Someone put these in my bag as a disgusting joke. I need to know these aren't human so I can try to get some sleep tonight."

She plucked the eyeball from the paper towel and held it in her bare hands. I'd seen her boiling carcasses of small animals before, so this would be nothing for her.

"Definitely not human," she said, turning it over so she could look at it from different angles. "Too small to be human, and the irises aren't right."

I felt a large weight fall from my shoulders.

"Do you mind if I cut it open?" she asked.

"Be my guest."

Mrs. Kenton went to a cupboard and grabbed a dissecting tray and scalpel, which she set on the table closest to me. I took a seat on a stool.

She put the eyeball on a tray and stabbed it with a T-pin to hold it in place, then made a careful incision. "Interesting. A pecten. It's avian, and probably a midsize bird. If it's local, it could be something like a magpie, or a crow or raven," she said. "If you find the sick kid who did this, please let me know, but I plan to speak to the principal, and you should go file a report with the front office."

I opened my bag and held it out for her. She threw the eyeball back inside. "I hope you catch that son of a—" Mrs. Kenton shook her head. "Mutilating animals is the sign of a possible future serial killer."

"Thank you." I fought against the current of students coming into the lab for class.

The bell rang on my way to the front office, and I entered, knowing I would probably make sweet Mrs. Davis pass out. It was busier than I expected, so I sat in one of the chairs and waited for my turn with four other students, two girls and two boys.

Mrs. Davis spotted me and hopped to her feet. "Well speak of the devil, Claire. Mr. Tama was looking for you." She motioned for me to come closer to the counter, so I stood and met her there. "He said he'd wanted to speak to you after class but was a little worried when you raced out of there. I was about to go chase you down and make sure you're okay when you walked through our door." She put her hands on her hips and leaned back, rolling her spine into a stretch. "It's a good thing too because this old thing ain't what it used to be."

"I'm fine," I said. "Really I am." I brought my knuckle to my lips.

"Good to know." She winked. "Run to the faculty lounge when we're done here. He only needs a minute, and he isn't teaching this period, so stop there on your way out. Where are you supposed to be right now? I'll let your teacher know you'll be late."

"Study hall."

Mrs. Davis nodded and said I could go sit back down. "How can I help you, Miss Granger?" She pointed to a petite girl with mousy brown hair, who looked too young to be in high school.

In an effort to have a little personal space, I chose a seat as far away from the other students as possible. Who would do this? It had to be someone from school. Probably the same person who had taken my pictures. No matter how many people I considered, Chase was the only one I could think of who would have motive to do something like this.

Ten minutes passed before my name was called. The office had emptied of other students. I warned Mrs. Davis before I even started that what I was about to say was disgusting.

When I told her the rest, she threw her hands in front of her face, even though I hadn't shown her my backpack. "Oh good heavens! Let me get the officer on site."

She went through a door behind the counter, and when she returned, Officer Clemmons was with her. Officer Clemmons was big and tall and the friendliest man on campus.

"Mrs. Davis says you received a present?" He set a form on the counter and pulled a pen from his front pocket.

I nodded and raised my open bag. "This is the box inside here. Mrs. Kenton says the eyeballs were from a bird."

Mrs. Davis went back to her desk and sat down. Officer Clemmons wrote some notes down on the form and asked a lot of questions regarding where I was, what time I found them, and who I thought might have put them there and why. After he finished, he put his pen back in his pocket.

"This probably isn't what you want to hear," he said, "but it's not going to be easy to find out who did this, so if you know or hear of anything, let us know because you're our best lead. Even if we do find out who did this, be prepared because it might be hard to prove that a crime was committed to the birds. If the person took them from dead birds, it would be sick, but not an actual crime. And it's probably harassment to leave them for you like this, but again, it's hard to prove."

"Are you serious?" I said, louder than I meant to. Mrs. Davis's head jolted up.

Officer Clemmons nodded. "If the person tortured a live animal or killed it without privilege, it would be a Class A misdemeanor, but there's no way for us to tell if these birds were alive or not."

"Oh good heavens," Mrs. Davis said again from her desk.

He walked around the counter, wincing. "I'm going to need to take the box and eyeballs so they can be submitted into evidence." He pawed at the opening of my bag, barely touching the zipper. "Ew."

My backpack still had some notes and pens along with the white box inside, but none of it was anything I needed. "Take the whole thing." I slid the bag off my arm and gave it to him. If he hadn't taken it, I'd have thrown it away anyway so I'd never have to see it again.

"I'm sorry this happened," he said.

Thanks for nothing, I wanted to say, even though I knew the idea of them immediately finding the person who'd done this and taking them out of the school in handcuffs was asking a little much. "Well, thank you."

"No problem," he said. "That's what I'm here for. Let me know if you think of anything that would help us find the kid who did this."

"I will." My lip stung — I must have bitten down on it. The muscles in my jaw wouldn't relax.

"I'll let Mr. Tama know you're on your way to the lounge," Mrs. Davis said over the top of her monitor.

Why was this happening to me? Had I done something to deserve this? No. No one deserved this. Blood pounded in my head and my chest. Whoever was responsible for this truly was sick.

The halls had emptied, the students already absorbed into classrooms. I pushed open the door to the women's restroom and washed my hands over and over again. I shut off the water and steadied both hands on the sink. Only twenty-five minutes of study hall remained and school would be out.

With thoughts ricocheting in a million directions, there was no point in staying. It was Friday, and after the day I had, I deserved an early weekend. Whatever Mr. Tama had to say, I'm sure it could wait until Monday since it was practically the weekend anyway. If I didn't get away from school, I was going to combust.

I could go to the front office and check myself out of school, saying I wasn't feeling well. It wasn't entirely a lie. Mrs. Davis said she wasn't feeling well either after that. She would probably ask if I'd talked to Mr. Tama, though.

Forrest would have happily given me a ride home, but I had energy to burn, and our house was less than two miles away. I pushed open the school's doors and walked into the sun. A light wind carried a mixture of smells: earth, decaying leaves, and wood. A few dark clouds gathered ahead with what I hoped was the promise of rain. I strolled along Franklin Avenue until I reached the first intersection.

As I waited to turn left and cross to Highland Drive, a black SUV crawled up the street. I hadn't seen it when I left the school. I couldn't see its license plates from here, so I told myself that it probably wasn't the same one. *There are black SUVs all over Utah,* I told myself. *You're overreacting.*

When the light turned green, I crossed at a steady pace. Highland Drive was always busy, and I would need to stay on the sidewalk near the road for a while if I wanted to get home as fast as possible. The SUV turned and pulled into the right lane. As it approached me, it slowed down, creeping behind me at a snail's pace. Other cars behind began to honk and change lanes to pass.

Maybe I was right after all.

My pulse picked up speed. Every muscle lit with a new intensity, and I sprinted forward. To the right of me was a tall concrete wall that continued up a small hill. If I could make it just after the hill crested, I could run into Reams and hope the grocery store was a public enough place that he wouldn't continue to follow me.

The car accelerated enough to keep up with me, allowing me to see into the front seat. Behind the driver's wheel was the same hooded man with sunglasses.

I reached in my pocket for my phone. My fingers slipped as I tried to keep up my pace and dial at the same time.

I typed 911 and was about to hit Send when the car sped off, driving so far it disappeared from my line of vision. After pausing a moment to cancel the call and look around to be sure the car was gone, I decided I wasn't going to wait for it to return. I sprinted the rest of the way, peeking over my shoulder every few seconds.

Running two miles was normally an easy jog, but I was desperate for air when I crossed through our back door. I threw off my shoes and wandered to the couch in the family room, where I collapsed. My heart continued to pound, so I rested until my breathing slowed to a regular pace. I stood and got myself a large glass of water. As I drank, I paced around the island, trying to put all the pieces together. So much had happened. I set the empty glass in the sink and fell back down on the couch.

The events at the school could possibly be connected. But what did the SUV have to do with all of this?

Somehow, during all of my questioning, I must have drifted off. When I opened my eyes, a shadow fell over me.

I gasped and looked up. My dad was standing above me.

"What are you doing home?" he asked.

"We need to talk," I said.

"Yes, we do," he said. "Where were you? You missed your meeting with Principal Alvarez, and I've been trying to call your phone for the past half hour."

Crap.

WE WALKED TO Dad's office and my mind churned over where to start.

"Well?" Dad asked as we walked. "Where were you?"

"The short answer is I was running home." I staggered my steps to make sure I trailed a little behind.

"And what's the long answer?"

I crashed into one of the leather chairs in the office. Dad sat across from me behind his desk, arms folded.

"I think someone might be harassing me at school. I don't know if all these events are connected, but it started with someone accusing me of cheating—"

"Which is why you were supposed to be at the principal's office."

Yes. We had established that already. "Anyway, someone broke into my locker last week and took all the pictures I had hanging up. And then today, someone put a box in my backpack with four eyeballs. Real eyeballs. Mrs. Kenton said they were from a bird, maybe something like a raven or a crow."

As I described the box and how it was all packaged, Dad's face grew dark, and he seemed more concerned than I expected him to be. "Do you still have the box?"

"No. I gave it to the officer at the school, and he said he would file a report and submit it into evidence."

"Did your brothers get boxes too?"

"I don't know," I said. "I didn't see them after class."

"Do you have any idea who would have done this?" he asked. The more he fired questions at me, the more it felt like my stomach was filling with sludge.

"Maybe Chase Phillips. I don't know," I said, my head in my hands. "I figure it has to be someone at school though, because I had my bag with me the whole morning. I never left the school. They must have slipped it in walking down the hall or something, and it would have been after fifth-period calculus, because I know it wasn't there when I closed my bag, and before sixth period, which was history."

Dad leaned forward, resting his weight on his elbows.

"Claire," he said. "I need you to think hard. Is there anyone at school who would know a lot about Japanese culture?"

"No one besides Fed." Up until this point, I had only been angry, but I began to wonder if there was something I had missed. "Why?"

"Nothing." Dad closed his eyes and massaged his forehead.

"You can't do that," I said. "You know I'm going to go crazy and try to figure out what everything means."

He glanced up and sighed. "Yes, I know." His shoulders dropped. "The Japanese are very superstitious people. They never give anyone anything in a group of four because the number four, *shi*, is a homophone for the word death."

"You're worried because there were four of them?" That could have been a coincidence. I still didn't understand why he was so concerned.

Dad shook his head. "Your name was written in red, which they don't do because red is the color used for names on graves. My guess is that the eyeballs were from a crow, not a raven or other bird. Japanese people believe if you catch a crow's eye, something bad is going to happen—although I would guess the saying refers to crows that are alive."

"So this is really bad." I shrank in the chair. "What do you want me to do?"

"I don't want to jump to conclusions yet, but I need you to be careful and make sure you call for help," he said. "If anything like this happens again, you need to let me know immediately."

I nodded. Because the eyeball incident had happened at school, I'd assumed another student had done it. But if there really were Japanese ties behind the present, I had to think it was possible that everything was connected somehow. The cheating, the stolen pictures, the eyeballs, and the black SUV. It felt like rocks had collected in the pit of my stomach. Any frustration or fear I had about the isolated events now added on top of each other, forming one big pile.

He rotated his chair, and I noticed he had changed the lock to the drawer I had broken into. The wafer lock had been replaced with what looked like a disk tumbler lock, which was a lot harder to pick, but he had completely underestimated my skills.

It occurred to me, and had on many occasions in the past few weeks, that I knew very little about the man in front of me—the man whom I had called "Dad" for over a decade. When he married Mom, I don't think I was old enough to understand what was going on or care where he had come from because I knew he was meant to be part of our family. But now I wasn't sure what he did or where he went for work. I didn't know how long he had known my father or how he had really ended up with Mom.

Something heavy took root in my stomach. Dad didn't seem to be letting on how serious he thought the situation was. And I hadn't even told him about the car yet. If there were a chance he had been involved in my father's death, could he also have been involved somehow with what was going on now? I didn't want to believe that, but too many things had been kept from us.

I took a deep breath and straightened my shoulders. "Why didn't you and Mom ever tell us that you knew my father so well?" I stretched my toes to the burgundy carpet.

Dad's eyebrows scrunched up, and he leaned forward. "Why do you ask?" His voice had an edge, and I knew I had to tread carefully, but I also needed answers.

"I saw the picture of you at my father's funeral holding a bone with your chopsticks. Grandpa said *family* members put the bones in the urn."

He nodded but didn't say a word. After a few moments, he straightened some papers on his desk and pushed them aside. "You remember how my father, your grandpa, was a Buddhist reverend?"

I nodded.

Dad steadied his arms on the desk. "Well, when your father came over from Japan, he literally had only the clothes on his back. I remember walking home one night after watching one of the high school football games. Henry, your father, was huddled in the alley next to the temple where Grandpa served. At that time your father was still Hideki Kawakami. I invited him into the temple and introduced him to my father, who gave him some food and a place to sleep. Grandpa always tried to help as many people as he could, but there was something different about your father. Perhaps it was that your father looked to be about the same age as I was at the time. Grandpa took him in and got him a job at the local diner."

How could they not tell us this before? There was only one reason I could think of and even then, I still didn't understand how all the secrets were related. "Did he . . . know my father was in the yakuza?"

Dad raised his eyebrows, blinking. "How did you find out?" His voice was low and serious, with a flat tone that unnerved me.

Why did it matter if we knew about our father?

I dropped my head and stared at a loose thread on my shorts. "I found a letter written to you by my father, and in a part that we translated, it sounded like he might have known he was going to die, but he couldn't have known he was going to die of a heart attack. Unless that wasn't how he really died."

To get a good read on his expression, I glanced up. Dad's eyes opened a little wider but only for a second. "Go on."

"I knew there were things you guys weren't telling us, so I thought maybe he hadn't really died that way, and I ordered a copy of his autopsy report. That's when I found out about all the tattoos. And then I found some pictures in the attic. One second. I'll be right back."

I ran to my room and gathered the pictures we'd been poring over from the middle drawer of my desk.

Back downstairs, I handed him the pictures of my father with Osamu Sekiguchi and sat back down in the leather chair.

He lowered his brow. "You found the letter and funeral pictures in my office, and then these pictures were in the attic?"

"Actually, I found the letter in one of those boxes in the garage with my father's old stuff." Well, I had. Just in a journal that I'd found years ago.

His chair creaked as he shifted and massaged the back of his neck. "And you didn't think it might be important to give the letter to us before Avery *ate* it?"

My parents had been lying to us, so it seemed reasonable to me that we wouldn't have given it to them, but the tense muscles in Dad's face suggested otherwise. "I guess I didn't know what to think when I found out you were hiding this from us, and I didn't know if there might be more we didn't know."

Dad leaned back in his chair and took a deep breath. "Sometimes your persistence is a little scary. I don't know if I should be impressed or angry."

The tight grip he had on the arms of his chair and his narrowed eyes didn't give a vibe that he leaned toward "impressed."

He held up the pictures and studied them one by one. "Yes," he said. "Your grandfather knew where your father had come from."

"And you were okay with that?"

His face relaxed into a smile. "At first I resented the way Grandpa cared for him and felt like he had brought Henry into our home because I had somehow failed him as a son. Hideki Kawakami became Henry Sato to hide from the yakuza, but changing his name also reflected the life changes he had made."

"I was able to get information by following paper trails," I said. "Wouldn't the yakuza be able to do the same thing to find him even though he had changed his name?"

"Oh, there were paper trails," Dad said. "Your father wanted nothing to do with that lifestyle when he left. But his rank in the clan was high enough that they would come looking for him if he escaped, so your father had help from someone who had access to a lot of money. They left paper trails that led mostly to Korea but some led to Brazil, Hong Kong, and Los Angeles. Airline tickets, real estate purchases, financial investments, fake documentation."

"Fake documentation?" I sat straighter. "Do you mean he wasn't really a citizen?"

"He was a legitimate citizen. His friend helped your father get a job so he could get a green card, and he started working at your grandfather's diner, and met your mom. And once he married your mom, it was easier to become a US citizen."

"That still seems fast, though. I swear Ashley Cheung once said it took her dad almost twenty years to become a citizen."

"The fact that his friend had a lot of money also made the process a quick one. Everything was legal, but his friend was very fluent in business politics and knew how to work the system."

I scooted to the front of my chair and leaned my elbows on his desk. "Are you sure my father changed when he came here? Not just his name, but as a person?"

"Positive. Over time, I grew to love your father like a brother, and when I left to attend college, we wrote to each other often. We were close."

I loved hearing about what their relationship had become.

Once Parker left for college, I'd probably email him, but I couldn't see myself taking the time to send anything handwritten. "Do you still have his letters?"

Dad nodded. "I do. I have the one when your father met your mother at the diner, one from when they were married, letters announcing the arrival of kids and other big events. They'd waited so long for children, more than ten years, and then all of a sudden it was like the stork dropped a big bundle. I was so proud of all he had done with his life. As you know, I entered the military immediately after college, but he would send me pictures of you guys all the time."

Behind him was a set of pins hanging on the wall. He had collected them from various places he had been assigned. Mom had laid them out on a piece of felt and then had them framed. She gave it to him as an anniversary present a few years ago.

"So how did *you* end up with Mom?" I asked, the most relaxed I'd been all day. I nearly forgot about all the strange recent events that caused me so much anxiety.

He leaned back until the leather chair groaned. "Claire, the day your father died was one of the saddest days of my life. When I saw your mother on the day of the funeral, standing with the three of you next to her, I felt . . . *compelled* to take care of all of you. It seemed like the honorable thing to do—something your father would have wanted. Through all of the letters and pictures your father had sent, I felt like I knew you—as if I had grown to love you and your brothers before I had even met you." His mouth curved into a smile, and his dark eyes sparkled.

I could have curled up in that story. Maybe there were bad

people out there who wanted to do bad things to me—and maybe the rest of our family and friends—but he wasn't one of them.

For a moment he stopped, perhaps unsure if he should continue. But finally he shifted his weight forward. "So I took a leap of faith and moved to be near your family, not knowing what would happen, and spent time with your mother. She had her hands full with you and the boys, and my support came at a time when she really needed it."

I stared at him, speechless. This seemed like a pretty important part of my history which should have been made known to me— us—much earlier than now. "When were you guys planning on telling us all of this?" I bit at a fingernail.

"It never seemed necessary, but I think you're old enough to understand now. Your father did a lot of things we had always hoped to protect you from. Mom thought if you knew how well I had known your father, you would ask too many questions, and you guys were so young. At the time we got married, we wanted to keep it fairly quiet, so we eloped. For your mom to get married so soon after your father's death seemed like a potential scandal for the people in Hawaii who knew both of our families. We didn't want anyone to think I had taken advantage of a widow, and many traditional Japanese people felt she had not been grieving long enough to consider remarrying."

"Do you think he knew he was going to die?" I asked.

He pushed up his glasses again and paused to gather his thoughts. "I don't know, Claire. For Henry to die at such a young age . . . I guess it's possible." His tired eyes sagged.

The story of how my parents had gotten together was not what I expected, although I didn't know what to expect anymore. It was definitely more information than I thought he would share. I stared out the window to our front lawn. I could visualize the car parked across the street and the man taking pictures. "Dad, is there any reason the mafia would want to hurt us now that my father's dead?"

"Not that I can think of," he said. "Why do you ask?"

I told him about the black SUV, from the first time I saw it, to the guy taking pictures of our houses, to how he followed me out of school just now.

"How long has this been going on?" he asked.

I shrugged. "Maybe a few weeks. About the same time I ordered the autopsy report." I showed him the top of my hand. "Here's the license plate number." The marker had faded to a grayish-purple. "It's a Nevada plate."

He squinted. "I can barely read it. What if it had washed away completely?"

"I wrote it down on paper upstairs just in case."

He took a pen from his desk drawer and copied the information in a notebook in front of him.

"I don't want you to worry about this. I'm going to take care of everything," he said. "But if you happen to see the car again, I want you to call the police for help immediately, then call me."

"I will. Do you think this has anything to do with my father?" I tugged at the loose thread on the hem of my shorts until it broke. "Do you think I started this when I ordered the report?"

"I don't know." He pursed his lips as he shook his head.

Maybe he was saying that to make me feel better, but I

could tell there was something he wasn't saying. "Do you have any idea who's in the car?"

"Perhaps. How's the team doing without you?"

The way he transitioned into questions about soccer so quickly made something prickle in my gut.

"Fine. I think. We haven't had any games, so I don't know. I've only been away a few days. At this rate I'll miss tomorrow's game, but I'm a little more worried about everything else."

He picked up his cell phone. "I'm going to call the school and have them tell your brothers to call home. I need to know if they received boxes."

"They're at soccer practice by now, so you'll have to tell the office to give the message to Coach Zindler."

"Noted. And I'm going to try to reschedule your meeting with the principal while I have them on the line."

"Okay." I put my arms on the chair and lifted myself up. "Am I in trouble then? For the autopsy report and all that other stuff?"

He edged around the desk to get to me. He perched on the front of his desk, leaned over, and clasped my face with both hands. "Yes, very much so. But I will deal with you later." He kissed the top of my head, already dialing the school.

"Love you, Dad," I said as I left him.

"Love you, too." He lifted the phone to his ear. "I'm going to take care of this. I'm not going to let anything happen to my princess."

His gentle tone and the look on his face said he was trying to be convincing, but his anxiety lit up the room.

Dear Otochan,

Today I was thinking about something that happened a long time ago. We'd only lived in Utah a few months, but Fed had spent so much time at our house he felt like my little brother—one I liked. Anyway, we were all playing soccer at the park across the street. Forrest had been in the neighborhood even less time than we had because he moved in a little after. So this was his first time playing with us. He ended up knocking Fed to the ground, and Fed started screaming. Nicholas started to make fun of Fed and called him a baby because he wouldn't get up. I finally went over and helped Fed roll over. Blood was everywhere. He'd fallen on a sprinkler head, and it had somehow sliced his leg open. I remember I started to cry because I was so scared. All I could think about was how he might die like you. I held Fed's hand and was probably crying harder than he was.

I don't know how I could have been so stupid. I was worried he was going to die, but rather than trying to stop the bleeding, I sat there and bawled. I guess I'm lucky that all Fed needed was stitches.

I only have a few memories of you, but one is that I held your hand as you were dying. Mom says she told me to wait with you while she called for an ambulance. I don't remember that, but I remember I was going to be turning seven in a few weeks. I was worried that you were going to be sick on my birthday and that I would have to wait to open my presents. I know that I wasn't that old, but sometimes I wonder if there's something I could have done to save you.

   With everything going on right now, I know I don't ever want to feel like that again. I don't want to question whether there was something I should or could have done. I want to know I at least tried.

   Love,

   Claire, age 16

AFTER I LEFT Dad's office, I sat down at the piano. I'd played the piano for as long as I could remember, first in Hawaii and then Utah. Once we moved, I studied under a professor at the University of Utah. I missed taking lessons, but I hadn't missed the four to five hours of practice each day required by Dr. McLloyd. It was nice not to wake up early so I could get a few hours of practice in before school, and I enjoyed having more room in my schedule for other things like soccer.

I chose the Warsaw Concerto by Richard Addinsell. The style reminded me of Rachmaninoff, but Dr. McLloyd had told me the song was composed for a movie. I imagined playing the music to a screenplay of someone else's life, someone else's problems.

I finished the piece and checked my phone. School was out, and I had multiple texts from Forrest asking where I was. I texted him briefly to let him know I was at home.

When his Jeep rolled into our driveway to drop off my brothers, I ran out to meet him. I never understood why he always gave us door-to-door service when he lived next door, but it was one of the things I found endearing about him.

My brothers jumped out of the car. "Good to *see* you," Parker said. "Get it? *See*? Eyeballs?"

"You're so stupid," Avery mumbled.

"Did you guys get boxes too?" I asked, making my way to Forrest's side.

Avery shook his head.

"*Eye* did not." Parker bent over, laughing harder than anyone at his own joke. They hauled their stuff inside.

I was the only lucky one. I didn't know how to make sense of everything.

Forrest rolled down his window. "Since when do your brothers know more information about you than I do?" He smiled.

I hung both of my hands on his door. "Yeah, sorry about that. They only knew I was home because Dad called the school."

"Hey, Kiki," Nicholas said from the passenger seat. "I'm going to pound the guy when I find out who did that." He hit his fist against his palm.

"You can have him after I do," I said.

"So Katie's party tonight?" Forrest asked.

"Yep," I said. "What time do you guys want to head over?"

"We'll be over once we drop off our stuff, and then we can go whenever we feel like it," said Nicholas.

"See you in a little bit," Forrest said, and backed out of the driveway.

I headed up to my room to get ready and threw open my dresser drawers. And then I stared.

Nothing stood out. Even though all of my time was spent with these guys, I was still a girl who did, on occasion, care what I looked like. After agonizing forever, I dressed in a gray T-shirt from my last soccer tournament and a pair of jeans, which wasn't different than what I wore on any given day. I probably should have asked one of the girls from the team to go shopping with me to help with my style, but the kinds of clothes other girls wore looked so uncomfortable. And if I asked Mom to take me, everything would end up being pink.

While I stood in front of the bathroom mirror deciding what to do with my hair, the kitchen below became filled with a chorus of the usual noise. I heard Avery and Fed raid the fridge, open and slam the pantry door, trade insults.

My black hair fell just below my shoulders. I tried to pin some of it up the way other girls did, but it was hopeless. In the end, I stuffed my hair in the usual ponytail, but the elastic snapped and I didn't have any more in the house. I gave up and left it down.

I brushed on some mascara and tried some eyeliner. Since I didn't use eyeliner often, I'd never learned how to hold my hand steady. The line looked decent on my left eye, but the right eye took a couple of attempts before I could draw a straight line.

A muffled bumping sound came from my closet. Looking in the direction of the noise, I stiffened. Something shifted again behind the door. I grabbed a hairbrush off the bathroom counter and clutched it until the blood drained out of my hand. Stepping out of the bathroom into my room, I stared at the knob. The rustle of clothing made me stop. I urged my hand to steady itself, but it continued to tremble. Most likely it was a mouse, I told myself. A big one.

I hated mice.

My heart sprinted laps inside my chest. I reached for the handle and yanked open the door.

A huge figure dressed in all black yelled and launched himself at me. I delivered a strong backhand to his face with the brush as I was tackled to the floor. Everything happened so fast that I only realized Parker was in my face when my brush found his cheek.

He rolled off me, gripping his side to contain the laughter.

"Stupid jerk," I muttered, and punched him in the stomach as hard as I could.

He folded in half. "Jeez! It was just a joke," he said, rubbing his stomach with one hand and his red cheek with the other.

I threw the brush at him and stormed out.

When I marched into the kitchen, Dad seamlessly interrupted his chat with the guys. "Too much makeup," he said and kept talking.

Wearing a little mascara and eyeliner hardly equated to "too much makeup," but the fact that I ever wore makeup at all made him upset.

Fed cracked a toothy grin, his freckled cheeks pushing against the bottom of his eyes. "I think you look great. A princess, like Asayahime."

"Thanks." I tried to contain my big smile. Fed was proof brothers could communicate with sentences that didn't include insults. He'd also never jumped out of my closet and tackled me to the ground.

He tugged my arm and asked me for advice on what to wear. I scanned his blue T-shirt with a picture of a caffeine molecule and assured him he didn't need to go home and change because he looked fine. I wasn't the best person to give fashion advice though.

Dad put both hands on the island. "Where are you going?" he asked.

"To Katie's house," I said. "All of us are going."

Avery motioned to Fed to go upstairs so they could avoid the conversation, but Dad stopped them. "Son, I need to speak with you."

"I'll meet you up there," Avery said to Fed.

Fed nodded and disappeared up the stairs.

"Parker," Dad called. "Can you come down here please?"

I sat on a stool at the island.

Parker lumbered down the stairs and into the kitchen. He seated himself on the stool next to me.

"Look, kids, I don't think you should go anywhere tonight until I can find out what's going on," he said.

Avery walked over and stood behind Parker. "Just because someone doesn't like Claire?"

Dad closed his eyes and took a deep breath. He opened his eyes and said, "Avery, I think we all know this could be more serious than that, and we can't say for sure if Claire's the only one being targeted. Hopefully it isn't serious, but until I know who did this, I'd feel better if you and your friends hung out here tonight."

"Okay, I admit it. I did it," Avery said. He clapped his hands together. "Who's ready to go?"

Dad stared at him in disbelief, and from the way his nostrils flared, he was crossing over into extreme irritation.

"We'll stay here," Parker said.

"Thank you, Parker," Dad said, still glaring at Avery. "I need to catch a plane for a business trip to Phoenix, but I trust you can behave yourselves until Mom gets home from work."

"Claire, you heard Dad," Avery said. "No pole dancing tonight."

Dad shook his head and rolled his eyes before he went to his room. I remembered the prickly feeling in my gut when I had talked to Dad earlier that afternoon. There was something he was holding back. I had never been sure where he went, but I planned to find out. His briefcase was in his office.

I sprinted to the front of the house, my pulse racing, and slipped into his office. He kept his briefcase by the side of his desk. By now, I knew he wouldn't place any documents in it until right before he walked out the door. I took the GPS off my necklace and slid the disk inside the luggage tag of the briefcase, behind the paper with his name on it, then ran back into the kitchen.

"Where'd you go?" Avery asked when I returned.

"To the bathroom."

"Well, thanks to you, we get to stay home tonight," he said.

"Do you have any idea how annoying you are?" I asked, trying to catch my breath. "It's not my fault someone sent me *eyeballs*." Or maybe it was my fault. Why were things happening only to me? I couldn't help but feel guilty they weren't allowed to go. If it only affected me, I wouldn't care as much because parties were never my thing. I didn't need the added stress of people expecting me to do social things like *talk*. And with Avery grating every nerve, I don't know why I cared at all that he had to stay home.

"What are we going to do, then?" Parker asked.

"Watch a movie?" I said.

"Boring," Avery said.

"I can't think of anything," Parker said. "Let's wait for Forrest and Nicholas to get here, and we can decide."

Dad came back into the kitchen wearing a dark suit and tie with a small travel bag slung over his shoulder and his briefcase in hand. "Claire, your meeting is scheduled for next Friday. That's the soonest the principal and I could find a time that would work for all of us."

"Thanks for doing that." I wanted to bang my head on the island counter in front of me. Missing the meeting was my fault, and I knew it, but it didn't make the situation any easier.

"Parker," Dad called over to the family room, "take care of your mom and your sister while I'm gone."

"Yeah, I know," Parker said.

Dad said this every time he left for a trip, and it drove me crazy. "I don't need to be taken care of." It was the same response I always gave, but it didn't seem to matter.

"I know," Dad said to me, "but it doesn't mean I'll stop trying. Bye, kids."

"Bye," all of us said, and he went to the garage.

We ended up in the family room watching a movie. No one could think of anything else. The movie had been playing about twenty minutes when the doorbell rang. Who could be coming over? Everyone was already here.

No one moved. The doorbell rang again.

"Is anyone going to get that?" I asked.

"Thanks for volunteering," Avery said.

I got up and went to the front door. I opened the door and found Katie on the other side dressed in a tank top and cutoff shorts. What was she doing here?

"Oh hey," she said. "Can you come help me get some stuff out of the trunk?"

"Um, sure?" I slipped on some shoes and followed her to the car in our driveway. "What am I helping you with?"

"Stuff for the party. It actually worked out well that Avery called," she said. "My parents were getting all stressed out that something might get broken at our house, so they were relieved when I told him we moved it to your place." This was news to me. Avery was going to be first in line for Mom's wrath if she found out.

"Hmm." I hoped Mom was working late. "Did you let everyone know the location has changed?"

She pressed a button on her keychain and the trunk of her Passat opened. "Lanie, Mika, Kimi, and Ashley took care of it." She handed me a box filled with graham crackers, marshmallows, and chocolate bars. "And don't worry, they're telling everyone about the no shoes in the house policy."

Shoes in the house was the least of my worries. Mom was going to kill us.

"I was thinking we could make s'mores," she said, "because Avery said you could get a fire going in your copper pit." We do have a backyard that's ideal for s'mores.

Katie rested a tub of drinks on her hip and closed the trunk. We trekked across the front lawn and up the stairs of the porch. In the entryway, Katie set the tub on the floor so she could untie her shoes. Then she followed me down the hallway, past the stairs, to the family room and kitchen area. I set my box on the island in the kitchen and motioned for her to do the same.

"Hey guys," Katie called over to the family room.

"Hi," Nicholas said, from his usual couch. Forrest and Parker waved from the other couch.

"What's going on?" Parker muttered.

"I'm going to run to the gas station and get some ice," Katie said. "I'll be back in ten."

"No problem," I said.

As soon as she left, I said, "Apparently Avery told Katie we could have the party here."

Avery was sprawled on the floor in front of the TV. He rolled to his side. "Dad said we could hang out here with our friends, right?"

"Avery!" Parker said.

"What?" Avery said. "It'll be fine!"

For so many reasons, this was a bad idea. Our parents were going to kill us if they found out. Dad had wanted us to stay home so we would be safe, and now we were potentially inviting trouble to our front door. I put my hands on my hips. "What if the person who sent me the box ends up at our house?"

"We're not inviting anyone we don't trust," he said. "And if something happens tonight, we'll know it's a student, and we'll have a smaller pool of suspects."

And possibly a dead bunny—you know, if we had a bunny. "You're unbelievable," I said.

Avery put a hand to his heart. "Thank you."

Parker stood up and stretched. "It's probably too late to cancel, right?"

"Everyone already knows the party's here," I said. "But I still think we should cancel."

"Even if we do, people will still show up," Parker said. "And since there's no stopping this, we might as well get ready."

I couldn't call the party off when my brothers were working against me. "Fine. But we need to keep an eye out for anything suspicious."

"I think you should keep *four* eyes out for anything suspicious," Avery said.

To avoid fratricide, I walked into the kitchen.

MOM BOUGHT A set of outdoor furniture years ago, but no one ever used it, so it was usually pushed up against the back of the house. Parker, Nicholas, and Fed set up the matching patio chairs on one side of the copper pit and the bench with the backrest on the side closest to the house. Forrest and I set up a small table outside next to the patio chairs with stuff to make s'mores. Avery said he was supervising.

When Katie returned, I thought I should set some sort of ground rules since this party seemed to be happening whether I agreed or not. We stood in the entryway, and I gestured to the french glass doors directly to my right. "This is my dad's office. If anyone goes in here, we are dead."

"Gotcha." She tilted her head. "Let's tape a 'Do Not Enter' sign to the doors to be sure."

I swept my hand to the left. "This is obviously the living room, and if you continue down the hall to the left of the stairs, you'll find my parents' bedroom. We should probably put a sign there too."

"Good idea."

Within an hour, the house filled with a mixture of people from the boys' and girls' soccer teams and a handful of others. Nicholas, Parker, Avery, and Forrest scattered to different rooms to hang out with people they knew—everyone except for Fed, who clung to my back like a dryer sheet.

The two of us sat on a couch in the family room, observing others mingling around us. Maybe I had been more worried than I needed to be. I could either sit around and be paranoid, or I could take control over my life. "Fed, how about we both try to get dates to the Halloween dance?"

"I thought you were going to help me."

I'd been thinking of girls I could set him up with but hadn't come up with the perfect match yet. "I will, but maybe you can put some of the work in yourself."

He rubbed his round nose with a knuckle. His big, brown eyes dropped. I sighed. Those eyes almost made me cave, but I needed to show some tough love.

"Our chances will probably increase if we split up." I stood up and pulled him off the family-room couch, nudging him forward with a hand on his back. "See those girls over there?" I pointed to a group in the kitchen. "Go talk to them."

With all these people, there should be an opportunity to ask someone to the dance. It was easy to push Fed, but not so easy to push myself.

Fed yanked the front of his ball cap down, hiding his eyes, and skulked off to join Parker, who had everyone around him roaring with fits of contagious laughter. I hadn't been paying attention to what Parker was doing, but as long as he kept his shirt on, I wouldn't die of complete embarrassment.

And he did remain fully clothed. But the laughter grew as I walked into the kitchen, where he stood on top of the island and started doing orations with his butt by squeezing his rear cheeks in sync to his version of the Gettysburg address. The back pockets of his board shorts flapped.

I about-faced toward the living room and pretended I was an only child. Nicholas caught me and draped his arm around me.

"What are you doing?" I managed to shove his arm away.

His eyes flickered around the room. "Making sure you're okay."

"Can you please make sure I'm okay from farther away?" The room was crowded, and I had to shout so he could hear me.

"Of course." But he didn't move.

Why did he have to do this? Even if I was still a tad bit anxious, the last thing I needed was to give everyone the impression that I couldn't take care of myself in my own house.

"The thing that happened today isn't a big deal," I said, even though I couldn't get rid of a nagging feeling I'd had since I'd looked into the box.

"Jury's still out on that one," he said. "There's a reason your dad didn't want you to go out tonight."

"He didn't want Parker or Avery going out either, and I don't see you hovering over them." I gently tried to wriggle away from him. Not that there was anyone here I was interested in, but a couple of cute guys had left the kitchen looking disgusted when Parker started his butt-show, and hey, I liked a man who didn't care for my brother's gross humor. If I could work up the courage, I could talk to one of them. "Just give me some space."

"I will. Promise."

But he wasn't listening, and his arm remained around my shoulders. "You know I can take you down any time."

"Yep." He smiled, unaffected, and went to join Parker.

I was serious, though, and began calculating some of my signature self-invented martial arts attacks. Lanie spotted me standing in the corner seething. She threw both arms around my stiff body, her strawberry-blonde hair whipping me in the face. I patted her on the back awkwardly. I hadn't seen most of the team since the accusation of cheating had happened, and it was embarrassing to talk with them about why I wasn't making it to practice.

She wore a white T-shirt emblazoned with RAVENS on the front and black soccer pants, as if she had come straight from practice. Releasing me, she said, "Coach told us you missed your meeting today." Her mouth formed an exaggerated pout. "We need you on the field."

"Yeah, uh, I wish that hadn't happened." I tried to relax my face, but it was hard to mask how stupid I felt. Even with the whole eyeball incident, I would have stayed if I had been in the right frame of mind to remember the meeting. "It's unfortunate."

She opened her green eyes wide, sparkles of glitter reflecting off her freckles. "Grab a drink and join us. We're all outside on the patio," she called out as her ponytail disappeared through our back door off the kitchen.

I hesitated. After all, I *hadn't* cheated. These girls were my friends, and none of them had been weird toward me since the accusation. I grabbed a bottle of water off the counter and exited after her, eager to get as far away as possible from Parker and his fan club.

A small group of girls from my team huddled around the copper fire pit in the middle of the deck. A cool breeze caught the hairs on the back of my neck, and I hurried to join them. Utah deserts might be warm in the fall during the day, but at night the temperature drops. That fire looked so inviting.

Lanie flopped next to her boyfriend, Roarke, draping her long legs across his lap, and started kissing him. One thing I did *not* miss about my team was the PDA.

"Hi, Claire!" said Kimi and Mika, huddled under a blanket on a picnic bench across the fire. The glow of the flames danced in their dark eyes. Everyone stared at me, taking their attention from Lanie and Roarke.

Ashley sat next to them in a camping chair, concentrating on toasting her marshmallow.

"Hey." I sat in the middle of an empty bench at a right angle to them. I smiled awkwardly at everyone. Where to start? I hadn't talked to most everyone on the team since I was benched except to say hi or wave at them in class.

As the awkward moment dragged out, the back door flew open and Fed burst through. Avery swaggered close behind in his skater shorts. He wore a black T-shirt underneath a large, half-buttoned flannel shirt and a tough-guy scowl on his face. He surveyed the group and went back inside.

Fed clunked his lanky body next to me. His eyes wandered to Lanie and Roarke, who were a tangle of hands and had yet to come up for air. Not that I knew for sure, but I didn't think I could do that if I knew people were watching.

I looked across from me and remembered I was supposed to be helping Fed, too. "Hey, Fed, do you know Ashley Cheung?"

Why didn't I think of this earlier?

Ashley took her marshmallow from the fire and glanced up.

"Ashley, this is Fed." I put my arm around Fed. "Ashley was that girl from *Avatar* last year for Halloween. *The Last Airbender*, not the movie with the blue people."

"Katara," Fed said, entranced.

"I was thinking you could take her to your house and show her your collection of . . . stuff like that," I said.

"I'd love that," Ashley said. She popped the marshmallow in her mouth. Fed asked her about her costume, and Ashley said something about using long strips of blue cellophane and wrapping them around a wire frame so it looked like she was bending water. Soon Fed was leading her inside the house to find a quieter place to nerd-talk.

Nicholas filled the empty space next to me as soon as Fed was gone, before Kimi could even open her mouth, probably to ask me when I was going to come back to practice.

With a smile at Kimi, I turned to Nicholas. "You promised," I whispered through my gritted teeth.

He shrugged his oversized shoulders and gave me an innocent look. "Parker told me what all that eyeball stuff meant," he said in a hushed voice. "Do you really think I'm just going to brush that off?"

"I'm in my own backyard, surrounded by girls on my soccer team. I think I'll be fine," I said.

He sighed. "Fine. I think I hear some girls calling my name anyway. Let me know if you need anything." He adjusted his Seahawks hat and went back into the house.

"So when are you coming back to the team?" Kimi asked.

"As soon as I meet with the principal next Friday," I said, "and I prove that I didn't cheat."

Kimi grabbed two skewers leaning against the chair and handed one to Mika. They both grabbed marshmallows from the bag and skewered them.

"Everyone knows you wouldn't do that," Mika said as her marshmallow caught fire. She yanked it out and blew out the flames.

"I hope so." A few girls from the team had mentioned they didn't think I had cheated, but I didn't know what the rest of the school thought. Either they didn't know or didn't care. But the other teachers must have heard about it by now. Would they always wonder if I was a cheater even if I was found innocent?

The back door opened, and Mumps walked through. He strolled to the bench and sat next to me. "I've been looking for you," he said, stretching his legs in front of him.

He was wearing a button-down shirt, which seemed out of character, but then I realized I didn't know him well enough to know what he would or wouldn't wear. I mean, I'd seen him before in class but hadn't really paid attention to him. I didn't even know his real name.

"I'm still not clear why you rejected me," he said, pulling at his chin.

Caught off guard, I stared at him for several seconds before I could muster, "I thought Nicholas put you up to it."

Mumps smiled. "Okay, I just wanted to make sure it wasn't my bad body odor or something that scared you off," he said, laughing.

My shoulders relaxed. "I think it might have been your breath."

"Touché." He leaned back. "Are you telling me that if I brushed my teeth . . . ?"

"I might be willing to reconsider," I said and laughed.

"I'll remember that." He reached into his shirt pocket and pulled out an imaginary notebook, writing with an imaginary pencil. "Personal hygiene."

I laughed again.

"Anything else?" he asked.

"I can't think of anything."

"Okay, because I asked this girl to the Halloween dance, and she said no," he said, feigning confusion. "Can you believe it?"

I giggled. "You should really avoid those mean girls," I said. Who was inhabiting my body right now? I never giggled.

He picked up his imaginary notebook and wrote some more. "Avoid mean girls."

I took a deep breath, not wanting to offend him, but needing to say it. "I'm kind of embarrassed to say this, but I don't even know your real name."

"Calvin." He wrote in his notebook again. "Make sure they know my name." He leaned back and put his arm behind me, resting it on the back of the bench. "But you can call me Mumps. It sounds a lot more professional."

He put the imaginary pencil behind his ear. "Let me try this again." He held out his hand for me to shake, and I accepted. "Hi. My name is Calvin, and I brush my teeth."

Mumps had me laughing so hard that I forgot for a moment about the eyes, the cheating accusations, the dark SUV that could be following me. From the corner of my eye, I caught Forrest standing by the door. I didn't know how long he'd been there, but the strained expression on his face gave my heartbeat a start. I pulled my hand from Mumps's hand, which I'd continued to shake for far too long.

Forrest motioned with his head for me to join him.

"I'm so sorry," I said to Mumps. "Can you excuse me for a second?"

Mumps grinned. "You sure make a guy work hard to keep your attention."

I smiled. Talking with him had been so easy. "I'll be right back." I stood and walked past Forrest into the house.

Instead of going into the kitchen, I took a detour into the garage, where it was quieter. He closed the door behind him.

"What's wrong?" I asked.

"Chase is here," he said. "I don't know who invited him."

"He needs to leave." Heat rose up my neck.

"I agree," Forrest said. "I just thought you should know."

I opened the door, marched inside, and started searching.

Chase stood in the front door, arguing with Katie. He had one hand in the pocket of his khaki pants and was using the other to gesture. The white golf shirt made him look even more like an entitled brat.

Katie stood blocking his entrance, both arms folded in front of her chest. She was as tall as Chase, and as our goalkeeper, she wasn't afraid to face a challenge. I weaved through the crowd in the living room until I made it to Katie's side.

"I was telling him he needs to go," she said.

I narrowed my eyes. "Why would you even want to be here?"

"Look, all I need to do is talk to someone, and then I'll leave." Chase scanned the room.

"Who?" I demanded. Forrest slid behind me and put a hand on my shoulder.

Chase combed his hand through his hair with tense fingers. "One minute and I'll go." He looked to Forrest for support. "I was trying to explain to this Amazon that it'll only take a minute, but she wasn't listening."

I stepped closer to Chase. "What did you just call her?" I clenched my teeth together.

"Get out," Forrest said.

Chase shook his head. He shifted his weight back and forth, shoving his hands in the front pockets of his pants and then taking them out again. "Give me one minute," he said. "Just one." He shoved his hands back in his pockets.

"You have two options." I took another step closer to him. "You can leave before I call the police, or you and I can throw down, and I can embarrass you in front of all these people."

Chase glared at me, but turned around and left. I slammed the door.

"Throw down?" Forrest asked. He and Katie broke into laughter.

"I was angry," I said as the heart pounding faded. After a few seconds I laughed with them. I suppose it was a little dorky. I touched Katie's arm. "Uh, thank you. You didn't have to do that."

She shrugged. "That's what teammates do, girlfriend," she said. "You pick a fight with one of us, you pick a fight with all of us."

With that, she bounced off and melted into the group in the living room as if nothing had happened. Something warm tugged at my heart.

I maneuvered my way to the stairs and sat down on the third

step. Forrest plunked himself next to me. "Who do you think he was here to see?" I asked.

"I don't know."

I tried to sort through everyone at our house, but I couldn't think of anyone who would want to talk to Chase, let alone need to. He wasn't on any of our sports teams, which made up most of the crowd here. Nicholas was on the debate team with him, but after the experience I'd had with Chase last year, there was no love lost between the two of them. Maybe he didn't come to see anyone, but was using that as an excuse to get into the house. What was he trying to do?

"So . . . you and Mumps seemed to be getting along pretty well," Forrest said.

"Mumps." I jumped off the stairs. "I completely forgot about him." I bobbed through more people. Before I got to the back door, I ran into Mom.

Her eyes were sagging and tired, but there was no mistaking the tightness of her lips and her close-knit eyebrows. "I have just walked two blocks to get into my own house because there are cars in my driveway and in front of the house and across the street and all the way down the street on both sides."

"People should really carpool more," I said, but she wasn't amused.

"Do you want to tell my why all these people are in my house?" she asked.

"Dad said we could," I said. "And it's Avery's fault."

Mom lifted her purse higher on her shoulder. "I'm going to my room, and if I find anyone in there using my bed, none of you will see the light of day again. Get these people out of here."

22

EVERYONE WAS SLOW to leave, but my brothers and I were able to clear the house and get everything cleaned up. By the time I checked the patio, Mumps had gone. I'd have to apologize to him on Monday.

I said good-bye to Nicholas and Forrest at the back door. Parker and Avery had already crashed on the couches in the family room.

Fed tugged on the back of my shirt before he left. "Hey," he said, his face puffed as if it might burst with jubilation. "I have a date to the Halloween dance."

"That's great," I said. "Is it Ashley?"

"Yep," he said.

"I knew you could do it." I pictured Fed's lanky, tall body next to Ashley, who probably wasn't even five feet in heels, and it made me smile. Seeing Fed happy made the world seem lighter.

I closed and locked the door behind them and headed up the stairs to my room. Halfway up, I heard music, a slow and haunting melody that sounded familiar. The sound was faint, but grew louder the closer I got to my room. I flipped on my light and found my stereo had been moved to my desk. Someone from the party? Why would they move it?

A Japanese song I recognized from my childhood was playing on the stereo. The English version was called "Sukiyaki," but my parents had always sung the Japanese words to me. This was neither—the version playing was wordless and featured a stringed instrument, the tempo much slower than I had heard before.

My curtain fluttered, carried by a breeze floating through my open window. I was pretty sure I had closed it. Had I left it open by mistake? Had Chase snuck in here when he couldn't get through the front door? Maybe someone else from the party had been in my room. I surveyed my bed. Maybe two someones from the party had been in my room. Ugh. I didn't really want to think about that one. Why didn't I put a sign on my door like I had my parents' bedroom and the study?

I slid the window shut and paced around the room, inspecting. I'd noticed the big things first, but those weren't the only things wrong. The closet door was open, with clothes about to fall off their hangers and a small pile already on the floor. There was an overturned garbage can by my desk. The books from my shelf were scattered on the floor. As I looked closer, I saw smudge marks on my carpet, a small tear in the curtain. A shiver rippled through me. Who would do something like this?

"Mom," I shouted into the hallway. "Someone broke into my room."

Mom hurried up the stairs. She looked around. "Is anything missing?"

My laptop was still on my desk. I checked the top drawer of

my dresser. My wallet was there. My phone was in my pocket. Nothing else I owned would be valuable to anyone but me. My mouth went dry, and the muscles in my neck and shoulders tightened. What was going on?

"I don't think so," I said. "But they moved the stereo and made a mess."

"Are you sure?" She walked over to the stereo. For a minute she closed her eyes and listened to the music, then turned it off. "Was this was here when you got to your room?"

I nodded. Chase had come to the house, but he'd barely made it inside. Maybe the person had climbed up the tree and come through the window. I'd done it enough times to know it was possible. Had someone played a prank on me after hearing about the cheating scandal? I couldn't see any of our teammates as people who might come up to my room and violate my personal space to mess with me. They were all good people. Weren't they? But if it wasn't a stupid joke, someone had really broken into my room. Like someone who was a real criminal. What if I had been in here when the person came through the window?

"I've always loved that song," she said.

I had too, even though I had no idea what the lyrics meant. The melody brought back so many good memories, memories I hoped wouldn't be tainted by the bristle running beneath my skin. I scanned the room again but couldn't think of anything that was gone.

"Nothing's missing, but they left a CD playing on your stereo," Mom said. "I don't know if there's much the police can do with that, especially when you guys were the ones who invited a houseful of people over." She sighed. "Let's at least file a report."

She made a phone call and two policemen showed up at our house. I expected them to wear rubber gloves and have their kits ready to dust for fingerprints on the stereo and CD or sample the dirt smudges on the floor. All they did was walk around my room. They checked the window for forced entry, but didn't find anything peculiar.

One of the officers, a woman with an athletic build and light brown hair, introduced herself as Officer Rodriguez. Officer Schwartz, a short, round man, took me aside. His belt was cinched tight and had probably seen better days.

"I think that it's good to be careful," he said, "and it's better to be safe than sorry, so calling us was the right thing to do." He leaned closer. "Would you feel more comfortable if we asked your mom to leave, so you can tell us what really happened?" The way he glanced down at me with his pudgy face made me feel smaller.

"No. That's what really happened," I said.

He shifted his focus to my mom. "Sometimes teens do stuff like this to make it look like something expensive has been stolen when really they've sold it because they needed money." He held up his chubby arm and glanced at his watch. "It's only eleven P.M., so it's pretty unlikely someone would have attempted to break in."

"I told you nothing was missing," I said.

He put his hands on his hips. "I can't find any real evidence of anything, but it's probably a good idea to keep your windows closed."

"I *did* have the window closed."

"Sure. Well, if you see anything suspicious, you can call us again, okay, sweetheart?"

He patted my head like I was a small child or a dog. Obviously he didn't believe a word I said, and it was all I could do not to punch him. My social graces kicked in, though, when I saw Mom's warning expression, reminding me it wasn't the best idea to give a police officer the middle-finger salute.

Officer Rodriguez sealed the CD into a plastic baggie for evidence, and Mom and I followed the officers to the door, where Mom thanked them and apologized if we had wasted their time. They reassured her, rather insincerely in my opinion, and left.

"I'm going to go call your dad," she said.

I walked up the stairs. Even the slightest creaks made me jump. I scoured every inch of my room, determined to find something the police had missed.

It took me a good half hour of searching, but eventually I found something. On the floor right underneath my open window, I noticed a business card and picked it up. At the top was the name of a place called the Waiawa Circle of Friends. Below that was their website address, their mailing address in Waipahu, Hawaii, and a phone number. At the bottom was written, "Healing by exploring forgiveness and repairing harm." I'd never heard of the place, and I had no idea what that phrase meant, but it sounded like a place for free-spirited granola lovers.

I wasn't sure where it'd come from, but it must have fallen from my father's notebook a few weeks ago. Rather than taking the effort to put it back in the box in my closet, I set the card in my desk drawer. I closed my window and climbed into bed. For all I knew, Dad could be halfway around the world, but I wished he were home instead.

COLD AIR WOKE me only a few hours later, the clock glowing 3:34 A.M. Twisting the covers tighter, I curled in my blanket and shut my eyes.

Leaves crackled in the trees. I flopped to the other side to get more comfortable. The wind swept past the house, growing from a faint whimper to a hum. As a light sleeper, even hushed whispers woke me, so trying to lull myself back to sleep was going to be next to impossible. I smashed a pillow around my head, but the noises outside my window grew louder.

And then I heard music.

The sound was weak. I told myself it was just my imagination. At first the music hovered as if outside my window. And then the eerie melody echoed from downstairs.

Ue o muite arukou

I could barely hear it, but I knew it was the same song that had played over my stereo, only this time a man was singing, his voice low and gravelly. The tempo was still slower than what I'd remembered as a child, the tone somber.

I dragged myself out of bed, hoping someone else had woken and for some reason turned on the stereo in the living room. But the chances were small. I was the only one who woke so easily.

Each step was a step away from going back to sleep. I got to the top of the stairs and froze. Mom's bedroom was only yards away below me. I sucked in a deep breath and willed myself forward, but my feet moved the opposite direction, backward, and didn't stop until I stumbled into Parker's room.

"Parker," I whispered, shoving his arm. "Wake up." He didn't budge. I shook him harder. "Wake up. There's something at the front door."

He grunted. Slobber trickled down the side of his mouth. "I don't want to go to the dentist. Dentist. Don't do that to me, dentist." He rolled away.

I whacked him on the chest with my fist. He bolted up, his arms in karate-chop position. He stared at me, blinking for a couple of seconds before he really woke, then let his hands fall to the bed. "What are you doing in here?"

I grabbed his arm. "I think someone's on the porch."

Normally he would have thrown me out of his room while yelling a few choice words. But he must have seen the fear in my eyes. Without any questions, he reached under his bed and pulled out a wooden bat. "Let's go," he said.

I crept behind him, hunched as if we were thieves robbing the house. At the bottom of the stairs, Parker and I tiptoed toward the front door, but I took a detour into the living room, where I crept to the picture window and peeked outside.

It was too dark to see anything but black shapes, which could just as easily have been porch furniture as a person. "I can't tell if anyone is there."

Parker lifted the bat, ready to swing, and pushed his cheek closer to the door's crack. He flipped on the porch light. "Who's there?"

The voice continued to sing, the muffled melody sneaking through the cracks around the door. As far as I could tell, nothing was on the porch, but beyond the lit area, it was now pitch black.

Parker moved from the door. "Okay, you keep talking to distract him. I'll go out the back door, sneak around the house, and launch a surprise attack," he whispered.

"On what? We don't even know what's out there," I said. "I'm going to get Mom."

"Coward," he muttered.

I raced into my parents' room to wake her and found Dad there as well. He must have come home late, after we were all asleep.

Dad woke with little effort and came out to the living room with me. "Stay behind me." He stuck out his arm and herded me and Parker to the side.

Parker clung to my back with both hands as if I were a human shield. "Get off me," I said, wriggling away.

Dad removed a gun from the back of his pajama pants, the kind you see on cop shows that have a clip that goes in the handle. Parker's eyes went as wide as mine must have been. When did he get a gun?

Dad pressed his bare back flush against the wall next to the door's frame. He checked the chain lock to make sure it was in place before he cracked open the door.

A ball of fire exploded out in the yard, lighting up the window.

Heat rushed into the house as Dad slammed the door.

"Parker, call 911!" Dad yelled. He rushed to the window and inspected the fire outside. "Give them our address, and tell them we might have a burn victim in the front yard."

My heart dropped to my stomach. A burn victim? Who? Through the living-room window I could see a fire blazing in the front part of our oak tree. My hands shook.

At the same time, Mom screamed behind me and ran into the room. "What was that?"

Dad waved her back toward Parker, who was on the phone giving our address to the dispatcher. "Claire, go get Avery and meet me at the back door. Parker, take Mom and wait for me. Don't leave the house until I get there."

Parker nodded. I unfroze enough to sprint up the stairs, tripping and catching myself all the way up. Avery was sitting up when I got there, dazed and half-asleep. "What's going on?"

"There's a fire," I screamed. "We've got to go."

The sleep disappeared from his eyes. He jumped to his feet and followed me down the stairs to the back door, where the rest of our family waited. Dad waved us down. "Stay out of sight."

Mom huddled us around her, and we crouched on the floor.

Dad motioned for us to stay where we were. Mom's eyes were wide and focused intensely on Dad, tears pooling in the corners of her eyes. He nodded at her, acknowledging her unspoken plea, then lifted his gun, cracked open the door to peek through, and ran outside, shirtless and barefoot.

My stomach dropped to the floor watching him go. I couldn't see the fire from here, but I could hear it crackle. What if it reached the house? It had been a dry fall with burn bans up the canyon. Would we be able to escape the house, or was someone out there waiting for us, someone who set the fire? Would Dad be okay out there all alone?

Mom closed her eyes. A tear trailed down her cheek.

"We're gonna die, we're gonna die, we're gonna die," Parker chanted.

"Shut up!" Avery growled.

Another five minutes or so passed as we sat quietly, each of us in an anxious world of our own. Dad opened the door, startling all of us. His gun had disappeared and his expression had changed from stressed to annoyed.

"It's safe," he said. "Whoever did this is gone."

I STOOD UP on shaky legs.

Parker groaned as he got up. "I just hate when someone lights your tree on fire in the middle of the night as a prank and ruins your beauty sleep."

Avery jumped to his feet and gestured to Parker. "There's not enough sleep in the world that can fix that." He pointed at his own face. "On the other hand, beauty like this comes naturally."

Parker took a playful swipe at Avery, but Dad pulled him back. "Parker, go get the hose and start spraying the tree in the front yard," he said. He gave Mom a quick kiss after helping her up from the kitchen floor. "Everything's secure outside. We're not in immediate danger. You can stay here with Claire and Avery."

Parker followed Dad to the front of the house, with me at their heels. If Parker was going, I wasn't about to be left behind. The large oak tree by my window was a fountain of orange and yellow on the side of the tree closest to the street. Flames lapped up the tree and along the branches.

The fire hadn't made it to the house yet but would get there soon if we didn't do something. A fire like this could light up the whole neighborhood given the right wind conditions. Parker grabbed the hose and turned on the water as high as it would go.

On the porch below the window to Dad's office, music blared from wireless speakers and a cheap MP3 player, the song I had heard as I came down the stairs. My hand trembled as I stopped it from playing. Who would know that this song was part of my childhood? A chill pierced deep, down to my bones.

"Spray the house first, so it's wet—it'll catch less easily that way," Dad said, "and then focus on the flames closest to the house."

Parker aimed an arc of water at the roof, but glanced back in the direction of the fire. His eyes shifted to the ground. "Dad, what's that?" Parker asked, pointing the hose.

At the base of the tree was a silhouetted lump that looked like a partially charred body. Parker's face blanched as the realization came over him as to what it could be, then rocked on his feet. "I don't think . . ."

He passed out, his shoulder thudding against the grass.

"Dammit, Parker," Dad muttered.

As Dad went over and picked up the hose from Parker's limp hands to finish spraying the house, sirens rang from down the street.

I pointed to the body. "What is that?"

"It's not real." He changed focus from the house to the tree, sweeping the hose from side to side, shooting water as high as possible to reach the flames.

A wave of relief swooped through me. I walked down the porch stairs to get a better look. At the edge of the grass, I crouched and squinted at a mannequin, its feet pointed in my direction.

"Don't get too close," Dad warned. "These branches could fall."

Leaves and wood crackled above. The tree had to be over fifty feet tall, its branches shading half our yard. I knew it was just a tree, and I should be grateful nothing more significant had caught fire yet, but seeing the billowing smoke rise from the blaze made me choke up. I'd grown up climbing its branches and playing underneath it. Our garden hose couldn't put this fire out.

Though Dad wasn't able to extinguish the fire, he kept the flames from getting to the house.

Forrest ran over to me, dressed only in his boxers. He grabbed me by my arms. "Is everyone okay?" His parents stood on their front lawn, and other neighbors had come out of their houses to see what had happened.

"Yeah. I'm fine," I said, shrugging. I mean, I was physically okay, but tonight my world had shifted.

Forrest shook his head. "You're not fine." He dropped his arms. "What about Parker?"

"He's a pansy." I bent down. "He fainted when he saw this."

Mom came out onto the porch and called, "George, what's going on?" The glow of the ambulance lights as it arrived danced across her face. Her gaze dropped from the fire to Parker on the ground, and she screamed. "Is he dead?" Mom collapsed next to him and cradled his head in her arms. "Parker's dead!"

The ambulance screeched to a stop in front of the house. Two paramedics jumped out and ran to where I stood.

"It's only a mannequin," I said. They turned their attention to Parker on the ground. Dad handed me the hose, told me to stand well back and keep spraying. Then he went over to Mom and grabbed her by the shoulders, stood her up, and moved her aside so the paramedics could take a look at my brother. "Parker just passed out," he said to her. "I'm sure he'll be fine."

Mom disappeared into the kitchen, then came back and started patting Parker's cheeks with a warm, wet towel. The paramedics kept asking her politely to move out of the way but she took every opportunity to insert herself when possible.

A minute later, the fire department arrived with a police car right behind them, so I stepped aside. A lump formed at the back of my throat when I saw the same police officers who had been at our house earlier step out of the car. Why did Officer Schwartz have to be one of the officers to respond? Hadn't we already been through enough? Hopefully he would take this situation more seriously than he had the break-in.

"You can leave the hose here, just in case," one of the firemen said to me. I let the hose fall to the ground, and Forrest and I went to sit on the porch swing.

The fireman talked briefly to Dad while the others attached their big hose to a hydrant. They moved with choreographed efforts, suffocating the fire systematically.

After what seemed like a long while, Parker started to moan. With the help of the paramedics, Mom took him into the house while Officer Schwartz talked to Dad. Forrest and I sat on the porch in silence, entranced by the colorful glow as the heat blew over us. It took about half an hour, but the firefighters got the flames under control. They continued to spray it, though, to be sure it was completely out.

Why was all of this happening? How was everything connected? When I considered the eyes and music, I couldn't help but think this was all tied to my father.

"Someone broke into my room," I said in a soft voice.

"What? Why didn't you tell me earlier? What did they take?"

Though the break-in had happened only hours ago, it seemed like a lifetime had passed. I gave him the details, tremors forging a manic path through my body and voice as the weight of everything sank in. Forrest reached over and took my shaking hand, tethering me and my urge to run and never look back.

An hour passed before the fire was completely extinguished. As firemen canvassed the lawn, they found what looked like bits of garbage and part of an aerosol can, which helped them determine the fire was started by a small homemade bomb and fuse. I overheard one of the firemen tell my dad the bomb was most likely supposed to set the mannequin's head on fire, but the explosion shredded the rope and catapulted the body to the ground.

I slid my hand out of Forrest's and stepped down the porch stairs to see what I'd been thinking was a body. On the ground lay a female mannequin wearing a black long-haired wig, sections of it singed to the scalp. She had a rope tied around her neck like a noose, the end of which was black and frayed from the fire, and parts of her plastic face and neck were misshapen and melted, dark smudges all over the body. Above me was the other half of the rope, knotted around one of the charred branches, barely hanging on.

The round policeman stopped talking to Dad and called over to me in a sharp voice. "Don't even think about touching anything."

Dad's brow quirked, and the corners of his mouth turned down.

"I wasn't going to."

I didn't realize Forrest was behind me until I heard him

curse at the officer under his breath. I kept my distance from the fake corpse, but walked close enough to get a better look.

The mannequin lay on its side and wore a white soccer jersey with the word RAVENS written across the chest and matching shorts, which matched our team's uniforms. The back of the jersey was emblazoned with the name TAKATA, written from shoulder to shoulder, and the number three below it. Both shirt and shorts were marred with burn holes and charred edges. "I guess I know what was stolen from my room."

Ice ran through my veins, numbing my body. That mannequin was supposed to be me. Me. All the events and information and questions seemed to slip into quicksand the more they churned in my head, swallowing the thoughts and leaving only thick sludge behind.

"What the hell is going on?" Forrest muttered to himself more than me.

It had been too long a night.

After Dad pointed out the MP3 player, Officer Rodriguez put it in a plastic baggie and wrote something in black marker. Dad invited the police into the office and told me to follow.

A chill set on my skin. Forrest guided me up the porch steps, his warm hand at the small of my back. I glanced down to where the MP3 player had been. The music haunted my thoughts. Was this only the first song on the soundtrack to my nightmare?

Not far from where the player had been was something round like the wooden counters used on an abacus. I picked it up and held it in my palm for Forrest to see, but it was just a button. The wood had bright gold and dark brown striations. The grain and patterns looked similar to the koa wood used on my father's funerary urn. It was common in Hawaii, but a rare wood here and easy to recognize. Most likely it was from one of Dad's Hawaiian shirts. I put it in my pocket so Mom could sew it back on for him.

"Since it's closer to morning now, I'll probably sleep past noon tomorrow," Forrest said, "but call me even if it's for no reason in particular, and I'll come right over."

"Thanks," I said. Dad hollered for me. "I'll see you tomorrow."

Forrest shivered and ran his hands up and down his arms to keep warm. "I'm serious. Don't worry about waking me up if you want me to come over."

I nodded and went inside.

Dad called for my mom to join us in the study, and gestured for both of us to sit in the chairs when she arrived. The officers stayed by the door.

"Claire, can you tell us anything about what happened?" Dad asked.

Before I could ask him why he thought I'd know anything, Officer Schwartz interrupted him. "Sir, we'll ask the questions," he said. "Can you tell us anything about what happened?"

Dad's face went tight.

"Is something funny, ma'am?" Schwartz asked.

"No." I hadn't been smiling. Between their accusations earlier that I made my bedroom look like someone broke in, just to get attention, and this guy's attitude now, I had a feeling he'd dismiss it as a prank, even though it was clearly arson.

"No nothing's funny, or no you can't tell us anything?" He puffed out his chest and adjusted his belt.

I folded my arms, wondering why they thought I would know

who did this. "All I know is the mannequin out there is wearing a soccer jersey stolen from my room, probably when someone broke in tonight. Which you already know happened."

"Oh this is awful. Just awful," Mom said to herself.

Officer Rodriguez walked to my chair and placed a hand on my shoulder. "Do you think this is a prank? We take arson pretty seriously, especially when it's this dry."

"There's a guy named Chase Phillips at my school who doesn't like me, but I don't know if he did this." Chase had been at the house, but would he have gone this far just to get back at me? If this was a prank, it seemed too elaborate to be carried out by anyone who went to school with us.

The police officers asked some more questions and even more questions when I told them about the eyeballs. *Why eyeballs? Was there a possibility that someone from outside of the school could have had access to my backpack? When did I notice my uniform was missing? Did the song have any personal significance? What reason would someone have to target me?* For over an hour, I answered them the best I could, but exhaustion swept over me, and my eyelids drooped.

When we finally finished, Officer Schwartz shook his head. "Boy, someone really doesn't like you." His mouth released a short whistle. "Well, we'll investigate, but I wouldn't be surprised if it turns out to be an ill-humored prank."

Officer Rodriguez held out her hand. "What Officer Schwartz means is that we consider arson, as I said before, a very serious matter. Depending on the damage done, this could be a third- or even second-degree felony, so please let us know if you think of anything later that might be helpful."

Mom thanked them and showed them out, but Dad stayed behind. Once we were alone, he shut the office doors.

"When did you get home?" I asked.

"I turned around right after your mom called about the break-in and caught a midnight flight straight back."

"I don't know if I think Chase did this," I said. "He's the only one I can think of who would even think to do this kind of thing, or want to hurt me, but I don't know when he would have had the opportunity to break in to my room. And I don't know if it would cross his mind to draw on Japanese culture to terrorize me, but I guess we should consider everything."

"I'm not sure I believe he did it either." He clenched his hand into a fist, and his eyebrows drew closer. "We used to sing that song to you when you were younger and you had a hard time going to sleep."

"I remember."

He narrowed his eyes. "Do you know if your father ever sang that to you?"

"I think he did, but—" I sighed. "Sometimes I don't know if the things I remember are really my memories, or if they're things I think I remember because Mom's told me about them so much, or if they're ideas I make up because it's what I would have wanted to happen." I bit at my lip. "Why do you ask?" And how would whoever did this to us know about that song, anyway? There couldn't be that many kids at my high school who knew the Japanese melody. Not even Fed.

He gritted his teeth, then relaxed his jaw. "The pieces don't make sense, but we'll get to the bottom of this."

DAD WOKE ME up earlier than usual the next morning. I moaned and pulled the comforter over my head, pleading late-night arson interrupted my sleep. He lifted the blanket off my face, unsympathetic. "Meet me in the garage in five minutes."

I grumbled, but I got out of bed and changed into a tank top and shorts, expecting more self-defense practice. I'm sure all the moves we went over every Saturday were beginner's stuff, but he still insisted we practice.

In the garage, the cars had been backed into the driveway, and a padded mat had been placed on the concrete. Dad was at the punching bag. His hair might have been peppered with gray, but I was proud of the way he kept himself in great condition. Beneath his white T-shirt and navy jersey-knit shorts were well-defined muscles.

"Where are the boys?" I asked.

"I thought we'd spend some one-on-one time." He stopped punching. "They're cleaning up the front yard."

What he meant: the boys hadn't gotten boxes like I had.

We both moved to center of the mat. Dad put his hands on his hips. "What are the parts of the body where you can do the most damage?"

By now, I knew this as well as the alphabet. "Eyes, nose, ears, neck, groin, knee, and legs," I said.

"What parts of the body are most effective for inflicting damage?"

"Elbows, knees, and head."

He nodded. "Today I want to practice choke holds." He faced me and placed his hands around my throat. I put my right hand on his esophagus, extending my arm to push off him as I took a step back with my left foot and twisted my body in the same direction to break free.

"What's another way you could break the hold?" He put his hands at my throat again.

In one continuous move, I swung my right arm up and across both of his arms and used the momentum to keep rotating counterclockwise until my back was at his chest. Then I was able to direct my left elbow backward to his face. "Good," he said. "Let's do that a few more times, and then we'll practice a choke hold from behind."

"So where were you?" I asked as we went through the moves.

"Phoenix."

"What'd you do there?" I swung my arm and broke his hold.

"Same old stuff," he said. "I had to check out an international antiques distributor to see if it's a worthy investment."

I raised a brow, unable to stop curiosity from beating out reason. "What's the name of the distributor?"

"The Copper Cactus." He dropped his arms. "What are you really trying to ask me?" His eyes narrowed, and he pushed his glasses up the bridge of his nose.

"I don't understand why something like that would be such an emergency," I said and twisted my body. "Seems like you've been gone more than usual lately."

"That's the job sometimes. When it comes to finance, everybody's in a hurry. And when you're dealing with people who have a lot of money, they expect you to be on their schedule even if it's not during usual business hours," he said. "Okay, let's practice some from behind."

Throughout all my questioning, he had answers for everything even when I thought I might catch him off guard. He never flinched. I realized I probably had been paranoid over nothing and let the subject drop. I would, however, check my GPS app later to make sure.

We practiced the same moves over and over again until Dad was satisfied.

"I've got to run to the hardware store," he said. "I shouldn't be too long. For now though, I think we should try to fly under the radar, maybe stick around the house instead of going anywhere."

"Sure." I agreed with him anyway. Last night's fire had me a little shaken.

He left, and I folded the mat and leaned it against the wall. I went upstairs and jumped in the shower, then sat at my desk and stared out my front window. The boys were still in the yard, picking up branches and raking leaves. I probably should have gone outside and helped them, but I couldn't bring myself to see the damage up close in the daylight yet. A big part of our tree had burned, but I hoped enough was left that it could survive.

The police had taken the mannequin with them so they could submit it into evidence, but the image of the charred body wearing my uniform stayed with me. Was that the future someone had in store for me? My mind whirled, not really catching on any one thought about the events of the last several weeks. Before I knew it, an hour had passed, my brothers had finished outside, and I was still no closer to any conclusions, except that I didn't want to remain a prisoner in my own home because someone thought they could scare me.

A soft knock hit my door. "Claire?" Fed pushed open the door slowly.

I spun the chair around. "Hey, Fed. What's up?"

"What happened to your tree? It looks like a bomb hit your front yard."

Fed flopped his gangly body onto the bed, and I noticed he was hanging over every edge in a way he hadn't last year. He wasn't quite as tall as Nicholas and was a lot skinnier, but he was definitely getting there.

I told him about the break-in, and the effigy, and the fire in the tree. "I don't know how you didn't hear all the sirens and everything, even at the end of the street."

"Crap, Claire. Are you scared?" He sat up, eyes wide, lips parted. "That's a stupid question. Of course you're scared. Uh, not that you're a chicken or anything, that's not what I'm saying, I mean, I would be scared if I were you."

"It's fine, Fed. I get it." I got off my chair and sat next to him on the bed. "And yeah, I'm kind of scared." Except I was more than kind of scared, and I didn't know what I could do to stop all of this, and that scared me even more. Would I always be afraid of what bad thing was coming next?

Fed stood up. "Okay well, never mind then. I was going to ask you for a favor, but that would be pretty uncool right now. Hang in there." He headed toward the door.

"What did you need?"

He turned back to look at me. "Nothing. Don't worry about it. I'd feel bad—"

"Fed." I got to my feet. "What do you need?"

He flashed his toothy grin, bunching up his freckled cheeks. "I need a ride to work because Nicholas abandoned me."

I tilted my head. "Abandoned you?"

"He's at a debate tournament and Mom's working. But seriously . . ." He waved both hands at me.

"Let's go," I said, grabbing my car keys and wallet from my top drawer. I told myself I could do this. I wasn't going that far. I'd be back before Dad got home. Maybe whoever was doing this wanted me to sit home and to be afraid, but I didn't have to let myself be bullied.

"Thanks." He put his arm around me like Nicholas always did, but it about knocked his featherweight body over when he pulled me next to his side.

Fed fidgeted in his seat, dancing to the music from the radio. Every few seconds, he'd change the station, dance around, then change the station again.

Normally I would have made him choose one station and stick with it, but my head crowded with questions. Chase had been at our house looking for someone, but why couldn't he have called or texted him? Or her. But it still didn't make sense. The most recent events made me think it was more likely everything was tied to my father rather than someone at school.

But our father had died more than ten years ago. What would someone have to gain by terrorizing us now? Hopefully it would remain terrorizing rather than escalating to something worse.

I eased the car down the winding roads of our neighborhood and made a right turn at the stop sign.

"Hey, so do you think you can take me shopping this weekend? I need to get a birthday present for Parker."

"Seriously? Are you forgetting someone else's birthday? Mine is before his, remember?"

Parker was a senior, and I was a junior. But in age, Parker was ten days shy of being a full year older than I was. I don't know why Mom had had us so close together, but for those ten days we were the same age, I made sure his life was miserable.

I checked my mirrors and signaled to get into the left lane.

"Relax. I already got your present," he said. "And you will totally love it. I think. So will you take me?"

"Maybe."

I rolled to a stop at a red light in the left turning lane. The phone rang over the speakers, and the touch screen displayed Dad's name. I pushed the button on my steering wheel to answer.

"Where are you?" Dad asked.

"I'm dropping Fed off at work. Why?"

"Because I got home and you weren't here," he said. "What part of 'flying under the radar' did you not understand?"

I threw a hand in the air. "Dad, all I'm doing is dropping Fed off like a mile away. I'll come right back. You'll see me in ten minutes."

"Come straight home after you drop him off," he growled, and hung up.

"Is that not what I said I would do?" I said to the dead phone line.

"Uh, sorry about that." Fed fiddled with the buttons again. "I knew I shouldn't have let you take me. This is getting serious, Claire. When someone blows up your tree, and they blow it up with you in it, you know, the fake you, and they violate your room, and all that other stuff too? Then I think you have to consider maybe they're trying to send you a message." His voice soared to a high pitch.

"You think?" I was often surprised and amused at how long it could take for someone so academically intelligent to conclude the obvious.

"Okay, maybe you already knew that, but in my experience — and by experience I mean manga and anime — usually someone only does stuff like this if they want something someone else has, so they intimidate you until you give it up, or they want revenge. Besides Chase, who do you know that would fit into those categories?"

No one would want anything I had, and even if this was tied to my father's days in the yakuza, what did that have to do with me or the rest of my family? "I can't think of anyone, and no one would want something of mine."

The light turned green, and I made my turn onto Highland.

I didn't need to look at Fed to know his forehead and eyebrows were pinched in, and he was biting his bottom lip—the expression he wore when his thoughts churned in never-ending circles like mine did. He stayed quiet for the next few minutes as I drove, but I could tell his mind was sifting through data.

I turned into the parking lot of the strip mall where Fed worked as a fry cook at Stan's, a popular hamburger joint where kids from our school liked to hang out.

"I'm sorry I made your dad mad at you," he said.

"It's not your fault. He's being paranoid, and I mean, I'm worried too, but I refuse to let someone control my life so much that I can't drive ten minutes away from my house."

"I get it," he said.

I pulled the car into a spot right in front of the fast food hot spot and put the car into park.

Fed undid his seatbelt, climbed out of the car, and yanked his bag from the floor. "Thanks for the ride." His thin lips broke into a big smile. "And I don't suppose you could send someone else to pick me up when I'm done so I don't get you in trouble?"

"I'll be here at five thirty. And I expect you to have a peppermint shake in hand for me. Don't be stingy with the candy pieces." I sighed. "Unless I'm not allowed to be outside the house for more than ten minutes, in which case I'll send my mom."

"Thanks." He gave me a big smile and closed the door.

The same thoughts reeled through my head as I started home on State Street. I outlined the chain of events. Was it possible that all of it was connected? I tried to imagine every event that had happened as a puzzle piece, but the pieces felt more like forcing circles into triangular holes.

I glanced in my rearview mirror before I signaled to switch into the left lane. The car behind me followed. I changed lanes a few more times. The same white car happened to be there in the rearview mirror.

Probably just a coincidence, I thought. Someone trying to beat State Street traffic. I was being paranoid.

I switched lanes again. With every movement I made, the car waited a second, then followed. Not likely another coincidence. It wasn't a black SUV, so maybe it was a police car, the kind that looked like a normal car until the headlights flashed red and blue. Mom and Dad would kill me if I got another speeding ticket. I was only going four miles over the speed limit.

I slowed down to exactly the speed limit and waited, semi-hoping for the car's lights to flash. When nothing happened, my pulse rate took flight. I changed lanes a couple more times, and the car continued to trace my movements.

New, disheartening thoughts slithered to the forefront of my mind, thoughts I wasn't allowing myself to entertain up until now. I muttered a string of curse words. There were worse things than a police car that might be following me.

At the next light, I made a right turn onto Franklin Avenue, swerving to make the turn at the last possible moment. The car followed. I accelerated, but our minivan wasn't known for its speed. I tried to catch a glimpse of the driver, but the windows were tinted to a dark shade that was most certainly illegal.

I sped up the street and ran a red light at Alta View Parkway, but the car followed, causing other vehicles to swerve. So I sped up the hill, passing Franklin High School. As soon as there was a break in oncoming traffic, I did a U-turn as fast as the minivan would allow me. My wheels squealed as I spun the car around to head in the opposite direction along Franklin Avenue.

The car kept driving the direction I'd come from, letting me drive back to the intersection before it followed suit and turned around. I tightened my grip on the steering wheel to keep my hands from shaking. When I got to the next light, I whipped into a right turn at Alta View.

All sounds around me faded. With fingers trembling, I picked up my phone to dial 911, but it slipped and flew to the floor of the passenger side.

My hands tensed at the steering wheel and my breaths quickened. I needed to focus. As long as Bluetooth was still connected, I could make a call. The keypad wouldn't be enabled on the touch screen unless I brought the car to a full stop, so I all I could do was dial one of the preset numbers. Why hadn't I added 911 to the car's speed dial list? I pressed the phone button on the steering wheel. The GPS map disappeared from the screen and my speed dial numbers appeared. I selected Dad's number.

Ring. Ring. Ring.

My heart beat faster.

Ring. Ring. Ring.

An automated voice came through the speakers. "You have reached 801—"

I ended the call with the button on my steering wheel. Mom was at her aerobics class and wouldn't answer.

I pushed the button on my steering wheel to make another call.

Ring. Ring. Ring.

Come on, Forrest, pick up the phone!

Ring. Ring.

"What's up, Claire?" He sounded as if I had just woken him.

"Forrest—" My voice broke. "There's a car following me."

"Are you sure? The black car?"

"I'm positive." I pushed the words through chattering teeth.

"But it's not the black car. Call 911."

"Okay, um . . . um . . . just . . . um—Can't you call them?" Only panicked breathing came from his end.

"No. Just call for me!" I swerved into the next lane. "I'm heading north on Alta View, and I'm about to pass the gas station on the corner of 8800 South."

"I'm calling the police on our other phone right now," he said. His voice trembled as much as mine. "Stay on the line with me."

I accelerated, until cars blocked me in on all sides. Alta View had too many lights. I had to get off this street. I checked my rearview mirror and saw three cars separating me and the white car. At the intersection I tried to change lanes to gain ground, even if it meant a gain of only one more car length.

Forrest yelled through the phone, but I could barely hear him. "What does the car look like? What else should I tell them? Keep talking to me," he said. "Are you there, Claire?"

"I'm here." My insides burned, heat blooming in my chest and radiating outward: neck, cheeks, stomach. I glanced in the side mirror and swerved into the right lane. The driver of the white car wove between cars and lanes, multiple horns sounding in complaint, and returned to my lane only two cars behind mine.

"Keep talking to me, Claire. Are you okay? Keep talking to me. Please say something!" Forrest yelled. "Claire, tell me what the car looks like." His voice was shrill—frantic.

I tried to steady my thoughts. "White . . . four-door . . . sedan— maybe . . . Ford . . . Taurus." I could barely keep it together enough to drive and speak at the same time. "Dark . . . tinted . . . windows."

The white car veered away from me into the left lane, then skidded into the middle of the road, driving down the turning lane separating the opposite directions of traffic. Without any cars in its path, it cut the distance between us by one car, and then another, until the nose of its car was even with mine.

"For—rest." His name barely escaped my lips and sounded more like grunts caught in gasps for air.

"I'm going to silent for a second to talk to the police, but I'm here," Forrest said.

For now, the left lane separated us, but it couldn't travel in the turning lane forever. Eventually, another car from the opposite direction would need to turn, obstructing the car's path. At least I hoped one would. All it would have to do is merge back into the regular lane in front of the car next to me, and we would be traveling side by side. Cars surrounded mine in every direction except to the right, the shoulder of the road. I yanked the steering wheel to swing the car into the shoulder. With no one ahead of me, I pushed the gas pedal to the ground. Each breath came faster.

The white car cut across all lanes amid blaring horns and screeching brakes, barely missing cars, until it was right behind me.

The steering wheel shook. I couldn't steady my hands. The car jerked and zigzagged. The pulse in my neck quivered.

I barely remembered how to drive now. The wheel slipped from my quaking hands. Every move came from some unknown instinct—impulse—inside of me.

The hum of the engine in the car behind grew louder. The whirring sound clawed into my ears.

Five minutes. About five minutes and I would be home. I cursed. If I hadn't taken so many detours trying to lose the car chasing me, I would have already been home. Ahead of me was an intersection, and several cars in the right turning lane. If they were turning right, I wouldn't be able to keep driving straight on the shoulder.

I whipped a sudden right turn onto Creek Road, barely missing other cars turning the same direction—legally. The car followed me down the hill, its hood edging closer in the rearview mirror. I could *feel* it creeping in. Breathing down my neck. I gulped for air.

As the road began to level, the car crashed into my rear bumper. My forehead slammed into the steering wheel. The steering wheel cycloned out of my control. I screamed as the wheels left the road and the world outside spun like a carnival ride. Forrest yelled.

Boom! The van hit a curb and flew into a landscaped area running parallel to the street. The decorative rocks filling the long distance between trees pinged like popcorn as the car skidded across the gravel. My head smashed into the side window and glass clinked against my face.

There was a tree.

The front end of the minivan jilted upward, clambering up the tree's trunk like a ramp with the bumper pointing straight at the sky. Creaking metal rang in chorus until the car flipped onto its backside.

The seat belt yanked against my chest. I tried to suck in air, but the wind had been knocked out of me.

The left side of my head felt like it had been thrown against a bed of nails. Warm liquid streamed down my face. *Up my face,* I thought blurrily.

The blaring horn. The groans of the engine. Glass shattering everywhere.

Complete silence crept in and I drifted into darkness. Forrest's screams slipped away.

26

PAIN LIT ACROSS my body like the wildfires that demolish the Wasatch Mountains on hot desert days. Throbbing pierced my skull and sank into my teeth. The torture burrowed down into places I never knew existed. Death could not possibly cause so much physical agony.

The smell of antiseptics overwhelmed me. I must have been in a hospital.

"Claire." Forrest's voice was much softer now.

I stretched my fingers to him.

"Claire, it's okay. You're okay. You're safe now." His familiar voice soothed my ears.

The room was shadows and darkness. I gathered my strength, moaning as I craned my head to catch a glimpse of his face, but realized my left eye was swollen shut. He leaped from a chair next to my bed, grasping my hand in both of his and pressing his forehead to my wrist. His breath felt feverish against my icy skin. "Claire, I'm so sorry this happened to you." His voice crumbled.

"Me too," I said in a hoarse whisper. I squinted, my right eye adjusting to the dim light, and could see his eyes, big puddles of blue, taking me in. I tried to crack a smile, but the swelling prevented me from moving too much. "Why am I here?"

His eyes opened wider. "You don't remember?"

I combed through my memories. "The last thing I remember is leaving the parking lot after I dropped off Fed at work."

He explained what had happened. From his end, I could see how scary that must have been to hear what was going on but not be able to do anything about it.

Why couldn't I remember? "Did I at least give you a license plate number?"

"No, but you said the car was white, and you couldn't see the driver."

I stared at the ceiling. Someone had tried to kill me. If they had wanted to kill me, they had failed. What was going to happen to me now? I looked around the empty room. "Where is everyone?"

He stroked the side of my head. "Getting lunch. I'm going to let the nurse know you're awake." He pressed a call button on a remote near the top of my bed.

I ventured to move a little more, figuring out what exactly had happened to me. The stitches along my left temple felt bristly under the pads of my fingers. Another row of stitches ran down my left arm. Everything on the left side hurt. I peeked under my hospital gown, and though the light was limited, I could make out purplish bruises the size of a small country. Another bruise ran along my neck and chest where my seat belt had been. I couldn't see my neck, but the mark on my chest led me to believe the rest of the bruise would be just as ugly. I didn't see a cast anywhere, so

I assumed no bones had been broken, yet it felt like every single bone in my body was shattered. If I even thought about moving, stinging flashes of pain ignited through my body.

Who would want to do this to me? Why was it so important for them to see me suffer?

The light flipped on and overwhelmed all of my senses. I squinted until my one open eye could adjust, wishing my arm worked well enough to throw it over my face.

"You had to wake up on *his* shift, didn't ya?" Nicholas burst through the door, hands flung in the air. "We've all been taking turns by your bedside waiting for you to wake up." He came over, kissed the top of my head and moved closer to the TV on the wall farthest from me.

"The waiting area totally looks like Camp Maboroshi," Fed said. He wiped his greasy hands on his wrinkled shorts as he came closer, the fresh-off-the-farm scent suggesting he had yet to take a shower.

I had no idea what Fed was referring to with his Camp whatever, but I got the idea. I wondered what people must have thought when the elevator doors opened to that circus. The idea of everybody holding vigil for me made me all warm inside.

Mom and my brothers piled into the room. Mom held my hand and told me how happy she was to see me awake before she assaulted me with questions. *Did I feel nauseous? Was I sensitive to light or noise? Did I feel numbness in my extremities? Was my mind foggy? Did I feel irritable?*

Yes, I felt very irritable. "Mom, I'm sure the doctors will know what to do."

She squeezed my hand, then sat in a small powder-blue vinyl loveseat against the wall. Parker hugged me, then headed straight for the TV. Avery only waved his hand and said, "Hey," before walking to the TV and stealing the remote from Nicholas.

Dad was the last to enter. "You've been unconscious for over a day, princess." His voice sounded relieved, but ache and fear found their way into his forehead and frown lines. He wore a T-shirt and black sweatpants, looking ready for training. Dad never dressed down like that, even at home, unless we were working out. Fed slid to the end of the bed to make room for him.

Forrest leaned across me from the other side of the bed. "She doesn't remember anything about the accident," he whispered to my dad.

Dad nodded, and Forrest sat back down.

I don't know why Forrest felt the need to whisper. Everyone else in the room would end up knowing anyway.

"Based on the CT, the doctor said you have a concussion," my dad explained. "You'll need a lot of rest." He went to the loveseat, putting an arm around Mom as he sat next to her. He placed his other hand on top of hers.

A white car was the reason I didn't remember anything. Had I seen the driver? If I had, I'm sure I would have told Forrest, but maybe I didn't have the chance to. Mom remained silent, but her tortured face said all I needed to know. Maybe I shouldn't have snapped at her. Without any makeup, her face looked wrinkled and pale.

A doctor entered the room with a nurse behind him. The doctor pulled over a rolling stool and sat at my bedside. He began to ask me a lot of questions similar to the ones Mom had asked while the nurse poked and prodded me. They finished and said they would let everyone talk to me for a few more minutes, but after that I had to rest. The nurse injected something into my IV, and I assumed I would have no choice but to rest.

The doctor and nurse left after giving Mom some advice on how much rest I needed, and I couldn't help but think about how long I'd been unconscious. The blinds were drawn shut, but light peeked through the only window—it was day outside, though I couldn't tell if it was morning or afternoon.

Nicholas came to the side of my bed, sweeping his hand to point from one side of the room to the other. "So? How do you like it?"

"Who brought all the plants?" I asked.

Nicholas directed my attention to a plant by the window with flat lobes at the end of the stems. "That ugly one is from Forrest." His finger shifted to the flowering plant next to my bed. "And that awesome one is from me and Fed. You always say bouquets of flowers are a waste of money." Plastered on the opposite wall was a banner of yellow butcher paper with "Get Well Soon!" written in blue poster paint.

Someone had tried to kill me. As much as I tried to be attentive to what he was saying, my mind drifted back to why I was there in the first place. Parts of my memory were black holes, and the accident itself was completely gone. I remembered Fed asking something about who would have something to gain if I were dead. Why me? What did I have that my brothers and parents didn't?

Forrest punched Nicholas in the arm. "Actually, my plant is way cooler because it's a Venus flytrap."

The mention of a Venus flytrap snapped me back to attention because I'd always wanted one. "Thanks, guys. I love them both." But I especially liked Forrest's and couldn't wait to see the carnivorous plant in action.

Parker pointed to the wall. "What do you think about that work of art? Avery and I made it."

"Wow. I feel so loved." I pulled the blanket to my shoulders, shivering. I wasn't sure if it was the coolness of the room, or the reminder that there was a strong chance the driver of that car intended me not to have this moment—that the driver intended for me to never wake up.

"We didn't say we *loved* you." Avery exposed a half smile. "It's just kind of cool, I guess, that you didn't die or anything." He fiddled with a wallet, connected to his belt loop by a long silver chain.

"Close enough." I motioned for them to gather in so I could give them all a hug, but I couldn't move far without an explosion of pain. In the end, they were the ones to reach over and give me individual hugs, even Avery.

The room contained all the people I loved most, but it was too small to hold this many. My chest grew tight, and my breathing became more rapid. As grateful as I was to have them by my side, the room felt too crowded. I glanced at Forrest.

Forrest stood and came closer to my side. "Maybe we should give Claire some space. She's just woken up, and I'm sure she could use some rest."

Mom gathered my brothers and the Russo boys. They said good-bye from the other side of the room, as Mom herded them through the door.

Before he left, Dad came back to my side. "You're very lucky." He laid a warm hand on my shoulder. "We'll have to see how the head injury plays out, but no broken bones or anything. We'll get through this." His dark eyes had a tired glaze. "I'm sorry I couldn't stop this."

"I never expected you to," I said. "What could you have done?"

But lucky? Had I survived only to be subjected to the next thing?

"I don't know, but something more," Dad said. Something about his black T-shirt reminded me of a training session together. I didn't remember everything, but I knew I had wondered whether he was somehow involved with these events. That seemed ridiculous now. Dad patted my arm and left the room.

Now that I was less overwhelmed with people, I realized how much I didn't want to be alone with my thoughts. With everything that had happened, and everything that could potentially happen, my mind would go into overdrive. I'd never wanted to be one of those people who overly depended on someone like a best friend or boyfriend, and I hoped I wasn't turning into one of them. But when I checked my gut, I knew I didn't *need* to have Forrest stay. I *wanted* him there.

Forrest got to his feet slowly. He gave me a hug and was about to leave, but I grabbed his hand. "Will you stay with me for a little longer?" I asked.

"Of course." His face lit up, reminding me of the first time he brought his dog Flirt home. "You're not going to push me away like you usually do when you need space?" He gave me a playful smile.

"I don't push. I nudge," I said. "And I do need space, but right now it would be nice if you filled it."

He motioned for me to scoot over, and he climbed on the bed and sat next me.

I don't know what I had ever done to deserve a best friend like Forrest, but Dad was right. I was lucky.

I COULD TELL the days were growing shorter because it was dark outside even though it was still early evening. Once Forrest and the Russo boys had gone home, Dad called the family together and had my brothers form a half circle with the loveseat and chairs at my hospital bedside. If there was ever anything my parents felt was important enough to say to the whole family, Dad called a meeting.

Sometimes I could get Dad to give up information if I cornered him, but only rarely did my parents volunteer anything unless it was in this setting. I wouldn't have been surprised if that's where Parker and Nicholas had gotten the inspiration for the Axis Powers Meetings. I was anxious to hear what they would say and worried about what they wouldn't say.

Mom and Dad sat on the loveseat, and my brothers sat in the chairs. I adjusted the bed so I was more upright.

"Those potted plants have to go," Mom said in a quiet voice. "They're bad luck."

I could tell from my brothers' expressions that none of us had any idea what she was talking about.

Dad released a soft sigh. "*Netsuku* means to take root, but it's also a homophone for the verb meaning to be laid up, like with an illness. Some people believe if you bring a potted plant to someone in the hospital, he might take root and stay for a long time."

"Now that you've seen them, we can get them out of here," Mom said to me.

Parker rolled his eyes. "I'll take them home when we leave."

"Thank you, Parker." Dad clasped his hands together and bent forward, resting his elbows on his thighs. "I've talked to your mom, and we think it's time you knew some things. So far, the recent events have seemingly targeted Claire, but that doesn't mean the rest of us won't be next." He furrowed his brows. "I've reviewed these occurrences many times, and while I'd hoped it wasn't the case, I'm concerned all of this might be connected to your father's past."

He glanced in my direction. "Claire, I don't know why this happened to you, and I'm not saying for sure the yakuza is behind this, but we do need to consider the possibility. I promise I will do everything in my power to protect you. All of you." He looked at my brothers. "You've known for a while your father was in the yakuza, and given that, I think it's only fair to him that you understand what brought him there in the first place and also why he left."

He patted Mom's knee, and she took a deep breath, closing her eyes before speaking. "I'm sure you have a lot of questions. But I hope you understand why I wouldn't want you to know your father was involved in some very terrible things before I met him. His father was very abusive and left your grandmother when your father was only eight."

She must have thought about this explanation a million times, but the sentences refused to flow easily. "Times were very hard in Japan for single mothers, and your grandmother worked tirelessly to take care of your father. When your father was sixteen, she died unexpectedly of a brain aneurysm, and he had nowhere to turn. A local businessman took him under his wing, but in doing so, introduced him to a life of crime."

She danced around the word that hadn't left my mind since I saw the autopsy report: yakuza.

"At first it was everything he had dreamed of," she said in a soft tone. "He'd heard rumors the businessman was the oyabun of a large clan, but all that mattered to him at the time was he finally had a father figure in his life. As an orphan and having come from poverty, he was easily lured into the idea of family, and having more money at his fingertips than he had ever imagined possible. There were many things he did that he was not proud of, but acceptance into the lifestyle meant a promise of unquestioning loyalty and obedience to the oyabun."

The idea of unquestioning obedience and why someone would voluntarily commit to that was something I'd never been able to wrap my head around. But he was my age when his mother died, and he was left with nothing. Excluding recent events, my life seemed pretty easy in comparison, and I had no idea what I would have done if I were in his position.

Avery leaned back in his chair and put his hands on the armrests. "So what kinds of things did he do?"

My brothers and I had seen enough yakuza movies to know

the kinds of things my father must have done, but Avery couldn't seem to help himself when it came to pushing buttons. Parker and I glared at him.

"What?" he asked, feigning innocence.

Mom didn't bite. "Things that weighed heavily on his conscience and made him struggle with the oath he'd made. The last task he completed finally broke him, and he vowed he would never go back." She stared at her lap and shook her head. "But because of his high rank, staying in Japan was not an option if he wanted to remain alive. While he had money, it still wasn't enough to get out safely, so he used everything he had, and his friend made up for the shortage and helped him escape to America. It was possible they would still find him, but it was worth the risk."

Scenes from an old movie Mom made us watch, *The Sound of Music*, popped into my head as I tried to imagine what it would be like to escape a country. Maybe his escape hadn't been as dramatic, but it had to have been scary.

She paused to wipe a stray tear. "I met your father when I was only fourteen. He was eighteen and could have easily taken advantage of his friend's money, but he didn't want any beyond what was absolutely necessary to get him set up in America. My parents gave him a job at our diner as a dishwasher, which he happily accepted because he said it was his first real step toward the new life he wanted to build."

This part of the story rang more familiar. Grandpa had run the little diner in Hawaii until the day he died, and Grandma moved to Japan soon after.

"I had never known anyone with so much determination and tenacity," she said. "After his shift, I would work with him on his English, and within a year he was able to get his GED. The local community college was the only school that would accept him, but he was so thrilled at the opportunity." Her eyes lifted, and her gaze went past me as if she could see the scenes playing on the wall behind me.

I had heard parts of the story from my grandfather and dad, but Mom had never shared any of this before. A faint grin lit her face. "I couldn't help but fall in love with his appreciation for life. My love for him grew every day I was with him, and I felt like the luckiest girl in the world when he made it known he felt the same way about me."

This description sounded more like the man—the father—I had once known. Avery acted like he was kissing someone. Parker shuddered.

Mom ignored them and slouched forward, letting her hands wring in her lap. "I still remember the day he got his acceptance letter to law school. He was the first person in his family to go to college, and when he got the letter it was like his every dream had been realized. We got married the summer before he started, he became a US citizen, and we moved to the mainland together. I was only eighteen at the time, and life was an adventure." Her head turned to Parker. "We had been married more than ten years before Parker was born, so we had a lot of time by ourselves, getting to know each other."

For years, I had wanted to know more about my father, but she would shut me out every time I asked questions. My chest tightened.

Her voice started to tremble. "Your father did a lot of things he regretted, but he was one of the best men I have ever known. Please remember that. He spent the rest of his life trying to make up for his mistakes. That's why he wanted to become a judge. He believed upholding justice was one way he could begin to repair everything he had done wrong. I don't know the man—the *boy*—your father was before I met him, but I know the man he became, and it was an honor to spend that part of my life with him." A steady stream of tears trickled down her cheeks.

"I don't understand," I said, fighting to still the tremors in my voice. "Even if I don't agree with how you guys hid his criminal past from us, I understand why you did it. But I don't understand why you hid everything else. Do you know how long I've wanted to know what he was like when you met? Or what he had to do to become a judge? It's not like I haven't asked questions. You didn't have to keep that from us." When I stopped speaking, I realized how loud my volume had gotten.

Parker and Avery stared at me with dropped jaws. Mom was silent. She trained her eyes on her hands in her lap.

Dad put a hand on my shoulder. "Claire," Dad said in a hushed voice. "I'm sure you can imagine how painful and difficult it might have been for your mom to talk about this."

I whipped my head so my eyes could meet his. "We loved him too. It wasn't easy for us either. We lost our *father*, and for *ten years* we've had no one to talk to."

For years my questions had been blown off or deflected, and every time that happened, I took whatever pain or hurt I had and pushed it deep inside. I did what I was taught. Gaman. Endure with dignity and grace. Accept the pain and don't complain. But maybe I hadn't done it the right way because those pains never disappeared, and the space where I had shoved everything was so full it was about to burst.

I shifted my gaze to Mom. "Everyone keeps saying what a good man he was, and we're expected to believe it, but no one's told us the stories that made him good! We don't talk about anything truly important because it might be painful or considered complaining and that's not helpful to anyone. Shikata ga nai. It can't be helped, right?" The words tumbled out before I could catch them, each trembling as they hung in the air. "We're taught that our ability to suffer in silence is a good thing. But it sucks. Can I imagine how painful this was for you to talk about? Yes. I think I can."

A tear escaped, rolled down my cheek, and landed in my lap. Then another. And then something broke, and my chest heaved with each angry sob. I clasped my hands together to keep them from shaking, and stared through the slats of the blinds into the inky black sky.

No one said anything. Parker and Avery hung their heads.

"I'm sorry," Mom whispered.

The darkness held my gaze. I waited for her to say more, but she didn't. If I could string together every story, every little thing she had mentioned about my father since we moved here, the sum probably wouldn't have added up to what she'd shared in this short time. Maybe she had used up all her words. Guilt crept in. My intent hadn't been to hurt anyone or be disrespectful. I only wanted things to be different.

"I'm sorry too," I said.

"Claire," Dad said in a gentle tone.

I turned to face him. His expression was smooth, comforting.

It occurred to me that hearing my mom's expression of love for another man must have been painful.

"We're not perfect. But we try," Dad said. "And there's always room for improvement."

Avery parted his narrow lips. "So what's the plan?"

Dad lifted his glasses with a finger and rubbed his eye. "I don't know. On the surface, it seems like a hit and run. When the police examined our van, they found the only damage done by the other car was a dent on the back bumper. There's not enough evidence to suggest it was an attempted homicide, unless you add everything together. They've assured me they will be taking this very seriously, and pursuing it keeping everything in mind, but they've also asked we exercise patience and not take matters into our own hands."

Dad pushed off the arm of the loveseat and rose to his feet to stand next to me. "But I'm not very good at being patient." He put his hand over mine. "And I plan to find out who did this to you, and I will make sure he doesn't come near you or the boys *ever* again. In the meantime, I think we just need to take care of each other like we always have, and I believe the best thing we can do is live our lives with caution, but not fear." He pointed his finger in the air. "Use your ingenuity, kids."

"I think we would be much safer not going to school anymore," Parker said.

"Nice try," Dad said. His expression silenced Parker's snickering. "Unfortunately, I need to go to New York for the next few days. I know the timing couldn't be worse, but this is pretty important. I want Claire to stay home the rest of this week so she can heal, but you boys aren't going to be so lucky.

I should be back by the time she returns to school, but Parker, I want you to get the guys together, and let them know I want everyone watching out for her like a hawk. We should be careful, but go on with our normal lives. People can do some very ugly, desperate things when they think you're on to them."

My instinct was to argue my ability to take care of myself and voice my need for independence, but it seemed inappropriate. And someone had tried to kill me. Knowing everyone was keeping an eye out for trouble was a good thing. I'm sure Dad knew as well as I did there was nothing the guys could do if someone was after me, but I had also never seen him frozen in worry for so long.

THREE DAYS PASSED before the hospital allowed me to go home. I was ready to be discharged after two days, but Mom made them run almost every test again with the exception of the CT scan and MRI. But I knew Mom better than that, and I'm sure the real reason for the delay was that the day I would have been released was on a "bad luck day" according to the Japanese lunar calendar. I'm sure the doctor could have refused Mom's request, but to my dismay, he placated her, and I was subjected to more tests on my vision and balance and memory and reflexes and concentration.

The doctor said I should resume activities slowly, returning to school after a week of rest. He then informed us I shouldn't return to the soccer field for at least a couple of weeks, but he'd want to see how I was doing at that time before he felt comfortable giving me clearance to play. Based on my test results, I would most likely be able to play after a week, but a longer absence from soccer meant a lesser chance of reinjury, and if it were his child, he'd probably keep them away from a contact sport for a full two months.

Once Mom heard that, I knew I would be out for the rest of the soccer season. I think I would have been more upset if I didn't have so many other pressing things to occupy my mind.

Dad helped me out of the car and inside the house. I didn't think I'd needed the help, but he insisted. The muscles in my neck and back ached, and the bruises all over my body screamed if I moved the wrong way.

Mom was skirting around the kitchen in her pink tracksuit when we walked in from the garage. She closed the door to the pantry. "I've got the family room all prepared for you," she said.

I hesitated. "Thanks, but I think I need to be in my own room."

She placed a hand on her hip. "We'll be able to keep an eye on you better if you're on the main floor, but fine."

Dad shrugged. "I'll help her up."

Every step up the stairs required more effort than I expected, but once I was in my room, my sanctuary, a feeling of relief washed over me. Dad left my bag by the closet and helped me into my bed.

Before long, my mind was at work again, still trying to put all the pieces together because I hadn't made any progress in the hospital. It made sense that my parents felt the recent events had been related to my father, but I wasn't able to figure out what that meant.

Parker brought a TV into my room to make my existence a little more tolerable.

"Thanks." I slumped in despair. "But day after day of watching television—twenty-four/seven? That may be your lifelong goal of achievement, but certainly not mine."

"I have goals." Parker set down the TV. "I just don't share them with you because they'd blow your mind." His expression turned serious. He plugged the TV into the socket and turned it on. "There you go—your entertainment for the week."

He left and came back with an armful of string and pulleys.

"What are you doing?" I asked.

"Trust me," he said. "You'll love it."

Even if I didn't trust him, I had learned I couldn't stop him once his mind was set on a tinkering project. By the time he finished, I had two strings hanging over my bed. They ran along the ceiling and down the wall to the light switch.

"Pull the string on your right when you want to turn the light off," Parker said. "And pull the other one when you want to turn it on."

The string on my right moved along pulleys on the ceiling and down the wall and tied around the toggle light switch from the bottom. I gave it a tug, and the string pulled the toggle switch down. The light turned off. I pulled the string on my left, and it moved along its own pulley system and pulled the toggle switch up. The light came back on.

"That's pretty cool," I said. "Thank you." I appreciated the sentiment and didn't mention how I was actually feeling pretty good, probably didn't need to miss a week of school to heal, and was perfectly capable of walking over to the switch myself. My brother would never do anything nice for me again if I did.

"I knew you would like it," he said.

"Hey, if you don't have a date for the dance, I was thinking you should consider asking Mika."

"Because?"

"She thinks you're cute and funny."

He nodded. "Smart girl."

I looked through the window and found Forrest waiting at his window. I motioned for him to join us.

In no time, Nicholas entered carrying pillows and blankets. "Party in Claire's room." He lunged at the bed as if to pounce on me.

I narrowed my eyes and signaled for him to stop. "Don't even think about it."

"Aw, I'm just playing with you, Kiki," Nicholas said and kissed the top of my head. "I'm on direct orders from your father to protect you, so I'll pulverize you another time."

"Bring it on," I said.

For a brief instant everything felt . . . normal—almost. The guys piled everywhere. Reality shows were on TV. Fed and Avery arm-wrestled on the floor.

Before long, everyone was out cold except for Forrest. He leaned against the wall with an unfocused stare. "You okay?"

Muscles and bruises groaned as I rolled over and faced him. I'd just taken my night pain med dose, hoping it might help me sleep, but it hadn't kicked in yet. "Everything hurts, mostly my neck and back, but I'll heal."

"But are *you* okay?"

"Go to sleep. I'm fine."

"You're a horrible liar," he said, making himself comfortable on the floor.

"I know." If this was related to my father's past, I couldn't help but wonder why everything was happening now. The only thing I knew for sure was it had all started with finding the note from my father to my dad. No one had sent me gross threatening packages or followed me in a black car before that. Chase had never done more than make fun of me in class.

"Forrest," I said, my eyelids finally getting heavy. "Do you think I might have called someone in the yakuza when I called that phone number?"

Silence hung between us awhile before he answered. "It seems possible. Or it could have been the autopsy report like you said before. Or it could be because they'd been looking for your family for a long time, and they've finally found you. Maybe they don't know your father's dead."

What if my father had done something they wanted revenge for? What if the story he'd told my parents was a lie and there was another reason he needed to escape? What if . . . ?

Eventually the pain medication began to take over, quieting my aching body, and my eyelids grew heavy.

After almost a week of rest, the pain had died down, but not completely. I could open my left eye again, but it was black and blue and looked like I had lost a boxing match. Sometimes I couldn't remember new things that had happened since being home. The doctor said that was normal and would hopefully be temporary, but to me it was only another reminder of the nightmare I was living.

I sat on my bed and stared through the window at the formless shapes in the darkness. The moon crept higher but hid with the stars behind a sky full of clouds.

Physically, I had healed enough to go back to school, but whenever I thought about my return the next day, my chest grew tight.

Outside of our family and the guys, the only thing anyone else would know is I had been in a hit-and-run car accident. No one would know it was completely intentional. Dad said the less information the public had, the better chance we'd have of catching the person who did this. We hadn't been informed there were any leads on the case. I didn't expect them to find the culprit overnight, but my experience with Officer Schwartz had me worried nothing was being done, and I hoped they would prove me wrong.

I hadn't seen the black SUV since the day it chased me home, and I could only assume the white car had somehow been linked. I tried to focus on the father I knew, the one I loved. But everything that had happened to me, every horrible experience in the past few weeks seemed to lead back to him. What other explanation could there be for the crow's eyes, representing bad luck; given in a set of four, which means death; my name written in red ink the way it is on Japanese gravestones; and the Japanese music? I guess I couldn't complain I hadn't been warned. Someone wanted me dead.

I reached underneath the mattress and retrieved my diary. The thoughts of all the bad things my father could have done while in the yakuza clouded my mind as I leafed through each page. If his rank in the clan was as high as Dad had suggested, it was a guarantee my father had done some pretty awful things. Most girls began their entries with "Dear Diary," but all of mine began with "Dear Otochan."

The first page was from my first day of middle school. I removed it delicately. But every rip after that became more and more careless until shreds of paper surrounded me. I only stopped when Forrest knocked on the door.

He entered and, without saying a word, bent down to help me clean up the pieces of paper, scattered like confetti. Then I slammed the diary shell into the garbage can.

I sat back on the bed.

Forrest sat down beside me. "Are you ready to go back tomorrow?" he asked.

"Not really." I sighed.

"You and Mumps seemed to be getting along well," he said.

"I guess. He's funnier than I thought he'd be." Talking about Mumps seemed a little random.

The back of his hand brushed across my cheek, then slid down my arm until his fingers intertwined with mine on the bed. His expression was somber.

Something whirred inside of me, soft and barely noticeable.

"Forrest?" I said.

His mind wandered somewhere else, and I wondered if he had even heard me. He stared at our hands, still together, and said, "Claire, I've known you since the second grade. And I don't even know at what point you became my best friend—"

"Middle school," I said. "All of you guys had been invited to a party Brooke was throwing, but she didn't invite me. You pulled me off the couch and said, 'Everyone knows I don't want to go anywhere without you. Get in the car because your mom's gonna leave us.' You were so bossy back then."

He moved his thumb back and forth along my finger. "Yeah, I guess that sounds about right. I mean the becoming best friends part. Not the bossiness." He sighed and wriggled closer.

"I don't even know where she goes to school now," I said, "but I guess I owe her."

"Do you think we'll always be best friends?" he asked.

"Of course. Why would you even ask me that?"

The way he held my hand, the strain on his face, and the torment in his eyes made the weight of what he was really saying start to register.

"I don't know if . . ." His forehead crinkled for a brief moment. "I don't want you to pick Mumps," he said in a soft voice.

I finally understood. Forrest was answering the question I never dared to ask him. He opened his lips to say more, but I put my finger to them.

"Why now?" I tried to slow my breathing as I lifted my finger from his lips.

"Because I was so scared. When I first saw you after the accident, your eye was swollen and you had bruises everywhere, and I kept thinking, *What if something had happened to her, and I never told her?*"

His words spilled out so quickly that I could barely keep up with him. He continued, "But even before that, I saw you laughing with Mumps, and I thought I was going to explode." His eyes were wide and I think his breaths were coming as fast as my own. "I literally thought I might rip him off that bench and beat him up. And I didn't understand how you could pick him over me. What does he have that I don't? I have been here this whole time, Claire." He took an exasperated breath. "Pick me."

I didn't know what to say.

"Pick me," he said louder.

There had been times I had wondered if he wanted something deeper than friendship. There were times I'd even wondered if *I* wanted something more. But I'd never considered what I would do if I knew for sure. I hadn't let myself hope. It was too much of a risk. What if it didn't work out?

I shook my head. "Mumps doesn't have anything over you." I looked away, gathering my thoughts. "How long have you known?" I asked softly.

"Since the second grade," he said. "Pretty much right after we moved next door." He raked his fingers through his hair. "I wanted to kiss you so badly."

"What?!" I hadn't meant for it to sound so loud.

"Do you remember the first time I played soccer with you guys, and Fed got hurt?"

I managed a nod.

"And you ran over to him and held his hand?" Forrest raised his eyebrows. "I remember wishing I was the one who had gotten hurt so you would worry over me like that."

I grasped for something to say, but came up empty. He pulled my hand onto his lap and turned it over. The bruises on the inside of my arm and wrist had lost their deep purple color and were fading into shades of yellow and green. He traced patterns on my palm with his finger.

"Why didn't you tell me before?" I said, still quiet.

"I did." His finger stopped. "Kind of." He lifted his eyes. "I asked you to marry me."

"We were in the third grade," I said, breaking into a nervous laugh. I bit at my lip to make myself stop.

"I got you a ring and everything. And it wasn't cheap either. I used a lot of tickets at Chuck E. Cheese's to buy that thing," he said. "And I told you in all those notes I wrote to you."

We had passed notes. Everyone had. But none of the ones from Forrest ever told me how he felt about me. I would have remembered that. I gave him a questioning look.

"And then never gave you," he admitted. "Or when my dog died, and I told you I loved you for loving her as much as I did?"

My heart melted, but the rest of me had never felt more complete. Excitement radiated through me, freeing my muscles from stiffness and aching.

He tilted his head to the side and sneaked a glance at me. "Or when you didn't get invited to Brooke's party, and I told you that I never wanted to go anywhere without you." He locked onto my eyes. "That hasn't changed."

I thought about how love can be shown in small ways, how long he'd been doing that. Like the way he'd trade lunches with me when I didn't want what Mom had packed or how he made Spritzkuchen to cheer me up. And how all those small ways can add up to something bigger, which I should have realized a long time ago. My whole body buzzed, a chorus of tingling sensations rising to the surface.

Forrest had reached into my heart somehow and given life to something slumbering inside of me, new and full of energy. His words danced in my head, sweeping out the worries that plagued me: the terrible events that had happened, the terrible events that could happen, the fear and uncertainty of what role I had played. And for the first time in a long time, my mind was clear, empty of noise and debris.

I glanced down at our hands together, electricity humming

between us. "Or how you stayed after school to clean the stall in the boys' locker room because Chase had written sleazy things about me."

"Or now," he said. He lifted my chin until my gaze met his. My pulse spun into a frenzy.

"I'm in love with you, Claire. Because you've been there for almost every good memory. Because you're the first person I want to talk to when I've had a good day or a bad one, when something embarrassing has happened, or when I need to complain. I love you because you make me happy. And sometimes frustrated."

His voice began to shake. "I love you because you care deeply for people, and I know when I make mistakes, you love me no matter what. I love you because I know there isn't a fight out there you wouldn't jump into the ring with me."

My heart swelled. I couldn't tell if it was from happiness or if it was about to explode and leave me dead. I knew I would love him no matter what. But being *in* love was something different.

"Sometimes I think you're waiting for this perfect, epic love to come along," he said. "But we're already epic. No one will ever have the history I have with you. And we're never going to be perfect, but I'm tired of being patient and waiting around for you to figure out love isn't perfect, and getting hurt is part of the deal sometimes."

I looked deep beyond the blue of his eyes and saw fear and passion and something so tender and fragile it made me want to hold him and never let go. He cradled my cheeks in his hands and pressed his forehead against mine. His hair tickled my face and his breath was sweet butterscotch as it washed over me.

"I'm going to kiss you for the second grade," he said.

Every part of me became still. No one had ever kissed me before. I had bungee jumped off a cliff before, felt the wind rush over my skin as I plummeted, and been less afraid than I was now.

Forrest leaned down and kissed the hollow space above my collar bone, then left a trail of kisses along my neck before his lips found mine, quieting an eagerness I hadn't realized was there. I felt like I was falling, and yet couldn't tell whether it was exhilarating or scary. Both. My mouth responded as if we had done this before, every movement natural, and I was sure if I caught my reflection, I'd find my face glowing.

He pulled away and raised his head, a cautious smile creeping across his face as if asking whether or not he should continue.

I waited for my head to tell me all the reasons why we didn't belong together. Tell me I wasn't in love with him. But when my mind stayed silent, I let my heart take over. I swept some blond hair from his forehead, then cupped my hands around the back of his neck and brought his lips to mine. I kissed him less tentatively now, sculpting my lips to his mouth as if secrets and lies and people who wanted to hurt me never existed.

He wrapped his arms around me, carefully pressing his palms into my back as I slid my hands along his neck and up the back of his head. I buried my fingers in his hair. Every touch ignited my skin. Every fear and every pain, every celebration and every victory that we'd shared were all wrapped in this moment, interlocked in a way only the two of us could understand.

He kissed me until our breaths were ragged, and when he

pulled away, he left my lips wanting more. I laid down on the bed, exhausted and spinning, and giddy. Somehow the aches and pains from the accident had been swallowed in the moment, but crept back, reminding me of their presence.

Forrest curled next to me and stroked my hair. Alarm crossed his face. "Are you hurt? I'm so sorry. I wasn't really thinking when—"

"I'm fine." I knew he would call me on that. "I mean, I'm in a little pain, but it's pain I would have been in anyway, and it was good to forget about it for a little while. Technically I'm allowed to do light exercise now, and I think that qualifies." I smiled and placed my hand on his chest. "You were gentle. And perfect."

His face relaxed. "It was perfect."

Until then, I hadn't been self-conscious, but Forrest had kissed more girls than I wanted to think about, unlike me. I had no idea what I was doing. "Really? Are you just saying that?"

Instead of answering right away, he leaned forward and kissed me again. "Do you remember when you asked me why I broke up with Olivia?"

I nodded.

"It's because she wasn't you." He held my chin and brushed his thumb across my lips. "I have been waiting so long for this that there's no way it could be anything but perfect." His eyes crinkled. "If anything, it went a lot better than I thought it would," he said. "But I also know you could freak out any minute now, so I'm not going to get too excited."

I paused and quieted everything in my head. "I think I'm okay. What are we going to tell everyone else?"

"They already knew how I felt," he said. "I think it was

obvious to everyone but you, so I think they'll probably be happy they don't have to listen to my whining anymore. Not that I whine."

"I don't know if I'm ready to say anything to them." I raised my eyes to the ceiling. "I need some time to adjust."

"Claire, I don't want anything to change between us." He scooted closer and carefully pulled my head against his chest. "I mean, this is a good change, and I like this change, but everything else, the way we are with each other, I don't want that to change."

"Will you go to the Halloween dance with me?"

"I'll need to check my schedule, but I think I can arrange that."

I reached up and kissed him. I listened to the beat of his heart, and for the first time in a while, I felt like I could fall asleep.

———

IT HAD BEEN a week since I'd last been at school. Mom had bought me a new backpack while I was in the hospital and had checked the lunar calendar to ensure I was returning to school on a good luck day. I woke up early so I'd have time to get everything ready. Since I'd turned my whole backpack over to the police, I needed to make sure I filled my bag with school supplies again. I opened my desk drawer to get a pencil and saw the business card for the Waiawa Circle of Friends.

With everything that had happened with Forrest the night before, I'd forgotten about it. I went to the website listed on the card to get more information. The Waiawa Circle of Friends was a nonprofit organization that worked with inmates at the Waiawa correctional facility. In addition to helping the inmates "explore forgiveness and repair harm" as the card stated, they provided classes in communication and conflict-resolution skills. At some point, my father must have worked with this group, probably offering counsel to help rehabilitate inmates.

I took the card and returned it to the notebook in the box at the back of my closet. To make sure it didn't fall out again, I placed it in the empty envelope that once held the letter from my father to my dad. Forrest's car horn sounded, so I grabbed my bag and headed downstairs with heavy feet.

That morning, the sky was gray and burdened with clouds. I dragged in a deep breath before Forrest helped me out of the car. He walked me to my locker, his hand on my back the whole way.

"I would've held your hand, but I'm guessing you're not one for PDA," he said.

I shoved some books into my locker. "You know me well." I glanced at him and saw his face radiating with a huge smile. "What's that for?" I smiled back.

"You. Me." He raised my chin with one finger. "I was beginning to think it would never happen." He bent down and sneaked a quick kiss. "When can we tell everyone? I feel like I'm going to explode, and I don't know if I can hide this any longer."

"It just happened last night," I said.

"I know. And I haven't said one word yet." He put a hand on his chest. "I'm pretty proud of myself."

I laughed. He was still Forrest, but he was mine in a different way. Part of me wanted to hold that close and keep it to myself forever.

"I'm sure it will happen soon," I said.

He put his hands at his sides. "I'll try to behave myself until then."

I hooked a finger in his belt loop and tugged him closer. "I didn't say I wanted you to behave."

"You are pure evil sometimes," he said. "In a good way." He

waggled his eyebrows. "Let's get to class before you tempt me too much." I sighed and closed my locker.

Even though Forrest had brought homework to me during my absence, I still had a lot to catch up on. Every class weighted me with more and more work to do. But I made it through the morning and lunch, even though the cafeteria was noisy and crowded as usual and I wanted to run. Seeing Forrest between classes helped settle my nerves and let me focus on something good for at least a few minutes before I went to the next class and my mind started to wander again.

I paused before I entered history class. Even if Chase hadn't been involved in anything that had happened, he was the last person I wanted to see.

Mr. Tama caught me hesitating outside the door. "Welcome back," he said, startling me. "Generally we hold class *inside* the classroom." He gave me a warm smile.

"I'm still adjusting," I said.

"Hey, I wanted to mention I've had time to review your previous quiz scores and essay grades. Your grades are stellar, and you don't have a history of problems with academic integrity. In addition, your accuser spoke to me voluntarily regarding the matter, and this person has said they might have made a mistake. I'm not sure how a mistake of this significance could happen, but I was able to petition to have the issue of cheating resolved. You can go back to the soccer team as soon as tomorrow if you want."

"Thank you," I said, exhaling a large breath. "That's the best news I've heard in a long time." I didn't bother telling him going back to the team wasn't going to happen. It wouldn't have made a difference. I was just happy there was one less thing I had to worry about.

He opened the door and motioned for me to go inside. Not even Chase could make me stop smiling as I went to my seat.

"Welcome back," Katie whispered.

"Kisses." Lanie blew a kiss. Mika, Kimi, and Ashley all whispered hellos before I sat down next to Forrest. I smiled back, happy to see them.

Right after I'd gotten home from the hospital, I'd called and told Coach I wouldn't be returning this season. He said he was sad, but he said he agreed with the doctor, and my spot would be waiting for me next year. After that I texted Katie, even though I knew Coach would tell her and the rest of the team. She was supportive, like I knew she would be, and said everyone would miss me. I would miss playing, but I was surprised to realize how much I had missed being around the girls on the team.

"As we discussed," Mr. Tama said, "you will be divided into two groups: Federalists and Anti-Federalists." He wrote those terms on the board. "Each group will be responsible for writing a newspaper article supporting your position, and then you will defend your arguments in class together against your classmates."

He went to his desk and unlocked the bottom drawer. He retrieved his messenger bag and removed a stack of papers. "Now that all of you have chosen partners," Mr. Tama said, "I want to talk about the grading criteria." He handed the stack to Chase. "Take one and pass it on."

I turned to Forrest. "Are we partners?"

"No. I tried to sign us up together, but you were already assigned."

I raised my hand, and when Mr. Tama called on me, I said, "I'm not sure who my partner is."

He went behind his desk and looked at the screen of his laptop. "In your absence, it looks like Calvin Harper offered to work with you."

"Who's Calvin?" Forrest whispered.

My throat tensed. "Mumps."

Forrest's body went rigid. He faced the front of the class and didn't look at me after that.

When class ended, I stood up and grabbed Forrest's hand. His shoulders relaxed a little.

"It's just a history project," I said. "Come on. Let's go." I threw my backpack on my shoulder.

Mumps had lagged behind to wait for me. "Howdy, pardner," he said under the weight of an overdone Western drawl.

I jumped, then tried to act like nothing had happened. "Oh hey, Mumps."

He tipped an imaginary cowboy hat in my direction. "Maybe we can get together after school?"

Forrest shoved his fists into the pockets of his jeans.

"We can figure something out," I said, wanting to get out of there as fast as possible.

Mumps tipped his nonexistent hat again and followed us out of the classroom.

When we got to my locker, Forrest's face remained bunched. "I'm going to punch him," he said.

"You sound like Nicholas." I tugged on his finger. It wasn't

Mumps's fault things had changed between Forrest and me. "Will it make you feel better if I tell him we're together?"

"Maybe," he said. "A little."

I glanced at both ends of the hallway, and when no one was looking, I raised my heels and kissed him.

I left Forrest and headed to study hall in the library. Fed had already claimed our usual table. Every now and then I glanced out the window despite my efforts to concentrate. Nothing was there, but I couldn't help myself. It felt like I was being watched. The police hadn't found anything yet, and until they did, I'd probably be jumping at every bump in the night. He was still out there, somewhere, lying in wait.

"Claire, how are you doing?" Fed grabbed my arm to bring me back to reality. "Like, how are you *really* doing?"

"Okay, I guess." I told him about the cheating scandal news, and how what had been a great weight suddenly disappeared with no fanfare, no hearing. "So that's great news, right? Everything is fine now."

He tilted his head, raised an eyebrow, and his lips bunched to the right.

Forrest had once called me a horrible liar. It looked like Fed agreed with him. I sighed. "Okay, not really. Sometimes I feel sorry for my father and everything he went through." I turned my head back to the window. "And then I think of everything I'm going through, and it's unfair."

Fed nodded but looked unsure of what to say.

I pulled a blank sheet of paper and pen from my backpack. "I've been trying to fit all these events together, and they just don't. But maybe if I could visualize it, I might be able to see what I'm missing."

I drew a table and labeled the first column EVENT and the second column POTENTIAL SUSPECTS.

"Maybe you should have a column for conflicting events," he said, "or notes that tell us what other things were going on at the same time that would give someone an alibi."

"Good idea." I made a third column.

In the first row, I noted my pictures had been stolen from my locker. "I would think the only suspects would be students, but it can't be Chase." I wrote *student* in the second column and noted Chase was sick in the third.

In the next row, I wrote *black SUV*.

"I guess this could've been a student," Fed said. "But most of the sightings were late at night or when we were at school."

I put a question mark in the suspects column and noted school would have been a potential conflict.

The third event was the box of eyeballs. "This would have to be a student," I said.

"Or a teacher," Fed said. "We need to consider everything and everyone."

I went ahead and wrote both of them down. "The possibilities are really limited for this one. I know it was on a day that started with B-Block classes, so history was after biology, which means he'd have to have access to my backpack either at the end of biology lab or at the beginning of history." I shook my head. "Chase is really the only one I can think of."

Fed pointed to the first event. "The only way all these pieces make sense is if Chase wasn't really sick that day."

"Or there's more than one person, and they're working together." A chill ran up my arms. I was drowning in all the possibilities, none of them good, and needed to come up for air.

"I'm sorry." I shook off thoughts of the events as much as possible. "We've been focusing on me this whole time. How's the prep going for the Halloween dance? Are you nervous?"

"A little." His upper lip twitched.

"You'll be fine." I jabbed him in the ribs with my elbow.

Fed rubbed the spot on his T-shirt where my elbow had connected. "Ashley's as pretty as the girls Nicholas goes out with." His eyes glowed with excitement.

"She is," I said. "Not that you're competing with your brother or anything."

"I dunno." He raised his eyes to the ceiling. "Nicholas always gets the pretty girls."

"Do you ever wonder why Nicholas doesn't have a girlfriend?" I asked. "It's because being pretty shouldn't be the thing that matters." I thought of Forrest, and warmth flushed my cheeks. He had definitely seen me on my better days and my not so good days, and he'd never given up on me through all of that.

Through the library door's window, I could see Parker. A group had gathered around him. His whole class must have gotten out early. Laughter rose from the crowd as he raised his shirt to reveal eyes he had drawn around his nipples and a belly button that looked like a whistling mouth. His hips swayed side to side, and a small spare tire swung as he moved.

Fed chuckled and shook his head.

"Let's trade brothers, and you won't have to worry about

competing with anyone to get all the pretty girls," I said.

"Sorry. No deal," he said. "Avery maybe. But Parker? No way. And Parker has actually dated quite a few pretty girls."

"Yeah, I know. They must be blind. And deaf."

I shaded my face so I could block out any sight of Parker and his whistling rendition of what was most likely *Amazing Grace*, his new favorite.

"Fed, you're the smartest guy I know," I said. "Girls are going to line up to go out with you when you get older. You know how much I love Nicholas, but don't be like him. Pick a girl that attracts you because she's interesting, and can keep up with your intelligence so you can have a meaningful conversation. Pick someone because she loves you on your good days and bad ones too."

Fed shrugged. "Thanks," he said in a quiet voice. "It's a lot easier to talk to you about this kind of stuff than Avery."

"Avery talks?"

Fed laughed. "Do you think she'll have fun?" His thin upper lip quivered.

"Of course she will."

"Thanks. Really."

"Just be yourself." I patted his back. "You'll be perfect."

"So you and Forrest, huh?" He gave me a sly smile. "I caught you kissing him this morning."

I leaned in, hoping no one heard what he'd just said. I still wasn't ready for it to be public, despite my PDA earlier, which was not as stealthy as I had thought. "For the record, *he* kissed *me*," I whispered. "Is this going to be awkward for everyone?"

"Why? You guys are always together anyway." Fed shrugged

a shoulder. "Do you have any idea how long he's been in love with you? 'Cause it's been a long time. Man, that party at your house, he was boo-hooing about Mumps so much I finally made myself go ask Ashley to the dance so I could get away from him."

The last bell rang. I flinched. I hated how skittish I had become over the last month or so since this all started. I pulled my backpack from the floor.

"Here," Fed said and stuck out his hand, "I can carry that for you."

"I got it," I said. "I hate when you guys treat me like I'm weak just because I'm a girl. It's not like you'd offer that to Nicholas if he'd been the one in the accident." I steeled my nerves and started for the door.

"I wouldn't offer that to Nicholas because he picks on me all the time. But fine. I'll ignore all of those stitches on your arm and the big bruise on your neck. Let's go." He let his hand fall to his side and followed after me. At the locker rooms, he said, "See ya later," heading toward the guys'.

"See ya."

The path to the soccer field was lined with trees. The uneasiness of being alone sent my mind to unhealthy places. I made my way, taking time to scout the dark shadows cast by the large branches ahead. The metal benches sent a chill through me when I finally got there. Fall weather in Utah was so unpredictable that way. I zipped up my sweatshirt but still shivered whenever the wind hit my face.

Even though I couldn't play, Coach had still wanted me to watch my own team practice, but Dad refused, and that was that. Dad thought I would be safer if I was in a place where my brothers could see me, and because he didn't want me driving myself home because I would be alone for the drive and alone when I got home, I was forced to endure ninety minutes of a practice that wasn't even mine. It's not that I didn't understand. But it was cold, especially when I wasn't running around, working up a sweat.

The team began their warm-up drills. I watched Forrest differently than I had before, noticing the way the muscles in his legs flexed as he ran, the concentration on his face when he took a shot on goal. He'd glance up every now and then with a knowing smile that something had changed between us. It would have been easy to keep my attention on him the whole time, but I knew I should try to be more productive. I took a copy of *The Great Gatsby* out of my backpack to get some reading done for my English class.

I had been reading for over an hour when the reddish-orange haze of sunset seeped into the sky, and the temperature dropped as the sun fell. I huddled tighter, exposed and vulnerable. I brushed away my sleeve to look at my watch. Fifteen minutes and we would be able to go home.

I put away my book and glanced around until I found Forrest standing at the corner nearest to me. He kicked the ball in a perfect arc in front of the goal, and Nicholas headed it into the net. Across the field, something scurried in the aspens. I snapped my head to the shadowed spot. I could have sworn I saw binoculars pointed my direction. What little bit of body heat remained left me. Before I could get a better look at whatever it was, it was gone. I stared in the same spot with laser-focused eyes, but only trees glowered back.

Wind swooped through, sending the colored leaves sputtering. Maybe my imagination had gotten the best of me—something that happened a lot lately. But still . . .

Clank.

I almost fell off the bleacher at the sudden sound. I hadn't noticed Forrest coming up to the bleachers. On the bench in front of me was a soccer bag he had thrown. He hiked up the metal stairs and sat next to me.

"Sorry," he said. With graceful movements, he took off his cleats and put on another pair of shoes.

"I'm fine. I just wasn't paying attention." Breath clouds spiraled in the cold air as I spoke. "It's freezing."

"Here." He clutched my hands between his.

My skin felt cold and numb against his palms. He rubbed back and forth to create some warmth with the friction, and my circulation began to return.

"Thanks," I said. With all the guys arriving now, I felt like my whole body could relax.

"Anything else need warming up?" Nicholas asked.

"You're sick," Forrest told him. He picked up his cleats and threw them in his bag.

"Aw, he's just jealous," Nicholas said to me.

Forrest scowled at him. "Of what?"

"One, that she'd pick me over you any day," Nicholas said to Forrest. He turned and spoke to me now. "And two, that you have a better-looking date for the Halloween dance than he does." He squeezed my shoulder.

"Not true," Forrest said. "I'm taking your mother." He wiggled his eyebrows up and down.

Nicholas delivered a playful but hard punch to Forrest's shoulder.

"Actually," Parker said, stuffing his soccer ball into his bag, "Your mom *is* hotter than Phil," he said to Nicholas.

"Wait, who said I'm going with Phil?" I asked, lost. I knew who my date to the Halloween dance was, even if they didn't.

Parker glanced at Nicholas, who only shrugged.

"For the millionth time, I don't even know who Phil is," I said.

Forrest put his hand over mine. "She's going with me," he said, "so it's kind of hard for her date to be better looking than me."

Nicholas shared a surprised expression with Parker.

"What happened?" I heard Parker whisper to Nicholas.

"I don't know. Phil said he would ask her," Nicholas whispered back, and then he noticed I was glaring at both of them. "Well, cool." He stood straighter. "Wait. So are you guys like . . ."

"Yes." I took a deep breath, squeezed Forrest's hand, and prepared myself for their reactions.

Nicholas and Parker both smiled. "It's about damn time," Nicholas mumbled.

"Amen, brother," Parker said. "Claire and Avery got all the slow genes."

Except for a light wind that fluttered the leaves, the area was still.

Nicholas shoved Forrest, and then Parker got involved as we climbed down the bleachers. They all pushed each other back and forth until we got to the car.

I swept my eyes across the parking lot, checking for anything out of the ordinary before I got in.

WHEN I GOT home from practice, Dad called for me. My hands and feet were still frozen, so I grabbed a blanket off the couch in the family room before I made my way into his office. His face was hidden behind a magazine when I walked in. I didn't know why he had called me to his office, but past experience said it wasn't for something good.

He closed the magazine and set it in front of him on the desk. "How was your first day back?"

Dad was dressed in a black golf shirt and khakis, and it seemed weird to see him not in a suit. I closed the door behind me and sat in front of him. His face warmed. "How are you holding up, princess?"

"I've been better," I said. "Am I in trouble?"

He chuckled. "No. I was told I should ask you about the Halloween dance."

I shifted, then shifted again, but couldn't get comfortable. Forrest and I hadn't even coordinated costumes yet. "Told by whom?"

"Nicholas." Dad's eyebrows weren't knitted together, so I knew Nicholas had only told Dad about the dance, not Forrest.

Why did Nicholas think it was so important for Dad to know everything? I hadn't even been home five minutes. Had Nicholas called him? Texted him? Sure, I would have told Dad eventually. Once I had graduated from high school. And moved far away.

"Yeah, uh, I'm going to the Halloween dance." I held my breath and hoped it wasn't too much to ask that he leave it at that.

Dad stood up and walked around his desk. He seated himself in the chair next to me and patted my hand. "I was hoping you would." He added, "That way we can all be there as a family. Mom and I will be there as parent chaperones."

They were going to be there. It would have been nice if they'd mentioned this earlier.

"What are you guys dressing up as?"

He shrugged. "I don't know. Your mom picked out something for us. So who's taking you?"

My stomach bunched in knots. Why didn't Nicholas tell Dad about Forrest when he had the chance? Maybe Nicholas thought he was doing Forrest a favor. If I told Dad voluntarily, it wouldn't look like I'd been hiding anything from him, and he might handle the news better than if he found out when he got there.

I took a deep breath, and my heart beat faster. I tried not to cringe in anticipation of Dad's reaction. "I was planning to go to with Forrest." The sentence came out all in a rush. I held my breath.

Dad's face was still wrinkle-free. "That's great."

"Okay." I exhaled. I don't think he understood me, and I

wanted to get it over with. "But what I'm saying is Forrest and I are going to the dance because we're . . . *together* together."

The color drained from Dad's face. "On second thought, maybe you shouldn't go."

I rotated my body in his direction and leaned against my armrest. "Dad, you like Forrest."

He stood up and walked behind the chair. "I don't like him very much anymore." He pursed his lips. "I always knew he was untrustworthy, and—and you're too young to date."

I threw my hands in the air. "I'm almost seventeen. You're being ridiculous," I said. "I've gone to other dances before with guys who make Forrest look like a saint, but now I'm not old enough? How old do you expect me to be?"

He crossed his arms. "Thirty." His expression was deadly serious.

I stood now and took a step closer to him. "It's Forrest," I said again. "Are you saying there's someone else out there you'd rather I be with?"

He supported his weight on the chair's back. "No one's good enough for my daughter."

"Dad," I said, exasperated. "You spend your life doing stressful business deals, and *this* is what gets you all flustered?"

He let go of the chair next to me and went behind his desk to sit down. "Just remember I'll be a chaperone, so no funny business," he mumbled.

THE DAYS FOLLOWING my confession were tense. On top of worrying about everything I had already been worried about, I had to add Dad's feelings about my social life into the mix. I made sure Forrest and I did our homework at the kitchen table in the open once we got home. When we weren't doing homework, I made sure one of my brothers or the Russo boys was with us. If I hadn't told Dad, he wouldn't have even known Forrest and I were together. But by the end of the week, Dad still stiffened every time Forrest came near me.

In order to reduce the number of things Dad could complain about on the day of the dance, I woke up early Saturday morning and backed the cars into the driveway, then waited for him in the garage, setting the mat on the ground. The doctor had upgraded the level of activity I could be involved in, but still suggested I stay away from anything that would involve contact with my head. The bruises were barely visible, I was off pain meds, and the stitches were long gone. All in all, I felt back to my normal physical strength.

Dad's face was frozen in the same strained expression I had seen all week. He was worried about a reinjury but felt it was more important to train in light of recent events. The new level of training wouldn't keep me physically fit, but he said it would help keep my mind sharp. Since he'd altered the training, my brothers got to sleep in, and I'd be training alone for the next few weeks.

He began the same way he did every time we trained. "What are the parts of the body where you can do the most damage?" he asked.

"Eyes, nose, ears, neck, groin, knee, and legs," I said.

"What parts of the body are most effective for inflicting damage?"

"Elbows, knees, and head."

"What's the first thing you do if you're attacked?" he asked.

"Yell," I said.

"Good. Let's work on being grabbed from behind. And remember, a lot of times the attacker can be someone you know, like a boyfriend, or a neighbor, or a date, or a boyfriend."

I rolled my eyes. "Dad."

"I'm quoting statistics," he said. "You'd be surprised how many women are assaulted by their boyfriends."

He grabbed me from behind and held me in what would have been a bear hug if he weren't being careful to avoid my head. I dropped my weight and stomped on his foot, going through the motions slowly. We continued with variations on the same thing, in which I elbowed him in the head or twisted out of his grip and poked him in the eye. Moving at a snail's pace made everything take twice as long.

Normally that would have been the end of our session, but

Dad worked with me more than usual. He held my wrists and made me describe what I would do to leverage his weight off of myself. After that I practiced striking him under the nose with the heel of my palm, throwing my weight into the move. Next I hit him on the side of the neck with a knifehand strike. I held my hand flat, keeping my fingers together tightly, my thumb slightly bent at the knuckle and tucked under, landing blows where the jugular vein and carotid artery were located.

We moved into wrist holds and finally choke holds. Dad placed his hands around my neck, and a scene flashed in my head almost like I was watching a movie. I remembered asking my dad where he had been, and he had said he had done business with the Copper Cactus in Phoenix. It was only a snippet, and then nothing else despite my efforts to fill in more holes in my memory. By the time we finished, I was exhausted. Nothing we'd done had gotten my heart racing, but all the slow movements made me feel like I'd been practicing Tai Chi for an hour and a half.

I dragged myself into the kitchen and plunked myself on a barstool. Even though it was late enough that most families were about to eat lunch, Mom was in the middle of making breakfast. She set a cutting board in front of me and sliced tomatoes.

"Your husband is unbearable sometimes," I said.

"He cares about you, that's all," she said.

"So I guess he told you about me and Forrest?"

Mom stopped cutting and looked like I'd insulted her. "I'm your mother. I know everything."

If I believed that, I would have stopped picking locks a long time ago. I plucked a diced tomato off the cutting board and popped it into my mouth.

She slapped my hand. "Go wake up the others, please."

"Yes, Mother."

Nicholas and Forrest were asleep on the two faux-suede couches of the family room, and Fed was rolled up in a blanket on the floor in front of the TV. But Nicholas was the only one brave and/or stupid enough to get my brothers out of bed on a weekend, so I woke him up first, kicking the couch. "Morning, cupcake."

His dark brown hair ruffled in every direction, and he still wore the same white T-shirt from yesterday, RAVENS emblazed across the front.

"Morning, squirt." He groaned and stretched, then hiked up the waistband of his navy basketball shorts. Without prompting, he automatically said, "I'll go get your brothers." He nudged Fed with his foot as he passed.

Fed rolled over and got to his feet. He walked to the couch Nicholas had left vacant, dropped onto it, and fell back asleep.

Forrest looked comfortable, so I decided I'd let him sleep a little longer. I wandered back into the kitchen and sat on a barstool across from Mom. It was just before noon, and the sun was high in the clear sky, promising warmth. But I knew Utah well enough to know looks can be deceiving. If I stepped outside, the cold air was waiting to bite me.

Nicholas staggered into the kitchen with my brothers behind him, groggy and grumpy. Parker dropped his head at the kitchen table and fell back asleep. Avery's hair looked like it could benefit from a shower, but he slapped on a bandana and tied the ends behind his head. He stretched his arms, released a big yawn, and opened the refrigerator door. "Morning, Mom." He poured himself a glass of milk.

I lowered my voice in a poor attempt to sound like Avery. "Good morning, Claire. Did you sleep well?" I resumed my regular voice. "Good morning, yourself. Yes, I did sleep well. Thank you for asking."

"Whatever. You're so lame." Avery shook his head and took a seat at the kitchen table next to Parker.

Nicholas situated himself on the barstool next to me and poured himself a glass of orange juice. "So what time are we leaving for the Halloween dance tonight?" he asked.

I pointed my chin to the family room. "You'll have to wait until Forrest wakes up, because he's driving."

Loud snores came from the couch where Forrest's long legs hung over the edge.

"I'll let him sleep a little longer," Nicholas said.

Dad came in from the garage with a towel slung over his shoulder. He wiped the sweat off his forehead and came into the kitchen to give Mom a kiss.

"Morning," he said. He glanced over to where Forrest slept. "Since when do we allow boys to sleep over?"

"Since forever." Mom patted his chest. "Back down, Papa Bear."

I sighed. Getting Dad to accept my relationship with Forrest was going to take a miracle.

Dad walked to the kitchen table. "Parker! Avery! Let's go."

Parker jolted awake, and Fed popped up from the couch. Avery stood slowly and took his glass over to the sink.

On Dad's way out, he tapped Nicholas on the shoulder. "Are you joining us for training?"

Nicholas hopped to his feet. "Yep. Just let me grab my shoes."

"I'm coming too." Fed folded the blanket and set it on the couch before he went to the garage.

"Breakfast will be ready in thirty minutes," Mom called to Dad as she hacked at some mushrooms.

Thirty minutes. My brothers only had to train for thirty minutes, while I was out there for an hour and a half. I set the table and put the clean dishes in the dishwasher away.

Forrest ambled into the kitchen as I was putting the last bowl away. His Ravens T-shirt looked clean, but the nasty sweatpants and his disheveled hair made him look homeless. He sat on the barstool across from Mom at the island. "Morning," he said to me and Mom. "Where is everyone?"

"Training." I sat next to him and rested my hand on his leg, hidden from Mom's view by the counter of the island. "I assumed you didn't want to join them."

He wiped the sleep from his eyes. "Yeah. I don't think it's a good idea to put myself in a situation where your dad can legitimately beat me up."

Mom moved the cutting board from the island to the sink. "You just have to be patient with him. He'll come around," she said with her back to us. She turned on the water at the sink and rinsed off the knife.

"Go home and shower," I said to him. "You kinda stink."

Forrest sniffed his armpits. He winced. "Okay, yeah. I'll be back soon. Save some breakfast for me." He sneaked a kiss while Mom's back was still turned, then slipped on his shoes and went out the back door.

By the time the boys had finished training, Forrest had returned, and we all ate together. Before everyone went to their respective houses, they helped clear the table and put the dirty dishes in the dishwasher. Dad's posture remained stiff throughout the whole meal, and I worried even more that my first dance with Forrest was going to be an awkward one.

I went to my room and wanted to crawl back into bed, but I knew my mind would only go into its whirlwind of unanswered questions. There were a couple of hours before I needed to start getting ready for the dance, so I pulled my backpack off the floor and sat down at my desk.

A couple of days after I'd come home from the hospital, I'd stopped having memory loss of new events that had happened after the accident. The doctor had called it post-traumatic amnesia, and the fact that it hadn't lasted very long was a good sign. But lapses in memory from before the accident were still there, and I always second-guessed myself about anything that came back to me. Before I started working, I decided to run a search for the Copper Cactus. Their website said they distributed antique furniture, and they were located in Phoenix, Arizona. That seemed to be consistent with what I remembered Dad saying. With my mind at ease, I was able to do research for my history project with Mumps for the next few hours until it was time to get ready.

Since I had only decided to go to the Halloween dance a week before, I didn't have much time to think about a costume. Mom said Forrest and I could use some of the kimonos in the attic, an easy enough solution for the both of us. Parker, on the other hand, had been planning for weeks. I had mentioned to Parker that it might be a good idea for him to ask Mika, and he'd agreed.

They'd decided Parker would go as a bowling ball, and Mika as a bowling pin. Fed and Ashley were going as Tuxedo Mask and Sailor Moon and I hadn't asked Nicholas or Avery what their costumes were, but I'd find out soon.

I took out the purple kimono Mom had put in my closet a few days ago and dressed it over a T-shirt and a pair of shorts. Even though I only wore kimonos on special occasions, like the annual Obon Festival, it was often enough that I'd learned how to tie the sash properly. I took the obi off the hanger and wrapped it around my waist, tying the bow in front of me, and then turning the sash around my waist until the bow was at my back. But I needed Mom's help with my hair, pulling it into a tight bun on the top of my head. She added a kanzashi as the final touch, sticking the flowered hair ornament through the bun so part of it hung over the left side of my forehead and ear.

The doorbell sounded, and Mom left to answer it. I heard her invite Forrest inside, which seemed strange because he always let himself in, and when he did, he came through the back door, never the front. I bounced down the stairs.

He caught me off guard when I saw him. I'd seen Forrest dressed up before, but he'd never been dressed up for me, and never in a kimono. His hair had a sun-kissed shine, and his deep blue eyes, full and fixed on me, seemed even brighter against the blue fabric of his costume. At his waist was Parker's samurai sword and an obi that hadn't been properly tied, but I didn't care.

Mom tugged on my arm. "Like seeing snow for the first time," she whispered.

She grabbed the camera and took lots of pictures. Parker wobbled down the stairs, the sides of the big black ball skimming the wall and stair rail, and Avery came down dressed as a skateboarder. His costume didn't look any different than the way he dressed every day: flannel shirt with a white T-shirt underneath, shorts hanging low on his waist, and a ball cap. They said their hellos before leaving to pick up their dates.

Dad entered the living room and pulled Mom to the side. I didn't catch much of their conversation, but I think Dad was complaining about his costume. Mom told him he could stay home if he didn't want to wear it. He took one glance at me and stopped. His face softened. "You look very beautiful." And then his face hardened. He scrunched his lips and looked right at Forrest. "Three words," he mumbled. "Concealed. Weapons. Permit." He left the room.

Forrest raised a brow. "I didn't know he had a gun."

"I only found out recently when the burning tree thing happened." I put my hand over my face. "And I'm sorry. I'm sure he meant to say hello," I said. "I'd try to explain, but there is no rational explanation."

Mom took Forrest by the hand and patted it. "Don't you worry about him. They're his issues, not yours," she said. "You may not be able to tell very well right now, but he loves you like a son. I'll talk to him." She patted him again then let go.

Forrest laced his fingers through mine. "I know your dad, and I knew what I was getting into a long time ago," he said. "I'm always up for a challenge."

Without knocking, Nicholas strolled through the door dressed in a pinstripe suit as a gangster. A lithesome girl hung on his arm in a nude-colored dress that looked like it came from the lingerie department. She had a fringe headband around her forehead and said she was supposed to be a flapper. I didn't recognize her as someone who went to our school, but Nicholas had always managed to meet girls from all over.

Mom told Nicholas how handsome he looked and then introduced herself to "Monet." She snapped more pictures of them and then took more of all of us together.

"You actually look presentable, Kiki," Nicholas said. "I can almost tell there's a girl inside there."

"You don't look half bad yourself," I said, "when you've showered."

Mom snapped more pictures and finally let us leave the house. "See you guys there."

Closing the front door behind me, I threw back my head. "Ugh, I thought she was never going to let us out of there."

Forrest stopped me and gave me a kiss on the front porch. "I have something for you." He pulled the sword from the sheath at his sash, then tipped the sheath until something rolled into his hand. Once he'd gotten the sword and sheath back into the right place at his side, he uncurled his fingers and held out his hand. In the center of his palm was a plastic ring, with a white plastic gem on top. With his other hand, he took the ring and slid it onto my ring finger. It was a snug fit, but I wasn't going to lose it unless someone pried it off my finger.

I held out my hand in front of me to get a better look. How had he held on to this for so long? If he had given it to me back then, I was positive I would have lost it by now. So many things he did and that I was still discovering made me love him that much more. "I love it." I pulled the front of his kimono toward me so I could kiss him. "Thank you."

He kissed me again. "You look really beautiful, Claire."

"Thanks. You too." I quickly realized what I had said. "Not beautiful—I meant you look good too—handsome. You know what I meant, right?" I couldn't believe I had tripped over my words. This was *Forrest*. It's not like we hadn't hung out a million times.

He laughed and gave my waist a squeeze.

"So where are we going to dinner?" I asked.

BY THE TIME we made it to the school, the sun had faded and the sky had filled with threatening clouds. The far wall of the gym had been decorated with a backdrop of a haunted castle, lit by red torches at the sides of the portcullis. Bales of hay and large pumpkins lined the pathway to the corner, where a scarecrow stood surrounded by cornstalks.

Katie, from my soccer team, spotted us and slinked over in a pioneer dress and boots. "Forrest is so hot!" she whispered. She smoothed her blonde hair underneath her bonnet as she eyed me from head to toe. "Actually, he's the lucky one. You look *great*! Where did you get that costume?"

"Thanks. I . . . you look pretty awesome yourself," I whispered back. Before I could answer her question, though, I was waving good-bye as Forrest pulled me to the dance floor.

Kimi, Mika, and Lanie were already dancing there in a big group with their dates. Mika, in her bowling-pin costume, waddled away from Parker, grabbing Kimi and Lanie's hands. The girls came up to me, squealing.

"You guys are so cute together," Kimi said in a hushed voice. Forrest stepped away, but he could still hear her. The sequins on her disco-queen jumpsuit reflected light, as she bobbed up and down to the rhythm of "The Monster Mash," an upbeat song that they couldn't help but sing along with as it played.

"Thanks," I said. "You too. With your dates, I mean."

Kimi winked at me. "Sure. I'm so jealous!"

"Love your hair," Mika said. She lowered her voice. "And thanks for putting a bug in your brother's ear."

"I'm glad he asked you," I said.

"We're on our way to the bathroom. Wanna come?" Lanie asked, tugging at a strawberry-blonde curl. She was a perfect Dorothy from *The Wizard of Oz*, and I'd heard rumors that Roarke was supposed to be Toto, but I hadn't seen him yet.

"I'm fine, thanks," I said, and they all ran off. I turned to Forrest. "I know I'm completely illiterate when it comes to female friendships and the associated social interactions, but that's something I don't think I'll ever understand. The bathroom doesn't seem like a fun place to kick back and gossip."

"I don't get girls either." He put his arm around me and squeezed my shoulder.

Mom and Dad were stationed underneath the backdrop at the table with drinks. Mom wore a bright green dress that fell just above her knees with a headband full of flower petals framing her face. I'd never seen Dad with such a dour expression, except for the time Parker had "borrowed" his car and gotten a "flat tire" which really meant a broken axle. His black suit was like the kind he wore almost daily, but on his head was a black-and-yellow striped bee hat that surrounded his head and tied underneath his chin. Bug eyes were attached at his forehead, and twelve-inch antennae protruded from the top with big black pom-poms at the end.

Mom probably thought it was hilarious, but I'm pretty sure I was as embarrassed as Dad was. Forrest took one look, and his jaw dropped. I pulled him far away to the wall so he could release howls of laughter. "Whatever you do," I said, "do not let him see you. He will never forgive you. And I'm pretty sure he will never forgive Mom."

Through a gym window, I saw a bolt of lightning streak across the dark sky. A crack of thunder shook the building and sent vibrations through the walls.

Forrest's lips grazed my ear, and he whispered, "It's raining."

I yanked on his arm, pulling him toward the door. "Let's go," I said, dragging him across the floor. The rest of the guys were headed to the exit too. Dancing in the rain had been an Axis Powers tradition that started years ago, the day after Nicholas and Fed's father left. It had been a hot summer day, and then without warning, the sky opened up, huge drops landing everywhere.

Nicholas had walked outside and stopped in the middle of the street. He looked to the sky, held out his hands, and closed his eyes, rain pouring down on him in torrential streams. We all knew how angry and sad Nicholas was, even though he wouldn't talk about it. Parker went outside and stood next to him, and the rest of us followed. Nicholas started to dance, so the rest of joined in, dancing like crazed lunatics. And when the rain stopped, there was still sadness underneath Nicholas's expression, but a lot of the darkness in his face had melted away.

There were only a couple of times it had rained when we were at a dance, but if we were all together, it didn't matter what we were wearing. With everything that had been going on, it was like the sky knew what we needed.

Like me, Forrest had worn a T-shirt and a pair of shorts underneath, and we shed our costumes at the door so they wouldn't get wet. Those who could do the same followed suit, leaving everything in a pile by the door, and tore outside. Before I left, I took my phone from my shorts and slid it into a secret pocket in my obi. Dad tugged Mom behind us with swift feet.

Outside, large drops of icy water pelted my face and ran down my neck. The cool wind blew clumps of my hair until it stuck to my cheeks. Parker and Mika both splashed in puddles, barefoot. Ashley didn't hesitate to join in the fun and tried to teach everyone else the foxtrot, but coordinated feet on a soccer field didn't necessarily translate to coordinated dancing feet.

Forrest spun me in circles until I almost fell over. Even Mom and Dad joined in. The fresh taste of rain sloshed across my tongue, and I laughed until my sides hurt.

The air gave us goose bumps, and before long we were all shivering, but we'd played soccer games in blizzards. After a few minutes, the downpour slowed to a sprinkle and then a mist. The clouds parted, and the moon created a silhouette of the Wasatch Mountains in the background.

Everyone started to go inside, but Forrest and I trailed behind. Water seeped into my shoes, so I kicked them off and drained them, using Forrest for a support.

When I stood back up, Forrest reached over and pushed some of my wet hair to the side. "It's good to see you happy again," he said. "I was beginning to think you'd kidnapped my best friend."

"You mean *girlfriend*?" I said, shivering uncontrollably.

His face lit up. "Yeah, that."

I laughed. "Sounds weird, doesn't it?"

"I think I can get used to it." Forrest tilted back his head and let the water slip down his face. He spun me out along his arm, then rolled me back in. His hand pressed into the small of my back, holding me against his chest for a moment longer than I expected. He sneaked a peek to see if my parents were watching, and then pressed his lips hard against mine before he spun me away again, laughing.

Forrest leaned in so close his long eyelashes tickled my forehead. "Let's go inside before you freeze to death."

He steered us in the direction of the building so we could go back inside. The school building's warm air rushed over me like a blanket. I'd have to stand under the hand dryers in the bathroom for a long time, but it had been worth it.

After we picked up our costumes, Forrest took my hand and pulled me away from the entrance and behind a cardboard mummy. I draped the kimono over my arm and held it away from my body so it wouldn't get wet.

"Let me take that," he said.

I handed him the kimono and obi, laying it over the top of his on his arm, and then he walked away. About five feet from us was a stack of baled hay where he set the kimonos and obis carefully and returned. "What did your mom mean about the seeing snow thing?" he asked.

"Mom grew up in Hawaii," I said, "so she'd never seen snow until she was a teen, when her family vacationed in Colorado for Christmas. She said she wondered how she could have missed out on something so beautiful for so many years, and when she first saw my father, it was like seeing snow for the first time."

For a moment, I thought about all the pain my father's death had caused her and wondered if she would have been better off if she'd never seen snow in the first place.

"Claire?" He cupped my chin and focused on my face, his lips stretching into a broad smile.

"What's so funny?" I asked, still shaking.

"You sort of disappeared on me there for a second," he said.

"Sorry."

He hooked his arm around my waist, and we swayed as if the music had slowed. "Your expression reminded me of a time last year in art class."

"I can't believe you convinced me to take that stupid class."

My rain-soaked clothes felt heavy. He rubbed his warm hands on my arms. "Remember how you picked a panda when we were assigned to paint an animal with fur? And it was turning out to be a lot more work than you had expected? You had this expression that looked like the one you had a moment ago. You looked stressed, and your eyes and nose were scrunched up." He mimicked my face.

I shivered again, and my lips trembled. "Glad my anxiety was entertaining for you."

He tapped his finger against my lips. "You're such a perfectionist. You had that look, and you kept muttering about how long the fur was taking because you had to paint each individual strand. You were getting so frustrated." He bent down, picked up one of my shoes, and slipped it on my foot.

I shoved my foot into the other heel. "Ugh, I remember trying to paint those stupid eyes."

"But the way you were worrying about it was adorable." Forrest put his arm around my shoulder and reeled me into his side. "I'd seen every side of you since we were kids, and I realized I still loved everything about you."

I stretched up and kissed him. Forrest wrapped his arms around me. His kisses were gentle at first and then hungry, and everything about him was like snow, and I wondered how I had gone so long without knowing how beautiful something can be. All the hurts in the world could never make me regret the experience of seeing for the first time.

By the time we came up for air, my body had stopped shivering, but I was still cold, and every bit of me dripped with water. "I'm going to the restroom to see if I can dry up some of this," I said, sliding my hand from his.

"I think I'm going to try to do the same," he said, "and then I'll get us something to drink."

As I made my way out of the gym and into the hallway, I overhead Mr. Tama on his phone. Like almost everyone else, he hadn't joined the revelry in the rain and was still completely dry. From what I could tell, he was costumed as someone from Hawaii. His Aloha shirt was the typical collared Hawaiian dress shirt with a wild floral print, shirt pocket, and buttons down the front. On the bottom he wore blue board shorts that ended below his knees.

"Ho, you seen dat show dah oddah night, brah?" he said.

I stopped and smiled. I'd lived in Hawaii long enough to

know that almost all the residents, no matter what their racial or cultural background was, spoke Hawaiian pidgin. And when I heard Mr. Tama speaking this simpler form of English, I knew he had lived there too.

"Ah, buggah," he said. "Okay, if can, can, if no can, no can." He ended his call.

He saw me and came over. "Hey, Claire."

"I'm sorry. I didn't mean to eavesdrop, but I kind of heard you on the phone. I didn't realize you were from Hawaii." I wiped at some drops running down my face. "I guess the Aloha shirt you're wearing should have been my first clue. I was actually born there."

"Fo' real?" He folded his arms. "No tell da oddahs I talk pidgin, yeah?" He winked and changed his pronunciation and intonation. "I wouldn't want anyone to think I was unprofessional."

I laughed. "My dad can do that too," I said. "He can turn the pidgin off and on like a switch. Your secret's safe with me."

His dark eyes swept over me from head to toe. "Why are you all wet?"

"We were messing around in the rain." I folded my arms across my chest, thankful I'd worn a dark T-shirt instead of a white one.

He nodded. "And are you fully recovered?" His fingers fumbled to return his phone to his shirt pocket as he kept his focus on me.

"I still have a few bruises, but—" I gasped as the phone fell in his pocket and he took his hand away. "But I'm much better, thank you."

"Is something wrong?" he asked.

"No," I said.

The pocket on his shirt was missing a koa wood button.

THE BUTTON LOOKED like a decorative one—not meant to keep the pocket closed—so maybe he hadn't realized it was missing. Was this a coincidence? The gears in my head kicked into full steam. My breaths were rapid, so I tried to focus and regain my composure. "So where did you live in Hawaii?" I asked.

"McCully area by da shopping centah, and Mililani little bit," he said, reverting back to pidgin. "How 'bout you?"

"Hawaii Kai," I said, drawing in large breaths to slow my pulse. I knew it might be a stretch, but he had a missing button, and I'd never been quite sure where the business card had come from. "Did you by chance ever live in Waipahu?"

His face stretched as if all the air had been sucked from his lungs. "Uh, yes. I did for a couple of years." The pidgin had vanished, and he sounded more formal. He paused. "Why do you ask?"

Crap. Why was I asking? What could I come up with that would be believable? "My uncle did some work with a nonprofit group there, and you kind of remind me of him." I caught myself swaying from side to side, and I stilled my legs.

He looked right at me with an intense gaze. "What was your uncle's name?"

Double crap. Crap. Crap. "Takeshi Kitano." It was the first name that came to my mind. I hoped he didn't recognize the name of the man who was famous for directing many of the yakuza films we'd seen. "Anyway, I'm going to go dry off. Good talking to you." Before he could answer, I turned around and ran.

Instead of drying off, I sprinted back into the gym, searching until I found Forrest standing next to Mom at the drink table. I practically leaped into his arms.

"Miss me?" he asked, and then he read my expression.

I pulled Forrest away from the table before Mom could see me, dragging him across to the opposite side of the gym. "Mr. Tama," I said. "I think he was the one who broke into my room."

I told him about the button, and I could tell he was still skeptical. "He's from Hawaii. Maybe that's how he knew my father."

"Claire, you have to be careful," he said. "All you have are coincidences."

"But it's not just any button. It's made out of koa wood. I recognize the patterns and the coloring," I said. My heartbeat raced faster. "I've only seen that wood used in Hawaii. It has to be his button. And I found this business card under my bed for a nonprofit group in Waipahu, which is a city in Hawaii, and I didn't know where it had come from, but there's a prison there. And when I asked him if he'd ever lived there, he said he had for a couple of years."

"You can't just go accuse a teacher of something like this."

"I know." I squeezed both of his hands in mine and looked him in the eye. "I need to get more proof." My grip on him had turned my knuckles white, and I realized I was probably cutting off his circulation too. I let go.

"Don't do this." Forrest shook his head and grabbed me by the shoulders. "I don't know what you're thinking, but stop. Get it out of your head right now. We should tell your dad."

"What if I'm wrong?" Ninety-nine percent of me was positive it was Mr. Tama. If I made a mistake, it could ruin him. I paused and let everything sink in. But charging ahead could mean ruin for me. "Okay." I looked toward the table of drinks, but only Mom was there. "Where is he?"

"Your mom said he had to run an errand, or go do something—I don't know—but he should be back soon."

The prickly feeling returned to my stomach. Where had Dad gone? Who needed to do errands at this time of night? I could call him and tell him to come back, but what would I be telling him to come back from? I remembered that GPS disk I had slipped into his briefcase. Chances are he didn't have the briefcase on him, but it was worth a try. "Wait here," I said.

I ran to the bale of hay, retrieved my phone from the pocket in my sash, and swiped at my screen as I returned. "This GPS app shows Dad's location is at the house, which means either he's there with the briefcase, or he's somewhere else and his briefcase is at home."

Forrest shook his head. "I don't even dare ask how you got that and what you did with it. You're scary sometimes, you know that?"

"Of course I know." If I confronted Mom about where he'd

gone, there was little chance I would know if she was telling me the truth. My only other option was to go home.

As much as I wanted to believe he really did have some errand to run, I couldn't escape that niggling feeling in the pit of my stomach. And then I remembered the app had historical data I had meant to check but had never gotten to because of the accident.

"On the night our tree was on fire, I had been surprised to see him home because he was supposed to be in Phoenix." I selected that date. An orange swoosh swirled on the screen as the data loaded.

My breath hitched.

Forrest looked over my shoulder. He gasped. "Oh no."

Dad hadn't been in Phoenix, Arizona. He'd been in Los Angeles, California.

My mind scrambled, trying to think of what good reason he might have to lie to us. I thought I was going to be sick, but I checked another date anyway, one after my accident, wetness pooling in the corners of my eyes. I gulped. A tear ran down my cheek.

Dad hadn't been in New York. He'd been in Honolulu, Hawaii.

Forrest grabbed me and pulled me into his arms, wrapping around me so tight I could hardly breathe. "Tell me what to do," he said, pressing his cheek against my forehead.

Run. I wanted to run. I breathed in Forrest's scent of rain and musk. People I loved could get hurt. "I'm going to call an APM. We need to find out if my dad is working with Mr. Tama."

Right after I had gathered the guys together by the wall on the south end of the gym, Dad carried a large tub full of ice across the gym and set it on the table of drinks. I recognized the tub as one from our cafeteria. Maybe his errand was legitimate, and he'd been scooping ice from the machine in the school's kitchen for the past five minutes. It didn't matter. He'd lied to us about being in Phoenix, New York, and who knows where else.

I couldn't even stand to look at him. "Keep dancing so Dad doesn't suspect anything." I had to speak up so everyone could hear me over the music.

Fed stood across from me, his lanky arms and legs swinging in every direction. "I can't dance and talk at the same time."

"Please stop," Nicholas said to him. He put a hand on Fed's shoulder.

Fed stood still and tugged his black Zorro-looking mask down, letting it hang around his neck.

"So what are we doing?" Avery asked.

"Whatever it is, I'm in," Fed said, flexing his muscles.

Forrest clung to my hand as I told them about the button and the business card and the Waiawa Circle of Friends and how Mr. Tama said he'd lived in Waipahu. No one was very close to us, but because of the loud volume we needed to speak with in order to compete with the music, I kept scanning the crowd, worried we would be overheard. If we moved outside the gym where it was quieter, Dad would notice we were all missing.

"A prison?" Parker flailed his hands, which were the only part of his body sticking out the sides of his bowling-ball costume. On any other day it would have been comical, but no one was in a laughing mood. "Our father *sentenced* people to prison."

"I know," I said.

Nicholas raised a brow, his nose scrunching up. "Are you sure? I mean, I get what you're saying, but he doesn't seem like

someone who would do something like this. I really like this guy."
His shoulders slumped. "He's the best debate coach I've ever had."

If I'd really thought he was second-guessing me, I might have been offended, but I knew he was processing his disappointment. And there were a lot worse things to be upset over. "I liked him too." I tilted my head up to meet his eyes. "But I need to search his messenger bag and possibly his classroom to see if I can find anything that links him to our father."

"There are teachers patrolling the whole school so that exact thing doesn't happen." Nicholas took the black fedora off his head and combed his fingers through his hair. He glanced over at my parents. "Not to mention your dad, who is going to tear this school apart if you are missing more than one minute. We should tell him so he can help us."

I blinked hard and blinked again. Forrest put his arm around my shoulder. I inhaled and released the air and then I told them what I'd discovered about Dad.

Nicholas's body went rigid. "No," he growled, shaking his head. "There has to be a good reason he lied to you."

Avery's eyes crumpled into an anguish I'd never seen on him before. He turned to Nicholas. "Don't you think we want to believe that? He's really the only dad I've ever known. But we don't get the luxury of giving anyone else the benefit of the doubt right now. The only people I know I trust are standing right here." He pointed in my direction, but kept his focus on Nicholas, fire burning in his cheeks. "Someone tried to kill Claire. I could be next. Parker could be next. I don't want to wake up thinking someone is trying to burn our house down. I don't want to be scared anymore. We need to find a way to put an end to this."

No one said anything. I barely recognized my little brother. Parker glanced at me. The soft look in his eyes told me his heart ached for Avery in the same way mine did. If anyone understood Avery, it was Parker and me.

"Tell us what you need us to do," Nicholas said, breaking the silence. His voice barely cut through the music.

I barked out orders, military style, not wanting to waste any more time. "Okay, the teacher's lounge is by the front entrance. We know from last year's Halloween dance that even if the door's closed, it should be unlocked because the door to the nurse's station is in the back."

"You're welcome," Parker said, bowing his head. Last year he'd come dressed as a vending machine, a costume he'd spent a month making. He'd surrounded himself in a clear plastic box with arm and leg holes, an open top, stuffed animals around his body. But because he couldn't see where he was walking, he'd tripped on an empty cup and cut his forehead open when he hit the drinking fountain.

"You guys need to stand guard. Text me if someone's coming, and cause a distraction so I have time to hide. I'm going to get in there, look for his locker, and see if his messenger bag is in there," I said. "If it is, I'll see what I can find. If it's not, I need to get into the history classroom in the west wing. Every dance so far, they've had two teachers patrolling each hall. Usually they stand at the entrance of the wing so no one can get past. Parker, you're going to fall down close to the west-wing entrance but far enough that you can draw them away. Fall on your back and act like you've hurt yourself again. It's not going to be a hard sell since, once again, you can't see where you're walking." I gestured in a circular motion to his bowling-ball costume. "If anyone tries to roll you, then start howling in pain."

I pointed to Fed. "You're going to call for help and draw the teachers in front of the west wing away from the hall. As soon as they leave, Nicholas and I are going to sprint to the classroom. Mr. Tama didn't have his messenger bag on him when I saw him, and if it's not in the teacher's lounge, it's probably locked in his desk drawer. I'll get into the drawer, and Nicholas will search the rest of the classroom."

"We're counting on you to get the door to the classroom *and* the desk drawer unlocked?" Nicholas combed his fingers through his hair again and put his fedora back on.

"Yeah."

Nicholas cursed. I hadn't shared any of my lock-picking skills with the guys, so I suppose I deserved that, but I didn't have time to explain.

"If someone starts to come back, you've got to text us, Fed, so we can get out of there." I looked at Avery. "If Mom or Dad even look like they're about to leave, you need to try and stall them."

"I can do that," Avery said.

Forrest raised his hand. "So what am I supposed to do?"

"I need you to get our kimonos, and then your job is to keep my dad away."

Forrest cursed.

I turned to Fed. "I'm going to need to borrow your date."

Fed cursed.

"And her costume," I said.

He cursed again.

ASHLEY MET ME in the girls' bathroom.

"So why am I doing this?" she asked. She took off her Sailor Moon costume and draped it over the stall.

I traded it for my kimono and sash. "Payback," I said.

We both knew she didn't care if I got payback. Ashley and I had been soccer teammates, but that wasn't the bond that brought her here. She was here because of Fed, and anyone who was willing to do something because it was important to Fed was someone who'd automatically earned a lot of my respect.

"Does this have anything to do with Chase?" she asked.

"I'm about to find out."

Ashley was a little smaller than I was, so it was a tight fit, but I squeezed myself inside. It hugged every curve of my body, which was disgusting because of the way it fit, and because the dress was still wet. She was in my wet shirt and shorts, so I shouldn't have been complaining when Ashley was the one doing me a favor.

I exited the stall and looked at my reflection in the mirror.

If I bent over too far, someone was going to get a show, and I'm not sure where she'd gotten the outfit, but the V-neck collar went much lower than I was comfortable with. I wasn't necessarily well-endowed in the chest area, but the tight fit of the costume made the top half more like a corset.

"Uh, I'm going to need help," she said from inside the stall. She opened the door and walked out.

She had gotten the kimono on, with my shirt and shorts underneath, but needed help with the obi. I wrapped the sash around her waist, and had to concentrate because tying it on myself was different than tying it on someone else. When I finally figured it out, I bloused the top half of the kimono over the sash so the bottom didn't drag on the floor.

Our hair was the same color and straight, but her hair was a lot longer than mine. She took the elastics out of her hair, then pulled it back and started to twist it into a bun.

"I'm going to need to hang onto some of these bobby pins," I said, "but you can use the rest."

Fortunately Mom had used a lot of pins to keep my hair in place. I pulled the pins and the kanzashi from my hair and set them on the counter for her. She gave me her hair elastics so I could put my hair into pigtails, and I stuck four bobby pins back into my hair, two at each pigtail. I helped stick the kanzashi in her hair, hanging the ornament to the right side of her head.

We checked each other out when we were finished. All in all, I thought we looked pretty good. She agreed, and we went outside, where the rest of the guys were waiting. Fed's face bloomed into a big smile when he saw Ashley. She pranced over to him and hugged his waist. Based on his reaction, I was pretty sure I was one of the only girls not related to him who'd given him a hug before. He didn't hesitate to embrace her back.

Forrest had changed back into his kimono by the time we exited. He grabbed me, tugging me closer, and gave me a sly smile.

I shoved him in the chest. "Can you please look at my face and not my boobs?"

Forrest continued to stare. "They're so . . . squished."

"Perv," Avery said behind him.

"Gross," Parker said, ducking his head into the bowling ball. Nicholas shoved Forrest's back.

"The dress is a little fitted, that's all," I said, twisting and adjusting myself so I didn't fall out. "Okay, Ashley, you go with Forrest and try to keep your back to my dad when you're dancing together. If Mr. Tama leaves the gym, you need to text us, Avery."

Avery nodded.

"The things I do for you," Forrest muttered.

Fed let go of Ashley, and Forrest led Ashley back into the gym.

I took a deep breath.

"Should we synchronize our watches?" Fed asked.

Nicholas rolled his eyes.

"Let's roll," Parker said, smiling.

Parker, Fed, and Nicholas kept watch while I sneaked into the teacher's lounge. I scanned the lockers until I found the one labeled with Mrs. Davenport's name. Apparently they hadn't gotten around to changing it yet. The door was secured with a cylinder lock. Some were harder than others to pick, but I wouldn't know until I started. The only locks I'd picked so far were family locks. My pulse beat furiously, but I knew I could do this. I took a pin from my hair and broke it in half. I bent one half and slid it into the bottom of the lock as the tension wrench, and the other half I slid into the top as the pick.

If I'd had my pick set, I could use a rake pick and jiggle this thing open, but as soon as I applied tension and moved the pick, I knew I'd have to move each pin individually. I maneuvered the pick, listening for each pin, and was able to open it in what I assumed was under two minutes. I cracked open the locker. Except for bread molding in a plastic baggie, the locker was empty. I grabbed the baggie and slammed it into the garbage can on my way out.

Parker, Fed, and Nicholas had hopeful faces when I exited, but I shook my head.

"We've gotta go to the classroom," I said. The longer we were gone, the greater the chance was Dad would notice. I didn't know if my dad or the teachers scared me more. We needed to hurry.

Parker and Fed were able to lure the teachers away as planned. Nicholas and I tore down the hall. I unclenched my hand with the bobby-pin tools when we got to the door and slid them inside the lock. Nicholas jerked his head up every few seconds to check for people.

"Could you be a little less obvious? You're making me nervous."

"Sorry," he said, jerking his head again.

I moved my left wrist, applying tension with my right hand and picked the door to the classroom.

"You are frightening." Nicholas shuddered.

"So I've been told," I said. "I've done this a few times. Desk drawers, cabinets, dresser drawers, glove compartments. Pretty much any place my parents might hide something." Come to think of it, it was surprising it had taken me nearly to my seventeenth birthday to stumble upon the picture of my fathers together, given what a snoop I was. But I couldn't think of either one of them, or my thoughts would be sucked into a downward spiral.

We slipped inside. I pushed those thoughts out of my head and focused on the desk. The room was dim, but there was enough light to maneuver around.

"Check bookshelves, behind posters, anywhere you can think of," I said.

"What am I looking for?"

"Anything that would place him in my room or prove motivation to break in to my room in the first place." I used the same pieces of the bobby pin to open the desk drawer. If nothing was here, I'd have to break in to his house.

Once the thought crossed my mind, I realized how far I'd gone—how far I was willing to go. What we were doing wasn't right, but breaking in to a house seemed to be a whole new level. Had I made the right decision?

The messenger bag was there. I exhaled the breath I'd been holding, and threw it open, going through everything as carefully as possible and remembering the order in which everything had been stacked. Lecture notes. Ungraded quizzes. In the left front pocket of the bag, I found his wallet.

"Nothing," Nicholas whispered. "We should get out of here."

Our phones buzzed. The time flashed 10:55. Fed had sent a text.

Someone is coming.

Our phones buzzed again.

Stay there.

"Underneath the desk," I said, throwing the bag into the drawer but keeping the wallet in my hands.

We scrambled under. With the two of us, it was a tight fit. I thought I might pop a seam in Ashley's dress. I hugged my knees close to my chest and could feel my heart pounding against my legs. I rolled the chair as close to us as I could. The dance would be ending in five minutes. They were probably checking all the doors before they left. If we didn't get out of here soon, the dance would be over, and Dad would definitely notice we were gone.

Voices came closer, and the doorknob jiggled.

"This one's unlocked," Mrs. Kenton's voice said.

"Probably just forgot," the other one said. Coach Cesar.

The door opened. A light turned on. "It's empty," Mrs. Kenton said.

The light turned off. The door clicked closed.

I let go of the breath I was holding.

We waited a moment, and then I pushed the chair away. I let my head rest against the desk, and exhaled. I opened Mr. Tama's wallet.

Beneath a clear plastic pocket was his driver's license. My heart stopped. My hands ran cold.

"Nicholas." I held the wallet in the light streaming through the window of the door and angled it for him to see.

Mr. Tama's picture was on the license issued in Hawaii, but with a different name. Nicholas read it and raised his head slowly. "His name is Lionel Bart?"

I knew that name from somewhere. From the Internet.

How could I have missed this? I'd read so many articles about my father and the people who had grudges against him in the last few months, but even the sheer number wasn't enough to assuage this feeling I should have recognized Mr. Tama from the pictures in the articles about his case. I should have known.

Behind the license was a piece of paper. Nicholas slid it out and showed me a temporary Utah license issued under the name of Marcus Tama. He stood up and extended his hand to help me off the floor. "Do you think this temporary license is a fake?"

"I have no idea. Maybe we should take the licenses as proof," I said.

He slid both licenses back in the wallet then shoved it in the bag. "Proof we broke in here?"

We heard Mrs. Kenton say something on the other side of the door.

I straightened the bag, put everything back in order, and locked the drawer with the pins.

"Let's go." I raced to the door.

"But the teachers are still out there," he said.

"Does it really matter at this point?"

He shrugged. "Guess not."

I opened the door, and we started to run.

"Mr. Russo. Ms. Takata," Mrs. Kenton called.

We stopped and turned around.

"What are you doing down here?" she asked.

Nicholas put his arm around me. "Looking for somewhere private." He winked at her.

"I suggest the two of you get back in there," she said.

We both nodded and resumed running.

Maybe we should have taken the wallet with us. I couldn't believe everything had gotten so bad that stealing had become okay.

Fed and Parker ran into us first, close to the entrance. Parker's right ankle was taped and shoeless. His costume was deflated and draped over his arm. "Mr. Tama isn't who he says he is," I said. "But I don't know what to do. We can't tell Dad, can we? We have to call the police."

My phone was in my obi, around Ashley's waist. We passed the faculty lounge, and I ran inside. I picked up the landline phone on a table by the refrigerator and dialed 911.

"911. What's your emergency?" the female dispatcher said.

I told them I was at Franklin High School, and there was a teacher there by the name of Marcus Tama who was a convicted felon, and I was worried he was putting someone's life in danger. When the person asked my name, I said, "Anonymous."

"I'll send someone over right now," she said, and I hung up.

Fed, Parker, and Nicholas stood behind me.

"They're on their way," I said.

We jogged at a slower pace to the gym, and I tried to explain as much as I could while sucking large amounts of air.

What if Officer Schwartz was assigned to this case? As far as I knew, he'd done less than nothing so far. I brushed the thoughts out of my head. I couldn't think that way. Everything was going to be okay.

I didn't stop until I found Forrest waiting for us with Ashley at the entrance. I tried to catch my breath. The gym had emptied except for the clean-up crew, which included my parents and some teachers. Mom and Dad were at the other end of the gym. Mom cleaned up the table with drinks, while Dad helped kids from student government take down decorations.

Nicholas caught Avery's attention and motioned for him to come over. I looked at Fed, who had his arms around Ashley, her back facing us, and lowered my eyes in her direction. He closed his eyes and nodded. I knew he felt like a jerk. I felt like a jerk, but she couldn't be here.

Mika and Avery's date pitched in, but I couldn't see Monet anywhere. Nicholas didn't seem to care. We'd need to find a way to make things up to them.

"Hey, Ashley," I said, struggling to catch my breath. She pulled away from Fed and turned around. "Thank you so much for your help. Really. And I want to explain everything, but I'm hoping it can wait because I'm about to keel over." That was not a lie. My breaths were almost too ragged to speak. I hadn't been working out since being off the team this last month, and it showed right now.

I was about to make something up to get her out of there when Fed said, "I want to go check out the scarecrow before they take it down." He led her in that direction. "Do you wanna come?"

They left, and the words started to pour out. Everyone circled around me, Forrest at my back. "It's him. Mr. Tama's the one who broke into my room," I said. "Underneath Mr. Tama's desk— It's not his real name." I bent over and caught my breath. And then I explained what we'd found.

"Lionel Bart has rants all over the Internet because he believes he was convicted unfairly, and he blames my father,"

I said. I'd read so many articles about him. How did I never match the pictures from the trial in the news reports to my nice history teacher? He was at least a decade younger in the pictures online, and he'd definitely gained a few pounds since then, but still . . . I should have made the connection.

"What about Dad?" I asked.

Avery's eyes narrowed. "We don't say anything until we have more information," he said across from me.

So many things didn't make sense, but Dad made the least sense of all of them. Didn't he love us? Was he lying to Mom too?

"Agreed," Parker said, and placed his hand on Avery's shoulder.

To the right of me, Nicholas nodded, but I could tell he wasn't thrilled about it. "I'll tell Fed." He motioned for us to go to the other side of the gym. "We should help clean."

Before I pitched in, I found Ashley, we exchanged clothes, and by the time we returned, the police had arrived.

I sidled next to Forrest and hugged his waist. Even though I was happy we'd found who was behind everything, prickles of fear still ran through me. This wasn't over yet until we were sure he was behind bars. Forrest put his strong arms around me, holding me up, and kissed the side of my head. Exhaustion started to settle in, but there was still work to be done. Forrest and I added to the efforts by peeling off cardboard pumpkins taped to the walls and piling them into a nice stack so they could be reused.

We had almost finished taking everything down when I saw the police talking to our principal. She pointed in our direction and motioned for my mom and dad to join them. My parents crossed the gym toward me, Mom's eyebrows knitted in puzzlement and worry, Dad's face contorted into something intense but not quite readable. Anger? Fear?

Two officers I didn't recognize brought a yellow manila envelope over. On the front was TAKATA written in black marker. "This was taped underneath Mr. Tama's desk," a tall officer with dark features said to my parents. He opened the flap and pulled out pictures. Nicholas and me at the watermelon-eating contest. All of us together at Lake Powell. Forrest and me at the county fair. My family with Grandpa in Hawaii for his birthday. Every photo was one that had originally hung in my locker.

He showed us a few more, and I bit down on my fist. Since Mr. Tama was a teacher, he would've had no problem getting my locker combination. "Those were stolen from me," I said. "The corners are ripped because someone tore them from my locker."

My stomach turned. Crosshairs had been drawn on all of our faces with a red marker.

"Do you mind if we ask her some questions?" the other officer asked my parents.

Dad rested a hand on my shoulder. "Go ahead."

The officer nodded and asked, "Does the name Lionel Bart mean anything to you?" He was almost as tall as his partner but had fair skin and pale gray eyes. I told them I recognized Mr. Tama's real name, and explained the connection to my father.

"Do you know why he would keep these here?" the officer asked.

"No," I said, shaking my head. "Maybe he thought it was the last place someone might look because it was the most obvious place to look." Mr. Tama hadn't seemed like he'd be that stupid, but I had misjudged a lot of people lately and the lies they were capable of telling.

The officer nodded. "Well, thank you for your time," he said. "We'll be keeping these for evidence."

In the hallway, Mr. Tama argued with a different pair of officers. First he denied everything, but eventually he let them lead him away for questioning at the station.

The police told Dad they'd be issuing a warrant for Mr. Tama's home. They'd let us know if there was anything we should know, and said they might need to contact us if they had more questions.

Forrest pulled away from my side. "I'm so happy, I could do something crazy." He balled his hands into fists. "Or beat up a shark or something. I'm so happy this is over."

I reeled him back to me. I closed my eyes and felt the beat of his heart against my ear, the rise of his chest with each breath. "Can you hold me like this forever?" I asked.

He kissed my head again. "Only if you promise to trade dresses permanently with Ashley."

NORMALLY WE WOULD have all crashed in the family room after the Halloween dance, but we were exhausted, and Forrest and the Russo boys wanted to change out of their wet clothes.

Forrest promised to call me when he woke up the next day, but I jolted awake at 5:30 A.M. With Mr. Tama locked away, I should have felt safer, but I didn't. And I probably wouldn't until I had answered all questions about my father.

I considered the GPS. Should I leave it in Dad's briefcase? If I did, we would have a better idea where he was. But if he found it, would he be able to trace it back to Fed? I had no idea what my dad did or what resources he had. I could be putting Fed in danger. The best decision seemed to be the one that kept Fed safe. I could always place the GPS on a case-by-case basis if we felt we needed to.

The house was silent. If I was going to get it out of Dad's briefcase, there probably wouldn't be a better time. I crept with light feet down the stairs and into his office. To help me see, I used my phone as a flashlight rather than turning the light on. The briefcase was at the base of his desk, where it always was. Crawling to reach it, I slipped my fingers behind the piece of paper in the luggage tag to slide out the disk. Pulling the disk out was much harder than it had been to slide it inside. I wedged my fingers underneath and wiggled it side to side until it flew out, high in the air, taking the piece of paper with it.

The disk hit the chair and bounced. I stood and shined my phone's flashlight to find where they had landed. Both the disk and the paper were closer to the door. I moved to the front of the desk and clipped the disk back on my necklace, but when I picked up the paper, it had the name Nobu Yamasaki. That was not the name I'd seen when I tried to get the GPS. I flipped the paper over. George Takata.

A big lump rose and fell in my throat. What was going on? Who was Nobu Yamasaki? I sat right there on the office floor and did a search on my phone. Too many links came up. I did a search with the name and added "Los Angeles." My dad's picture appeared in two of the images that resulted. I didn't know if I wanted to click on the link. This was a man I loved. Did I really want to know, or could I pretend none of this had ever happened? I knew what I needed to do.

I clicked the picture. A man named Tony Akiyama had posted a picture on a social media site of him and my father at what looked like a birthday party held in a bar six months ago. In the background, a woman in a string bikini held a tray of drinks. He'd tagged my dad as Nobu Yamasaki. Tony looked much younger than my father, maybe midtwenties. He had a black leather jacket and sunglasses. Dad was in his suit, also wearing sunglasses. I clicked on the other image and found Tony Akiyama had tagged my dad again as Nobu Yamasaki on the day Dad was supposed to be in Phoenix.

This couldn't be happening. How many lies were there?

The picture showed the two flanking another man in the middle, who hadn't been named. This man was about the same age as my dad, dressed similarly in a dark suit and sunglasses. Above was an arched metal sign that read Santa Monica Pier. Tony wore a black short-sleeved T-shirt. I enlarged the image. Peeking out from the collar of Tony's shirt were tattoos. They were hardly noticeable, and if he hadn't had his arm around the man in the middle, his shirt might not have pulled in a way that would have shown them. The man in the middle had his arms folded, a pinky missing from his left hand.

What was Dad doing with these men? Especially with Tony? I clicked on Nobu Yamasaki to see where the tag would take me, and it revealed a simple profile with basic information. Nobu had a profile picture that was definitely my dad, but he had listed himself as a single man, divorced but no children, living in West Los Angeles. Was Dad dating other women while he was out there?

I thought I might throw up. Was Dad in the yakuza? Did he have something to do with my father's death? Had Dad been working with Mr. Tama? Could this have anything to do with what happened to me? He was supposed to love me. He was supposed to take care of me.

My throat felt closed off almost completely, and I could barely breathe. I tried to slow the thoughts pinging in my brain. What did this have to do with me? What would Dad have to gain if I were gone? He could have killed me at any time. Was there a reason to drag it out? Why me and not my brothers? The only thing that made me different was I was a girl. Why did that matter?

I was a girl. *That* was the difference.

In my father's notebook, he'd written an entry on how I was his only daughter. My father had been an extremely traditional man, and he had written about how he had put away money in my name for a dowry. He didn't say how much, but it might be worth killing me for, especially if it had been accruing interest for almost seventeen years.

If I was dead, I had to believe the money would go to my mom. And then, he could kill off the rest of my family, and he would walk away with whatever money was there.

But why all these events? Was it to throw suspicion onto someone else?

Before I could think of an answer to that, the office light flipped on.

I screamed and fell to the ground, my phone and the luggage tag paper tumbling to the floor next to me.

Dad stood at the door, pointing a gun at my head.

HIS FACE WAS gnarled in an angry expression, and then recognition seemed to set in as he realized it was me.

"What are you doing in here?" He lowered his gun.

I scrambled backward in a crab walk as fast as I could until my back hit one of the leather chairs, pushing it aside, and then the desk. My heart beat against my chest, pounding so hard it rang in my ears. "I know who you are," I said, my body shaking.

"I'm your dad." He slowly put the gun in his waistband at the back of his pajama pants. "And whatever you're thinking, I'm sure you're wrong." He took a step in my direction.

I tried to back up, but there was nowhere to go. "Don't come any closer!"

Dad held his empty hands up in surrender position. "I'm not going to hurt you, Claire. I promise. I love you."

A tear rolled down my cheek. I choked back a sob. "You've been lying this whole time. Why would I trust you now?"

He took another step closer.

"Stop!" I screamed, hoping to wake someone up.

Mom came running, eyes wide. "What's going—" She stopped when saw me on the floor. Her focus moved to the small of Dad's back where he'd placed the gun.

"I don't know exactly what she knows, but it's probably best if I handle this by myself." He waved her away.

She nodded, put her hand to her chest, and started to back up. How could she trust me with this man?

"Mom, don't leave me." I stared into her eyes, begging, pleading.

"You'll be okay," she said. "I don't know what's going on, but I have a guess. Just trust your dad." She nodded at Dad and continued backing into her room.

Was she in on this too? "Why did you send her away?"

Slowly, he lowered his hands to his sides. "Because this is about my relationship with you."

I reached for my phone, but his eyes caught me.

"Don't," he said, holding out a hand. "You need to trust me."

I stared into his dark eyes. "If you want me to trust you, you'd better start answering my questions, or I will call the police. I swear I will. And then I'll find a way to contact Tony Akiyama, and I'll tell him who you really are." The luggage tag paper was within reach, so I snatched it and waved it at him. "Does he know who you are? Does he think you're single? How many people are you lying to?"

Dad's eyes closed and his brows pinched together. He massaged the wrinkles on his forehead. "Go ahead. What do you want to know?"

Now that I had my chance, I didn't know where to start, didn't know if I really wanted to know what he would say. I'd been in this same position before, asking questions about my father, wanting to know more. Could I even trust him to tell me the truth?

"Do you have any tattoos?" The question wasn't the one burning at the front of my mind, but I needed to wade into the water slowly to see how deep I was willing to go. As much as I had loved my father, I knew the answers my dad might give me had the potential to rip my heart in ways that couldn't be fixed.

"I do. One on my hip."

No wonder I'd never seen it. "What kind of tattoo?"

"The Takata mon." He reached around his back and steadied his gun with his left hand. With his right, he tugged down the waistband of his flannel pajama pants and boxers to reveal our family crest, about two inches in diameter, low on his hip.

Relief washed over me, allowing me to steady my nerves. "Have you ever killed anyone?"

Dad paused for much longer than I expected. My sinking feeling plunged somewhere even deeper and darker. Too many times, my gut had told me all of his business trips didn't make sense, but I could never come up with a realistic answer for why that would be. Thinking he was a member of the yakuza still didn't make sense to me either, but what other explanation could there be?

"You don't deal in antiquities, do you?" I asked at last. He never seemed to bring any antiquities home. For all I knew, he'd never dealt with the Copper Cactus at all.

He didn't say anything. He only shook his head, confirming

what I'd known all along but never voiced, never truly wanted to know. My father and Dad, both involved in nefarious schemes. At least my father tried to right his wrongdoings. What kinds of horrible things had Dad done? But I was done asking questions. I knew all I needed to know.

Dad reached out slowly and grabbed the back of one of the leather chairs, sliding it closer to him. He glanced through the glass of the french doors, and then pulled them closed.

My heart thundered. I stared at my feet, and hugged my knees to my chest, the paper wilting in my hand. A stabbing pain tore through me. I had loved and trusted a man I'd never really known at all.

He perched himself at the chair's edge and scooted it closer to me. "Claire, I need you to look at me."

My shaking body stayed frozen in the same spot, but I let my eyes drift up.

"Do you trust me?" he asked.

I swallowed hard. "I thought I did, but I don't know," I said and shifted my focus to the floor.

"Do you know that I love you?" His voice was soft, and his expression sincere.

In the past, I'd known and never questioned it. I still wanted to think he loved me, but too much had happened. "I don't know."

"Claire, look at me." He said each word as if it were its own sentence.

I forced myself to raise my eyes until they met his.

"Do you *feel* that I love you?"

There was a slight tremble in his voice.

Whether he deserved it or not, I knew I loved him. Could

I trust myself to see what was really there rather than what I *wanted* to see?

Dad rested his hands on his knees, and his face was soft, crinkles at the corners of his eyes. When I bored my eyes into his, trying to glimpse his soul, I couldn't ignore the warmth that swelled inside of me. "Yes. I feel you love me."

He pointed to the other leather chair. "Then come sit next to me."

My legs wobbled as I stood. What was I doing? If I felt his love, did that also mean I trusted him? I slid the chair to its original position, and let myself sink into the leather.

Before he started to speak again, he eyed my closed fist and held out his hand. I gave him the scrap of paper with both names on it, and he set it on his lap. "I deal with some very dangerous people," he said in a soft voice. "People who trust me and consider me a friend. People who would hurt me and our family if they knew I wasn't who I say I am."

A small tear rolled down my cheek. "Who are you?" I asked in a voice that was barely audible. My knuckles had gone white from gripping the sides of the chair. "Who is Nobu Yamasaki?"

He closed his eyes and rubbed his forehead.

I thought of the autopsy report, and how my father had died. I hadn't let myself really *think* before about how something was suspicious with his death, and how even though the cause of death was listed as a heart attack, the manner of death was undetermined, which meant something else must have caused the heart attack, and it could've been medicine that caused it, or it could've been something he did on purpose.

Or it could have been *someone*.

My heart raced and my voice trembled. "Did you kill my father?"

He reached over and put his hand on my arm. His grip felt strong. "No," Dad said. "Claire, I loved your father. I love your mother. I love you and your brothers. I would never hurt any of you."

The room felt as if oxygen had become scarce. I tried to breathe, but my throat was too tight.

"Did someone else kill him?"

"Yes."

I had to ask again. I needed him to say it out loud. "Who— who are you?"

"I'm your dad." His voice was hushed. "And that won't ever change."

Some of the knots in my stomach began to loosen. I fixated on the trees outside the window. The sun had begun its rise, but it was still so dark. Every now and then the wind rustled the fading night, and a silhouetted leaf glided gently to the ground. I focused on a falling leaf, focused as if it was the most important thing in the world. My eyes traced the descending path, and by the time it fell below my view, I could breathe again.

His hand remained steady on my arm. "Claire, when your father died," he said, "I vowed to take down the man who did it. I had already been working with the government, but when he died, I switched divisions, and I am in very deep with the organization behind your father's murder. As far as they know, I roam between L.A. and San Francisco. To them, people like Tony Akiyama, I am Nobu Yamasaki. But if they found out who I really am, it would be bad for all of us."

He lifted his hand off my arm, took the crumpled paper tag from his lap and stared at it. "As Nobu, I am single and childless so no one tries to get to you to get to me. It's one of the ways I keep you safe. Your mother is the only other person who knows." His fingers curled around the tag until it disappeared in his fist. He raised his eyes to capture mine with a tight expression. "I need you to promise you won't say anything to anyone, including your brothers."

"I promise," I said. "Why are you only telling me?"

Dad moved his grip from my arm and rotated my chair so I was directly in front of him. He took both of my hands into his on my lap. "Because your brothers are content in their ignorance, but you are a much higher liability when you don't know something." He shook his head. "A real pain in the ass." He smiled. "I like to think you got that from me."

I bit my lip, then returned the smile. "I am your daughter."

"I'll tell your brothers soon," he said. "When the time is right."

I sat for a moment, taking in what Dad had said, my hands still in his. Could I believe him? My intuition said I could—that he'd never do anything to hurt us. And when I looked into his eyes, there was something there, even if I didn't have proof, something told me he loved me even though I had doubted him. Even though I'd made mistakes. That had to be proof. And it wasn't like the CIA had badges . . . did they?

The heaviness in the air lifted. If Dad wasn't working with Mr. Tama, then we should be safe.

"Dad, this should all be over, right? Now that Mr. Tama's been arrested?" I asked.

I noticed Dad's eyes were red and his face sagged. He sighed.

"I hope so, but I'm going to make sure I check out any other possibilities to make sure he wasn't working with anyone."

I let the chair swallow me. As I sank, I stared at the light on the ceiling, counting the dead bugs caught in the domed glass.

Mr. Tama could have been behind the cheating accusation. Maybe there had never been a student involved in the accusation in the first place like he'd suggested. Was he trying to ruin my life in every way possible? He must have known I wouldn't be allowed to play soccer if that happened, and when he saw how easy it was, he probably moved to the next thing. I'd already concluded getting into my locker would have been easy for him. In fact, I remembered it was his first day there, and he was late to class. He could have stolen my pictures before he'd gotten to the room.

On the day I received the eyeballs, he'd actually stopped me on the way in and said he wanted to speak to me. That's probably when he slipped the box into my backpack—probably a little trick he learned in prison. He'd seen me take off running after class. Maybe he thought I was already on to him. Had he left school and chased me down in the black SUV when I hadn't met him in the faculty lounge? And then run me down in the white car later? Obviously he broke in to my room and started the fire because that's what led me to him in the first place. It seemed possible he could have done everything by himself, although how would he know about all the Japanese superstitions? How did he choose the Japanese song?

A thought made me bolt upright. "Do you think he had ties to the yakuza? Maybe he met someone in prison. How else would he have known about all the Japanese stuff?"

Dad had reclined in the seat next to me and stretched out

his legs to the side of my chair. The back of the chair supported his neck, and his eyes were half closed. "If he had ties, I would have known about it because he would've been on my radar a long time ago."

I sat up and folded my legs under me in the chair. "How could the school even hire someone like that?" Weren't there laws to protect us—to make sure this exact thing didn't happen?

Dad stayed in the same position but scrubbed the sleep from his eyes so he could look at me. "He did everything he was supposed to do. He was only eighteen when he was arrested and charged for credit card theft." He gestured with his left hand, up and down, in a chopping motion. "He was sentenced to three years, but he worked with a group called the Waiawa Circle of Friends, who helped him petition the governor to get a pardon, and after that his record was expunged."

I gazed out the window. The sun had moved higher. The sky was gray, washed with pockets of pale blue. I expected to feel happier, knowing the man who had stalked me and sent me such nasty "presents" was behind bars. But something wasn't right.

I couldn't stop questions from poking at me. I rose from my chair and wandered to the window. "So if my father is dead, why come after me? Why now, and why me, and not my brothers?" I asked, glancing back.

Dad grabbed the ends of the armrests and pulled himself upright, folding his legs back toward him. "I'm not sure why he chose you, but it could have been as simple as you were the one he had the most access to because he was your teacher." He removed his gun from the back of his waistband and checked the safety before he set it on his desk.

Before long, he was next to me, his expression pensive. "When a person feels like he's been wronged, he can lash out in ways that don't necessarily make sense." Dad shifted his focus to something beyond me. "From what I've seen since your father died, there isn't a statute of limitations for revenge. Sometimes the desire to make things fair or right only gets stronger over time. Sometimes this gets expressed in irrational ways."

Even with all the evidence, I still couldn't imagine Mr. Tama trying to hurt me, much less trying to kill me. I knew it sounded naive, but I still had to ask. "What do you think he was planning to do to me?"

"I don't know." Dad put his arm around my shoulder and tugged me close enough that he could rest his chin on the top of my head. "I don't even want to think about it. I'm just glad you and the rest of the family are all safe."

"Me too." I wrapped my arms around his waist, and we stared out into the street, facing the mountains as the sun climbed higher above the peaks. The window glowed a slightly greenish tint in the rays from a film Dad had specially ordered so our windows on the first floor would be resistant to baseballs or rocks. "That special film you had put on the windows? It wasn't because you were afraid one of us would throw a ball or something at it and accidentally break it."

"No."

"Are they bulletproof?"

"Yes." He rubbed his hand along my arm. "But in the event of a fire, the structure will change, and you'll be able to break through. Otherwise, no."

Silence hung in the air. There were so many things I had

yet to learn about my dad. About our house. About our past.
About our futures.

"Claire, what were you thinking when you broke in to his classroom? Why didn't you come to me first?" His chin dug into me when he exhaled a tired breath. "Never mind. After this morning, I think I understand what was going through your mind." He lifted his head from mine and pointed to the side of his head with the arm that wasn't around me. "Do you see this gray hair?" he asked. "It has your name written all over it."

"I know." I dropped my cheek into his side, so I didn't have to look at him. "I'm sorry."

"The good news is we know who did this, and we can get on with our lives."

"That is good news," I said, but my stomach ached. I didn't understand how Mr. Tama's hatred could be so strong.

Dad took me by the shoulders and rotated me until I faced him. "Claire, for my peace of mind as well as our family's, I'm going to make sure Mr. Tama acted alone. For a time, I worried whatever is going on had more to do with me and what I do, but none of this is in line with anyone I have relationships with. And from what I've gathered, my cover is still solid. I promised I would keep you safe, and I have resources to do that. But even if this is over, there's always a possibility of danger because of what I do. If I ever think it's too much of a risk to stay here, I may have to move you guys to a safer place. I've been lining one up."

"Move? Forever?"

He stepped closer and hugged me. "If I have to. The most important thing is we're all safe, but there's nothing to worry about yet. I'm going to be taking a few trips soon to make sure, but I really believe none of the people I or your father associated with have any idea who I am or where our family is."

I nodded. I understood, really, but the idea of having to leave everything here, everyone, brought an anxiety that made it hard to think. What would that mean for me and Forrest?

"Dad?" A lump formed at the back of my throat. "Promise me you'll be safe. I don't want anything to happen to you."

The sound of his laughter rippled through me as his body shook against my cheek. He pulled away, still holding on to my shoulders. "I promise. The closest I've come to having my cover blown is by my teenage daughter."

"Was that supposed to make me feel better?" If I came that close, who knew what could happen?

Dad folded his arms. "I hate to brag, but I'm good at what I do. Scary good. So I'm certain you'd give most agents a run for their money." He exhaled. "But let's not try and find out."

I WAS SURPRISED how many students hadn't heard about Mr. Tama by the time school started Monday morning. An announcement was made over the loudspeaker. No one mentioned his arrest. All the principal said was Mr. Tama needed to take a leave of absence.

The halls filled with whispers and murmuring about what had happened to Mr. Tama anyway. I heard students say he'd embezzled money. Others said there was a family emergency, that he was dealing drugs, or had been caught sleeping with one of the students while at one of the debate tournaments. They were the kinds of things I had expected.

I walked into the US History classroom with a heavy heart and took my seat at the back. No matter how hard I tried, I couldn't shake the same thoughts about him. Mr. Tama was a good teacher. I actually enjoyed his class. How could he be the same person who wanted to hurt me? The governor wouldn't have pardoned him if he hadn't really changed. But what plagued my mind the most was why I kept trying to defend him.

"Hey, Claire," Mumps knocked on my desk.

My head shot up. "Oh, hey." I hadn't even seen him approach.

He plopped himself into Forrest's desk and scooted until our desks butted against each other. "So I was thinking we should get together and work on our project," he said. "Maybe after school at your house today?"

I thought through my schedule and everything else that was going on. Dad was out of town again, and Mom would be at the office. As long as Parker was home, I didn't think my parents would mind.

"That should work," I said.

"Cool. I'll see you then." Mumps pushed Forrest's desk away and strolled back to the front, his arms swinging.

The seats around me filled. I waved to my teammates, and Forrest arrived. It surprised me how happy I was to see him even though I had seen him on the way to school today and between class periods and, of course, every day we had this class together.

He kissed my forehead before he sat down. "Who do you think our teacher's going to be?"

I shrugged.

Everyone was in their seats when Coach Cesar walked in. He stood in front of the class with his feet shoulder-width apart and his arms folded. "I'm going to fill in for Mr. Tama until a replacement is found."

He looked around the classroom. "Pelo."

Katie sat straight and glanced up with questioning eyebrows. "Yes?"

"Why don't you lead us in the discussion?"

Her eyes wandered around to the other students, confused and unsure.

Coach pointed at me and Lanie. "Takata. Ward." He pointed at Kimi and Mika and Ashley next. "Miyashima squared. Cheung. You guys help her out."

We all gave each other wide-eyed, raised-brow expressions. What were we supposed to do? We'd just finished a section and had a test right before the Halloween dance, so we were all at a loss as to what Mr. Tama had been planning next. I hoped for Nicholas's sake that Coach wasn't replacing Mr. Tama for the debate team too.

We could probably work on our projects, but I wasn't in the mood to do anything. I raised my hand. "Maybe we should have a study hall today."

He nodded. "Good idea, Takata. You guys can take care of yourselves, right?" Everyone agreed, and he left, even though I'm positive he wasn't supposed to do that.

Katie burst into laughter when the door closed. "Did that really just happen?" She turned to me. "Thanks. I don't know what I would've done if you hadn't suggested that."

I shrugged. "I got your back."

No one studied, but it was nice to have a break. I rested my head on the desk.

Forrest scooted his desk over until it touched mine. He smoothed the wrinkles on my forehead with a soft touch. "What's wrong?"

I gazed at Mr. Tama's desk. "I don't feel good about what happened."

"Do you regret turning him in?"

"No," I said. "But something doesn't feel right. It was too easy."

"That doesn't seem like something to complain about."

"I guess not."

He reached over and rubbed my back. "You trusted him. Give it some time."

After school got out, Nicholas met Fed and me at the school's entrance.

"Wish me luck." Fed slung his messenger bag over his shoulder and headed in the opposite direction toward the gym.

"Good luck," I said even though I didn't know where he was going.

"Where is everyone?" I asked. Forrest had said he'd meet me at the car, but where were my brothers?

Nicholas held open the door. "Avery's at basketball tryouts with Fed. The rest of the guys are at the Suburban."

"How is it everyone else knows so much more about what my family is doing than I do?" I asked.

"Because it's hard for girls to keep too much information in their heads at one time," Nicholas said. "We keep things from you to make your life easier." He laughed and ducked out of reach before I could punch him.

"Don't even start with me." I knew all he wanted was a reaction, but I was in no mood to deal with the sexism he thought of as "jokes." I should feel better about Mr. Tama, but I didn't, and I didn't understand why. If this was what I wanted, why was guilt tying my insides in knots?

"Aw, you know I only say it because you're so easy to rile up." He ruffled my hair, and I flicked his hat to the ground.

We had to dodge a few careless drivers to make it to the Russos' Suburban, where Parker and Forrest were waiting for us. Then Nicholas dropped me and Parker off, and Forrest promised to come over after he had grabbed something to eat.

"I've gotta pick up a poster board from the store, and then I'll be there in a little bit too," Nicholas said.

Parker hurried ahead of me into the house, but I took my time.

Even though there wasn't a wind, the air pinched at my skin, and I wrapped my scarf tighter around me. The sky was bright and calm. A snowstorm must be coming.

Inside the front door, I took off my shoes. The house was quiet. I knew we were safe, and the quietness was because my parents were at work, but an uneasy feeling washed over me.

But I couldn't let myself worry. Instead, I walked up the stairs and to my room. I opened the window facing Forrest's room and let the fresh air sweep through. Outside, the neighborhood was calm, quiet. I lay down on the bed and gazed at the ceiling.

Everything was still. I closed my eyes, wondering if the unease I was feeling was actually peace I couldn't recognize. The worries about Mr. Tama were still bubbling, but a lot of the noise that had clouded my head for weeks had finally started to wane.

A clunk sounded from down the hall. "Parker?" I called out. No one answered. "Parker, what are you doing?"

The back door opened and closed. "Parker?" I called out again.

"It's me," Forrest said. His steps approached up the stairs.

Over the past decade, we had seen each other almost every day, never growing tired of one another. It seemed somewhat of a miracle that after all these years, a relationship could grow into something surprising.

Forrest smiled at the door, then situated himself beside me, scooting on my bed until my shoulder and side were snug against his. "What are you thinking about?" He twined his fingers with mine.

"You," I said.

He waited for me to elaborate.

I pondered some more. "What would you have done if I hadn't kissed you back?"

"Cried." Laughing, he loosened his hand from mine so he could turn on his side and face me. "I would have tried the next day, and the next, until we were old . . . or you got a restraining order."

I brushed back some hair from his face and rested my hand on his cheek. Training my eyes on his, I leaned in and kissed him. He reeled me against him with a firm hand and kissed me back hard, as if trying to make up for lost time.

My skin flushed with heat, burning at his touch. Remembering a time when this wasn't the most natural thing in the world was hard.

As my hands explored the muscles in his arms, his back, his chest, a perfect breeze floated through the window and into my lungs. He let a soft moan escape when I kissed his neck and bit at his ear. Even though I thought I knew everything about him, there were suddenly mysteries and things undiscovered. I'd surprised myself with how unafraid I was despite the risk of everything and how I could let go of any anxiety that I wasn't as practiced. Maybe he'd done this many times before, but he had a way of making me feel like he was experiencing everything for the first time too. His hands tangled in my hair, brushed the skin on my neck, traced the curves of my hips. I could have kissed him forever.

The doorbell rang.

Forrest pulled back, fighting for breath. "Let Parker get it." He crushed his mouth against mine. The doorbell rang again.

I threw back my head. "Ugh. It's probably Mumps. We're supposed to work on our history project together tonight."

Forrest's face tensed.

Reluctantly, I climbed off the bed and combed through my hair with my fingers. The room had grown colder, so I closed the window. "Come on. You can study with us." I leaned in one last time and crushed my lips against his and let them linger. Grabbing his hands, I pulled him up, still sneaking little pecks as we walked toward my bedroom door.

At the door, Forrest pulled away and straightened his shirt. "There's something about this guy that . . . I don't even want to be in the same room with him. And I can't stand the way he talks to you—like he thinks he's so funny. I'm funny, right? That monkey joke I tell is really funny."

I started to laugh. "Yes. You're very funny." Mumps was too, but Forrest was the kind of adorable funny that had won over my heart. "I picked you, remember?" I kissed him again.

I tugged him down the stairs, reminding him every few steps with kisses and assurances that this was only a history project. By the time I answered the front door, I was almost out of breath.

Mumps stood on our porch wearing a black long-sleeved shirt and a black leather biker jacket that was almost as tattered as his jeans. "Hey, girlfriend." He handed me a bouquet of white flowers.

Confused, I hurried and took the flowers from him, crushing the cellophane in my anxious grip. "Uh, thanks. You really didn't need to bring flowers for a homework assignment."

He looked over at Forrest. "What's up," Mumps said and took off his shoes. "I didn't realize you'd be here."

"I'm sure you didn't," Forrest mumbled.

I needed to say something to Mumps about Forrest, and I had meant to say something, but I hadn't pictured saying something with both of them there, in a situation where Mumps had just called me girlfriend and handed me flowers. It's not like I'd ever been in this position before, and I didn't want to say anything that sounded too presumptuous to Mumps. For all I knew, he was flirty with lots of girls. I'd only told Mumps not too long ago Forrest and I were just friends. Would he think I'd been lying to him?

And I loved Forrest — in a new way now — but introducing him as my boyfriend still felt like trying to speak a foreign language for the first time. After shifting and going in circles in my head, I grabbed Forrest's hand and tugged him forward.

"So . . . Forrest and I aren't really complicated anymore." Had that sounded as stupid as I was pretty sure it had?

Forrest let go of my hand and stepped to the side. "Maybe you should clarify what you mean by that."

Could he possibly have made the situation more awkward? And if Forrest thought I didn't catch the pleasure he was taking out of watching me squirm, he was wrong.

This wasn't even a big deal. Why was saying the word "boyfriend" so hard? I hadn't used it in reference to Forrest to anyone yet, not even when I told my dad. What if we broke up tomorrow?

We *weren't* breaking up tomorrow. I inhaled a deep breath of air. "I mean . . . What I mean to say is I kissed Forrest. We kissed. He kissed me." That sounded so stupid I wanted to hide under a rock.

Mumps narrowed his eyes. "So you're saying Forrest is your boyfriend?"

"Yes. That." I exhaled. "Let's go work on our project."

"Ooookay," Mumps said.

Forrest took my hand, and we walked toward the kitchen. On the way, he leaned close to my ear. "Now that wasn't so hard, was it?"

I glared at him. He knew I wasn't good at stuff like that. I'd spent a lifetime of *not* sharing anything too personal with anyone in my family for my entire life. Sharing things with people I didn't know very well was a big leap. For me, anyway.

Mumps followed us into the kitchen. I let go of Forrest's hand and hurried and set the flowers on the far corner of the counter so they were farther out of view. Forrest had left his backpack by mine at the back door. He grabbed both our bags and brought them to the kitchen table.

I sat next to Mumps and took a notebook from my backpack. Forrest sat on the other side of me.

"We need to write a newspaper article supporting our arguments for the Federalists, so I was thinking we could brainstorm four arguments together," I said. "And then we each take two and work on finding support for the arguments."

"Sounds like a plan," Mumps said. He dropped his history textbook on the table. "We can write up our two paragraphs and then put them together for the article, but we also have to defend them to other people in the class. How do you want to handle that part?"

My phone rang. I fished around my backpack and pulled it out. Nicholas. "Sorry," I said to Mumps. "I'm sure it'll be quick."

"Go ahead," Mumps said. "I've got time."

I answered the call. "What's up?"

"I'm trying to reach Parker," Nicholas said, "but he's not answering."

"He's probably sleeping." I stood and walked out of the room so I wouldn't bother anyone.

"What are you doing?" he asked. "Can you do me a favor since your brother's useless?"

"Depends on what it is," I said and sat on the couch in the living room. "I'm working on something with Mumps."

Nicholas went silent. I thought the call had dropped. "Nicholas?"

"What is he doing there?" he asked.

"We're partners on a history project," I said.

"Why would you ask him to be your partner?" he said.

"I didn't," I said. "He asked me while I was in the hospital. I didn't have much to do with it." I put both feet on the coffee table.

"Why would he ask you?" Nicholas asked, his voice tense.

I felt my chest inflate. "Why *wouldn't* he ask me?"

"Because he's friends with Chase. I can't stand the guy."

"So you're *not* friends with him?"

"Hell no," he said. "They're both on the debate team with me, and I've never met two more arrogant people."

"Why didn't you say anything when he was at the party at our house?" I asked.

"He was at your house? I never saw him there." Nicholas

growled, "Because if I had, I seriously would have had some words with him. That very morning he said he had to miss our debate tournament because he was going out of town after school and would be gone all weekend."

Maybe there were too many people there. Now that I thought about it, I had no idea who would have even invited Mumps. Katie hadn't, and it was originally her party. As far as I knew, the only one who knew him remotely well was me, and I know I hadn't invited him.

As I processed the information, a lump ballooned at the back of my throat. I sat up and set my feet on the ground.

I hurried to my dad's office and closed the doors behind me. "On the day I got into the accident, you were at the debate tournament," I whispered, "which means Mr. Tama would have been there too, right?"

"'Course he was there. He's our coach." He paused. "And that means Mr. Tama wasn't the one who crashed into your car."

I had been so focused on the evidence against Mr. Tama. I'd been so sure—at least I thought I was, until now. Either Mr. Tama was completely innocent, or he had help.

To steady myself, I pressed my hand on the back of one of the leather chairs. "Mumps could have stolen pictures from my locker," I said, words tripping over each other. "He could have put the white box in my backpack. He was probably the person Chase was looking for the night of the party, and he could have broken into my room and stolen my uniform, and if he wasn't at the tournament the day of my accident . . ."

"Go wake up Parker," Nicholas said. "Is anyone else there?"

"Forrest," I said, my voice tight.

"I'm at the store, but I'm coming over right now."

"Okay," I said in barely a whisper. "I'm going to go get Parker, and then we'll get Mumps out of here."

I opened the office doors. My mind felt heavy with confusion, my feet heavy with hesitation. I willed myself to go back to the kitchen, where I collided with Mumps.

"Is everything okay?" he asked. "I was coming to check on you."

"There's actually been a family emergency," I said, struggling to keep my voice even. "I'm sorry, but you're going to have to leave. Can we reschedule?"

"Yeah, no problem," he said. He lowered his eyes. "Is there something I can do? I can stay and help." He looked concerned, but it felt false.

"I appreciate the offer, but I really need you to go." I pushed myself around him and into the kitchen. "Let me help get your stuff."

Forrest caught my expression and stood. "Is everything okay? Who called?"

"Uh, something happened to my mom," I said.

From the way Forrest looked at me, I could tell he knew I was lying, so he didn't ask more questions.

I handed Mumps his backpack, and he put his textbook inside. Practically shoving him outside, I said, "I'll be in touch," and closed the door. I turned the deadbolt and struggled with the chain lock. Forrest lifted it from my shaking hands and slid it into place.

I ran to the kitchen and grabbed the flowers off the counter. I hadn't paid much attention when Mumps had handed them to me.

Peeling back the cellophane and tissue paper, I found four white flowers. Four. Shi. The homophone for death. White, the color of death. A tag hung from a ribbon tied around the middle of the bouquet. I turned it around.

My name was there, written in red. Red, like the color they used for people's names on gravestones.

Forrest wrapped his arms around me, tucking me to his chest. "What's wrong?"

I swallowed a cry. "It's not over. I need to call my dad."

Something landed upstairs with a thunk.

"Parker?" I shouted.

No one answered.

"Parker?" My stomach dropped. I ran to the base of the stairs. "Parker, you'd better answer me."

I dialed Dad's number. His phone rang and rang. I realized I couldn't remember the last time he'd actually answered the phone when he was on a business trip. He always called back, and usually it didn't take too long, but—voicemail answered.

How careful did I need to be? Were there bad people out there like Tony Akiyama who might hear my message? I didn't want to do anything to compromise Dad or our family, especially when I wasn't exactly sure what was going on, but Dad needed to know.

The tone sounded, and signaled me to begin. "Hello, I'm, uh, calling from the Copper Cactus and this message is to *Claire*-ify that the matter in regards to the Tama deal might not be finalized. It's possible something was missing from your order, but um, Calvin Harper can provide the information required. We did have a little scare there, but I really don't think it's anything to worry about. Mrs. *Parker* is mostly likely lying in wait to pounce on me for no good reason at all except to be annoying. At the present, the warehouse is filled with a *Forrest* of antique furniture, and I'm sure other items will be arriving in the *Nick* of time. But you should call when you have the chance. Good-bye."

That was stupid. I shouldn't have emphasized everyone's names. Why did I do that? Would he even know what I was talking about? Maybe he had a completely different cell phone he used in the field. I should have asked him when I had the chance. Wait. I'd left messages—normal messages—for Dad before when he was out of town, hadn't I?

Forrest stared at me, brows bunched. "What in the hell kind of a message was that?"

As I returned my phone to my back pocket, I realized no one else knew what Dad did, and I didn't have the time or permission to explain. "I'm under a little stress right now, if you can't tell. I think Mumps might have been the one who tried to run me over with the white car." Unless Parker answered me soon, I was going to hurt him. "Parker!" I shouted from the bottom of the stairs.

Forrest stayed close as I made my way toward the steps. My eyes scanned every shadow and dark corner.

"Parker, this isn't funny." I clutched Forrest's hand, gripping until the circulation left. My fingers searched blindly for the light switch in the hallway. The beats of my heart grew stronger.

"I swear I'm going to kill you if you jump out and try to scare me," I yelled. Each time silence responded, my stomach flipped. If Parker wasn't playing a joke on us, then . . . no, he had to be. No one would have had the chance to come into our house without one of us noticing.

Unless someone had gotten inside before we came home. I didn't want to even consider that. We'd already been through so much.

To my left, through my bedroom door, I could see my curtain flapping in a wind that rushed into the house. Had I not closed that window?

Forrest drew me nearer to his side.

I approached Parker's door past mine and turned the knob slowly.

I pushed open the door.

I looked at the floor.

And screamed.

THE FIRST THING I saw was Parker's limp body on the floor.

The next thing I saw was a red Japanese demon mask with horns and sharp teeth. A beat passed before reality sank in. I froze.

"What did you do to my brother?" I demanded. "Is he still alive? Mumps? Is that you?" I screamed as the intruder launched himself at me.

Out of instinct, Forrest countered and tackled him to the ground. The man grunted and broke free. He shoved Forrest off, but Forrest charged at him again. I broke out of my stupor and launched myself at his legs.

Neither of us saw the gun the man was holding.

When Forrest leaped at him, the man flung out his arm and hit Forrest across the face with a strong backhand with the hand holding the gun. Forrest went flying backward, landing at the top of the stairs.

Everything slowed as I turned on the floor, several feet away from the intruder, to watch Forrest. As his feet flipped over his head from the momentum, his body hit the staircase wall, which flipped him sideways. Then he rolled down the stairs until he crashed into the wall at the bottom.

"Forrest!" I screamed. Each thud punched me in the gut as his body hit the steps. Now he lay crumpled and still at the base of the stairs. The silence crippled everything inside me. I didn't know if Forrest was alive, but I knew part of *me* would die if he didn't get up.

Forrest didn't move.

I needed to get him help. If I tried to call 911, the intruder would reach me before I completed the call. I'd have to find a way to put more space between me and this monster.

A rush of heat flooded my chest. In order to get downstairs, I'd have to get past this demon—obstacle—blocking my path. I drew in a deep breath and tapped into my dad's voice, the one he used every Saturday morning to coach my self-defense moves. I stood from the floor with a new sense of bravery. I fixed my gaze on the deep void of the demon's dark eyes behind the mask.

What is the first thing you do when you're attacked?

I screamed and screamed. I yelled and called for help.

When he charged at me, I rolled to the side to lure him away from the stairs, but he was too fast. His elbow caught me across the chest and flung me on my back.

What are the most vulnerable parts of his body?

Pointing the gun at me, he tugged at the collar of his black turtleneck where a scratch across his neck trailed blood.

Then he adjusted the hood of his black sweatshirt and pulled it tighter around the mask. His body was shorter and thicker than Mumps—much closer to Chase's build. Had they been in this together with Mr. Tama?

Eyes, nose, ears, neck, groin, knee, and legs.

He had a gun. My only chance was to attack one of these areas.

"Chase?"

A spray of spit flew out of the mask's mouth with each exhalation. I could almost picture his hidden lips forming a sick smile as he reached down, yanked me to my feet by the front of my shirt, and directed the gun in my face.

"Why?" I swallowed back tears. "Why would you do this?"

A wicked laugh escaped from the mask's angry mouth, but he didn't answer. Now that I was under his control, he pointed down the stairs as if commanding me to walk down.

I glanced down at Forrest and then at Parker and felt my nerves strengthen, but my legs shook as I spoke. "No." I stiffened my back and willed myself straighter.

The man raised his weapon and pointed it at me. "Go," he said in a gruff voice—a voice I couldn't be sure, but thought I'd never heard before. Spit collected at the corners of his demon mouth.

I stared straight into the barrel and refused to budge. Whatever he was going to do to me, he would have to do it right here. Worse things could happen if I let him take me to another location. That's what Dad had said in our trainings. This was the time to fight back. Fragmented thoughts tore through my mind as I faced what would certainly be my final moments—would he hurt the rest of my family after me? Would Parker live? Forrest wasn't moving. Could I at least do enough damage to buy time and give everyone a better chance?

"Nicholas will be here any minute," I said, shutting down that line of thinking. "He'll never let you get away with this."

"Nicholas." He sneered.

"He'll call the police. He's big. He'll hurt you. He'll . . ." There was nothing Nicholas could do against a gun, and this man knew it too. If there was any chance of getting away, I needed to take it.

I turned and raced down the stairs, hoping he wouldn't shoot me. I missed a few steps. Stumbled on others, and had to jump Forrest. He bounded after me, almost tripping on Forrest's lifeless body.

I sprinted to the living room, whipping my phone out of my pocket to call 911, but as I reached the front door, he tackled me from behind. The phone flew from my grasp, crashing to the floor and shattering as it landed. I wriggled from his grasp and grabbed a lamp on the end table next to the couch. He started to stand as I swung at his head. His body collapsed in front of the door.

Almost immediately, he tried to rise, the mask still attached to his face. Balancing himself on one knee, his head swayed.

I didn't stop to see if he recovered—I ran past Dad's study and into my parents' bedroom, where I searched for a place to hide.

Under the bed.

In their closet.

Through the window.

But I couldn't break through on the first floor. And they weren't made to be opened. I couldn't think straight. My heart pounded and my hands shook.

I tore into their bathroom and climbed in the cabinets beneath their sink. I had used this as a hiding place before, as a kid, but was surprised and grateful that I still fit. I shut the door as quietly as I could and scooted to the back.

As I had done many times when I was younger, I sat on the left side and grabbed the toilet-paper rolls on the right to build a wall in front of me. My hands trembled, and I worried I was making too much noise. It felt like the loud thumping of my heart might give me away.

His footsteps grew closer, and as they did, I could hear his voice singing. The tempo was slow, and his voice was low and mournful.

"Ue o muite arukou . . ." The melody grew louder as he opened doors and searched around.

First the coat closet, then my dad's study.

My parents' bedroom door creaked as it swung wider.

Their closet door opened. The hangers swished and the clothes ruffled.

The comforter and sheets crumpled. I could picture him searching in the bed. And then underneath.

His shoes tapped against the bathroom floor as he crossed closer to the sink. His song grew stronger, the tempo remaining slow, but my blood coursed faster and faster.

The shower-curtain rings scraped against the metal rod as they slid from one side to the other.

The cabinet door where I was hiding opened. I froze behind

my toilet-paper wall, holding my breath, and struggling so that a whimper didn't escape.

The door closed. I wanted to exhale, but didn't dare.

And then the singing stopped. His footsteps faded. Everything was silent.

I began to breathe again. A minute passed. And then another. I didn't dare move.

The cabinet door ripped open. My toilet-paper wall crashed as his hand broke through. He yanked me out by the hair.

I struggled against him, punching and kicking, as he dragged me out of the bedroom, still pulling me by the hair. At the edge of the kitchen, he grabbed me from behind by the waist.

I dropped my weight and twisted my torso to connect my elbow to his head. He fell backward, but grabbed the back of my shirt and pulled me to the ground with him. Pain jolted through my body. I bit his hand. I gouged into the mask's eyeholes.

He let out a sharp yelp as I sent a hard kick to his left knee and then followed the kick with an elbow to the throat. His gun skated across the floor.

But the demon recovered quickly and charged at me. He caught my shoulder and upended me on the ground. Before I had the chance to catch myself, my chin hit the hardwood floor, my teeth crashing against each other with a loud crack. I flipped onto my back. He crawled closer and straddled me. With his arms pinning my shoulders, and his face so close I could smell tobacco on his breath, I delivered a head butt to the mask.

My forehead exploded in regret.

A deep, throaty snarl erupted behind the mask's sharp fangs. Blood flowed down the side of the demon's mouth. As I reeled in pain, he got up and retrieved the gun and lunged at me, propelled by feral fury.

The front of my head screamed, but I jumped to my feet and charged to the back door. But the door was locked — I'd locked the door. It took time to unlock it, precious seconds that slowed me down. As I pulled the door open and took a step, he caught up and tackled me again. With my stomach against the ground, I pawed at his tight grip.

A sharp pain exploded on the back of my head. The world around me became gray and ragged shadows.

I wasn't out entirely, but I wasn't entirely conscious either. I could tell what he was doing, but everything was fuzzy. Out of the corner of my eye, I saw him take something out of his coat pocket, with which he tied my hands and feet behind me. I struggled to break free. His footsteps faded into the kitchen. The door leading into the garage opened. Then shut.

The sound of his shoes treading toward me grew louder.

A cloth covered my mouth.

The odor was sweet and chemical and made everything even fuzzier.

When I woke, I wasn't sure how much time had passed. My cheek was flush against the floor by our back door. The room spun. I didn't know if he expected me to be conscious, so I closed my eyes and lay still, too groggy to do anything anyway. With enough time, whatever he gave me would wear off, and I'd have a better chance of freeing myself from whatever he had used to bind me.

Before long, he returned and tied something around my mouth that forced me to suppress a gag. He hefted me onto his shoulder and headed to the unlit garage, where he dropped me into the trunk area of a black SUV.

Inside, I could feel myself rolling over another body that lay still at my back. Forrest? I couldn't speak around the gag to call to him.

I opened my eyes long enough to take in our surroundings. With the two of us in there, the space was cramped because the seats weren't laid down, and there wasn't enough room to turn and see who was locked in there with me.

Although I tried to tell myself it wasn't Forrest, the only picture that filled my imagination was his lifeless body at the bottom of the stairs.

Dad would tell me to try to kick out the taillights so a cop might pull over the driver or someone could see me through the hole, but they were impossible to reach. Every time I moved, the rope chewed into me. A moan escaped my lips.

The man growled, and I knew he'd discovered I was awake. Within a minute, the cloth returned to my face. I swept my head from side to side, held my breath, and tried to fight. But the scent was sweet.

And then there was only darkness.

MY SKIN PRICKLED as if small shards of ice stabbed from all angles. Every muscle tensed. I struggled to open the heavy and swollen lids of my eyes. As moonlight fell on them, I winced.

How long had I been unconscious?

The first thing I saw was high, broken windows — I seemed to be in some sort of dusty industrial room, lit only by the bright moonlight falling in from outside. Tipping my head backward to this view as I awoke, my neck could barely hold any weight. The back of my head felt as if a jackhammer had pounded on it. I tried to move anyway, but my hands were numb, bound behind a cold metal seat, my ankles tied to the legs of a chair.

The room smelled of rusted metal and old motor oil. Stretching my neck, I saw layers of dust blanketing old engines. Propellers, wings, parts with gauges, and large pipes cluttered the floor in front of me. I was in an abandoned warehouse or factory somewhere, filled with airplane parts. This room was huge, maybe a hangar of some kind.

Unlikely we were anywhere near home. Were we anywhere *anyone* could hear? Images of Forrest on the stairs loomed in my head. I opened my mouth to scream.

The safety of a gun clicked behind my head. I clapped my mouth closed.

"Scream. No one will hear you, Kimiko." The man spoke in a low, raspy voice.

Kimiko.

"How do you know my middle name?" I asked.

He sneered and freed an evil laugh.

The man walked around, leaning in closer until the mask was only an inch from my face. I tried to stare him down, but the muscles in my neck gave way, and I lowered my head.

Untying the strings of the mask with one hand, the man lifted it from his face with the other. He threw it to the ground, pulled back his hood, and dragged the zipper down. The hoodie fell from his shoulders, revealing a black fitted T-shirt. He slipped his arms from the hoodie sleeves, letting it fall to his feet.

In front of me stood a Japanese man. From the gray in his hair, I guessed him to be in his sixties. Every muscle from his neck down his arms was sculpted, stretched over sun-spotted skin, but even more toned than my dad's. Beneath the tight fabric of his shirt was a sculptured chest and abs.

"I know more about you dan you know about yourself." He shuffled away across the dirty concrete floor, kicking up dust clouds until he was a good twenty feet from me. Resting a worn boot on a stray piece of machinery, he lit a cigarette. The embers glowed a fiery red in the darkness. With each drag, my heart accelerated faster.

"Who are you?" I asked, my voice trembling.

He stared upward, watching the smoke dissipate into nothing. "Jiro Arakaki," he said, emphasizing each syllable.

But the name meant nothing to me.

"This is a mistake," I said, shivering. "You must think I'm someone else."

His head snapped in my direction, and he slid his boot from the machinery, letting it thud as it landed. With slow steps, he crossed the floor, one boot stomping, a pause, and then the other, decreasing the distance between us. Thud. Pause. Thud. "No." Thud. Pause. Thud. He drew even closer, surveying me with creepy eyes.

Each thud—each pause—echoed in the hollow space, making my heart hammer in sync.

"Dis no mistake. I know who you are, Kudayah."

The way he said my name punched me in the gut. *Kudayah.* Only my mom's family in Japan had struggled to say Claire that much. Did he know my father? My dad?

He puffed his cheeks and blew in my face. His tobacco breath warmed my skin but made my eyes water.

Something rustled to my side maybe three feet away. I dropped my head to find Nicholas unconscious on a flatbed cart, bound and gagged. His flannel shirt was ripped, and I could see his bare chest. He barely moved, and from the bruises on his body, I could tell he was badly beaten.

"Let him go!" I cried. "You don't want him. You want me. Do whatever you want to me, but please . . . let him go!"

The Japanese man stared at me and smirked as if he took pleasure in my anguish.

"Let him go!" I screamed. "Why are you doing this?"

"Honor." The word rolled off his tongue with little effort. He leaned his head back and closed his eyes.

"How can this possibly have anything to do with honor?"

"Do you know who I am?" he asked.

"You're yakuza," I said in a quiet voice.

"Stupid, stupid girl." A wicked smile crossed his face. "Do you have any idea the kinds of things your father did? Do you know how long I waited for dis moment?" He paced around the chair and puffed the cigarette. Small spirals of smoke left his nostrils and rose in the air, drifting to the ceiling.

"Do you know who I am?" he asked again, so close I could see the wrinkles on his forehead stretch wide when he spoke. I choked on his smoke-filled breath as he glared and asked, "Do you know who *you* are?"

Claire Takata. Daughter of loving parents. Devoted sister. Loyal friend.

He struck me with the back of his hand, the force almost tipping the chair I was tied to. The sting sent a burning shiver down the side of my face.

"Answer me," he said. His voice was soft—quiet, like the purple sky before a snowstorm. He paced around, waiting for my answer.

Did *he* have any idea the kinds of things my father did? How he'd left behind a life of violence to have a better life, to leave a legacy for us, where decisions were our own and not the dictates of someone else's idea of loyalty or obedience?

I lifted my head, my hands behind my back, hidden from his view. "I am a child," I said. The thought of my father made me struggle to get free, but the rope cut into my wrists. I swallowed hard and tried again.

I thought of Nicholas on the cart. Fed. Mom and Dad. Parker. Avery.

Forrest.

Desperate to locate an escape, I scanned the gray brick walls. Mr. Arakaki blew smoke in my face again. I coughed as the taste hit my mouth and made my eyes burn. His shirt smelled rancid, and every time he moved, the smell of stale urine mixed with vinegar, sulfur, and rotting vegetables filled the air.

"I tell you why you are here," he said. He stood and corrected his posture as if readying himself for a speech. "Almost three decades ago—"

"I don't care!" I yelled. I jerked my shoulders and tried to break free. "Help! Help! Somebody help me! Somebody—"

He slammed the back of his hand against my cheek. The chair rocked and almost fell over. The jolt made my head pound harder. I tried to hold back tears, but the salty liquid slid down my throat.

He clenched his yellow, rotten teeth and tapped a finger on my forehead. "Don't try dat again." He straightened himself. "Years ago I have daughter named Kimiko—just like you. I run a dry-cleaning business, and your father show up on first business day of every month at 8:00 A.M. to collect protection money."

His eyes shifted to the wall behind me, and for a moment his face softened. "My wife and I have Kimiko when we were only teenagers. We work hard to make a living. I gave a lot of money to your father, but I never complain. We had daughter, and I do anything to protect my family."

Though his English was broken and hard to understand at

times, every phrase flowed as if it had been rehearsed for many years. "One day my wife collapse. The doctor told me she would die of brain cancer. She argued to me, but I willing to do anything to save her."

A few patches of hair peeked through his half-buttoned shirt. He tugged at a thick gold chain around his neck. "We use all our money, but she died. Just as doctor said she will do."

His shoulders slumped forward.

"On first day of month, your father came, but I didn't have the money," he said, shoulders still sagging. "I promise he have payments by end of month, and I thought he have pity for me because he left. But I was fool. They came back and tore apart our house."

Tears slid down his face, but he pressed on with determination. "My Kimiko work at bakery after school, but she never came home dat day. Police call and say she in hospital. Someone hit her on her bicycle with car. They haven't kill her. They just hit her hard enough to send warning. I beg your father and promise to get money even if I have to steal." He opened his hand in the air, then closed it as if trying to catch something.

He clenched his fist and moved his face nearer to mine — close enough I could see dirt in his pores, his stained teeth, his soulless dark eyes.

"By next day I have enough money from family dat I able to pay debt," he said. "But first of the month came too soon. And your father came to store. I have only half of the payment ready for him. Kimiko would get paycheck next day. But your father become angry."

He grabbed my shoulders and shook until I thought my neck

might snap. "Your father hit me so hard I fall to floor. He yell and say his boss grow impatient because I always late. The next night they burn a doll, dressed in Kimiko's clothes, on doorstep of our house."

Arakaki-san hung his head, chin against his chest, as if still experiencing the humiliation he'd endured so many years ago. "And then I receive envelope, filled with pictures of Kimiko at work and school, and pictures of her with friends. All their faces crossed out." His chest heaved. "I promised to protect her."

His voice grew quiet. "For weeks we scared. And then she was gone. I run to Miya's house. But Miya missing too. I search all night, knocking on doors, but no one had seen them. My Kimiko have just become eighteen."

The tears turned to sobbing as he relived the events of that fateful day. "Kimiko Arakaki and Miya Okano. Eighteen years old and best friends. Always together from day they met. Found in abandoned warehouse. Both shot. Both dead."

ARAKAKI-SAN WIPED TEARS from his face with the dirty sleeve of his sweatshirt.

"Your father is coward." His finger stabbed my chest. "He disappear right after dat. His boss give up trying to find him after only few years, but *I* motivated by something much stronger dan money."

He took another drag of his cigarette and exhaled. The wisps of smoke hung in the air, before melting into the nothingness above us.

"Nicholas." I looked at my friend, then turned to the man. "Please let him go. Do what you want with me . . . just let him go."

Nicholas, who must have woken up in the last few minutes of this exchange, moaned through his gag, his eyes begging me not to ask for such a trade.

"Quiet!" the man shouted. He pressed his lips together. Deep wrinkles marked the sides of his mouth.

But I couldn't let Nicholas go through this for my sake. "Don't do this. Don't bring shame to Kimiko's name." I twisted and again the rope burned into my wrists.

"Quiet!" the jaded man shouted again. Spit flew in every direction. "What do you know about shame? I am not to blame." He shook his fist in the air. "You are stupid like your father. I search for him for years, and I would not have found you if you had not call me."

This was my fault. I had called him. He was the man from the letter—the man on the other end of the phone. A sick acidic taste rose in my throat.

"Poor Mr. Tama. You completely ruin his life."

Mr. Tama? I raised my eyes to meet his. "What are you talking about?"

"All he wanted was new start." Arakaki-san shook his head. "He make it too easy."

"Because he hated my father as much as you," I said.

"Did he?" His face quirked as if he were reveling in something I didn't know. He pointed at my chest. "You are hated as much as your father, so what dat say about you?"

I shifted my focus to the ground.

"It not hard to find someone who hate you. Do you know things people say about you on Internet? Finding help was easy."

I had a pretty good idea.

He twirled the gun in his hand. "This is your fate. *Unmei.* This is your destiny—to die like my Kimiko and her friend Miya."

"Chase and Mumps may hate me, but even they wouldn't want me murdered," I said through quivering lips. At least I hoped they didn't. Were they murderers? When I thought Mumps was the man in the mask, I'd thought him capable of it.

Had they helped this man, knowing what his plans were?

"My father's dead. If you thought killing me would make him suffer, you're too late."

"I know he is dead. I learn dat when I got here." He leaned closer. "But I wouldn't have killed him even if he were living," he whispered, "so he could see what he caused." He stood upright and paced the length of the room. For a moment I thought he would leave us there to die of thirst and starvation where no one could hear us call for help, but he circled back, following the same path again and again.

I refused to believe this was my fate, that there was no other way. How could Jiro Arakaki's only destiny be to kill me, as if he had no choice?

The man continued to pace around the cold, bare room. At moments his bass voice would break into song, the same sad ballad he had used to haunt my house. The Japanese melody floated in the hollow room. I wondered if he even remembered we were there with him.

"Do you know what those words mean?" he asked without looking at me.

He didn't wait for me to answer. "It is about a man who looks to skies so dat tears will not fall. Spring, summer, autumn he looks up because he is alone. He counts stars with tearful eyes because he is alone."

Arakaki-san continued to walk and lifted his gaze to the light of the moon streaming through the broken windows. "And tears collect in eyes as he walks because sadness lies in shadows of stars and in shadow of moon. And he looks up so tears do not fall. For he is all alone."

A twinge of sympathy struck me, but I pushed it away. Sympathy wouldn't save us.

"Do you know what it is like to be all alone?" he asked.

My chin dropped. Exhaustion weighed on every muscle. It had to be past midnight. Dad would tell me to conserve my energy, and I wasn't about to waste any answering this man's questions.

The tears had dried, but strands of hair remained matted to my face. I couldn't break free to brush them away.

Arakaki-san finally fell against a large metal barrel and crumpled to the ground. Shadows hid his face, yet I could still feel his eyes piercing the darkness. The sky was blank without stars, but cloud silhouettes unrolled into wisps across the moon, high, but hidden from my view.

The man stayed slumped on the floor. Every now and then he would wake himself with a loud snore, jerk his head, then fall back asleep. In the stillness, I stared at Nicholas. Guilt washed over me. We needed to get out.

The tops of my ears burned from the glacial air. All feeling in my hands and feet had been gone for at least an hour. If I felt this way, how did Nicholas feel?

I winced when I looked over. Seeing Nicholas sent panic through me. He barely moved. The shallow breaths that escaped his lips and materialized as he exhaled were the only evidence I had he was even alive.

But all I could do was look, and my strength betrayed me. My mind started to wander in and out of consciousness, until all I could see was Forrest. My worries for Nicholas and my worries for Forrest melded into one great ball of fear, which turned to nightmares in my dreams.

I JOLTED AWAKE when Arakaki slapped my face. My skin was near frozen before, and now the shivers were uncontrollable. Hypothermia was setting in. Outside, snow had started to fall against the black night.

I mustered enough energy to lift my head. "Please don't do this. You have a choice."

He stared at me with sharp eyes, ignoring my pleas. "I did not choose for Kimiko to die. Dat choice taken from me." Greasy strands of black-and-gray hair fell in his face.

In the faint light of his cigarette, I could see red lightning-like lines streaking the whites of his tired eyes.

"I'm sorry for what my father did," I said. "For what he put you through. If you think it will make you feel better, you can kill me, but there's no honor in retaliation. Please let Nicholas go. You can't respect the life she led by taking the life of another."

"You." He pounced at me until his face was right in mine.

"You are shame to our people. You have no idea what honor means. Things I have been through are things you cannot understand."

His shouts hurt my ears, but I had no way of escaping. I shut my eyes. "How are we different?" I cried. "Both of us are suffering because of decisions my father made. We had no choice regarding the consequences of his actions, but we have a choice now. I refuse to believe his poor judgment defines the kind of people we become."

He lunged and wrapped his hands around my throat, squeezing as I struggled for breath. Blackness closed in. Just when I thought I would pass out, he let me go. I choked and gasped for air.

But he wasn't done yet. He stepped back and delivered a flying kick to my side. The chair crashed to the ground, its metal legs screeching across the floor. My cheek slid along the concrete like sandpaper. When I finally came to a stop, blood pooled around my ear.

The side of my face flared with pain. "I'm sorry he did this to you," I said. My voice was weak, and I couldn't stop shivering. "But Nicholas and I are innocent. Like Kimiko. If you kill us, you only take more innocent lives. For the past several months, you have tortured me, recreating all the events that happened to your daughter. This has nothing to do with honor."

He threw back his head. "You don't understand! She is gone."

"I do understand. He did this to all of us, not just Kimiko. I'm sorry he did this to you," I whispered. I couldn't help but resent my father in this moment, resent how his past still haunted us. I wished I'd never seen that letter.

But now wasn't the time for regrets. I slid my wrists back

and forth, over and over again, cutting my skin against the rope to loosen it. "I'm so sorry."

He yelled what sounded like Japanese profanities. In complete madness, he spun around and around, his eyes possessed. He stomped across the floor, picked up a small metal pipe, and swung at a barrel. The booming, hollow sound filled the empty space. He flung the pipe at a window. Shattered glass rained everywhere.

I tugged at the rope harder. My wrists were raw and bleeding, but the rope had started to loosen.

Arakaki-san stormed to a large shelf full of machine parts and shoved it to the ground. Gears, nuts, bolts, cylinders, and small pipes toppled in all directions, deafening me as metal clanged against the concrete floor.

He picked the gun back up and waved it in the air, firing a couple of shots. Part of the ceiling crashed to the floor, narrowly missing my head. He stretched both arms high and spun in slow circles. Without warning, he recklessly aimed it at Nicholas.

And then he pulled the trigger.

Nicholas's body jumped and slammed back down against the cart.

"Nicholas!" I screamed. "Nicholas!" I jerked side to side and tried to fling myself toward him.

Nicholas thrashed in agony. Blood streamed above his heart and blanketed his shirt in a bath of red. I moaned pangs of anguish, still shivering uncontrollably.

"Please don't let him die!" I cried. "Don't become my father. Just kill me now, but don't let him die. Let me go. Please. I need to get to him. You wanted revenge on my family, not his."

The Japanese man froze. "Revenge? This much more than

revenge. If I want revenge, I would have killed your whole family and all your friends. Dis," he said, gesturing with the gun, "is about bringing back my family honor. Dis is for the months your father shamed me. And when he kill my daughter, he send message dat I am weak and cannot protect her."

He shifted his eyes to the ground.

"Look at me!" I screamed. "Is this what you wanted? Please don't let him die! Don't become the kind of man my father used to be. Please."

I pulled against the rope as hard as I could. My hands broke free, but I kept them behind my back as if still bound. A fiery pain burned my wrists where they'd been tied, but I readied myself.

Arakaki-san collapsed to his knees and began to sob. Large tears splashed to the ground. *"Gomen nasai... Gomen nasai, Kimiko!"* he howled. "Please forgive me, my Kimiko. I could not save you. Please forgive me." He lifted the gun and pointed it at my head with a trembling hand.

"Don't do this," I said.

He closed his eyes and bowed his head, gun still pointed in my direction.

I leaped up, my feet still tied to the chair, and knocked the gun from his hands, then delivered a punch to his throat. He put his hands to his neck and crumpled over, fighting to catch his breath.

The punch threw me off balance, and I fell over. I reached down and slid the rope and my legs off the chair. The metal feet scraped against my calves. I screamed and wiggled and kicked until my legs were free, then planted the chair over his face.

He raised his head, hands at his throat. My eyes met his. I

lunged to reach the gun. He grabbed at my ankles, but I kicked his face.

He rolled onto his back, cradling his nose. Blood streamed through his fingers.

I picked up the gun and forced my tired legs to stand. I aimed the gun at him. "Don't move," I said. "Or I *will* shoot."

The gun trembled in my hands.

He rolled over onto his knees.

"I. Said. Don't. Move." I steadied my hand with the other.

He looked up and trained his dark eyes on me.

All the terror he had put me through made anger storm inside me. I pictured Parker's limp body on the floor at home, and Forrest as he lay broken on the stairs. Nicholas writhed on the ground next to me, still bleeding.

I wanted to hurt this man as much as he had hurt me. I could kill this man right now.

Without guilt.

He stood up slowly. Rage coursed through me. My finger tugged at the trigger, the gun ready and aimed at him, but stopped at the last second.

He hurled himself at me, clasping my hand holding the gun. We crashed to the ground, the gun firing on impact. The bullet hit a metal tank, causing it to explode. Balls of fire lit the air. A rush of heat blew across my face. The force sent us flying across the concrete floor.

When I glanced up, Arakaki-san's body lay still on the ground ten feet away. The flames started to catch across the room slowly, but moving inexorably nearer.

I ran to Nicholas and ripped the gag from his mouth. He

yelled in excruciating pain. I searched through my pockets but couldn't find my phone anywhere, then remembered it was in the entry at home, lying in pieces.

With as much speed as I could manage, I untied his hands and legs. The rope was unrelenting. The bindings were tight, and his hands and feet had started to swell and turn purple. I bit at it to loosen the knots.

"Nicholas, stay with me. Don't leave me." I held his face. "I need a phone."

"Back pocket," he said. His voice was feeble.

I fumbled around, wet and cold. But there was nothing in his pocket. Arakaki-san must have taken it from Nicholas when he tied him up.

"No one's going to find us," I cried. And then I remembered the disk Fed had given me, sliding along the chain of my necklace. I squeezed it hard and hoped Fed could help the police locate us in time.

IN THE BACKGROUND, Arakaki-san started to groan. For a second, I caught his face.

"Kimiko! I'm so sorry, Kimiko," he said. "Forgive me. I bring shame to our family." He tried to stand, but his left leg collapsed beneath him, blood blooming on his pant leg.

The flames rose to the ceiling along a wooden beam. I had to get Nicholas out of there before the roof caved in on us. I leaned my weight against the cart, but looked back. Arakaki-san would never make it out of here on his own. After all he had done to terrorize my family, I was under no obligation to help him. But if I left him here . . . I would be the one condemning him to die.

I ripped open Nicholas's shirt with shaking hands and found his chest covered with black powder and reddish-brown splotches, a sight that would forever stain my memory. Arakaki-san's hoodie lay on the floor. I ran to retrieve and used it to press against Nicholas's wound. Nicholas shrieked in pain. Blood ran everywhere, even though I applied pressure. I pushed his side, listening to his deafening shrieks as I lifted him enough that I could see blood spill from underneath. The bullet must have gone through.

I raced to the door where I'd seen some airplane passenger seats. Flames lapped up the beams and started to reach the room. One of the seat belts wasn't connected to the seat, and I tore it off. The others were sewn into the seats or glued. I wasn't sure.

We were running out of time, and one seat belt wouldn't be enough for what I had in mind. I found a metal pipe about eighteen inches long and used Arakaki-san's hoodie as a hot pad. I held one end of the pipe close to a flame by the wall about six feet away, and when it glowed, I placed the hot end of the pipe on the seat belt, close to where the belt was attached. After several quick repetitions, I was able to singe the seat belt enough to remove it.

I brought the hoodie and the seat belts back to Nicholas, coughing from the smoke. To connect the straps together, I used the seat-belt buckles, and then wove the strap underneath Nicholas, lifting one side and shoving the strap as far under as it would go, then running to the other side, lifting him, and pulling the strap through. Sounds of fire crackled loud in my ears. I wrapped the hoodie around Nicholas's body on the side of the wound, top and bottom the best I could, and used the straps to hold the hoodie against his body, pulling the belts as tight as possible. Each movement caused Nicholas to wail.

Once I had taken care of Nicholas, I rushed over to Arakaki-san, beads of sweat streaming down my face.

I bent down, lifting and tugging at his arm until it was around my shoulder.

He moaned. "Leave me."

"I can help you out. Here we go." I pushed off the ground with my legs, screaming as his weight pulled at my shoulders. He forced himself to stand, and we were able to hobble and limp to the cart.

"Hang on to the handlebar for support," I said.

Slowly we pushed the cart to the door. Nicholas's long legs dangled off the end and scraped the floor as we moved, but we reached the door and pushed. I was right—this had been a hangar of some sort. The door went directly outside. A trail of blood snaked behind us in two trails—one from Nicholas and one from Arakaki. Using me as a crutch, Arakaki helped me push Nicholas, and we fought our way out.

The air outside was even colder. A gust of wind cut through me. As it blew, the flames devoured the warehouse, spiking higher in the snowy air. I followed the silhouette of the mountains. We had to be somewhere west of Salt Lake City.

Nicholas moaned. For a brief moment, he stared at me, but his deep-set brown eyes had a hollowness behind them.

The icy wind whipped across my face. The heat of the fire had only dried my shirt a little, and the wetness turned to frost against my skin.

The old man lifted his head, terror in his eyes. *"Gomen nasai,"* he said. "I'm sorry. I will repay my debt." His tears turned to sobs. He bowed his head. *"Gomen nasai. Gomen nasai.* I'm sorry."

"Me too." Using my elbow, I delivered a blow to his temple.

He dropped to the ground.

Little rivers of blood forged through the fresh snow around the cart where Nicholas lay. His face had lost all color. I pressed down, applying as much direct pressure as my weak body would allow.

"Nicholas, don't leave me," I said. My words sounded clumsy. "I love you. We're family. Stay with me."

He moved his lips to speak, but was only able to utter my name before he began to lose consciousness.

I clutched his cheeks tighter between my hands, but my fingers were numb. "Nicholas! Please! You can't leave me."

Nicholas tried to focus, but his eyes fluttered and closed. He didn't open them again. His head lolled away as if surrendering. His body fell limp on the cart. I pressed my head to his chest and held his hand, the memory of my father's heart attack beating down on me. Stubbornly, I kept pushing on his wound to stop the blood flow. I was no longer shivering, but my fingers stopped working. Everything stopped working. "Don't die. Don't die," I wanted to say.

I heard faint sounds all around me. The weight of my body was too much. And it was so cold. I climbed on the cart and curled up next to Nicholas with my head on his chest and the weight of my shoulder pressing down on his wound.

Thick, heavy clouds settled in my head. Different experiences danced in front of me—past occurrences, flashes of what could have been. Mom. Dad. Parker scoring the winning goal on the soccer field, and Avery slaying someone with a one-line quip. Fed. Nicholas. How could Nicholas be in front of me, when he was right next to me?

"Look, Nicholas," I whispered. "Everyone's here. Even you. And it's not cold anymore."

Forrest approached me, dressed in his dark suit and tie.

His sandy-blond hair reflected the light of the full moon in the clear sky, and he lifted me from the ground until we rose to the ceiling of the warehouse. A stream babbled, and the pitter-patter of quaking aspen leaves rippled in the air. In the far distance, sirens sounded. He smoothed my hair with his hand, closed his ocean-blue eyes, and then he kissed me.

His lips sculpted softly around mine. "I would see only you," he said.

When he let go, I floated in the halls of the courthouse. The statue of Lady Justice pointed her double-edged sword at me—not in a threatening way—but as if she was beckoning me to follow her.

Her white robe swished and waved, caught in a gentle wind, but before I could take a step in her direction, I saw my father—my real father—standing underneath the blue-domed ceiling, smiling, arms outstretched to receive me. The tattoo of a Japanese carp, a koi, representing perseverance, bled through his sheer shirt.

He opened his mouth to speak. "Look Claire. The rings. They're gone."

But I only caught a glimpse, and before I could express how happy I was for him, before I could say anything, he disappeared.

Only five black rings remained in the place where he stood.

"NICHOLAS!" I GASPED. The pounding in my head throbbed so much I thought it would explode. The air felt cool, the smell familiar. I raised my heavy eyelids.

Mom and Dad rested on the couch by the window and rose when they saw me awake. Forrest sat in a chair next to my hospital bed, like a bad case of déjà vu.

"Nicholas is going to be all right," Forrest said, sporting a cast in a sling and a couple of stitches across his forehead. He scrambled to my side.

"Forrest." I reached for him. "You're alive. I'm so glad you're alive."

He grabbed my hand and kissed it. His hands trembled around mine. "Ditto." He leaned down and left a gentle kiss on my forehead.

I glanced over at Dad. His eyebrow was raised, but he didn't say anything.

I shifted my focus back to Forrest. "When I saw you on the

stairs . . ." Tears pricked behind my eyes. "I can't imagine—I'm so glad you're here."

"I couldn't live without you either." He squeezed my hand again. "Good thing you're so indestructible."

I swallowed more tears before they could escape. "Is your arm okay?"

Forrest shrugged. "Well, it's not going to be as cool as Nick's scar, but I'm hoping the cast will draw some sympathy from a certain attractive girl because I might need someone to kiss it better." He wiggled his eyebrows up and down. "Did I mention she's smart and athletic too?"

"Who is she?" I said. "I'm going to punch her."

He laughed.

"Can you take me to see Nicholas?"

Mom got off her chair and walked over. She pressed my shoulder so I would lie flat against the bed. "You might have suffered another concussion, so the doctor wants to monitor you a little bit longer. Not to mention the hypothermia and your other injuries."

Forrest spoke in a quiet voice. "I think you should listen to your mom and take it easy."

"I'm fine," I said even though I wasn't. Everything ached. From what I could see and feel from where I lay, my wrists and ankles still bore the marks of being bound. Bruises decorated my skin everywhere—even if I couldn't see them, I could feel them. And there were stitches under my chin and on the back and side of my head.

Avery strolled through the door with a large stack of hospital bed pads in one arm and a bedpan in the other.

Mom went over to him and held out her hands to relieve him of the load. "Oh, that was so thoughtful of you, Avery," she said, "but I don't know if Claire needs them. I think the nurses have got it handled."

Avery pulled his stash closer to his chest. "Claire? I didn't get these for her. These are for me." He walked to the loveseat and stacked everything into a nice pile next to Dad, oblivious to Dad's look of death.

"Son," Dad said, putting a hand on the top of the pile. "What do you think you're doing with these?"

"I think I'm going to be playing video games a lot longer without needing to leave for a break." Avery smiled.

"Avery," Mom said, smoothing down her hair. "You know, sometimes, you just . . . I—I don't know what to do with you."

"I need to get out of here." I shifted my legs to the edge of the mattress. "I need to get away from him," I pointed to Avery, "and I need to see Nicholas."

"Claire, get back in the bed and wait until we can get a wheelchair." Dad stood and folded his arms. "I don't want you to get hurt again. Nicholas is fine. The police were able to use Fed's phone and find you before anything too unthinkable happened."

Avery tugged at the hip of his skater shorts and postured himself as if he was about to deliver a monologue. "The patient was shot medially, just under the clavicle—where subclavian and brachial arteries and veins are located," he said in a British accent. "It almost required surgery, but luckily we were able to explore the area without surgical intervention." He gestured to a chart above the bed. "Fortunately, the patient didn't suffer any fractures, so we're hopeful that he'll avoid long-term nerve damage."

Mom and Forrest laughed at his impression. Dad shook his head. I didn't even know how much of that was true.

I settled beneath the blanket, skin crawling, and restless. Staying still was almost impossible. Unlike after the car accident, I remembered almost everything and hoped scans showed I hadn't reinjured myself with another concussion. Enough of me had been damaged already. Forrest held my hand, stroking his thumb against my skin.

"You're here," I said, unable to believe how fortunate we'd all been.

"I'm here," he said.

The events of the past weeks had seemed almost dreamlike. A nightmare I had endured but survived—that all of us had survived. "Dad," I asked. "What happened to the Japanese man?"

Dad left the couch and came to sit closer to my bedside. "They couldn't find him," he said, his voice deep and gravelly.

"He was on the ground," I said. "Right by the door. I knocked him out."

Mom pulled herself next to Dad, near the side of the bed. "Claire, the man who did this was the father of the last person—"

"I know," I said with a quiet voice. "Jiro Arakaki."

"Hmmm," Mom said. Her black hair brushed her chin when she leaned closer. "Do you remember how I told you your father was asked to do something that weighed on his conscience? That something was to take Kimiko's life. Your father told me he tried to convince the boss that Kimiko's father deserved a pass."

Mom rested her hand on mine. "But his boss was relentless.

The yakuza demand unquestioning loyalty and obedience to their superiors, so your father carried out the assigned task, but he couldn't bring himself to return and continue more of the same actions. He cut off his pinky to show absolution and sent it to his boss before escaping to America. It was the most honorable way to leave, in his mind. When you were born, he insisted we give you the middle name Kimiko, in honor of the person who had impacted his life so profoundly. I'm sure you would have made your father and Kimiko proud." She closed her watery eyes.

I melted into the pillow behind me and imagined what it would be like to have my life back. Forrest gave my hand another squeeze, and Parker bounded into the room.

"Dude, you should have seen what I did to that Arakaki guy, Claire!" Parker said. "Couldn't even recognize him afterward. They had to check the dental records to identify him." He flexed in front of the mirror at the sink, and his thick neck disappeared.

"Whatever," I said. "The last time I saw you, you were knocked out cold on your floor."

Parker ignored me.

Fed skipped into the room with a look of ecstasy. "Do you guys realize how many different TV channels they have here? It's like a million, and I don't know why people complain about cafeteria food. It's awesome." He came to my side and gripped the bedrail. "I hope Nicholas never gets released."

The room became crowded, and Mom and Dad stepped out.

I tugged at Fed's wrinkled shirt. "Your GPS thing saved our lives. Thank you."

"Oh man," he said. "I'm so sorry. If I'd remembered you had it, I could have found you sooner."

"I'm just glad you helped them find us at all."

He shivered. "Man, it was so scary. At first I had no idea what was going on because this alarm kept beeping. It was tsuchigumo scary. And my mom. Whoa. You totally freaked her out because her phone was doing the same thing."

"I'm so sorry," I said. "How is Nicholas? I need to hear it, one more time, that he's going to be fine."

"He'll live. I just came from his room. They've been giving him like all this pain medication, and he is way out of it. Reminds me of Fujiyama from this manga series, and whenever he gets drunk, he says all these crazy things." Fed pulled at the bedrail, his eyes dancing with excitement. "It's awesome. I may have to record him."

"Leave your poor brother alone," I said.

Fed sat down on a stool with wheels and inched next to the side of the bed. His clothes were a mess, and he smelled like he hadn't showered in a few days.

I shifted my head on the pillow so I could face him. "You're my hero."

"I know," he said.

Mom and Dad returned with an empty wheelchair. Mom brought it to the side of the bed. "As soon as the nurse comes, she said you can go visit Nicholas."

I tried to stand. "Thanks, but I can walk."

"Would you like to visit Nicholas or not?" Dad asked. He folded his arms across his chest.

I huffed, but sat in the wheelchair after the nurse had hooked my IVs to a pole with wheels.

NICHOLAS WAS ASLEEP, but his mom, Anne, stayed at his bedside. Her dark brown hair was pulled up from her face. Unlike her boys, she had a short, petite frame.

Anne was one of my heroines. She had been through so many different hardships in her life as a single mother, and I envied her quiet strength. The way she had raised Nicholas and Fed to be such wonderful people was proof of her supernatural abilities. I had never meant to be the cause of more grief.

As soon as I saw her, I fell apart. "I'm so sorry—"

"I can't say you didn't give me a scare," she said. "But Nicholas . . . Claire, he wouldn't have had it any other way." She took my hand. "You're all part of our family. Nicholas and Fed would do anything for you guys. This is not your fault. You know that, right?"

I nodded, not sure whether I was in agreement with what she had just said. How could I feel this wasn't my fault? But words caught in my throat. Nicholas and all the guys had been there for me so many times. I wondered if my friendship and love could ever be an even trade for what they had endured.

Mom wheeled me to Nicholas's side, and I rested my chin next to his face, staring at the steadiness of his breathing. He was covered in so many bandages.

I wanted Nicholas to sleep so he could recover, and yet I wanted him to wake up so I could hear his voice and know he truly was going to be all right. I needed proof beyond the rhythmic heartbeat on the monitor and the rising and falling of his chest as he inhaled and exhaled. "He's going to be okay, right?" I asked.

He'd been bleeding so much, I'd worried he'd die. To hear he didn't even need surgery because the bullet had passed through cleanly was such a relief.

Anne smiled. "He's well on his way to recovery," she said.

Dad stepped behind me and grabbed the handles of my chair. "Twenty minutes is long enough for today," he said. "I think it's time to go back to your own room and get some rest."

I grunted. "Fine."

I tugged at my gown and pulled the corners underneath me as he wheeled me out into the hall. "So how long do I have to be here?"

Dad pushed me into my room and secured the brake before he helped me out of the chair. "The doctor wants you to stay one or two more nights as a precautionary measure," he said. "Most likely you'll be able to go home tomorrow."

All the rest of the guys gathered in my room.

Dad situated himself near the side of my bed and cleared his throat. "I've spoken to your parents," he said to the guys, "but I need all of you to know what you may see in the media will be a different story than what has taken place. As much as possible, we must tell them this was a random event."

He looked directly at me and my brothers. "For our family's safety, it's important no one connects you to your father's history, or we will always be in danger." He then turned to Forrest and Fed. "I know we have asked a lot of you guys, but I'm sure you understand how important it is that this information be kept from *ever* seeing the light of day."

They all nodded. I felt for them. They would be living the same lie I was every day. At times it had seemed like an impossible burden. I had a feeling Dad's request had as much to do with not blowing his cover, too, which could put us all in even more danger.

Dad removed his glasses and rubbed his eyes before he set them back on his face. "As far as I know, what you will be hearing is that this was a case of mistaken identity. Nicholas and Forrest were both hurt because they tried to prevent the abduction." He raised a hand and motioned in the air. "We'll try to make sure that never happens again, understand?"

Everyone nodded.

"Sure," Parker said, and he patted Dad on the back.

Forrest nodded. "We'll make sure your secret's safe," he said.

"Whatever," Avery said, tossing back his hair.

Dad's face darkened. "It looks like Mr. Tama might be innocent," he said. "He says he was a stupid kid when he left those comments on the Internet. From what I can tell, he seemed to have reformed his life completely when a headhunter contacted him about a teaching position at your school."

He rested his foot on the bottom of the stool. "The only reason he changed his name is because he wanted a new start. Marcus

Tama is his new name. He'd gotten the Utah temporary license, but was waiting for the permanent one to arrive. The police are looking into what made Mrs. Davenport leave in the first place though. Mr. Arakaki had help from one of your classmates. Calvin, is it? Please do not take this issue up with him at school. Let the law handle it. He has been very cooperative so far, and I suspect he was conned like the rest of us were."

He gestured to the boys. "I'd like to talk to Claire alone if you don't mind." They ambled out of the room.

Dad rolled the chair next to my bed. "Claire." He hung his head. "I promised to protect you." His voice began to tremble. "I let my defenses down." He seemed to mumble more to himself than to me.

"We all let our defenses down," I said. "Once Mr. Tama was arrested, we thought we were safe. We played our roles exactly the way Arakaki-san wanted us to."

"I can't help but feel this is my fault," he said. "I knew who Arakaki-san was way before you ever found that letter. But his profile never suggested he would do anything like this."

I wanted to throw my arms around him, but could barely move. "How can this possibly be your fault? You can't be there by my side for the rest of my life. Dad, you do more for me than you will ever know. At some point you have to let me go, not knowing all the things that could happen to me."

"I don't know if dads ever let go of their daughters completely."

"This is *my* fault," I said. "I'm the one who led him to us."

"I think there were a lot of factors that led him to us."

"Are you worried Jiro Arakaki is still out there?" I asked.

He shook his head. "Now that I know who he is, I can find him. He won't come near us again."

"He said he did this out of honor and because my father had shamed him and made him look weak."

Dad nodded his head. "Shame is about the worst thing a Japanese person can experience. Back in the samurai era, warriors would rather take their own lives when they lost a battle because it was shameful to be captured or killed by the enemy."

"Like the kamikaze pilots."

"Like the kamikaze pilots. Japan resorted to suicide tactics to evade the humiliation of defeat. The Japanese have lived with this culture of shame for thousands of years. The things your father did caused Arakaki-san a lot of shame, and to have that be known publicly made things worse. He probably felt the only way he could restore his family's honor was to commit some of the same offenses and show he wasn't weak."

I explained how I had pulled Arakaki out of the warehouse. "He said he would repay his debt."

Dad crossed his legs, resting his ankle on his thigh. "Because you saved his life, he is in your debt. If he ever had the opportunity to save your life in the future, he would do so because of this unspoken code of honor."

"Even though he wanted to kill me?"

"Even if he hated your guts, he would still save you. I don't know for sure, of course, but that's the way the culture tends to operate because it would be the honorable thing to do."

I gathered my thoughts together. "Dad, I wanted to kill him. I almost shot him. What does that say about me that I almost murdered a person?"

"But you *didn't*. That says a lot about you," he said. "I can't say I would have been as generous. And I think the thing that speaks the most highly about you is not only did you not shoot him, but you risked your life to save his."

"That could also be construed as reckless," I said. "Or plain stupid."

Dad placed his hand on my shoulder. "It was a little reckless. And stupid. But it was also brave." He closed his eyes. "Please don't try to be brave again. You're going to kill me. I wish I could keep you in a bubble." He stood and walked over to the loveseat. From the side he lifted a gift-wrapped box. "I have something for you."

What present could he possibly have gotten me? He set it on my lap, and I unwrapped the plain silver paper. Inside was a leather-bound journal.

"Seemed like you could use a new one." Dad leaned over the rail and pointed to the front cover. "I had your name engraved on it."

"Thank you." Tears pricked at my eyes. "How did you know?"

He smiled. "I'm in the business of knowing things."

Someone knocked on the door. I looked over and saw Mumps.

"Can I talk to you?" he asked.

"No," I said.

He shoved his hands in his pockets and hunched his shoulders. "Please."

"Fine," I said.

"I'm going to stay if you don't mind," Dad said to Mumps. "And even if you do, I'm not leaving."

Mumps walked in. "That's fine." Dad pushed the rolling stool over, and Mumps sat down. His shoulders slouched and his head hung low.

"I owe you an apology," he said.

"You think?" He nearly got me and several people I love killed.

He inhaled a deep breath. "When Chase made that bet that started your whole feud, it was because he had liked you for a really long time. I thought the bet would motivate him to do something about it. But, then you found out, and you punched him, and you know how that all turned out."

"I do," I said not even trying to hide my irritation that he was here, wasting my time. "But what does that have to do with anything?"

"Chase was upset, but not as much as I was. I posted some things about you online anonymously. I tried to ruin your reputation the same way you ruined Chase, but—"

"Hold up. *I* ruined Chase?"

"After you sent Nicholas and your brother to threaten him, they told some of the teammates what had happened and to keep an ear out and let them know if Chase was saying anything bad about you. Rumors started, and suddenly a lot of people, girls especially, thought he was a scumbag."

The corners of Dad's mouth turned into a proud grin.

"Number one, I've never wanted Nicholas and Parker to fight my battles. If you'd taken the time to get to know me before you did all of this, you would know that." I flicked my eyes to Dad so he would get the message too. "And number two, Chase ruined his reputation by himself. If he had help in that department, it wasn't from Nicholas or Parker, or me. It was from you."

Mumps lowered his head. "I know. I didn't realize that then."

"So then what happened?" I asked, but it sounded more like a command.

"I couldn't get any of the girls on your soccer team to turn on you, so I switched your test and told Mrs. Davenport you cheated."

Hearing about my teammates made me feel warm inside, but I wanted to hurt Mumps.

"And then out of nowhere, this guy emails my anonymous account," Mumps said, "and he says he'll give me a thousand dollars to steal pictures from your locker. And then he says he'll give me another thousand to put this box in your backpack."

"So you asked me to the Halloween dance," I said, "because you thought it would help you get closer to me."

He nodded and rested his hands on the bedrail. "Claire, it was such easy money. So when he said he'd give me five thousand dollars to steal your soccer jersey and leave a couple of things in your room, I didn't hesitate."

"It didn't occur to you to question *why* he wanted you to do these things?" I asked.

"Yeah, but they didn't seem like a big deal. I didn't think anything I'd done could hurt you." Mumps put his hands on the sides of his head. "Chase started asking me questions about where all this money was coming from. All I told him was I was being paid to play pranks on you, and I thought he'd be happy, but he wasn't. He came to that party at your house to try to stop me."

"That's why he was there," I said more to myself than Mumps.

"And then I talked to you, and you weren't at all like I expected. I thought you'd be mean and cold. But you're funny, and I liked talking to you. The guy had already given me half the money upfront, so I had to finish the job even though I didn't want to."

I glared at him. "That's supposed to make me feel better? The fact that you did it, but you didn't want to?"

He shook his head. "No, but I really did feel horrible after that. And even though he asked me to do one more thing for him, I didn't," he said. "I'm not the one who taped those pictures under Mr. Tama's desk."

"Who did?"

"I don't know, but I've told the police everything," he said. "Claire, I'm so sorry. I never would have done any of that if I knew what was going to happen."

"What about the flowers?" I asked.

"Those were on your doorstep when I got there. All I did was pick them up and hand them to you. I don't even know what kind of flowers they were."

"White chrysanthemums," Dad said. "They're used at funerals."

Mumps tugged at the front of his shirt with both hands. "I didn't know. I promise."

I looked away. He touched my arm, and I flinched. "Can you at least look at me?" he asked.

I turned my head enough to see him from the corner of my eye.

"I'm so sorry," he said. "I will find a way to make this right. What I did was stupid, but I didn't know. I'm sorry." The misery on his face seemed genuine.

I glanced up and saw Forrest in the doorway. "Mumps," I said. "I think you need to leave."

"I think what she means," Dad said, his posture straight and his arms folded, "is she will take your apology under considera- tion, but I would strongly advise that you give her some space when she gets back to school."

Mumps nodded and stood up. He turned slowly and started to leave. Forrest walked right up to him and, with his good arm, punched Mumps in the jaw.

Mumps dropped to the floor, grabbing his face. He wobbled as he tried to get back on his feet and looked at my dad. Dad shrugged. Mumps scrambled out of the room.

Dad leaned over and whispered, "I think I like Forrest a little more now."

"I've wanted to do that for a while," Forrest said. He shook his hand and winced. "But ow! That really hurts."

Dad patted him on the shoulder. "I'll give you guys some privacy," he said, then pointed at Forrest with a squint. "But no funny business." He left.

FORREST PUSHED DOWN the rail of the bed.

I scooted over. "Sit next to me."

He struggled with his one good arm to crawl into the bed. "I have something for you," he said, reaching into his pocket and producing my grandmother's necklace. He held the familiar silver chain, but along with the bead it had a new pendant attached: a cloisonné panda.

I patted my chest, and realized it had been taken off me. "My dad has gotten me jewelry like this on his business trips to Japan," I said. As soon as the words left my mouth, I realized his business trips were something different than I had previously imagined them to be. "I didn't realize you even knew what cloissonné is."

He turned the panda in his hands. "See how the fine metal wire details the intricate features of the animal and encases the brilliant colors of the enamel?" He laughed. "Okay, I didn't. Your mom helped me."

"It's beautiful. I love it," I said. "Can you hang on to it for me until I get home?"

"Of course. And one more thing." He reached into his pocket again. "Your ring." He slid the plastic ring on my finger and leaned in closer. His mouth skimmed my ear. "You smell amazing," he said.

He stroked my hair and trailed his hand along my cheek as if he couldn't resist. "It's nice to see you awake." He spoke with a soft voice. "I'm so sorry this happened to you."

His eyes crinkled at the corners when he smiled, and I couldn't believe how happy I was we were both there, together and alive. I stared deep into his eyes. They reminded me of the color of the ocean, with thin whitecaps stretching over waves of deep blues and greens.

"I would only see you too," I said.

Forrest raised an eyebrow, puzzled.

"When I was hallucinating at the warehouse, I saw you, and you said you would only see me." I took his hand in mine. "I would see only you too. If you were one of the trillions of stars, I would only see you."

He leaned in and his lips brushed mine.

He pulled back. "I'd like to do a lot more right now, but this cast is getting in the way, and I don't want to do anything that would delay getting you home."

"I'm fine," I said through the pain. "Get back here." I grabbed the front of this shirt and pulled him closer.

He kissed me again, then pulled away. "Trust me. I plan to ravage you later." He laughed. "I'm kidding. You know I'm kidding, right? What does 'ravage' even mean?"

"You'd better not be," I said and tugged on his shirt again.

"Shhh," he said. "Your dad's probably standing right outside the door."

"Just one more then," I said.

He kissed me longer this time.

"Nicholas is up!" Fed shouted.

Forrest shot up straight. "Euh. For a second, I thought it was your dad."

"You're adorable," I said. "Let's go see Nicholas." I squeezed Forrest's hand.

Forrest jumped off the bed and then helped me get down. Fed navigated the wheelchair over to the bed. "How fast does this thing go?" He inspected the wheels.

In Nicholas's room, Fed gathered with Parker and Avery in front of the TV to watch the University of Utah football game. Nicholas's bed was fully elevated. He shouted at the referees as if he were completely healthy.

His attention shifted when I wheeled in. "How embarrassing! We wore the same outfit today," he said.

My face lit up when I saw him. I threw myself at him like a wild animal, attempting to balance hugging him with all my might and respecting his fragile state, not to mention my IVs. He tried to hide the fact that he was wincing in pain. I must have erred on the hugging-him-with-all-my-might side.

He cringed back from me a little. "Ease up a little, Kiki."

I loosened my grip, but I couldn't bear to let go.

He pointed his chin in the air. "Not many guys can say truthfully they'd be willing to take a bullet for you." The corners of his mouth reached into a wide grin.

"I'm hoping no one ever has to say that again." I fixed myself next to him. "I didn't even know what to do when I thought—"

"I know," he said in almost a whisper. "I can't tell you how helpless I felt when I saw you tied to the chair, and I didn't know what he was going to do to you." He grabbed my hand and clutched it tight against the bed. "Kiki," he choked. "I owe my life to you."

I stared at him as if he had gone completely mad.

The seriousness in his expression didn't waver. "I lost a lot of blood. They say I would have bled to death if you hadn't been there. And if I didn't bleed to death, the cold would have gotten me, but having your body next to mine helped. He was going to leave us to die, Kiki, or maybe something worse, and you saved us."

"You wouldn't have even been there if it weren't for me."

He wiped a stray tear off my cheek. "True, but then I wouldn't have this scar to impress the ladies." He grinned as he yanked down the shoulder of his hospital gown and revealed the bandages covering his wound. He patted the back of my head.

He tilted his head to the side. "We make an unbeatable team, our three families, don't we?"

"A powerful triumvirate."

Nicholas raised a brow. "A what?" He nodded, but his eyes wandered, trying to figure out where he had heard it before.

"The first triumvirate was during the Roman Empire, a regime dominated by three powerful individuals, or in our case, three families. I've been thinking the Axis Powers is due for a name change."

"A powerful triumvirate." He gave a nod in agreement. "Axis Powers unite!"

We shared silence for a moment. I closed my eyes and sighed. "I'm so glad you're okay."

"You too." He clasped my hand again. He sneaked a look at the rest of the guys. "I'm glad you gave Forrest a chance," he whispered. "Life's too short."

"It is," I said.

He sighed. "And man, you've made my life easier."

I shot him a questioning look.

He gave a sly smile. "Haven't you wondered why we always set you up with total losers? It takes a lot of work."

"I knew it." I drew my hand back to whack him, but saw the bandages and thought I should probably give him a break. I let go of Nicholas, and Forrest wheeled me back to my room with his one good arm.

"I'm hoping I only have to endure one more night of hospital food," I said.

"It'll be nice to get you home," he said. "I'm sick of sleeping on the waiting room floor." Forrest helped me climb back into bed and pressed the nurse call button to let her know we had returned. She came within minutes to inject some more sedative into my IV so I could rest.

I made myself comfortable on the pillow. Forrest draped a blanket over me.

"Do you think things will ever really get back to normal?" I asked.

"I think it will take some time, but I think we'll be all right."

"You're still my best friend," I said.

"And you're mine." He kissed my forehead. "I hope that never changes." He relocated to the guest couch.

"Best friends forever?" I asked.

"And beyond." He propped pillows at the end and covered himself with a blanket.

I fought to keep my eyelids open long enough to agree with him. But I knew my life would never be ordinary again.

GLOSSARY

anime (ah-nee-meh): Japanese animated production

Arakaki-san (Ah-rah-kah-kee sahn): Refers to Jiro Arakaki. The addition of -san to the end of a surname is a Japanese honorific, or title of respect, similar to Mr. or Mrs.

butsudan (boo-tsoo-dahn): a Buddhist altar or shrine, which can be found in temples or homes

Dobash (doh-bash) **cake**: a cake made of alternating layers of cake and pudding

gaman (gah-mahn): enduring what seems unbearable with dignity and grace

gomen nasai (goh-men nah-sahy): Japanese phrase meaning "I'm sorry"

irezumi (ee-reh-zoo-mee): traditional Japanese method of tattooing by hand

itadakimasu (ee-tah-dah-kee-mahs): Japanese saying to express gratitude for the food about to be eaten

juzo (joo-zoh): prayer beads

kanzashi (kahn-zah-shee): Japanese hair ornaments used in traditional Japanese hairstyles

katana (kah-tah-nah): a type of Japanese sword

kimono (kee-moh-noh): a traditional Japanese garment that is a T-shaped, straight-lined robe

koa (koh-ah) **wood**: comes from a flowering tree, Acacia koa, which is endemic to the Hawaiian islands.

kolohe (koh-loh-hay): Hawaiian word meaning "rascal" or "naughty"

manga (mahng-gah): Japanese comics

Maori (mah-aw-ree): a member of the native Polynesian population of New Zealand

moshi-moshi (moh-shee moh-shee): in Japanese, means "hello" when answering the telephone

netsuku (neh-tsoo-koo): to go to bed, or being in bed for a long time

obi (oh-bee): Japanese sash used as a belt

Obon (Oh-bohn) **Festival**: A Japanese Buddhist celebration to honor the spirits of one's ancestors

oma (oh-mah): German for grandma

otochan (oh-toh-chahn): Japanese for father

oyabun (oh-yah-boon): the leader or godfather of a yakuza clan

shi (shee): Japanese for the number four

shikata ga nai (shee-kah-tah gah nahy): Japanese phrase meaning "it cannot be helped" or "nothing can be done about it."

Spritzkuchen (shprits-koo-ken): German fried pastry similar to a donut

tsuchigumo (tsoo-chee-goo-moh): a spiderlike mythical Japanese creature

"Ue O Muite Arukou" (oo-ay oh moo-ee-teh ah-roo-koh): A Japanese song released in 1961, and to date, one of the only Japanese-language songs to hit the Billboard Hot 100 charts in the United States.

unmei (oon-meh-ee): fate or destiny

yakuza (yah-koo-zah): Japanese organized crime syndicates

yubitsume (yoo-bee-tsoo-meh): a ritual to atone for offenses by means of amputating one's own finger

*Americans have incorporated some of these words into the English language, but they pronounce them differently. While there can be slight variances in pitch or intonation, the Japanese language does not put stress or emphasis on individual syllables in a word. The pronunciations in this glossary reflect the Japanese pronunciation.

** The sound for R in the Japanese language is similar to the sound of a Spanish R, between an R and L sound.

AUTHOR'S NOTE

I am a fourth-generation Japanese American, yonsei. Because my family immigrated to the United States just after the turn of the century, in the early 1900s, the Japanese practices I grew up with might differ from those practiced in Japan. After so many years, I'm sure certain aspects and understandings of traditions were lost or convoluted. Although my family isn't Buddhist, we participated in Buddhist rituals because of my extended family, and some traditions became more cultural rather than religious.

In addition, many Japanese Americans, whose families immigrated over a hundred years ago like mine, were affected deeply by World War II. Some were placed in internment camps where they were not allowed to speak Japanese. There were also Japanese people who were not interned, who chose voluntarily not to speak Japanese to their families and/or participate in rituals in order to avoid persecution or prove they were loyal Americans. As a result, there are traditions that have not been preserved in the way they might have been under different circumstances.

Before writing this book, I'd asked my mom why we weren't supposed to pass food with our chopsticks to someone else's chopsticks. She said all she knew was that it was bad manners. This story allowed me to learn more about my heritage and the meaning and purpose behind some of the things we did. However, I chose to depict the Takata family with the same partial understanding I grew up with because I'm sure there are children out there like me. This experience has given me a deeper appreciation for my ancestry and culture as well as a desire to learn more. I hope there are readers who feel the same yearning to learn about and embrace not just the Japanese culture, but all kinds of diversity.

ACKNOWLEDGMENTS

As a debut author, writing acknowledgments has been an overwhelming task. Admittedly, each one of these was punctuated with tears of gratitude.

P.W., Pucca, Sunshine, & Punky, for your long-suffering and love. Let's go to Disneyland.

Mom & Dad, for supporting me through the hard times, even harder times, and the hardest of times. Thank you for believing in me and never giving up. Kristen & Cristi, for being amazing beta readers and even better sisters. To Ashley, for making our family complete and for turning eighteen. To Kellie-Ann & Kristie-Ann, for being my cheerleaders and for loving my characters.

My brothers, for all the priceless memories. Thank you, Todd, for filming/producing my book trailer; Troy, for medical explanations; and the Langfords & Russos of my life: Jacob, Andrew, Sam, Ben, Derik & Isaiah.

The SIX: Brodi Ashton, Sara Bolton, Kimberly Webb Reid, Emily Wing Smith, & Bree Despain, for helping me get here. You are my dearest friends and the best & most talented writing group in the world.

Christian McKay Heidicker, my rotten better half, for being a dream to work with and one of the most talented writers I know. We did this together, and I can't imagine making the journey without you. Many of the times I have laughed the hardest have been moments we shared. I love your guts. Literally.

The book trailer crew, for helping me bring my book to the screen even though this story was still in its infancy. Brian Ray, for your amazing artwork and undying friendship. Kimiko Miyashima, for letting me claim you as my little sister & donating your acting skills. Chris Luker, Jeff Miller, Jacob Cavanaugh, Ben Lonsdale, Sam Lindeman, Alex Runolfson, Andrew Hercules, Jake Lindeman, Jon Orr, for lending me your time & talents.

All my mentors: A.E. Cannon, Kimberley Heuston, Carol Lynch Williams, Cheri Pray Earl, Martine Leavitt, Ann Dee Ellis, Louise Plummer, Sara Zarr, Sydney Salter, Mette Ivie Harrison, & Rock Canyon for teaching me the basics of writing and even more important, the not-so-basics.

Dusty Heuston, for everything. Thank you for your words of wisdom, support, inspiration, guidance & for allowing me to be a mother first.

Mark Bromley, for your infinite biology wisdom, and Masaji Watabe, for help with the Japanese translation.

John M. Cusick, for taking on the burden of "hottest agent ever" and saying the title was pretty much standard boilerplate at the agency. John, you had me at "If anyone tries to steal you from me, I will garrote them." I knew immediately it was a perfect match.

Everyone at Lee & Low and Tu Books, for your faith in my writing, your hard work, & your mission to diversify children's literature so kids can see themselves in books in a way I never did. Thank you for "picking me" as the New Visions Award winner! There are no words adequate enough to articulate what an honor it is. Stacy Whitman, my fearless editor, for raising my book from the dead and breathing life into its words. Thank you for your patience and for carting my manuscript with you on the train, on the weekends, through the rain, and in your heart. You are brilliant, and it's been a privilege to work with you.

And to all my readers everywhere, for taking the time to read my book.